# LISA GARDNER

# Catch Me

headline

First published in 2012 by
HEADLINE PUBLISHING GROUP

1

Cataloguing in Publication Data is available from the British Library

Hardback ISBN 978 0 7553 8822 6
Trade paperback ISBN 978 0 7553 8823 3

Typeset in Sabon by Avon DataSet Ltd,
Bidford-on-Avon, Warwickshire

Printed and bound in Great Britain by Clays Ltd, St Ives plc

Headline's policy is to use papers that are natural, renewable and
recyclable products and made from wood grown in sustainable forests.
The logging and manufacturing processes are expected to conform to the
environmental regulations of the country of origin.

HEADLINE PUBLISHING GROUP
An Hachette UK Company
338 Euston Road
London NW1 3BH

www.headline.co.uk
www.hachette.co.uk

# Catch Me

# Prologue

The little girl woke up the way she'd been trained: quickly and quietly. She inhaled once, a hushed gasp in the still night, then her eyes fixed on her mother's drawn face.

'Shhh,' her mother whispered, finger to her lips. 'They're coming. It's time, child. Move.'

The girl threw back her covers and sat up. The winter night was cold; she could see her breath as a frosty mist in the glowing moonlight. The little girl was prepared, however. She and her older sister always slept fully dressed, layering T-shirts, sweatshirts, and coats regardless of season. You never knew when *They* might come, flushing their prey from warm sanctuary into the treacherous wild. Unprepared children would fail quickly, succumbing to exposure, dehydration, fear.

Not the little girl and her sister. They'd planned for such events. Their mother, from the time they could walk, had trained them to survive.

Now the little girl grabbed her backpack from the foot of her bed. She slipped the wide straps over her shoulders while sliding her small feet into her loosely laced sneakers. Then she followed her mother onto the darkened second-story landing. Her mother paused at the top of the stairs, finger on her lips, as she peered down into the gloom.

The little girl halted a step behind her mother. She glanced toward the back of the hall, where her sister usually slept. The tiny rental didn't allow for her older sister to have her own room, or even her own bed. Instead, her sister slept on the floor, with her coat as a mattress and her backpack as a pillow. As a good soldier should, their mother said.

But the spot against the far wall was empty – no sister, no coat, no frayed red pack. Fully awake now, the little girl felt the first tingle of fear and had to resist the urge to call out her older sister's name.

Her mother's instructions on this subject were firm: They were not to worry about each other, they were not to wait for one another. Instead, they were to get out of the house and into the woods. Immediately. Once they'd managed to safely evac and evade, then they would meet up at the predetermined rendezvous points. But first priority, get out of the house, elude capture.

And if they did not . . .

As their mother had told them many times, thin features pinched, face too old for her years: Be brave. Everyone has to die sometime.

The little girl's mother descended the first step, staying to the far right, where the riser was less likely to groan. Her oversized wool coat swirled around her legs as she moved, like a black cat weaving around her ankles.

The little girl followed in her mother's wake, placing each foot with similar care while she strained her ears for sounds from the darkness below. Their tiny two-story rental used to be a farmhouse. It was located away from town, down a long dirt road on a dusty brown patch of land at the edge of the woods. They had no roots in the community, no ties to their neighbors.

Everything the girl owned, she wore on her back. From clothing to water bottle to dried fruit and almonds to one battered Nancy Drew novel she'd bought for ten cents at a garage sale to a quartz rock she'd found two years ago along another road in another town where her mother had also woken her and her sister in the middle of the night and they'd never seen that house again.

Maybe other children had toys. Pets. TVs. Computers. School. Friends.

The little girl had her backpack, her older sister, her mother, and this.

Her mother had reached the first floor. She held up her hand, and wordlessly, the little girl halted. She still heard nothing, but watched silvery dust motes swirl around her mother's boot-clad feet.

Now the little girl could hear a noise. A rattle, followed by two thumps. The old furnace, finally registering the chill and kicking to life. After another moment, the distant thumping ceased and the midnight hush returned. The little girl looked. The little girl listened. Then, unable to determine any sign of danger, she peered up solemnly at her mother's pale face.

Sometimes, the little girl knew, they didn't flee in the middle of the night because of the infamous evildoers, the nameless threat lurking in the shadows.

Sometimes, they fled because training didn't allow time for working, which didn't allow for money to pay for rent, or heat, or food. *They* had a lot of strategies, and keeping the little girl's family hungry, cold, and tired was the most effective of all.

At this stage of her life, the little girl could drift as soundlessly as a shadow and see as keenly as a cat in the dark. But maybe her stomach would growl, or her body would shiver. Maybe, in the end, being too hungry, too cold, and too tired was all it would take for her to give her family away.

Her mother seemed to register her thoughts. She half turned, taking the little girl's hand.

'Be brave,' her mother whispered. 'Child . . .'

Her mother's voice broke. The rare and unexpected show of emotion scared the little girl far more than the dark, the cold, the too-quiet house. Now she clutched her mother's hand as tightly as her mother held hers, realizing this wasn't a drill. They were not practicing. They were not planning.

Something had happened.

*They* had found them. This was the real deal.

Her mother moved. Pulled the little girl toward the small kitchen, where the bank of windows allowed the moon to pool on the floor and cast rows of finger-thin shadows around the edges.

The girl didn't want to go anymore. She wanted to dig in her heels. Stop the madness. Rush upstairs and bury herself beneath the blankets on her bed.

Or bolt out the door. Flee from her home, the tension, her mother's harshly lined face. She could race to the old white house on the other side of the woods. A young boy lived there. She watched him sometimes, spied on him from the sprawling oak tree. Twice, she caught him watching her back, expression thoughtful. She never said a word, though. Good girls didn't speak to boys. Soldiers did not consort with the enemy.

SisSis. She needed her older sister. Where was SisSis?

'Everyone must die sometime,' her mother was muttering. She'd reached the middle of the kitchen, stopping abruptly. She seemed to be studying the moonlight, maybe listening for sounds of further danger.

The little girl spoke for the first time. 'Mommy . . .'

'Hush, child! They could be right outside the kitchen. Did you think of that? Right there. Outside that window. Backs resting against that wall, listening to our every footstep. Already getting hard and hungry with the thought of what they'll do to us.'

'Mommy . . .'

'We should light it on fire. Torch the wall. Listen to them yowl in fury, watch them dance in pain.'

The girl's mother turned abruptly toward the windows. The moonlight caught her fully in the face, revealing eyes that were huge, dark pools. Then her mother smiled.

The girl shrank back, letting go of her mother's hand, but it was too late. Her mother still clutched the little girl's wrist. She wasn't letting go. She was going to do something. Something horrible. Something terrible.

Something that was supposed to get *Them*, but that the little girl already knew, from past experience, would hurt her or her big sister instead.

The little girl whimpered. 'Mommy,' she tried again, searching those too dark eyes, trying to find a flicker of familiarity.

'Matches!' her mother cried now. Voice no longer hushed, but booming, nearly gay. They could be at a birthday party, lighting candles on a cake. What a grand time! What a great adventure!

The little girl whimpered again. She tugged on her arm, trying to pull her wrist out of her mother's grasp, struggling more forcibly.

But it was no use. At times like these, her mother's fingers were talons, her entire body radiating a taut, wiry strength that was impossible to break. She would have her way.

Her mother yanked open the first kitchen drawer. Her left hand still clutched the little girl's wrist, while her right hand raked through miscellaneous contents. A glossy white shower of plastic silverware rained down on the peeling linoleum floor. Sprays of ketchup packets, mustard pouches, bags of free croutons the little girl sometimes crept out of bed to eat, because her mother believed hunger would make them stronger, but mostly it made the little girl's stomach ache, so she would pop croutons and suck on ketchup, before stuffing her coat pockets with mustard for her older sister, whom she knew was also starving but couldn't move nearly as quietly through the house.

Soy sauce. Chopsticks. Paper napkins. Wet wipes. Her mother pawing her way furiously through drawer after drawer, dragging the little girl in her wake.

'Mommy. Please, Mommy.'

'Aha!'

'Mommy!'

'*This will teach the fuckers!*' Her mother held up a matchbook. Shiny silver cover, fresh black strike stripe.

'Mommy!' the girl tried again, desperate. 'The front door. We can go through the front door. Into the woods. We're fast, we can make it.'

'No!' her mother declared, voice righteous. 'They'll be expecting that. No doubt have three, six, a dozen men already waiting. This is it. We'll torch the curtains. Minute the wall's fully engulfed, they'll flee the property. Fucking cowards.'

'Christine!' The little girl cracked her voice, changing tactics. She planted her feet, drew herself up as tall as her six-year-old frame would allow. 'Christine! Stop it! This is no time to play with matches!'

For a moment, the little girl thought it might work. Her mother blinked, her face losing some of its overbright luster. She stared at her daughter, right arm falling lax to her side.

'The furnace shut off,' the little girl declared boldly. 'But I fixed it. Now go to bed. Everything's all right. Go to bed.'

Her mother stared at her. Seemed confused, which was better than crazy. The little girl held her breath, chin up, shoulders back.

She did not know about *Them*. But she and her older sister had been preparing, planning, and strategizing to survive their mother for their entire young lives. Sometimes, you had to play along. But other times, you had to seize control. Before their mother went too far. Before they really were running for their lives, their mother having done the unspeakable in order to combat the unseeable in her mind.

Years ago, the little girl had suffered from bad dreams. She would hear a baby crying, and the sound haunted her. Her mother, calmer then, softer, rounder, would come into her room to comfort her. She would brush back the little girl's hair and sing, in a sad, pretty voice, of green grass and sunny skies and faraway places where little girls slept through the night in big soft beds with warm, full tummies.

The little girl had loved her mother during those moments. Sometimes, she wished she would have bad dreams just to hear her mother sing, feel the gentleness of her mother's fingertips tracing across her cheek.

But the little girl and her older sister didn't have nightmares anymore. They lived them instead.

The boy, in the woods. Maybe, if she jerked from her mother's grasp hard enough, ran fast enough . . .

The little girl drew herself up. She didn't really believe a boy could save her. Never had. Never would.

'Christine, go to bed,' the little girl ordered.

Her mother didn't move. She let go of the little girl's wrist, but her right hand still clutched the matches. 'I'm sorry, Abby,' she said.

The little girl's voice softened. 'Go to bed. It's okay. I'll help you.'

'Too late.' Her mother didn't move. Her voice was quiet, sad. 'You don't know what I did.'

'Mommy—'

'I had to. You'll understand someday, child. I had to.'

'Mommy . . .'

The little girl reached out a hand. But it was too late. Her mother was already moving. Dashing to the yellowed lace curtains. Match cover popping open, flipping back. First match ripped from the cardboard prison.

'No, no, no!' The little girl gave chase, clutching at her mother's oversized coat, trying to grab the thick wool fabric and yank her mother back.

They were dancing, whirling around in beams of moonlight, twirling around long, quivering shadows, except her mother was bigger, faster, stronger. Her mother was powered by madness, and the little girl had only desperation on her side.

The first match flared to life, a beautiful lick of orange in the dark.

Her mother paused as if to admire her accomplishment.

'Isn't it gorgeous,' she whispered.

Then she tossed the match at the dangling curtain. Just as the little girl's older sister stepped out of the shadows of the family room and swung a brass candlestick lamp into the back of their mother's head.

Their mother stumbled. Looked up. SisSis struck her again, this time across the left temple. Their mother dropped like a rock.

The ancient candlestick lamp fell to the floor beside her, while with a faint whoosh, the hem of the lace curtain burst into flame.

The little girl got the curtain first. She beat it out with her bare hands, flattening the flames against the dirty wall, smacking it until, with a charred sputter, the fire was extinguished and only the palms of her hands burned.

Breathing hard, the little girl turned at last to her sister, the two of them on either side of their mother's fallen form. The little girl looked up at her older sister. Her older sister looked down at the little girl.

'Where were you?' the little girl spoke first.

Her sister didn't answer, and for the first time, the little girl noticed something else. The way her sister studied her left side. The way the gray nylon of her winter coat bloomed with a dark flowering stain.

'SisSis?'

The little girl's sister clutched her side. She splayed the fingers of her hand, and the dark rushed out, racing across the gray of the jacket, stealing the moonlight from the room.

The little girl realized now why her sister hadn't met her on the upstairs landing. Because their mother had woken her first. Brought her downstairs first. Listened to the voices telling her what to do to her older daughter, first.

The little girl didn't speak anymore. She held out her hand. Her older sister took it, swaying, falling to her knees. The little girl went with her, down onto the grimy kitchen floor. They held hands, across their mother's still form. How many times they had crept into this kitchen together, scrounging for food, hiding from their mother, just meeting, just being together, because everyone needed an ally in war.

The little girl was not dumb. She knew their mother hurt SisSis worse and more often. She knew that SisSis accepted the punishment, because when her mother was in one of her moods, someone had to pay. So SisSis was the good soldier, who kept her little sister safe.

'Sorry,' SisSis whispered now, a single world of apology, a single sigh of regret.

'Please, SisSis, please,' the little girl begged. 'Don't leave me . . . I'll call nine-one-one. Help will come. Just wait. Wait for me.'

In response, her older sister tightened her grip. 'It's okay.' Her breath left her in a soft, hiccuping rush. 'Everyone has to die some-time, right? Be brave. I love you. Be brave . . .'

Her older sister's grip weakened. Her hand fell to the floor and the little girl sprang for the phone, dialing 911 just as SisSis had taught her, because they'd known it might someday come to this. They just hadn't thought it would be so soon.

The little girl gave her mother's name and address. She requested an ambulance. She spoke clearly and without emotion, because she had practiced for this, too. Together, she and her older sister had prepared, planned, and strategized.

Their mother wasn't crazy about everything: Everyone did have to die sometime, and you always had to be brave.

Task completed, the little girl released the phone and raced back to her sister. But by the time she returned, SisSis didn't need her anymore. Her eyes were closed, and nothing the little girl did made them open again.

Her mother stirred on the floor.

The little girl looked at her, then at the old brass lamp.

She lifted up the heavy lamp, thin arms straining, eyes watching how the silvery beams of moonlight gleamed across its dull surface.

Her mother moaned again, regaining consciousness.

The little girl thought of lullabies and matches; she recalled soft hugs and hungry nights. She remembered her older sister, who had genuinely loved her. Then the little girl clutched the top part of the shadeless lamp, stood above her mother's body, and one final time, hefted its weight into the air.

# 1

My name is Charlene Rosalind Carter Grant.

I live in Boston, work in Boston, and in four days, will probably die here.

I'm twenty-eight years old.

And I don't feel like dying just yet.

It started two years ago, with the murder of my best friend, Randi Menke, in Providence. She was strangled in her living room. No sign of a struggle, no sign of forced entry. For a while the Rhode Island cops thought maybe her ex had done it. I guess there'd been a history of domestic assaults. Nothing she'd ever told me, or our other best friend, Jackie, about. Jackie and I tried to console ourselves with that, as we wept together at Randi's funeral. We hadn't known. We just hadn't known or of course we would've done . . . something. Anything.

That's what we told ourselves.

Fast forward one year. January 21. The anniversary. I'm at home with Aunt Nancy in the mountains of northern New Hampshire, Jackie's returned to her corporate life as a VP for Coca-Cola in Atlanta. Jackie doesn't want to mark the occasion of Randi's murder. Too morbid, she tells me. Later, in the summer, we'll get together and celebrate Randi's birthday. Maybe we'll hike to the top of Mount Washington, bring a bottle of single malt. We'll have a good drink, have a good cry, then sleep it off at the Lake of the Clouds AMC hut.

I still call Jackie on the twenty-first. Can't help myself. Except she doesn't answer. Not her landline, not her work line, not her mobile. Nothing.

In the morning, when she doesn't show up for work, the police finally give in to my pleas and drive by her house.

No sign of a struggle, I will read later in the police report. No sign of forced entry. Just a lone female, strangled to death in the middle of her home on January 21.

Two best friends, murdered, exactly one year and roughly one thousand miles apart.

The locals investigated. Even the FBI gave it a whirl. They couldn't find anything definitive to link the two homicides, mostly because they couldn't find anything that was definitive.

Bad luck, one of the guys actually told me. Sheer bad luck.

Today is January 17 of the third year.

How much bad luck do you think I'm going to have on the twenty-first? And if you were me, what would you do?

I met Randi and Jackie when I was eight years old. After that final incident with my mother, I was sent to live with my Aunt Nancy in the wilds of New Hampshire. She came to fetch me from a hospital in upstate New York, two relatives, two strangers, meeting for the first time. Aunt Nancy took one look at me and started to cry.

'I didn't know,' she told me that first day. 'Trust me, child, I didn't know or I would've taken you years ago.'

I didn't cry. Saw no purpose for the tears and didn't know if I believed her anyway. If I was supposed to live with this woman, then I'd live with this woman. Not like I had anyplace else to go.

Aunt Nancy ran a B&B in a quaint resort town in the Mount Washington Valley, where rich Bostonians and privileged New Yorkers came to ski during the winter, hike in the summer, and 'leafpeep' in the fall. She had one part-time helper, but mostly my aunt relied on herself to greet guests, clean rooms, set up tea, cook breakfast, provide directions, and all the other million little odd jobs that go into the hospitality trade. When I came along, I took over dusting and vacuuming. I could spend hours cleaning. I loved the scent of Pine-Sol. I loved the feel of freshly polished wood. I loved the way I scrubbed the floor again and again, and each time, it looked pretty and fresh and new.

Cleaning meant controlling. Cleaning kept the shadows at bay.

First day of school, Aunt Nancy personally walked me down the street. I wore stiff new clothes, including black patent Mary Janes I polished obsessively for the next six months. I felt conspicuous. Too new. Too fresh out of the box.

I still wasn't used to all the noise and clamor that came with 'village' life. Neighbors, everywhere I looked. People who made eye contact and smiled.

'Your tea set is tarnished,' I informed my aunt, one block from my first ever school. 'I'll go home and polish it for you.'

'You're a funny child, Charlene.'

I stopped walking, my hand rubbing my side and the scar that still itched sometimes. I had more scars, spiderweb fine, on the back of my left hand, let alone the ugly surgical mark on my right elbow, burn marks on my right thigh. I was pretty sure other kids didn't have such blemishes on their bodies. I was pretty sure other children's mothers didn't 'love' them as much as mine had sworn she loved me. 'I don't want to go.'

My aunt stopped walking. 'Charlie, it is time to go to school. Now, I want you to march through those front doors. I want you to hold your head high. And I want you to know, you are the bravest, toughest little girl I know, and none of those kids have anything on you. Do you hear me? None of those kids have anything on you.'

So I did what my aunt said. I walked through those doors. I kept my head high. I slid into a desk at the back of a room. Where the little girl on my left turned and said, 'Hi, I'm Jackie.' And the little girl on my right turned and said, 'I'm Randi.'

And just like that, we were friends.

But I never told them everything.

You know what I mean, don't you?

How sometimes, even with best friends, even with the sisters of your heart who laugh with you and cry with you and know every single minuscule detail of your first crush and final heartbreak, you still can't tell them *everything*.

Even best friends have secrets.

Take it from me, the last one standing, who's spent the past two years learning most of our secrets the hard way.

We grew up in the last days of real childhood. Spending our summers running wild in the woods, where we built tree forts out of downed limbs and had tea parties featuring acorn soup and pinecone parfaits. We raced leaf boats down eddying streams. We discovered secret swimming holes. We wired soup cans with twine in lieu of cell phones.

I'd help Aunt Nancy every morning and every evening during the summer. But afternoons were mine, and I spent every minute with my two best friends. Even back then, Jackie was the organizer. She'd have our afternoons all mapped out, probably would've developed a marketing plan and forecasted future opportunities for play if we'd let her. Randi was quieter. She had beautiful wheat blond hair she wore tucked behind her ears. She preferred playing house in the tree fort, where she always had the perfect finishing touch for her tree stump, maybe some creative combination of berries and leaves that made a random pile of decaying limbs feel just like home.

I recommended her skills to Aunt Nancy, and for much of our high school years Randi helped out in the B&B on the weekends, hanging holiday ornaments, preparing fresh centerpieces for the dining room, decorating the front parlor. Jackie would come along as well, hooking up Aunt Nancy's first computer and, when the time came, introducing my aunt to the Internet.

I didn't have Jackie's drive, or Randi's artistic skills. I thought of myself as the glue. Whatever they wanted to do, I did. Whatever hobby they had, I took up. I'd been raised at an early age to go along, so going along was what I did best.

But I meant it. I loved them. I'd grown up in the dark, then I'd come to the mountains of New Hampshire and found the light. Randi and Jackie laughed. They asked my opinions, they complimented my efforts, they smiled when I walked into a room.

I didn't care what we did. I just wanted to do it with them.

Of course, small town kids inevitably have big city dreams. Jackie started the countdown our junior year in high school. She was sick of nosy neighbors, community theater, and a post office that doubled as the biggest gossip center in town. She had her sights on Boston College, gonna hit the big city and live the glamorous life.

Randi, in her quiet way, upstaged Jackie. One snowy weekend in January, she met a Brown University med student on the ski slopes. We graduated high school in June, and she was married July 1, packing her childhood into four cardboard boxes and heading for Providence, content to spend the rest of her life as a doctor's wife.

Jackie got her scholarship. She was gone by September, and for the first time in ten years I didn't know what to do with myself. I stripped, sanded, and refinished Aunt Nancy's hardwood floors. Steam cleaned all the drapes. Shampooed all the furniture. Started organizing the bookshelves.

End of September, Aunt Nancy took me by the hand.

'Go,' she said, firmly, gently. 'Spread your wings, and then, when you're ready, come home to me.'

I ended up in Arvada, Colorado. Followed some guy I never should've followed. Did some things it's best that Aunt Nancy never knows about. I learned the hard way, you can't always just go along. Sooner or later, you have to find yourself, even without your beloved aunt and two best friends to help show the way.

After the breakup, determined not to slink home with my tail between my legs, I applied for a job as a 911 operator. Biggest attraction of the job: You didn't need a college degree, just a high-school diploma, fast typing fingers, and an innate ability to think on your feet. Given those were about the only skills I possessed, I decided to give it a whirl. For thirty thousand dollars a year, I worked long hours, surrendered any hope of having a personal life, and actually discovered a calling.

I worked at a command center with twenty-two phone lines, four radios, and nearly two hundred thousand calls a year. Requests for police, fire, emergency services, animal control – it all came to us. We transferred the calls for emergency services and fire to a second dispatch service, but animal control, police, the prank calls, the incoherent calls, the genuinely panicked and hysterical calls were all ours.

I once worked a shift where my fellow dispatch officer saved a woman's life by having her scream until the home invaders panicked and ran away. Another shift, my colleague got a terribly injured teenage girl to describe the car that ran her down. The girl died before the police got there, but her statement was recorded on our call lines and became the evidence that put the drunk driver away. I cried with people. I screamed with people. Once, I sang lullabies to a five-year-old boy while his parents shattered glass and hurled insults just outside the closet door.

I don't know what happened to the boy. I think about him sometimes, though. More than I should.

Which is why after six years, I left Arvada and returned to the mountains. I guess I'd lost some weight. I guess I didn't look so good.

'Oh, Charlene Rosalind Carter Grant,' my Aunt Nancy said quietly when I got off the plane.

She took me in her arms. I stood in the middle of the airport and cried.

My aunt had been right: I'd needed to go away, and now it was good to be back. I embraced the mountains; I welcomed my community, where I was surrounded by neighbors and everyone looked you in the eye and smiled. Aunt Nancy had become my family, and this one town, had, finally, become my home.

I didn't plan on leaving again. But I guess someone else had other ideas.

Standing at Randi's funeral, I didn't feel any sense of danger. My childhood friend was dead, but the more Jackie and I learned about her rat bastard ex, the more we thought we knew the perpetrator. Just because the police couldn't charge him, didn't mean her abusive, alcoholic ex hadn't done the deed. Doctors are probably wise enough in the general workings of forensic science to cover their tracks. Plus, Randi was softhearted. We could see her letting her ex through the front door, despite her best judgment.

I spent some time with the Providence detectives, trying to advocate on my friend's behalf. Jackie sprung for a private consultant from Oregon, some retired FBI agent to analyze the scene. Neither one of us got anything to show for our efforts.

Then, one year later, Jackie . . . Who lived in downtown Atlanta, who was city-smart and corporate battle-hardened, and, in many ways, forewarned. Who would she have welcomed into her home that night? Who would she have stood quietly and allowed to strangle her in her own living room, without putting up a fight?

Certainly not Randi's ex-husband.

Meaning, maybe the abusive ex didn't do it. Meaning, maybe it was someone else.

Someone who knew Randi and knew Jackie. Someone they knew and trusted.

Someone who, by definition, would have to know me, too. Because there were no such things as Randi and Jackie. For ten years, in our town, it had always been Randi Jackie Charlie. Just like that. One name for one entity. The three amigos. All for one, one for all.

With two dead, did that mean there was now one left to go?

In contrast to Randi's memorial service, I stood dry-eyed next to Jackie's cherrywood coffin, searching the crowd in the tiny, tastefully decorated Victorian funeral parlor. I peered into the faces of my grieving neighbors, community members, friends.

I wondered if someone standing beside me right now was already counting down until the next January 21. Except why and how and who? So many questions. I figured I had 362 days left to find answers.

We concluded Jackie's service at 9 p.m. I was in my car by 9:15. Luggage in the trunk, the feel of Aunt Nancy's dry kiss fresh on my cheek.

I drove to Boston. Ditched the car, tossed my cell phone, and turned my back on Aunt Nancy, my community, the mountains, and the only shot I'd had at a real life. As the saying goes, hope for the best, but plan for the worst.

So that's what I'm doing. Hoping for the police to do their thing, and catch the bastard who murdered my best friends. But planning on January 21 rolling around, when sometime around 8 p.m., according to the police reports, someone may come looking for me. Because once there'd been Randi Jackie Charlie, then Jackie Charlie, then just Charlie. And soon maybe none of us at all.

I don't have friends anymore. I don't encourage acquaintances. I live in Cambridge, where I rent a single room from a retired widow who needs the income. I work a solo graveyard shift as a dispatch officer for a thirty-man PD outside of Boston. I work all night, sleep all morning.

I run ten miles four times a week. I attend firearms training courses. I box. I lift weights. I prepare, I plan, I strategize.

In four days, I believe someone's going to try to kill me.

But the son of a bitch has gotta catch me first.

# 2

Boston Sergeant Detective D.D. Warren was on the case. And she was not happy about it.

This was unusual. A born workaholic, D.D. lived and breathed her job. Nothing made her happier than a high-profile homicide case that demanded endless nights of cold pizza as she and her squad racked up round-the-clock hours, targeting their prey.

Granted, she was a mother now, and baby Jack was proving as big an insomniac as his mom. Teething? Probably not at ten weeks. Colic? Maybe. It's not like babies came with an instruction manual. D.D. had tried singing to him last night. He'd cried harder. Finally, she'd rocked and cried with him. They'd both fallen asleep around four; her alarm had woken her at six. But two hours of sleep wasn't the reason D.D. was cranky.

True, her life had undergone another major sea change: Given the unexpected news that she was forty and pregnant, she'd decided to roll the dice toward domestic bliss and actually move in with the baby's father. She'd sold her North End condo, said sayonara to the four pieces of furniture she'd managed to acquire over the years, and moved into Alex's tiny suburban ranch. He'd graciously given her the entire closet. She was trying to stop hogging the covers. They both loved the nursery.

Alex was supportive, caring, and most importantly, as a crime scene expert who taught courses at the police academy, wise enough to allow her plenty of space to do her job. He'd spent the previous night taking his turn being up all hours with the baby, so Alex definitely wasn't the reason she was cranky.

Granted, this was also her first major case after her eight-week maternity leave, but given the past two weeks of office paperwork, fieldwork seemed a great idea and definitely was not the reason she was cranky.

Frankly, she didn't want to talk about it. She just wanted others to feel her pain.

D.D. pushed her way through the growing crowd of gawkers piling up on the sidewalk, then flashed her shield at the uniformed officer standing outside the crime scene tape. He dutifully entered her name and badge number in the murder book. Then she was ducking under the yellow tape and slipping on shoe booties and a hair net, before finally mounting the peeling wooden steps of the faded gray tenement building.

Scene was on the second floor. One-bedroom unit of the low-income housing project. Victim was a forty-something Caucasian male, which from what D.D. could tell, made him the only white guy in an eight-block radius. Apparently, he lived alone, and they'd only gotten the call when neighbors had complained of the smell.

D.D. hated tenement houses. If you could take despair, give it four walls, leaking ceilings, and very few windows, this is what it would look like. She hated the punk ass teenagers that eyed her boldly as she approached, already so grim they might as well piss off a Boston cop, because what else did they have to lose? She fretted over the shrunken, eighty-year-old grandmothers, forced to carry heavy bags of groceries up three flights of stairs to a bone-cold efficiency unit in the winter, or a 120-degree boiling kettle in the summer. She despaired over the packs of feral kids gazing distrustfully out of doorways, because at the ripe old ages of four, five, six, they'd already been taught to hate all authority figures.

Race relations in Boston. Inner-city socioeconomics. Label it whatever you wanted; tenement buildings stood as a constant reminder to D.D. of all the ways her job was still failing a significant portion of Boston's population.

Guy here had been murdered. D.D. and her squad would investigate. D.D. and her squad would arrest the killer. And life for everyone in this building would suck just as much tomorrow as it did today.

Sergeant Detective D.D. Warren was cranky. But she did not want to talk about it.

D.D.'s squadmate, Neil, met her on the second-floor landing. The thirty-two-year-old lanky redhead used to work as an EMT before joining the BPD, and was their go-to man for all things gory. Currently, he was holding a handkerchief over his mouth and nose, which D.D. took as a bad sign.

He took one look at the expression on her face and recoiled slightly.

'The baby?' he asked tentatively.

'Not why I'm cranky,' she snapped.

He had to think about it. 'Alex left you?'

'Oh for heaven's sake . . .' She loved her squad and her squad loved her. But just working with her was enough for them to believe that Alex, who lived with her, must be a saint. 'Not why I'm cranky.'

'You don't have to go inside,' Neil ventured. 'I mean, if you're worried about the smell, or, or . . .' His voice trailed off. The warning look in her eyes was enough; he stopped talking.

'My parents are coming!' D.D. blurted out.

'You have parents?'

She rolled her eyes at him. 'Florida,' she muttered. 'They live in Florida. Where they play golf and bridge and do all the things old people do. They like being in Florida. I like them being in Florida. Just because I have a baby is no reason to mess with a good thing.'

Neil nodded, then waited. When it became clear she was done speaking, he leaned forward slightly. 'Do they have names?'

'Patsy and Roy.'

'Oh. Well, that explains it. Can we talk about the murder vic now? Please.'

'Thought you'd never ask. What do we got?'

'Two GSWs to the head. Probably three to four days dead.'

D.D. raised a brow. 'Bloated, gassy?' she asked, meaning the corpse.

'Well, been brutally cold, which helped,' Neil offered.

True. A four-day-old corpse in the heat and humidity of August D.D. would've smelled a block away. As it was, standing three yards from the door of the apartment, she caught only the dull undertones of something rancid. Thank heavens for the mid-January deep freeze in Boston.

Then she thought of something. 'What about the apartment's heating unit?' she asked with a frown.

'Turned off.'

She arched a brow. 'By the victim, or the killer?'

Neil shrugged, because of course he couldn't know that yet, which didn't mean he hadn't wondered himself. D.D. often thought out loud, which, out of sheer self-preservation, her squad had learned not to take personally.

'Who's here?' D.D. asked now, meaning the other investigators.

Neil rattled off several names. Their other squadmate, Phil, the family man. A couple of crime scene techs, latent prints, photographer, the ME's office. Not too big a party, which D.D. preferred. Space was small, and extra officers, even so-called experts, had a tendency to mess things up. D.D. liked her crime scenes tight and controlled. Later, if things went wrong, that meant it would be on her head. But D.D. would rather shoulder the blame than ride herd on a bunch of uniforms.

'What else do I need to know?' she asked Neil.

'Won't tell you,' Neil announced stubbornly.

She glanced at him, startled. Their other squadmate, Phil, was known to go toe-to-toe with her. Neil not so much.

'If I tell you and I'm wrong, you're gonna be pissed,' Neil muttered, no longer looking at her. 'I don't tell you, and I'm right, you can feel good about yourself later – and take the credit.'

D.D. shook her head. Neil would be an excellent detective, if only he didn't hide behind her and Phil so much. He seemed content to let them be the forward members of the crew, while he spent his days overseeing autopsies at the morgue.

She wondered if the medical examiner, Ben Whitley, was here. Neil and Ben had been dating for a little over a year now. Not an office romance, per se, but an industry one. Made D.D. uneasy about what might happen in the event of a breakup. On the other hand, given that she was forty, unwed, and now mother to a ten-week-old baby boy, she figured she wasn't in any position to give personal advice.

Life happened. All you could do was ride the ride.

She sighed, pinched the bridge of her nose, and felt the full weight of her ride's current sleeplessness. Jack had been snuggled into his carrier when she'd left him this morning. All wide blue eyes and fat red cheeks. When she'd kissed the top of his head, he'd waved his pudgy little fists at her.

Did a ten-week-old baby know enough to miss his mommy, because a ten-week mommy sure knew enough to miss her baby.

D.D. sighed one last time, squared her shoulders, and got on with it.

First scent that hit D.D.'s nostrils was the overwhelmingly astringent odor of ammonia. She recoiled as if she'd hit a wall, her eyes already tearing up as she frantically waved at the air in front of her, an instinctive motion that made no difference.

She glanced down and noticed the rest of the story: piles and piles of animal feces, which accompanied at least a dozen pools of urine.

'What the hell?' she demanded.

'Puppy,' Neil supplied. 'Cute floppy-eared yellow lab. Was shut up for multiple days with the body. Obviously, not good for house-breaking. Puppy survived on toilet water and a box of crackers it chewed its way into. Animal control already took her away, if you want a puppy for Jack.'

'Jack sleeps, eats, and poops. What's he gonna do with a puppy?'

'Hmm,' Neil said, nodding sagely. 'It's probably just a phase.'

D.D. stepped carefully over the puppy piles and followed Neil through the tiny living area into the even tinier kitchen. She waved to a couple of crime scene techs as she went, easing around them in the tight space. Each nodded in greeting but kept working. Given the smell, she couldn't blame their desire to get in, out, and done.

Off the kitchen was an open doorway that appeared to lead to the single bedroom. Inside, D.D. spotted her other squadmate, Phil, sitting at a tiny desk with his back to the kitchen. He was wearing gloves, his fingers flying over the keyboard of the vic's laptop. As their technical expert, he was the most qualified for preliminary data mining. Later, of course, he'd deliver the laptop to the techies for a full-scale forensic eval. But in any investigation, time was of the essence, so Phil liked to see what he could learn sooner, rather than waiting for the full forensic analysis, which would follow weeks later.

'Hey, Phil,' she called out to her older squadmate.

He glanced over his shoulder at her, raising one arm absently in greeting, then, spotting her face, performed a double take.

'Is it Jack?' he asked. Phil had four kids.

'Not why I'm cranky,' she gritted out.

'Alex . . .'

'Not why I'm cranky!'

'Her parents are coming,' Neil supplied from behind her.

'You have parents?'

D.D. glared at Phil. He quickly returned his attention to the victim's computer, which allowed her to return her attention to the kitchenette, where a small wooden table had been shoved against the far wall. It featured two rickety wooden chairs, one of which was currently occupied by a corpse.

The ME, Ben Whitley, was leaning over the body. He looked up at D.D. as she approached, but she noticed he was careful to keep his gaze away from Neil.

*Hmm*, she felt like saying. *It's probably just a phase.*

She switched her attention to the vic, an either really fat or really bloated white guy with greasy brown hair and twin bullet holes through the left side of his forehead.

'No one heard the shots?' she asked. Her eyes still stung from the stench of urine. She understood Neil's handkerchief now and resiliently forced herself not to gag.

'In this neighborhood?' Neil replied wryly.

D.D. pursed her lips, acknowledging his point.

Dead guy's considerable mass was just beginning to contort inside the sausage-like casings of his jeans and button-down red flannel shirt. The force of the shots had sent his head back, where his features had probably locked in the first two to six hours due to rigor mortis. Within two to three days, however, rigor had passed, the muscles slackening, the flesh of his jowls seeming to slide down his face like wax melting from a candle. Next step in the decomp process: putrefaction. Within twenty-four hours, bacterial action inside the body produced gases, leading to swelling and a very distinct odor known to homicide detectives and MEs the world over. Skin around the lower abdomen and groin turned blue-green, while stomach contents started to leak out through the mouth, nose, and anus.

Nothing pretty about decomp, which meant that all in all, D.D. was pleasantly surprised by the corpse's intact condition. Bacterial action was just starting up, versus already running amok through the dead guy's intestines. Made the scene more bearable, though she still wouldn't want to be standing as close to the body as the ME was.

'So you're thinking three to four days?' she asked Ben now, the doubt obvious in her voice.

He pursed his lips, considering. 'Cold temperatures impede decomp. Given the apartment's chilly ambience, I think that explains the slow putrefaction process. But won't know for sure until I open him up.'

'First thoughts?'

'Cause of death is most likely twin GSWs to the left side of the forehead,' he stated. 'Double tap, up close and personal. Notice the powder burn ringing the entry wounds, as well as the tight pairing. GSW one and GSW two are not even half an inch apart.'

'Execution style?' D.D. asked with a frown, venturing closer in spite of herself. 'Any defensive wounds?'

'Negative.'

D.D. trusted Ben implicitly – he was one of the best MEs the city ever had. But she couldn't stop from glancing at the vic's hands because the lack of defensive wounds didn't make any sense. Who sat at his kitchen table and just let himself be shot?

'You're sure it's not suicide?' she asked Ben.

'No gun at the scene. No GSR on his hands,' the ME reported, then added, as a slight rebuke for her questioning his findings, 'unless, of course, he was wearing gloves which he kindly removed after shooting himself to death and hiding the murder weapon.'

D.D. got his point. She glanced back at Neil. 'Forced entry?'

The lanky redhead shook his head. He appeared smug. 'First responders had the building manager let them in. No sign of tampering with the lock. Windows are intact, not to mention too warped to open.'

D.D. eyed her squadmate. 'You're not going to tell me, are you?'

'Nope.'

'All right, all right,' she muttered. 'Game on.'

She continued her analysis of the scene. Entry wounds to vic's forehead appeared tight and round. Given the lack of exit wound, she assumed a small-caliber weapon, such as a .22. Easy enough handgun to conceal until the last minute, especially this time of year when everyone was bulked up in winter jackets. But also a questionable choice for a murder weapon – not much bang in a .22. Gun aficionados generally referred to such handguns as 'plinking' guns. Good for shooting at cans and squirrels, or maybe hurling at an opponent if all else failed. But plenty of people got shot by .22s and lived, making the small-caliber handgun a dubious choice for an execution-style homicide.

D.D. moved on with her analysis: Shooter was most likely someone the victim knew. Victim not only opened the door, but let the unknown subject into his apartment. Furthermore, sitting at the kitchen table implied hospitality. Would you like something to drink, that sort of thing.

D.D. crossed to the kitchen sink. Sure enough, two chipped blue mugs sat inside the grimy stainless steel basin. With gloved hands, she lifted the first mug and peered inside. No noticeable dried residue, so either a clear liquid or the mugs were rinsed.

She returned the mugs, which would be bagged and tagged by the evidence techs, then did a double take.

Mugs had been rinsed, then placed in the sink? Because nothing else inside the apartment looked like it had been rinsed, wiped, or otherwise tended in at least six months. The countertops were sticky and grungy. Ditto with the urine-splattered floor, grime-covered floorboards, and stained walls.

She glanced back at the wooden table, which also appeared suspiciously pristine. She ran a gloved finger along the battered surface. Old yes, battle-scarred definitely, but clean. So two mugs rinsed, one wooden table wiped.

She looked up at Neil, who was smiling even more broadly now.

'Shooter cleaned up after himself,' she murmured.

He wouldn't reply, but given his terrible poker face, he didn't have to.

Next up, D.D. wrenched open the refrigerator door. She discovered an opened can of dog food that smelled even worse than the rest of the apartment, a six-pack of beer, wine coolers, Hostess Twinkies, containers of leftover Chinese, half a dozen condiments, and the remains of a rotisserie chicken dated ten days prior.

So the victim liked fast food and had a sweet tooth.

D.D. tried some of the cupboards, discovering paper products in lieu of plates, plastic products in lieu of silverware, as well as multiple shelves of chips, crackers, cereals, and store-bought cookies. Last cupboard seemed to be for the dog – bags of dry puppy food, plus more canned food.

D.D. continued to build her mental profile. Middle-aged single white male, living a bachelor life in a low-income housing project.

Why this building? White guy had to stand out, feel uncomfortable. Lonely? Was that why he got a puppy? But he entertained. Had someone here, whom he invited in for a drink, perhaps, maybe come over, see my new puppy. Have a drink, have a snack.

D.D. got that feeling. It was a distinct physical sensation that started at the base of a good detective's spine, before zipping straight up the vertebrae to the back of her neck, where the tiny hairs stood up and made her shiver.

She glanced at Neil, who beamed larger.

'No fucking way!' she said.

'Way.'

'What's Phil found?'

'Don't know about the computer, but we already discovered two shoeboxes of photos tucked beneath the bed.'

'Is the vic in the system?'

'No hits thus far, though we're still running his name and prints through the national database.'

'But the photos?'

'All boys, all under the age of twelve, mostly black, but other ethnicities as well. I'd say he selected his victims based on opportunity, rather than race.'

'Son of a bitch!' D.D. exclaimed. 'He's a pedophile. Set up shop right in the middle of his target population – unloved, unsupervised, highly vulnerable kids. Gets their attention when he's walking his puppy, then invites them up for a cookie, chips, a bottle of beer. Son of a bitch.'

'D.D.'

She glared at the dead guy, the twin holes in his forehead, the melted wax face. 'Kid struck back,' she muttered, then considered the carefully wiped down surfaces. 'Or maybe a parent or an older sibling or a friend. Someone got wise, then he got dead. Good.'

'D.D.'

'What?'

'It gets better.'

'What's better than one less pervert in the city?'

Phil came walking out of the bedroom, snapping off his gloves. 'You tell her yet?' he asked Neil.

'Tell me what?'

'You were on maternity leave,' Phil said, as if that explained everything.

'Tell me what!'

'Not one less pervert in the city,' Neil said happily. 'Mr Wanna See My Puppy over there makes two.'

Phil and Neil had to walk her through it. It was four weeks back, meaning Jack had been six weeks old, a plump little form that spent his days curled up on her chest, feeling like a hot water bottle except fragile and in need of constant diligence, so she'd spent hours just sitting in the rocking chair with him, counting fingers and toes and touching the impossibly soft wisps of hair that cradled his skull – so she'd definitely *not* been watching the news, because she'd been *being* with her baby in a way she'd never been in any moment before. Totally. Completely. Without word or thought or interest in anything else. Alex would come home from work each day, glance at her and Jack in the rocking chair and smile at her in a way no man had ever smiled at her before. Then she'd get a strange feeling in her chest. Of belonging. Of being. Contentment maybe.

For her eight weeks of maternity leave, she'd reveled in it.

So, four weeks prior, D.D. had been nesting with her baby in Waltham, while a level 3 sex offender had been shot in his apartment near the Suffolk County hospital. Not in his kitchen, Phil was quick to add. In the entry. As if he'd answered the door, and boom. Double tap from a .22, expertly placed.

No witnesses, though a couple of neighbors reported having seen a young man, maybe a teenage boy, loitering about. Further search of the vic's home had revealed pornographic videotapes as well as an extensive collection of photos on the vic's computers, all showing boys and girls between the ages of six and twelve involved in various sex acts.

Just owning the computer was a violation of the victim's, Douglas Antiholde's, parole, so investigators felt it was safe to assume the vic had gone off the straight and narrow and was back in the business of destroying young lives.

'Leads?' D.D. asked now.

Phil shrugged. 'If you see a white male between the age of sixteen and twenty-five in a dark winter coat with a navy blue knit cap, let us know.'

'Bet the hotline's ringing off the phone with that one.'

'Please, the neighbors are just doing the happy dance he's dead. No love lost there, and that was *before* they heard what was on his computer.'

D.D. pursed her lips. 'Did he have a puppy?'

Phil shook his head.

'We'll have to cross-reference the photos of the victims,' she mused out loud, and immediately felt something inside her recoil. To go from Jack to those images . . .

She hesitated. Beside her, Phil, father of four, appeared equally queasy.

Neil spoke up. 'I'll do it.'

Phil and D.D. looked at him.

'It's not like I *want* to,' he said, shrugging awkwardly. 'But I don't have kids. And both of you . . . So, you know, it'd probably be easier for me to study them. 'Sides, I handle the bodies all the time. How much harder can this be?'

'Way harder,' Phil said immediately. 'Dead people . . . worst has already happened. These kids . . .'

Neil shrugged again. 'Somebody's gotta do it, right? Better me than you.'

Phil nodded slowly. 'I think he's growing up nicely,' he told D.D.
'Obviously we've raised him right,' she concurred.

Neil rolled his eyes at both of them. 'Since it's my first time
through, any advice?'

'Don't just look at the people,' D.D. informed him. 'Cross-
referencing the victims is step one, but you also want to examine the
backgrounds of each photo – look for patterns in curtains, carpets,
bedding. Sometimes, it's not the who that matches, it's the where.
Either one gives us a link between our dead pervs. When you're done,
we'll send the photos to the National Center for Missing and
Exploited Children, where they have trained experts who will do the
same thing all over again, except comparing them against a national
database. They also have some facial recognition software, which
helps them get the job done.'

Neil looked at her.

'We gotta get you to the National Academy,' she informed her
younger partner, as she did at least once every six months. The
National Academy was a ten-week course in advanced police training
offered at Quantico, considered de rigueur for any up and coming
cop. When D.D. had attended, she'd spent an entire day with the
folks at the National Center for Missing and Exploited Children,
which not only helped her understand the resources they had to offer
for local law enforcement agencies such as the BPD, but also made
her grateful she was a city detective and not a criminologist swimming
against the tide to rescue sexually abused children.

She stared at Neil now. He looked away, as he did every time the
subject of the National Academy came up.

'Perpetrator's right-handed,' he mumbled, changing the subject.
'Given the angle of the gunshot.'

'Doesn't limit our suspect pool that much,' D.D. retorted with
a shrug.

'Daytime shootings,' Neil offered next.

'How do you figure?'

'Because in both neighborhoods, nobody would open their doors
after dark.'

'But no witnesses,' D.D. pushed back.

'Because in both neighborhoods,' Neil repeated, 'people are

trained not to see anything. And they certainly aren't gonna tell us about it if they do.'

'True.' D.D. turned to Phil. 'While Neil handles the photos, I need you to oversee both victims' computers. Pedophiles are net-workers. They visit chat rooms, post blogs, seek out others like themselves. Even if our two victims never met each other in person, doesn't mean they haven't crossed paths online. Find that common denominator, and maybe we can get some traction.'

'The Antiholde computer has already been processed,' Phil informed her. 'Meaning we just gotta dissect this one, and I'm ready to rock and roll.'

'We'll pull local video,' D.D. mused out loud, referring to the various video cameras that dotted any Boston city block, whether owned by the city or an area business, or even in some cases by a concerned citizen trying to protect him- or herself against crime. 'You never know, maybe we can find footage of a sixteen-to twenty-five-year-old white male in a black winter coat with a navy blue knit hat.'

Phil and Neil smiled at that, but D.D. wagged her finger at them. 'Seriously! Forget the wardrobe and age range. Think white kid. How many of them do you see outside? In this neighborhood, Caucasians stand out. Let's use that to our advantage.'

'Gonna get the media involved?' Phil wanted to know.

She had to think about it. 'Maybe, if we can get a better profile of the shooter. Until then, I don't see the point.'

Neil seemed surprised. 'But there have been two shootings, second one already half a week old. Meaning, maybe even now, we got a perpetrator out there, targeting a third victim.'

'Third pedophile, you mean,' Phil muttered.

D.D. was more circumspect. 'Two homicides performed by the same shooter? Are you sure? Do you have a witness telling you he or she absolutely saw the same person here and there? Do you have a report from Ballistics stating the slugs recovered from this crime scene absolutely positively match the slugs recovered from the Antiholde crime scene?'

Neil shook his head.

'Well then,' D.D. declared briskly. 'Let's not get ahead of ourselves. I wouldn't want to panic the good citizens of Boston unnecessarily. And . . . maybe I wouldn't want to encourage the city's pervert population to practice undo caution either.'

Neil's eyes rounded slightly. He got the implication of D.D.'s decision, glancing quickly at Phil, whose face was just as stony as D.D.'s.

'Wow,' Neil murmured. 'And I wondered if motherhood would make her soft . . .'

His voice trailed off. At the last minute, the youngest member of the squad seemed to realize he probably should've kept that thought to himself.

But D.D. just clapped him on the back. 'Missed you, too,' she informed him cheerfully. 'Now then. Nothing personal, but I gotta be home by five, which gives us –' she glanced at her watch – 'about six more hours to catch a killer. Let's do it.'

# 3

Hours later, D.D. finished overseeing the processing of the murder scene. She'd long stopped registering the ammonia-like scent of urine, let alone the rank odor of puppy poo. Instead, she clambered back down the stairs of the tenement building and out the front doors contemplating many thoughts at once: She should get home soon, she should contact the lead investigator from the first shooting, she should order a rush on the ballistics test from this shooting to compare with the previous shooting. What were the odds of her boss, Cal Horgan, letting her have an extra body to help view all the video footage? Or maybe she'd just have to do that herself. Phil, after all, would need days to pore through all the computer data. Neil would probably soon be in a state of depression going through all those photos, the kind of work D.D. and Phil had done before and would probably do again, but not any sooner than they had to. Didn't matter how objective and analytic you made yourself, photos of kids hurt. So adding to her mental list, check on Neil, see how he was coping with his assignment; did he require any mental health resources, or even a therapeutic night out over beers? Sergeants managed their people as much as their cases, and D.D. prided herself on both.

She cleared the building steps and hit fresh air, inhaling several deep breaths. No flash of media cameras awaited her; a shooting in a Boston tenement hardly rated coverage. Of course, once the media caught wind of what they'd found in the vic's photo boxes and, not being dumb bunnies, connected this incident with another shooting four weeks prior . . .

But for now, all was quiet, and D.D. was gonna enjoy it while she could.

She pushed through the last of the gawkers, most of them looking bored, an actual murder investigation not being nearly as exciting as what they'd seen on TV. D.D. buried her hands in her pockets, ducked her head against the biting January chill, and headed down the block to her car.

Fifty yards away, she spotted it. White, like a blot of snow, at the bottom of her windshield. Except when the wind caught it, it started flapping, and she realized it was half a piece of paper, shoved under the left wiper.

Maybe an advertisement or flier. She didn't pick up her pace, just kept walking, huddling inside her BPD field coat for warmth.

As she hit the hood of her car, she could see enough to realize it wasn't a flier – the letters were handwritten script, not block printed. She faltered, footsteps slowing. Keeping her hands in her pockets, she leaned forward, studying the half sheet of paper more closely.

The script letters were thin, almost spidery looking but curiously flat at the bottom, as if the person had used a ruler to set an edge. The note wasn't addressed or signed. It contained two sentences:

*Everyone has to die sometime.*

*Be brave.*

Immediately, D.D. glanced up, looked around. There, across the street, a figure disappearing around the corner in a black down coat.

D.D. started to run.

As she sprinted across the street, D.D. had two thoughts at once: Running was not a good idea for a woman who'd given birth ten weeks ago; things bounced that had not bounced a year ago and none of it was comfortable. Second, chasing a potential suspect all alone was not a good idea for a new mom who hoped to kiss her baby boy on the cheek in approximately three hours.

Bad news: Uniformed officers might carry radios, but detectives did not. Meaning she should've stopped at her car for the radio, yelled over her shoulder at another officer, something.

Ah fuck it. D.D. rounded the corner, saw the fast-moving figure in black preparing to cross the next street, and yelled out her Hail Mary pass: 'Boston Police. Stop or I'll shoot.'

Not even remotely close to appropriate use of force, but given that most of the public grew up on *Dirty Harry*, who were they to question such a threat? The figure in black obediently halted and turned around.

'Keep your hands where I can see them!' D.D. boomed, slowing to a jog, right hand inside her coat, on the butt of her handgun, still nestled in her shoulder holster.

The person of interest stuck his arms out, splaying black gloved fingers in a comic parody of *I didn't do it*.

D.D. settled into a walk, approaching more carefully. She homed in on the pale oval face she could just make out between the high collar of the black down coat and the low brim of the black wool hat. This close, she could see that the features were too small, too delicate to be male. In fact, once she adjusted for the bulky winter coat, she realized that the person in front of her was probably only five one, maybe a hundred, hundred and ten pounds.

Female. Young, early to mid-twenties would be her guess. Caucasian, with dark hair and hollowed out blue eyes that currently looked simultaneously wary, fearful, and defiant. Basic response of most of the general population when being confronted by a cop. The initial *I didn't do it* warring with the deeper knowledge of *but I have done something*.

D.D. came to a halt three paces back from the lone female. She kept her gaze hard, right hand still resting on the butt of her gun.

'Name?' she asked crisply.

'Why?'

D.D. narrowed her eyes. 'You always talk back to cops?'

'I'd like to see your badge,' the woman said firmly, but her voice wavered at the end. Tough, but not that tough.

D.D. said nothing, did nothing. Always the best offense.

In response, the girl sighed and seemed to settle in herself. A woman of experience.

D.D. let an entire minute drag out. Then, slowly, deliberately, she unclipped her badge from the waistband of her jeans with her left hand and held it out. 'Sergeant Detective D.D. Warren, Boston PD. I've told you mine, now you tell me yours.'

'Charlene Rosalind Carter Grant.'

'Say what?' D.D. blinked a few times at the long string. 'Rosalynn Carter . . . You're a former First Lady?'

'*Rosalind* Carter. Charlene. Rosalind. Carter. Grant. But you can call me Charlie.'

D.D. stared at her harder. 'You're not from around here, are you, Charlie?'

'No, I'm not.'

'Then what are you doing at my crime scene?'

The young woman stared at her. Her expression seemed to waver then, all at once, harden in resolve. 'I'm checking you out.'

'Excuse me?'

'Four days from now, I'm expecting to be murdered. I've read that you're one of the best homicide detectives in the city, so I'd like you to handle the investigation. I figure you're the only shot at justice I'll have left.'

D.D. took Charlie down to BPD headquarters. One, because that was the craziest damn story she'd ever heard, and that made D.D. deeply suspicious right there. Two, Charlie happened to match the very general description of the shooter from the first dead pervert scene, not to mention she'd been walking away from D.D.'s car at about the same time D.D. had spotted the windshield note. Finally, it's not like D.D. had any better leads to pursue, so one lone female in a bulky black winter coat it was.

D.D. patted down her suspect, then made her remove her hat before dumping her in the backseat of D.D.'s Crown Vic. Policing 101. Eye contact and facial expressions were everything, meaning D.D. never let suspects, interview subjects, or witnesses hide beneath hats and scarves.

D.D. bagged and tagged the note on her front windshield. She placed that on the seat beside her. Then, with Charlie in the back, D.D headed to HQ while working her phone in the front. In a matter of minutes, she was able to establish that Charlene Rosalind Carter Grant worked the comm center for the Grovesnor PD and was not listed on any outstanding warrants. Two points in the girl's favor, she supposed.

Next up, she checked her messages. One from Alex, just seeing about her day. Second was her mother, and D.D. instinctively cringed. Her parents would be arriving in just two days, Thursday night. Her mother wanted to know if D.D. planned on meeting their plane or was going to force them to find their way to Alex's house on their own. Her voice made her opinion on the subject clear. Also, the way she said '*Alex's* house'.

D.D. cleared the message, didn't immediately call back.

Not too late to panic, she thought idly. Maybe she, Alex, and baby Jack could all run away and join the circus. Personally, she thought Alex would look handsome in clown stripes, and Jack would be adorable in polka dots. And given the choice between confronting her clearly disapproving *You had a baby out of wedlock* mother and wearing a red clown nose for the rest of her life . . . well, D.D. thought that choice was clear.

D.D. sighed. Her parents hated coming north. No doubt, they'd been waiting for her to be a dutiful only child and bring their first grandchild to Florida. But Jack had been born almost four weeks premature, in mid-November versus mid-December. He'd had to spend his first week of life in neonatal intensive care, finishing baking, as her obstetrician had said. D.D. hadn't been capable of dealing with her parents at that time. She hadn't even called them until ten days after her own son's birth, a fairly unforgivable sin, she was informed later. But during those first few days . . .

By the time the crisis had passed, and D.D. had connected with her parents, it had been Thanksgiving. Too chaotic for travel, her mother informed her, voice filled with disapproval and dismay. D.D.'s selfishness had already cost them the first two weeks of their grandson's life, and now they'd be forced to delay even longer . . .

More phone calls, more holiday season churn, more guilt. Until here D.D. was, counting down to her parents' January 19 Boston flight.

Then her parents, who'd never planned on having kids but late in life ended up with her, and herself, who never planned on having a family but late in life ended up with Jack, could all sit together in one room.

If Alex had any sense at all, he'd start running now.

D.D. neared headquarters, started the search for parking. BPD headquarters was situated in the middle of inner-city Roxbury, where parking spots and drug-free neighborhoods were equally difficult to find. She performed her usual loop. Third time was the charm.

She parked, got out, opened the back door, and contemplated the girl again.

Charlene Rosalind Carter Grant simply climbed out and stood up.

'You don't talk much,' D.D. said.

'You don't believe me. What's there to say?'

D.D. nodded. 'Fair enough. Want coffee?' She strode across the street, keeping the girl beside her.

'Yes please. Are you charging me with something?'

'Should I be charging you with something?'

The girl sighed. 'Have you spoken to the Grovesnor PD?'

'Yep.'

'Then you know I'm not a total fruitcake.'

'Why'd you leave a note on my windshield?' D.D. asked.

'What note? I didn't leave a note.'

'Note you watched me bag and tag.'

'Not my note,' the girl said. 'Didn't even see it, let alone know that car was your vehicle. Trust me, to us non-law-enforcement types, all Crown Vics look alike.'

D.D. didn't comment, but thought it was a fair observation. In a street chock-full of police cruisers and Crown Vics, had the author of the note known enough to target D.D.'s car specifically, or a detective's vehicle generally? Something to consider for later.

D.D. escorted Charlie inside HQ, then upstairs to Homicide. The homicide department was a nice space, D.D. always thought. More business suite than gritty cop show set. As a squad leader, D.D. had her own tiny office, complete with a laminated wood desk, laptop, and plush black leather desk chair. Very civilized.

D.D. didn't take her charge there, but instead led Charlie to a small interview room, where she took the girl's coat, then plunked her down at the table. D.D. went off in pursuit of beverages. Coffee for the girl, which made D.D. waver, eye the pot. But no, she'd been decaffeinated this long, she could make it another hour.

She'd initially given up coffee during her pregnancy, or rather, Jack had rebelled so insistently she couldn't stomach the dark brew. Then, she'd stayed off the caffeine as she'd breast-fed for the first six weeks, surprising herself by desperately wanting to nurse, and had only weaned Jack at the six-week mark because she had to return to work and no way her schedule allowed for all that pumping and stuff other working moms heroically endured.

She missed it. Didn't talk about it, not even to Alex, because what could she say? She had to return to work. So her baby took a bottle and was now being watched eight hours a day by a nice lady down the street. That was life. If D.D. could walk a homicide scene, surely she could handle parenthood.

D.D. poured a cup of coffee for Charlie, grabbed a bottle of water for herself.

Ninety-three minutes before she went home.

She reentered the interview room, took a seat across from her person of interest, and got down to business.

'Where you from, Charlie?'

'J-Town, New Hampshire.'

'Never heard of it.'

'Three hours north, near Mount Washington. Small town. One of those places where everybody knows your name.'

'Why'd you leave?'

'Because I believe the person who will try to kill me on January twenty-first will be someone I know. So, first line of defense is to run away from everyone I know.'

The girl grimaced. She'd taken the coffee from D.D. but wasn't drinking it. Just holding it between her hands as if for warmth.

According to the preliminary background report, Charlene Rosalind Carter Grant was twenty-eight years old. In person, with her long brown hair scraped tightly into a ponytail, she appeared even younger. She had a slight frame, D.D. decided, further hollowed out by nerves or stress or something. The girl's pale cheeks were gaunt, her blue eyes bruised from sleepless nights. She wore an oversized shapeless black sweatshirt, the kind favored by street thugs and vandals, paired with broken-down jeans and cheap snow boots. An outfit guaranteed to blend into almost any urban landscape.

A good ensemble, D.D. figured, to be either predator or prey.

'Why January twenty-one? And why do you think you'll know your killer?'

The girl started talking then. It was impressive really. About her first childhood friend murdered two years ago on the twenty-first, then her second friend murdered one year later on the exact same date, leaving Charlie as the last man standing. Charlie had names of lead detectives, even volunteered a report written up by a retired FBI profiler, Pierce Quincy, analyzing the crime scenes.

'Findings?' D.D. had to ask, not that she trusted some Feebie's report, but, then again . . . She took some notes. One of the investigators, Rhode Island State Detective Roan Griffin, she knew from training exercises. Maybe she'd give him a call.

'Given the lack of physical evidence,' the girl said, 'no forced entry, no sign of struggle, Quincy theorizes the killer is of above-average intelligence, methodical in thought and appearance. Perhaps someone known to the victims, but at least someone who would initially appear nonthreatening. Probably above-average verbal skills, hence the killer's ability to talk his way into the home and control his victim's responses until the last possible moment.'

The girl recited the sentences flatly. Someone who'd read the crime scene analysis so many times, the words had ceased to refer to people she once knew and loved, and instead had become stock phrases repeated to trained professionals over and over again. D.D. had worked with family members from other cold cases. She knew how this drill went. The slow migration from wounded loved one to staunch advocate. How some family members ended up knowing more about forensics than the experts involved.

'Sexual assault?' D.D. asked.

'Negative.'

D.D. frowned. That surprised her. Most murderers were sexual predators at heart. Particularly given these dynamics, a crime that involved intimate stalking, then occurred up close and personal. Now, in cases of murder-for-hire, or a homicide for personal gain, lack of sexual assault was more typical. Motivation then was materialistic in nature, not sexually driven.

'Signs of robbery?' she asked now.

'Negative.'

'Anything missing at all? Even a special artifact, something meaningful to each victim?'

Charlie shook her head. 'But hard to be definitive,' she supplied. 'My friends lived alone, meaning it's hard to confirm every item in each household. If something small were taken, it could be easily overlooked.'

'What about inheritance?' D.D. asked. 'Anyone obviously better off from your friends' deaths?'

'I'm not sure. I don't think Randi had much, being recently divorced. I guess it went to her parents, maybe? Probably the same for Jackie. She was doing very well for Coca-Cola, but even then, I wouldn't call her rich. She probably had some equity in her house, her car, a retirement account. But tens of thousands, I'd guess, not hundreds of thousands.'

'You get anything?' D.D. asked her bluntly.

The girl shook her head.

'Life insurance?'

'I never heard of anything. Though,' Charlie caught herself, 'it wouldn't surprise me if Jackie had a policy. She liked to plan ahead. I would guess, however, that her parents or her brother were the beneficiaries.'

'No husband?'

'No partner,' Charlie corrected.

'Lesbian?'

'Yes.'

D.D. stared at her. 'You ever get involved with her?'

'We were best friends,' Charlie said evenly. 'Lesbians can have female friends you know, just like guys can have female friends.'

'Gotta ask the question,' D.D. said mildly. 'It's what I do.' D.D. pursed her lips, continuing to mull the matter. Two homicides, a thousand miles apart. Link between the victims, the methodology, and the date, but not enough evidence to provide traction. Hell of a story, she had to admit. Interesting. Intriguing. The kind of thing to tickle a workaholic detective's crime bone.

'So what do you want?' D.D. asked finally.

Charlie blinked. Stared at D.D., held her coffee cup again. 'What do you mean?'

'You came to me, remember? Lurked outside an active crime scene. Why?'

The girl hesitated. Her gaze flickered away.

D.D. took a swig of water. She enjoyed obvious liars. Made her job easier.

'I wanted to see you,' Charlie said at last.

'How'd you know where I'd be?'

'Police scanner. I'm a dispatch officer, right? I hear all the calls come in. Heard about the shooting, gambled you'd be there.'

'Why?'

'Because I Googled you.'

'Excuse me?'

'I Googled you. I searched for homicide detectives in Boston and your name was the one that kept coming up. You helped rescue the state trooper's little girl, solve the string of family annihilations, find the missing wife in South Boston. I did some research, and . . .' The girl pushed away her coffee mug, looked up at D.D., and shrugged. 'I don't know what's going to happen in four days. I guess, I just want to meet the person who might handle my murder. And I want you to meet me because maybe that will help. Maybe, having met me, you'll try harder. And that will finally catch him. Someone has to.'

'Won't be me,' D.D. said.

'Why not?'

'You rent a place in Cambridge, right? Not my jurisdiction.'

'Oh.' Apparently, Charlie hadn't known this. 'Perhaps I won't be murdered there.'

'Your friends were. In their own homes, right?'

'It's not really my house,' the girl said. 'I just rent a room.'

'Semantics. Your profiler describes these murders as an intimate crime, right? Not stranger-to-stranger. Known perpetrator to known victim.'

'Yes.'

'So he'll strike where you feel comfortable. That's part of the process, the methodology. Sneaking up on you on the subway won't do it for him. You gotta see him coming. You gotta welcome him with a smile. It's part of the drill.'

'Then I guess I won't go home on the twenty-first.'

D.D. was curious despite herself. 'So you left your town, came to the big city. Figured it was easier to get lost here, maybe hide in a crowd?'

The girl nodded. 'And I run, and lift weights and box and train with firearms. I'm not defenseless.'

'Licensed to carry?' D.D. asked sharply.

'Yes.'

'How'd you manage that?' Unlike other states, where it was legal to have a gun in one's vehicle, home, or business, Massachusetts required a gun license to even possess a firearm. A license to carry was one step above that, granting the person permission to carry the firearm outside his or her home or business. The license usually required some kind of underlying reason – the person seeking the license worked in security, was a business owner who routinely carried large amounts of cash, that sort of thing. Being young and paranoid probably wasn't a check mark on the form, D.D. guessed.

The girl, however, had her jaw set in a stubborn line. 'I'm legal,' she said, and folded her hands in front of her.

D.D. continued to regard her levelly. 'All right. You're legally armed and training to be dangerous. But you kept your name, Charlene Rosalind Carter Grant. Why take all those steps and *not* change your name?'

Girl looked away. 'I have to work. And the only experience I have is in dispatch, which means I have to pass a background check. Even if I invented a new identity, I don't know how to create one that would stand up to that level of scrutiny.'

'No.'

The girl startled, looked up at her.

'Come on, don't waste my time. You lie about one thing, then I gotta worry about you lying about other things and for the record –' D.D. glanced at her watch – 'you have only three minutes left, so let's not waste it on games.'

'I have only three minutes left?'

'Yep. It's called lifestyle,' D.D. informed her gravely. 'Forty years later, I've decided to give it a chance. So don't fuck with me. Look me in the eye, and tell me why you kept your name.'

'I want to go home.' And the way the girl said it, D.D. understood she didn't mean to a rented room in Cambridge. She meant her town, her people. She meant the place she had belonged in the days before her childhood friends had started dying.

She meant a place that D.D. herself was just starting to identify, and that spooked her a little, made her shiver, because there was a plaintive tone there, a longing that D.D., with three minutes to go, understood.

'You want the killer to find you.'

'I can't go home until he does.'

'Has he made contact? Notes, phone calls, any kind of warning or threat?'

The girl shook her head. 'I understand,' she said, almost kindly, 'that there's nothing you can do. No threat, no assault, no murder, means no crime, means no jurisdiction. I'm just a fairy tale you're listening to today.'

'You should change your name,' D.D. said. 'Or at least tell your story to your own officers. You're dispatch. You have their backs, they'll watch yours.'

'It will be someone I know, someone I trust,' Charlie said.

'Ah, but the Grovesnor PD didn't know your friends. No link, making them your safest bet.'

But, for whatever reason, Charlie still seemed unconvinced. Just because you were paranoid, D.D. thought, didn't mean they weren't out to get you.

She glanced at her watch. Three minutes were up. Interview was over. Time for the new and improved D.D. Warren to report home. She stood.

'Charlene Rosalind Carter Grant, what kind of firearm do you carry?'

The girl regarded her mutely.

D.D. returned the stare.

'I carry a Taurus twenty-two LR pistol,' the girl supplied crisply. 'I train with J.T. Dillon at the Massachusetts Rifle Association in Woburn.'

'Yeah? How good a shot?'

'I can hit bull's-eye at fifty feet.'

'Sounds like you'd be really good at a double tap to the forehead.'

'Risky target,' the girl replied levelly. 'Center mass is a better bet.'

D.D. digested this, still not sure what she thought of the girl's presence outside an active homicide scene, and still not liking all her answers to D.D.'s questions. But seeing as gawking at crime scenes still wasn't considered a criminal offense . . .

D.D. pushed away from the table. 'All right. We're done.' She paused a beat. 'For now.'

The girl blinked a few times. 'Meaning?'

'Go home. Take care of yourself. Avoid future crime scenes.'

'Including my own?' Charlie smiled wanly, then rose to standing. 'You can't help me.'

'You were right before. No crime, no jurisdiction.'

'I keep my room spotless. I plan on bleaching the floors, walls, sheets the night before. Know that, on the twenty-second, when there is a crime, when you do have jurisdiction, or can consult with the detective that does. Anything found at the scene is from him. Plus, check my nails. I've been growing them out, and you better believe, blood, hair, skin, I'll be going for all the DNA I can get. I won't give up. Remember that, on the twenty-second. I've been preparing, planning, and strategizing. He catches me, I'm not going down without a fight.'

D.D. stared at the girl. She believed her. At least this much was true.

'I'm gonna die trying,' Charlene Rosalind Carter Grant informed her. 'Remember that, Detective Warren. After that . . . it's up to you.'

# 4

'Mommy, I'm home!' The boy burst through the front door of the apartment, tossing his Red Sox backpack to the left, while kicking his snowy boots to the right. Navy blue snow coat he dropped dead ahead, then amused himself by leaping over it in his stocking feet. He landed with a satisfying thump, then flipped his hat into the air. He didn't wait to see where it landed, but bolted to the kitchen for a snack.

'Jesse,' his mother chided him from down the hall. 'Not so much noise. I'm on the phone.'

Jesse didn't answer back; he knew his mother didn't expect him to. His entrance, her response, was as much a part of his after-school ritual as, say, grabbing Twinkies for a snack.

Jesse's mother worked on the phone. Sales stuff. Lucky she had the job, she'd told him many times. Lucky she could work from home, so he didn't have to do the dreaded after-school program, where they fed you, like, granola bars and not even the good chewy kind, but the hard crunchy kind no self-respecting kid liked, but parents bought 'cause they were cheaper by the box.

In the kitchen, Jesse climbed onto the countertop, opened the top cabinet, and grabbed a blue plastic cup. Cup down, he leapt from the countertop onto the floor – another satisfying thump. This time, the floor thumped back.

Mrs Flowers, the gazillion-year-old lady who lived beneath them. She didn't like it when Jesse bounced around. 'Sounds like you're raising an elephant!' she'd complained to his mother many times. His mother would then laugh uncomfortably. 'Boys will be boys,' she'd say, while shooting Jesse a look that meant he'd better straighten up his act, *or else*.

Jesse sighed, tried to use his quiet feet as he padded to the fridge and tugged hard on the door. This was the deal: He could eat Twinkies, but only if he drank a glass of milk.

Good deal. Jesse poured himself a glass of milk, then sucked the cream filling out of his Twinkies.

First after-school ritual completed, he went into the family room. He wasn't allowed TV or video games after school. TV rots the brain, his mother always said, and Jesse would need his one day if he wanted to have a *better life*. Plus, TV and video games made noise, which wasn't good for his mother's job.

So, another deal. He was allowed on the computer, which sat on the kitchen table in the corner of the family room. The table sat four, but since there was only him and his mom, that left two open spots. The computer occupied one. He was supposed to put his homework and school papers in the second spot. After dinner, his mother would review his school papers, then it was homework time. He'd do his, his mother would do hers.

She was in school, too. Nursing. One more year to go, then she could have a better job, she told him. One with more money and benefits, and maybe they could move to a better apartment in a building with a playground, where boys could run around and be boys, without ancient Mrs Flowers pounding her ceiling with a broom handle.

Jesse took a seat. Booted up the laptop. It was old, a gift from his mother's last boyfriend, who'd been okay. He'd liked the Red Sox, would play catch in the park, and had bought Jesse his first stuffed bear (holding a ball and bat), which he'd registered on the Athlete-Animalz site. Homerun Bear, his bear was called, and Jesse liked that. He wanted to be a baseball player, too, some day. Be just like Big Papi.

That boyfriend had lasted a whole year. Then apparently, he'd met someone else and Jesse's mother had cried and Jesse had stopped liking Mitchell, had started hating him instead. One night Jesse had even taken scissors to Homerun Bear and done his best to destroy him. In the morning, however, he'd felt bad. It wasn't really the bear's fault, after all. And Jesse didn't have that many toys, given the 'bad economy' as his mother always said.

Jesse had used silver duct tape to fix Homerun Bear as best he could. Attaching each limb, then the bat, then the ball, then the ears. He thought it made his bear look pretty cool. Zombie Bear, he called him now. A homerun hitter, raised from the dead.

Zombie Bear was currently sitting next to the laptop, waiting for their latest after-school adventures. Under Zombie Bear's steady gaze, Jesse finally got the old computer booted up and launched the AthleteAnimalz website.

Jesse was only allowed to go to three websites on the computer. His mother had checked out each one before giving her approval. He was not allowed to deviate from the list, and once, when he'd accidentally typed in the wrong Internet address, she'd known and asked him about it the next morning. Jesse had heard a TV commercial talk about spyware. He figured his mother had some.

Jesse liked AthleteAnimalz. He liked the games, especially baseball. Course, in the world of AthleteAnimalz, it was never Jesse online, it was Homerun aka Zombie Bear. So Jesse would log in and magically become his bear. As Homerun Bear, he could then move around the site – make friends, join games, compete to collect the most points.

Jesse wanted a million points. But he was only seven, and some of the games confused him. So far, he had 121 points. Not bad, he thought. When he hit 150, he'd get a trophy. He wanted that trophy. So lately, every day after school, he logged onto AthleteAnimalz.com and played baseball. He got to join a team with other Athlete-Animalz, including some pink poodle with a soccer ball that was the best homerun hitter Jesse had ever seen. He wasn't sure a pink poodle should be the best one at baseball, but there you had it. The world of AthleteAnimalz.

Today, he found a baseball game already in play. Each team had enough members, but you could 'sit on the bench' and wait for a team to draft you. Generally, you were picked based on points. Animals with lots of points got drafted quickly. Animals with fewer points, the 'rookies', had to wait longer.

Jesse checked out both teams. Their rosters revealed a long list of monkeys, dogs, cats, bunnies, two snakes, and one hippo, with a wide range of points. Not too bad then; he'd get drafted sooner versus later, he thought. And if his team won, they'd all score ten bonus points, plus one point for every fifteen minutes they spent online. In two hours, Jesse would get that much closer to his 150-point trophy.

A box opened on the screen. A hippo with a batter's helmet wanted to know if Jesse would join his team. Staring at the computer screen, Jesse's eyes widened. Helmet Hippo had like a gazillion points. Like, the grandmaster of AthleteAnimalz. Jesse had played with him a couple of times before. Helmet Hippo knew all the moves. Helmet Hippo never lost.

Jesse couldn't believe his luck.

He quickly accepted the invitation, and on screen, a little icon of his bear appeared on the baseball field. His team was currently fielding. Homerun Bear appeared in center field. Jesse could 'catch' the ball by clicking on the mouse once, and throw it by using the directional arrows to aim, then click again. Catching wasn't so bad, but throwing was more challenging for him – he had a hard time lining up his throw using the arrows. But for Helmet Hippo, he would do his best.

For Helmet Hippo, Jesse was determined to be a winner.

Sometime after four, Jesse's mother got off the phone. She wandered into the room, but he barely noticed. Pink Poodle had appeared and immediately been drafted by the rival team. She'd already hit two home runs, and now, in the final inning, Jesse's team was behind, six to seven, and coming up to bat. By virtue of points, Helmet Hippo was their team leader. He was urging them to be strong. They could do this!

Jesse's mother paused behind him. 'AthleteAnimalz?' she asked.

Jesse nodded absently, eyes glued to the screen. Almost his turn to hit. He was nervous. Didn't want to let his team down.

His mother nodded at the approved website and made her way toward the kitchen. 'Dinner in fifteen, Jesse.'

He nodded again, barely registering. His turn. One out, Helmet Hippo on second base. Right hit, and Jesse could drive in the tying run. Better hit, and Jesse and Helmet Hippo would both score, taking the lead.

To hit, Jesse had to watch the ball coming at him and time the click of the mouse. Except sometimes the ball would speed up, sometimes slow down, and sometimes drift wide – a walk. Just like in real baseball, judgment and timing were everything.

First pitch, Jesse clicked too soon. Strike.

Second pitch. Ball drifted wide, but Jesse had already clicked. A swing and a miss, strike two.

A dialogue box opened above Helmet Hippo's head. Players couldn't type in anything they wanted – the website didn't allow that. Security controls, his mother had said approvingly. Instead, you could select from stock expressions – a lot of sporting stuff, basic conversational stuff. The website was also patrolled for bullying. Jesse knew, because his mother had told him that. He didn't see how the players could bully one another, given that the stock phrases were all *Go Team Go* kind of stuff, but maybe there were ways around the phrases. Things the other, more experienced kids knew how to do. Jesse didn't care; he was still learning how to write, so he liked being able to select a whole phrase for his bear to say with a click of the computer mouse.

'Eye on the ball,' Helmet Hippo said now. 'You can do it. I know you can.'

Jesse took a deep breath. He would do this. For his team. For Helmet Hippo.

Ball came, a tiny black dot traveling down the computer screen, first slow, then fast, fast, fast . . .

Jesse clicked his mouse. On the screen, his bear swung a bat, the sound of thwacking came through the speakers, and suddenly, the tiny black dot was moving again, flying away from Jesse's bear, over Helmet Hippo into the green of the outfield, but still going, going . . .

The word 'GONE' lit up across Jesse's screen. Virtual confetti rained down, triumphant music blared. Home run. Jesse had done it. Home run!

The graphic explosion cleared, and now Jesse could watch his bear and Helmet Hippo run the bases. Scoring once, scoring twice, as Jesse's team took the lead, eight to seven.

'Jesse, five more minutes,' his mother called from the kitchen.

'Okay!'

Jesse remained glued to the screen. His left hand now clutched Zombie Bear. All his teammates were talking, conversation bubbles appearing everywhere as they congratulated him on his game-winning hit.

But Jesse had eyes for only one teammate: Helmet Hippo.

'Way to go! You are a champion!'

Jesse was still smiling, beaming really, when a new icon lit up on the bottom panel of his screen. The mailbox. His bear had just received mail.

Jesse obediently clicked. Generally mail came from the site itself. Notification of bonus points, presents for Zombie Bear on his birthday, or announcements of weekly specials on the site – play this game, earn this many bonus points!

But the message wasn't from the website administrator. It was from Helmet Hippo. They could send mail to each other. Jesse hadn't known that, but now he did.

'Homerun Bear,' the message began (only Jesse called his bear Zombie Bear, after the scissors incident). 'Congratulations on your winning hit. I knew you could do it! Want to play again? Tomorrow, 3:30, I'll be here. I always wear my Red Sox hat for good luck. You?'

There was a button for reply.

Jesse hit reply, watched a fresh window open up. Helmet Hippo's name automatically appeared, but the rest of the message was blank. No phrases to pick from. He'd have to do it. Type it in all by himself. But he could use the first message to cheat a little, look at those words for spelling.

Jesse's mother was banging around in the kitchen.

Jesse stuck his tongue between his teeth and began to laboriously type. 'Yes. I'll be here. I like the Red Sox, too.'

Later, after dinner, after homework, after bath and bedtime stories, Jesse curled up beneath his Star Wars sheets and clutched Zombie Bear. He thought again of his homerun hit. He thought again of Helmet Hippo.

And he felt warm all over. Like someone special.

Tomorrow, 3:30. Jesse couldn't wait.

# 5

'That dog that's not your dog is waiting for you on the front porch,' my landlady called through my bedroom door. It was 9 p.m., time for me to start thinking about heading to work.

My bedroom was located in the back ground level of a 120-year-old triple-decker. At first I'd been concerned about this. I would've preferred a second- or third-story unit, but those larger apartments were all taken and, frankly, out of my price range. It turned out, however, that my landlady, Frances Beals, was security savvy. She'd been born in this house, she'd told me the day of my interview. Good Irish Catholic family with eleven kids. Half the siblings were now scattered to other states; the other half were already dead.

Having lived her whole life in Cambridge, Frances wasn't blind to its shortcomings. A university town, Cambridge featured an eclectic mix of multimillion-dollar grand old mansions and barely maintained brick apartment units. There were sprawling green spaces and quaint dining opportunities for upwardly mobile young families, as well as Laundromats, pizza joints, and trendy clothing stores for the college kids. Some of Cambridge's residents, like Frances, came from families who'd lived here for generations. Most simply passed through for a summer or semester or four-year degree. Meaning the town offered interesting pockets of well-established security, surrounded by other pockets of petty crime, vagrant lifestyles, and drunken debauchery.

Before I could rent the room, I had to pass a two-hour interview with Frances, to determine which of these categories I fell into. When she ascertained I had no pets, no boyfriends, and most likely, no body piercings, I'd passed muster. My only requirement for her was a double-bolt lock on my door, and I asked permission to inspect all door and window locks on the lower level.

She seemed surprised by this request, then pleased. Like maybe that proved I had some common sense after all.

The most Frances and I had ever spoken was during the interview. I figured she was married once, because there was a wedding portrait on the mantel. Next to it was a picture of a baby, but Frances never mentioned kids and no family came for Christmas. Maybe that told its own story. I wondered, but I never asked.

By mutual agreement, Frances came and went through the front entrance, while I accessed my room via the rear, garden door. I tried to keep out of her way, which wasn't too hard as I worked graveyard four nights a week, then slept till midday.

My room was small, but I liked the battered hardwood floors, the nine-foot ceilings, the historic bull's-eye molding. A female professor had rented the room before me. She'd left behind an Ikea bookshelf filled with romance novels. So that's what I did in my free time. I sat in my room and devoured Nora Roberts novels. I figured with everything I had going on in my life, I deserved at least a few hours a day with a happy ending.

Now I pulled on a bulky gray hooded sweatshirt, then reached under my pillow for my .22. A year ago, I'd never so much as touched a handgun. I couldn't have told a pistol from a revolver, a rimfire from a centerfire, a .22 from a .357 Magnum.

Now, I gotta say, I'm a hell of a good shot.

A .22's not the best self-defense weapon in the world. Most people choose this gun as a 'concealment' weapon – its small size and light weight make it easy to carry. Tuck it in your pocket or belt holster, or, as I'd been told, hang it from a chain around your neck like a true gang banger.

In public, I kept mine in my leather messenger bag, as Massachusetts frowned on citizens being openly armed. In private, however, and certainly on January 21, the semiauto would be in a holster on my left hip. I'd practiced many, many times, drawing it quickly and opening fire. In fact, I practiced that at least thirty minutes twice a week.

My Taurus semiauto had a nickel finish with rosewood grip. It weighed twelve ounces, fit snug in the palm of my hand, and I'd come to welcome the feel of the warm wood against my fingers. It was a pretty gun, if I do say so. But it was also reasonably priced, and inexpensive to arm.

A year ago, I wouldn't have considered that either. Not just that firearms can be expensive, but so are boxes of ammo. And let me tell you, just because I feared for my life didn't mean I had unlimited resources.

These days, I was a walking advertisement for safety and security on a working girl's budget. Hence the real reason I had a two-hundred-dollar .22, and not something much more commanding, such as a two-thousand-dollar Glock .45. My instructor, J.T. Dillon, let me fire his one day. I thought the recoil was going to blow off my arm, but the hole in the target was something to behold. SWAT guys and Special Forces commandos often carry .45s. I wondered how that must feel, confronting an unknown threat while surrounded by buddies you know have got your back and carrying a weapon designed just for a guy like you to get the job done.

For the past two weeks, I'd been trying to picture January 21. J.T. kept walking me through it – visualization as a form of preparation.

I stood in the middle of my charming little bedroom. Twin bed was pushed against the wall to the left, blond Ikea bookshelf behind me, old microwave stand topped with even older twenty-inch TV stationed beside the door. Room to move, fight, defend. Space to fully extend my arms, two-handed grip, my Taurus a natural extension of my body. My pistol was loaded with match-grade .22-caliber long rifle, or LR, cartridges. The rounds may not pack the biggest boom, but I had nine shots to get it right.

During my twice-weekly training sessions, J.T. ordered me to empty my clip every time. Never practice hesitation, he instructed me, over and over again. Evaluate the threat. Make your decision. Commit to defend.

I still couldn't picture January 21. Mostly, I remembered the police reports – no sign of forced entry, no sign of a struggle.

*You gotta see him coming*, Detective Warren had said this afternoon. *You gotta welcome him with a smile.*

I holstered my Taurus, donned my heavy black coat, and headed for work.

*

The dog that was not my dog was waiting for me on the front porch. The rear of Frances's narrow lot was barricaded by a five-foot-high wooden fence; otherwise I was pretty sure the dog would wait at the back door for me. She was that smart.

I called her Tulip. She'd started hanging around six months ago. No collar, no tags. At first she'd just followed me down the street when I went for my afternoon runs. I figured she was hungry, hoping for a treat. But back in those days, I never gave her anything. Not my dog, not my problem. I just wanted to exercise.

So Tulip started to run. All five miles, tongue lolling out, sleek white-and-tan body pounding out the miles. Afterward, it seemed cruel not to provide at least a bowl of water. So we sat together on the front porch. She drank a bowl. I drank a bottle. Then she sprawled beside me and put her head on my lap. Then, I stroked her ears, her graying muzzle.

She looked like some kind of hound. Harrier, Frances had muttered one day. When I looked it up on the library's computer, the breed turned out to be a small to mid-sized English hound dog. Tulip shared many of the markings – a short tan coat with white stockinged legs and broad white collar. Wire whip tail, floppy ears, broad, handsome face. Tulip was definitely an older dog. A grande dame who'd been there and done that. The stories she could tell, I figured, and knew exactly how she felt.

Tonight, Tulip sat in the middle of the covered porch, away from the snow. She was a very patient dog; Frances said she sometimes sat there for hours waiting for me.

I hadn't seen her for several days – that's the problem with a dog that's not your dog. I didn't know where she went, or even if she had another home. Sometimes, I saw her daily; sometimes a couple times a week. I guess I got to practice patience, too.

She was shivering when I came around, and immediately I felt bad.

'You can't keep doing this,' I told her, rounding the corner, watching her rise in greeting and wag her whiplike tail. 'January is no time to be homeless in Boston.'

Tulip looked at me, whined a little.

I'd started buying bags of dog food five months back. She was just so skinny, and then when she kept running like that . . . The first vet visit was two weeks later. No fleas, no ticks, no heartworm. The vet gave her shots, gave me Frontline, then wrote up a bill that made my .22 semiauto look cheap.

I paid. Worked some overtime. Kept running with the dog that was not my dog. Started pouring dry food into a bowl.

I had a Baggie of food in my pocket, had filled it when Frances had told me Tulip was waiting on the porch. Now I emptied the kibble on the front porch. Tulip advanced gratefully. She looked skinnier to me. I saw a fresh mark near her hindquarters, a tear on her right ear.

I'd put up posters in the fall, trying to see if anyone had lost a dog. I'd even spent precious cash on an ad in the local paper. Once, I'd called animal control, but when the officer started to ask me too many questions, I panicked. I just wanted to know if Tulip had a real home, somewhere where she was loved and missed and needed to get back to. Because I understood that sort of thing, felt it myself.

But I didn't want her carted off to a pound, then killed, just because somewhere along the way she'd become her own creature instead of someone else's.

'You need a coat,' I murmured to her now, smoothing back her ears and scratching the heavier folds of skin around her neck. She leaned against me, pressed against my legs, and I could feel her body shiver again. Nineteen degrees and dropping. Couldn't take her inside, 'cause my landlady would kill us both. But couldn't leave her outside, quaking with the cold.

I checked to see how much cash I had in my wallet. Enough, I figured.

Then I looked down at the dog that was not my dog, still leaning against me, her eyes closed as she exhaled her exhaustion and worry over some misadventure I'd never know.

'This has to be our secret,' I told her seriously.

I hailed a cab and both of us went to work.

'Nine-one-one. Please state the nature of your emergency.'

No response.

I studied my ANI ALI monitor in front of me, as the information started to scroll. 'Nine-one-one,' I repeated, shifting slightly in my desk chair. 'Please state the nature of your emergency.'

'I got a big butt,' a male voice said.

I sighed. Like I hadn't heard that one before. 'I see. And this enlarged gluteus maximus resides at ninety-five West Carrington Street?'

'Dude!' the voice said. Laughter in the background. Giggles really. This is what happens, I reminded myself, when you work graveyard shift.

I continued, in a professional manner: 'And does this enlarged posterior belong to Mr Edward Keicht?'

'Man, *how* did you know?'

'Sir, are you aware that when you dial nine-one-one, your name and address appears on our monitors?'

Awestruck silence. 'No way, dude!' Apparently, Mr Keicht had been imbibing a little more than just beer this evening.

'And are you aware that a prank call to nine-one-one is a felony offense that could land you in jail?'

'Cool!'

'Say hi to the nice policeman at your door, Mr Keicht.'

'All right!'

'And remember, this is your brain on drugs.'

I clicked off line one, then contacted one of my officers to do the deed. All calls to nine-one-one required an officer response. Hence that whole felony offense thing. In approximately three to five minutes, Mr I Got a Big Butt wasn't gonna be feeling so grand about life.

One twenty a.m. My twin monitors remained blank, the phone lines quiet. Not too bad a night, but then it was only Wednesday. Call patterns had a tendency to pick up as the week went on. Friday and Saturday were madness, a deluge of domestic assaults, drunken disorderlies, and OUIs. Sunday around five was the second busiest time. The witching hour, we called it: five o'clock being the hour when most noncustodial parents were required to return the 2.2 children to the custodial parent. Except judging purely by call volume, feuding parents enjoyed screwing with each other more than being responsible caretakers. By 5:01, we'd have the first call and the first officer involved in the weekly game of 'No, ma'am, you may not shoot off his balls just because he's two minutes late', to be followed shortly by 'Sir, a visitation agreement is a legal document; I suggest you read it'.

I tried to avoid Sundays. Domestic disputes made everyone cranky – the callers, my officers, me.

Overall, the city of Grovesnor, all twenty-five thousand people, was tame compared to my time in Arvada. There, I'd worked in a major call center, handling hundreds of calls an hour. These days, it was me, sitting alone in a darkened room with the dog that was not my dog. I generally received between ten and forty calls a shift. Ten on a night like tonight, forty on a weekend.

Number one call I handled every night – wrong number. Number two call – Mr Big Butt, or Mr Pepperoni Pizza to Go, or whatever latest thing a bunch of bored kids thought was funny. And yeah, I dispatched a uniformed officer to each and every address. Hey, I didn't make the rules.

Only a third of the calls to 911 are for actual emergencies. More typically, I got reports of reckless driving, a dead or injured animal in the road, the occasional complaint against noisy neighbors. Information came in on my ANI ALI screen – ANI standing for Automatic Number Identification, ALI for Automatic Local Identification. Landlines were the easiest calls, with name, phone number, and address winking across my screen. Cell phone calls and Internet-based phone carriers (think Vonage) automatically went to the state police for them to sort out location, as such numbers weren't linked to a physical address, making it difficult for me to dispatch an officer.

In addition to my ANI ALI monitor, I had a second system, the Dispatcher Event Mask. I entered all the information from the call into this system – details of an accident, description of an intruder, whatever. Then, I could shoot this information straight from my computer to an officer's Mobile Data Computer in his police cruiser. Push of a button and ping, we were all on the same virtual page.

Assuming the system didn't crash. Assuming I had the where-withal to multitask between two monitors while simultaneously soothing a distressed caller, asking all pertinent questions, and typing in all relevant answers.

But other than that, easy breezy.

My ANI ALI monitor blazed to life. Name, phone number, street address appearing on the screen. I put on my headset and hit the button.

'Nine-one-one. Please state the nature of your emergency.'

'I . . . I don't know.' Female voice this time. Quivering.

'Ma'am? Do you need assistance?'

'My husband is angry.'

'I see. Are you at home, ma'am?' I rattled off the street address from my screen; she confirmed. 'And your name, ma'am?'

'Dawn.' She didn't offer a last name. My screen listed the number as belonging to Vincent Heinen. For the time being, I didn't press her.

'Dawn, nice to meet you. I'm Charlie. Is your husband at home?'

'Yes.' Her voice had dropped to nearly a whisper. I took that to mean he was someplace close.

'Are there kids in the house?'

'No.'

'Pets, dogs?' Officers like to know about dogs.

'No.'

I settled in, got down to it. 'Has he been drinking?'

'Yes.' Very soft now.

'Dawn, is he in the room?' Then, when she didn't immediately answer, my own voice dropping low: 'Are you hiding from him? You can hit a button on the phone. One beep for yes. Two beeps for no.'

I heard a beep, and I took a deep breath. Okay, so the makings of a genuine call. At my feet, Tulip stirred. She seemed to sense my tension, sitting up.

'Dawn, are you afraid of him?'

Beep.

Still monitoring the call, I got on the radio. 'Four sixty-one to nine twenty-six,' I said into the radio.

Nine twenty-six, aka Officer Tom Mackereth, tagged back. 'Nine twenty-six to four sixty-one.'

'Four sixty-one to nine twenty-six, I have a female party online,' I informed him crisply. 'States husband is angry. States husband has been drinking. States she's afraid of him.'

'Nine twenty-six to four sixty-one, location of caller?'

'Four sixty-one to nine twenty-six, sending through.' I updated my Dispatcher Event Mask with the extremely limited data I'd collected thus far and shot it through to Officer Mackereth's mobile computer. 'Four sixty-one to nine twenty-six, caller states they are at home, no kids or animals present.'

'Nine twenty-six to four sixty-one, can you get more details? Description of both parties, is the male party armed, are we talking alcohol, or also drugs?'

*No shit Sherlock*, I felt like saying. But our radio dialogue, plus the 911 call, was being recorded for posterity, so I kept to the script.

'Four sixty-one to nine twenty-six, will do.'

Back to my caller, who'd remained disturbingly silent.

'Dawn, it's Charlie. You there?'

Beep.

All right, contact reestablished. I leaned closer to my event monitor, adjusting my headset. I could hear the woman better now, the rapid sounds of her distressed breathing as she tried desperately not to make a sound.

'Dawn, are you in the bedroom?' I asked quietly, wanting to keep her communicating.

Another beep.

'Are you locked in the bathroom?'

Two beeps.

Two beeps meant no. I pictured a bedroom, tried again. 'The closet?'

Another beep.

I played the odds in New England colonial architecture: 'Dawn, is your bedroom upstairs?'

Beep.

I added the details to the call profile, moving along. 'Dawn, is your husband armed?'

Silence. Not a yes, not a no. Did that mean maybe?

I worked to clarify: 'Dawn, Mrs Heinen, is it you don't know if your husband is carrying a weapon?'

Beep.

'Officer Mackereth is gonna love that,' I murmured to Tulip, who was sitting straight up and staring at me now. Situation unknown – an officer's most typical and most dangerous kind of call.

I got back on the radio, summoned 926 and provided the short update: Caller was in the upstairs bedroom. Husband was within listening distance and may or may not be armed.

'Drugs?' Officer Mackereth wanted to know, because a drunk husband was bad enough, but a cokehead or meth addict was even worse – beyond the reach of logic *and* pain. Officers got tense about that.

I returned to Dawn Heinen.

'Dawn, does your husband do drugs?'

Beep.

I wasn't surprised. I added to the profile.

'Dawn, has he done drugs tonight?'

Silence.

'You don't know if your husband has done drugs tonight?'

Beep.

My fingers stilled on the keyboard and I closed my eyes, starting to feel the pressure. My job was to get information. I was Officer Mackereth's eyes and ears. If I did my job right, he walked into a situation forewarned and forearmed. If I failed at my job, a lone officer got to approach a darkened house at one thirty in the morning, with nothing but his quick wits to save him.

I got back on the radio. 'Four sixty-one to nine twenty-six. Caller states she doesn't know if husband is armed. Caller states she doesn't know if husband has done drugs tonight, but states he has done drugs in the past.'

'Nine twenty-six to four sixty-one, roger that,' Officer Mackereth replied. I felt the weight of his disappointment in those words. He was counting on me, and I was letting him down. He notified me that his position was one block from the address. He was cutting his sirens and going dark. Meaning I hadn't given him enough informa-tion. Meaning he was approaching quietly, in order to assess the situation for himself.

'Come on, Dawn,' I murmured under my breath. 'We gotta do better. For all of us, we gotta do better.'

I returned to my caller, listening to the sound of her shallow breathing and straining now for other noises in the background. A husband calling a wife's name? Shattering glass from a man in the throes of a violent rage? Or maybe even a knock on the downstairs front door marking Officer Mackereth's arrival. I heard nothing.

'Dawn, is your husband still in the room?' I asked now.

Beep.

'An officer is approaching. He's almost there, Dawn. Help is on its way.' I hesitated, struggling. My next order of business should be to establish a description of the offending party. That way if he tried to flee the scene, Officer Mackereth could identify him and give pursuit. I didn't know, however, how to engage in such a conversation with phone beeps.

The tension again, my shoulders creeping up, a low ache developing in the back of my neck. Officer Mackereth should be at the address by now. Opening his door, looking up at the residence, trying to get a bead on the situation.

'Dawn, is your husband still angry?'

Beep.

Then what's he doing? I wanted to shout. What kind of enraged man didn't make a sound?

Then, just like that, I knew. I could picture in my head exactly what kind of angry man could stand so quiet, so still, right outside a closet door.

I grabbed the radio. 'Four sixty-one to nine twenty-six,' I nearly shouted. 'Don't ring the doorbell! Do not approach! Stop immediately!'

A pause. I didn't hear Dawn anymore, just my own ragged breathing.

'Nine twenty-six to four sixty-one,' Officer Mackereth came over the radio, his voice as dry as mine had been heated. 'Nine eight two?'

Nine eight two was our own code. The numbers corresponded to the phone digits for WTF. What The Fuck? Hey, in this job, you had to have a sense of humor.

I took a deep breath.

'Four sixty-one to nine twenty-six,' I said. 'Please hold.'

'Dawn,' I whispered into my headset, 'does your husband like pizza?'

Silence, then beep, then the first noise I'd heard in a while: Dawn, weeping. 'One more minute, Dawn,' I promised her. 'Hang in there for me. Just one more minute.'

Quickly, I ran Vincent's name through my system and came up with a second number, a cell phone registered to his name. Keeping my fingers crossed, I picked up my prepaid cell and dialed those numbers. Not a move from the training handbook. One of those things that, in this job, you just knew when to do.

For a surreal moment, I got to hear ringing in stereo. My mobile ringing in my ear. Vincent's cell phone ringing in the bedroom. One, two, three times.

I was clutching my cell too tight.

Then my radio crackling to life: 'Nine twenty-six to four sixty-one—'

'Shut up!' I hissed, just as Dawn's husband connected with my mobile.

'What?' he said, one word, loaded with menace and threat and the icy cold kind of rage that kept his wife sobbing silently in their bedroom closet.

'Dude,' I shot back. 'Want your fucking pizza? 'Cause I'm not standing out here any longer. Been ringing your fuckin' doorbell for five minutes now. We're charging your credit card whether you take it or not, so get your fuckin' pie, or I'm eatin' it myself!'

I jabbed off my phone, then switched to my headset.

'Ass wipe,' I heard Dawn's husband mutter, outside the closet door. Then, finally, sounds of movement. A distant door being yanked open, pounding footsteps.

Belatedly, I grabbed the radio.

'Four sixty-one to nine twenty-six. You are pizza delivery. I repeat. You are pizza delivery. Male subject is most likely armed and coming to you in five four three two—'

'Fuck!' a male voice exploded through the radio.

'Police!' Officer Mackereth shouted. 'Hands where I can see them, hands where I can see them!'

Sounds of a scuffle, more banging, another shout.

I stood up, couldn't help myself. Grabbed my headset, squeezed my eyes shut in the middle of my darkened call center as if that would help my officer, somehow give him the advantage. Tulip started to whine. I bit down on my lower lip.

Then: 'Nine twenty-six to four sixty-one.' Officer Mackereth, sounding out of breath. 'Male subject subdued. Male subject disarmed.' Then, in a break from script, 'He was carrying a Glock nine. How the hell did you know that? Holy shit, Charlie. Holy shit.'

I closed my eyes. That's what I'd been picturing, what I'd just known. That Dawn's husband was standing there, on the other side of the closet door, waiting for his wife with a loaded gun. And the moment a third party arrived, sirens at the scene, a uniformed officer, ringing the doorbell . . .

That's what he'd been waiting for, good old Vincent. The final provocation to justify pulling the trigger.

Officer Mackereth came in over the radio. He'd pulled it together now, returning to script. I did my best to follow suit. 'Nine twenty-six to four sixty-one, is it safe to enter the home?'

I got back on my headphones. 'Dawn, it's Charlie. A uniformed officer is at your front door. He has your husband detained and disarmed. You can come out now, Dawn.'

Then, for the first time since the call began, the sound of her voice. 'Is he . . . is he okay?'

'The police officer or your husband?' Though sadly, I already knew the answer to that.

'My husband,' she said shakily.

'You know, Dawn, why don't you go downstairs and see for yourself.'

'Okay. Okay. I think I can do that. Charlie . . .'

I waited. But she didn't say thank you. Few of them ever did.

Dawn hung up the phone. She went to check on her drunken husband, who five minutes earlier had been prepared to kill her.

And I resumed my seat, my hand now on Tulip's head, stroking her silky ears.

'Glad to have you here, girl,' I whispered. 'Glad to have you here.'

She placed her graying muzzle on my lap, and I kept petting her head, until eventually my hands stopped shaking and both of us sat silently in the dark.

*

You'd think that would be enough for one night, but it wasn't. Two thirty-three a.m., the other relevant call came in. I saw the info on the ANI ALI screen and was immediately agitated. Then, I squared my shoulders, took a deep breath, and answered.

'Hey,' I said, slightly surprised to be receiving the call through official channels and not on my prepaid cell.

Silence at first, for so long, I thought maybe the caller couldn't answer. But then, finally, a voice. Small, quivering, scared. The girl then, not the boy. Too young to remember my cell number, so reverting back to the number of first contact: 911.

She was crying and at this stage of the game, I didn't need her to speak to know why. Dispatch officers . . . we are more than backup for our men and women in uniform. We are Ma Bell's version of social services, audio first responders to battered wives, overwhelmed new parents, drunken teens, and terrified children. We hear it all.

Then we transfer the call and walk away. Not our problem. We're simply the messengers that yeah, life really sucks out there.

Now, here's a question for you: If you only had four days left to live, what would you do?

Remain on the sidelines? Or get in the game?

And if, say, you'd spent the past year learning how to run, fight, shoot, how to stop being and start doing, would that change the answer? And if, say, you had insider's knowledge of the kind of crimes the system can't handle, where the perpetrator wins and the victim loses, would that change the answer?

I'd spent months contemplating this question. Then I'd arrived at a decision.

It helped me now, as I reached out and tapped my keyboard. As I deliberately and consciously broke the law, disconnecting my caller from the recorded dispatch system and picking her up on my prepaid Wal-Mart phone instead.

'Hey,' I said again. 'It's okay. It's me, Charlie. I'm going to help. One more day, sweetheart, and you will never be hurt again.'

# 6

'Bad news,' D.D. informed Alex over dinner. 'In the war over sanity in the city, the lunatics are winning.'

She'd done the honors of picking up Jack from day care at five forty-five. By six thirty Alex had made it home, where, being an enthusiastic cook, he'd put the finishing touches on a Crock-Pot version of chicken cacciatore he'd started that morning.

Now they were seated across from each other at the kitchen table. Alex had a glass of red wine; she had a glass of water. Alex had two hands for eating and drinking. She had one hand cradling Jack against her shoulder, the other wielding a fork.

Jack was currently asleep, half of his chubby face smashed into the curve of her neck, where he was making the most ridiculously adorable snoring sounds. This was probably as close to domestic bliss as she was ever gonna get, D.D. figured. Her baby snuggled against her chest, while she and Alex enjoyed a leisurely Italian dinner and talked shop.

'First I was wrapping up a shooting that may or may not be part of a broader vigilante crime spree,' she was telling Alex now. 'Then I end up chasing down a suspicious woman, who claims she wants me to investigate her own murder, four days from today.'

Alex paused with a forkful of chicken in midair. 'She's planning ahead? I don't remember ever seeing a spot for appointing your own homicide detective on the estate planning forms.'

'Oh, they're there. The beautiful young trophy wives just white 'em out before having their husbands sign on the bottom line.'

He thought about it. 'Makes sense.' He resumed eating, then paused again. 'Seriously, this woman is planning on being murdered?'

'Her two best friends were each murdered on January twenty-first. First one died two years ago, second one last year, meaning this year . . .'

Alex stared at her, clearly perplexed.

D.D. sighed. She set down her fork and stroked Jack's plump cheek. 'This is the crazy part – I looked it up on the computer when Jack and I came home and she's right. Randi Menke was murdered in Providence two years ago on the twenty-first, Jacqueline Knowles in Atlanta same date last year. How creepy is that?'

'Creepy,' Alex agreed, and set down his own fork. Alex taught crime scene analysis at the police academy and had a tendency to take a cerebral approach to homicide. D.D. appreciated that. Figured it was a good balance for her own shoot-first-question-later style.

'No jurisdiction,' he said now, opening salvo of an ongoing analysis.

'Yep. I asked about threatening letters, phone calls, contact. Nada. Sounds like her life is very quiet, if you exclude the annual funerals. Two murders in two different states complicates matters, as well. She said the FBI gave the homicides a cursory glance, but couldn't find any obvious connections between the two. Ironically enough, third time has a tendency to be the charm, meaning this year, after the twenty-first . . .'

Alex nodded. As a former investigator, he understood crime was really a numbers game. Twice was a coincidence, and no one blew their budgets on coincidences. Third murder, however, established a pattern. That got investigators more excited.

'Girl paid for a report from a retired FBI profiler,' D.D. continued now, readjusting Jack's snuffling form. 'I'm thinking of maybe contacting him, or perhaps the Rhode Island detective involved in the first murder. Asking a few questions.'

Alex nodded abruptly, conclusion reached. 'I would.'

'You think she's in danger?'

'Unknown,' he said crisply. 'But here's the second angle to consider – there is a link between the first two murders. The girl herself. Knew both victims.'

'I would assume investigators looked into that . . .' D.D. began.

Alex shook his head. 'Never assume. Also, you found her loitering outside a shooting, which is . . . odd. Either she's scared enough to want protection, in which case she'd most logically plead her case at headquarters. Or, she realizes, as she claims, there's nothing the police can do, and she continues to go at it alone. But stalking a homicide detective outside a crime scene . . . From a rational point of view, how does that gain her anything?'

'Personal connection,' D.D. informed him. 'Now that I've met her, I'm supposed to try harder to find her killer.'

Alex arched a brow. 'She's networking?'

'I'm telling you, it was a day defined by fruitcakes.'

'Tell me more about the note on your windshield,' he asked now.

D.D.'s eyes widened. 'The note! Crap. It's still sitting in my car. I totally forgot to deliver it to the crime lab. Oh my God! How do you forget something like that? How could I . . . How could I . . . Oh. My. God . . . !'

D.D.'s voice trailed off. The enormity of her mistake was too large, nearly incomprehensible. She stared at Alex wildly. 'That's homicide one-oh-one. First-year-out-of-the-academy, don't-get-yourself-fired basics. I'm an idiot. I went on maternity leave, and I came back stupid!'

'You're not stupid,' Alex stated calmly. 'You're sleep deprived.'

'I *failed* to deliver evidence. How could I have done such a thing?' Her voice broke. She was less hysterical, more genuinely panicked. Sergeant Detective D.D. Warren didn't make mistakes. Sergeant Detective D.D. Warren certainly didn't forget things like evidence handling 101.

Having children did change you; apparently it had made her worse.

'D.D.,' Alex said evenly.

'I'm going to have to quit my job.'

'D.D.'

'Maybe I could resign from being sergeant. Put Phil in charge of the squad. He has four kids, and still, brighter than me.'

'D.D.'

'Will the brain cells come back?' she asked Alex plaintively. 'I mean, all the baby books mention sleep cycles, so I'm assuming someday Jack will have one. He'll sleep through the night, and I'll stop making major mistakes that may or may not allow a murderer to go free.'

'Gee,' Alex interjected more forcefully, 'if only the father of your child was an expert on crime scene analysis, who could assist with evidence handling. And, say, even call an expert on forensic hand-writing analysis who happens to be a fellow teacher at the academy.'

D.D. stared at him. 'Really?'

'Really.'

'Oh.' She looked down at her plate, realized belatedly that she hadn't eaten much, and picked back up her fork. 'Huh, all that and you can cook, too.'

Alex smiled faintly. Done with his dinner, he pushed away from the table, stood, and cleared his plate. 'Careful,' he said, his back to her as he crossed to the kitchen sink. 'Some girls might be impressed enough to marry me.'

D.D. regarded his retreating form. She said, equally soft, 'Yeah, but I think we just established those girls are smarter than me.'

Alex didn't say anything more. He went to fetch the note from her car.

D.D. remained seated at the table, holding Jack. She kissed the top of his head. 'Sorry,' she murmured, though she couldn't have told either one of them what she was apologizing for.

Alex returned with the note, encased in clear plastic. With gloved hands, he carefully removed the plain white paper and shot several digital photos. Then he called his fellow academic. They exchanged pleasantries, after which Alex secured permission to email a photo of the note for preliminary analysis.

'He'll call us back in twenty to thirty minutes,' Alex explained to D.D., sliding the piece of paper back into its plastic cover. 'Of course, for a more thorough analysis you'll want to submit the note to the crime lab in order to fingerprint the paper and run tests on paper and ink type.'

'Thank you,' she said.

Jack was awake now. She sat with him on the sofa, where she had him sprawled on her lap. He peered up at her with wide blue eyes.

When Alex came over to join them, Jack turned to his father and waved a pudgy fist.

'Look at that,' D.D. declared triumphantly. 'He can already wave hello. Knew he'd be smart.'

'He gets that from me,' Alex said, settling onto the sofa, his right arm around her shoulders. 'I've always had dynamite greeting skills. Wipe the globe, wipe the globe.' He used his left hand to demonstrate his best Miss America wave. Jack responded by kicking his feet.

'Soccer star,' D.D. said immediately. 'Check out the muscle on him!'

'Soccer? Hmm, that must be from you. Given my own coordination skills, I make it a point never to walk and chew gum.'

'My parents were teachers,' D.D. said absently. 'College profs before they retired.'

'Then Jack definitely better watch that whole walking and chewing gum thing.' Alex touched her cheek. 'They still coming this weekend?'

She finally looked up at him. 'It's not too late to run away,' she said seriously. 'Or I could just tell them I buried your body in the backyard. They'll believe me.'

He grinned, but she could see the gentleness in his eyes. It bothered her that he seemed to think she needed such a look. It bothered her even more that he was probably right, that she had become a woman who required patient smiles and tender glances. Sleep deprivation, she tried to tell herself, but wondered if it wasn't one of those children-change-you changes, meaning she was doomed to forever be a frazzled, domesticated, slightly more inept version of herself.

'I don't hate them,' she heard herself say. 'I know I don't have the same relationship with my parents that you have with yours. But I don't hate them.'

Alex fingered a curly lock of her short blond hair. 'How do you feel about them?'

She shrugged, fidgeting with Jack's tiny fingers in much the same way Alex played with her hair. 'I respect them. They're two intelligent, well-meaning adults leading their own busy lives. They do their thing. I do mine. We're happy.'

'You didn't want your mom in the delivery room,' he said quietly.

D.D. shook her head vehemently. 'God no. That would've been terrible!'

'How come?'

'Because.' She shrugged again, looked down at her plump little baby who smiled back up at her with a big, toothless grin. He had her blue eyes, she thought, but would most likely end up with his father's dark hair.

'I love him,' she said suddenly. 'I love . . . everything about him. The way he smells, the way he feels, the way he smiles. He is the most perfect baby in the whole entire world. And I can tell you for a fact, my mother never felt that way about me.

'I was an afterthought. A late-in-life oops that happened to two very cerebral people who'd never planned on having kids. And after all that, I wasn't even a quiet, well-behaved bookish kid. I was a total hellion who climbed trees and crashed bikes and once hit Mikey Davis so hard he lost a tooth.'

'You punched a boy?' Alex asked.

'I was seven,' D.D. said, as if that explained everything. 'Split my knuckle, too. My first thought was that I needed boxing lessons. My mother's first thought was that I should be grounded for the rest of my natural life. We haven't moved much beyond those positions since.'

'They don't like you being a detective?' Alex ventured.

'Detective isn't so bad,' D.D. granted. 'Detectives, even in my parents' universe, command some respect. But when I first became a cop . . . I believe my mother was just relieved I was on this side of the judicial system.'

Alex smiled at her. 'A comment I've thought about many of my associates in uniform. Nervous?' he asked evenly.

She looked at him. 'Nobody makes me feel as ugly and stupid as my mother does,' she said simply.

'Then we will keep their visit short and focused on Jack. Maybe your mother has never appreciated your right hook, but how can she argue with him, sweetheart?' Alex gestured down to their kicking, gurgling baby. 'How can anyone argue with him?'

\*

The phone rang ten minutes later. D.D. put Jack in his bassinet, where he'd hopefully sleep for a bit, then it would be time for his next feeding. She dug out her spiral notepad and mini-recorder as she put Alex's teacher friend on the speakerphone.

'Professor Dembowski? Sergeant Detective D.D. Warren. Thanks for calling me.'

'Ray. Please, call me Ray.'

Dembowski had a pleasant voice. Deep, smooth, maybe fifty to sixty years of age, D.D. thought. She settled in at the kitchen table, the note in its clear plastic sheathing before her.

*Everyone has to die sometime.*

*Be brave.*

Alex sat across from her with a fresh glass of wine.

'So my first question,' the forensic expert spoke up, 'is do you have more samples? In my line of work, I'm generally comparing an exhibit against several exemplars. This note would be the exhibit. But where are the exemplars?'

D.D.'s eyes widened. She glanced over to Alex, who shrugged, equally perplexed.

'Exemplars?' she ventured.

'Other handwriting samples to be used for comparison. For example, if you suspect this note was written by subject A, you would submit three other handwriting exhibits from suspect A to serve as exemplars for my analysis.'

'Ummm . . . I don't have subject A,' D.D. volunteered. 'In fact, I was hoping to work the other way – you could analyze the handwriting on this note to help me find subject A.'

'You mean, judging purely by the script, I would provide age, gender, and probable occupation of subject A?'

'That would be perfect,' D.D. assured him.

In the silence that ensued, it occurred to her she might have taken a misstep. 'Ummm . . . assuming such an analysis is possible?' she asked belatedly.

'No,' Dembowski said.

'No?'

'That's called graphology, a pseudo-science if you will, where experts claim to read subconscious clues buried in a person's handwriting. I am not a graphologist. I am a forensic handwriting expert, meaning I scientifically compare documents to determine if the same person authored all the exhibits or not.'

D.D. didn't know what to say. She glanced across the table at Alex, who shrugged as if to say, *Who knew?*

'I'm sorry, Ray,' D.D. attempted at last. 'I only wish I was far enough along in the investigation to bring you multiple samples. Where things stand right now, however, I have one dead body and this note, left on the windshield of my car outside the shooting. Now, we have reason to believe the shooter is not yet done, so any insights would be greatly appreciated.'

On the other end of the phone line, Dembowski sighed heavily. 'You understand, we're moving beyond the field of science into the realm of conjecture?'

'You prefer to speak off the record?'

'Have to. I'm a forensic handwriting expert, not a graphologist, meaning even if a court of law were willing to entertain the notion of graphology, my analysis still wouldn't meet standards.'

'Okay.' D.D. nodded, starting to understand how her expert wanted to play it. 'Let's call this a chat between colleagues. I got this fascinating note. Say, what do you make of it?'

Another pause, a deep breath, then Dembowski got down to basics. 'As someone who studies handwriting, there are several aspects of this note that strike me. First off, the note is written in cursive, versus the more commonly used print. Furthermore, the letters are fairly large in scale, and looping, with the exception of the bottom of each letter, which has been flattened, as if the writer used a straight edge for guidance.'

'I noticed that myself,' D.D. said. Across from her, Alex craned his neck, reexamining the plastic-covered note. *Everyone has to die sometime. Be brave.*

'Few other anomalies – the average person creates letters of un-even size. For example, common letters, particularly vowels, have a tendency to be smaller in scale, more rushed in execution. In your exhibit, however, each letter is nearly identical in size and scale. Notice the crossbars on the two t's. They are exactly the same width, down to the millimeter. This indicates someone with a high degree of attention to detail. The use of a straight edge to set the bottom line further supports a writer with a high need for precision. From a graphology point of view, the author of this note is most likely someone with a significant need for control in every aspect of life, a type A personality, a tightly wound anal-retentive, my first ex-wife –' Dembowski laughed hollowly – 'etc., etc.'

D.D. pursed her lips, made a note. Given the scene, that made sense to her. The wiped down kitchen, the two mugs carefully placed in the sink. Even the shooting was direct and clean, double shot to the forehead, precisely placed to ensure instant fatality. So a murderer who possessed above average attention to detail and was a neat freak. Interesting.

'When analyzing handwriting, one of the things I always look for is letter slant. A left-handed person almost always has a backward slant to the letters, a right-handed person a forward slant. These letters are nearly perfectly perpendicular. To play the odds, I'd theorize your letter writer is right-handed, but again, exercising rigid precision in the formation of each letter.'

D.D. made another note.

'Next up, let's examine the open parts of letters such as m, n, y, h. Some people scrawl with a tight, cramped script that closes up these spaces. But your letter writer has produced full, open shapes, very elegant. Also, looking at the m's and n's, each hump is fully formed and rounded on top, while in contrast, the v in the word "everyone" is sharply angled. This level of precision, each letter being fully and accurately formed, doesn't just imply control, but also a great deal of practice, someone well schooled in penmanship.'

'You mean someone of higher education? Above average intelligence?' D.D. asked.

'I mean Catholic school,' Dembowski said bluntly. 'I mean no one learns to write this beautifully without wearing a plaid uniform and being beaten by a nun.'

'Makes sense to me,' said D.D., who was the product of public education and wrote with a tight, cramped scrawl only a doctor could love. Across from her, Alex, who had attended a private Catholic school and regularly teased her about her illegible handwriting, grinned.

'Of course,' Dembowski continued, 'the accurate spelling and correct use of punctuation, grammar, and capitalization all indicate a well-educated, intelligent person. Then again, the note consists of only two lines, meaning we have limited material for analysis.'

'Understood.' D.D. was starting to enjoy this. For better or for worse, Dembowski's pseudo-science was starting to create an image of a killer in her head, and she liked it. The note agreed with her crime scene; her crime scene agreed with the note. That worked for D.D.

'Finally,' Dembowski said, 'it's important to look at the tail of the y and the ending hook of the last letter of each word. These flourishing touches can tell us a bit more about psyche. For example, while the consistent size and accurate form of each letter tells me your letter writer is practiced and precise, the tail of the y gives us the first insight into style. In this case, the y has a distinct loop, above and beyond what is strictly necessary for form. Likewise, each word ends with an upward flourish, a sort of graceful finishing touch.'

'You mean refined,' D.D. said sharply. 'As in, I'm not only looking for someone well educated, but also upper class? Higher socio-economics?'

'Possibly. Attending a private school, however, would seem to indicate that. Overall, my highly unscientific opinion is that the person who wrote this note is right-handed, very neat in appearance, detail-oriented, well educated, possibly Catholic, and of course . . .'

He paused a beat, as if the last piece of the puzzle should be obvious to D.D.

'Rounded letters,' Dembowski prodded. 'Finishing flourishes.'

D.D. finally got it. Her eyes widened. 'No way!'

'Oh, I'm nearly positive. And when it comes to gender, studies have shown even a layperson can accurately predict the sex of a letter writer nearly seventy per cent of the time. Men and women are different, even when it comes to penmanship. So, assuming the person who did the shooting is the same person who wrote this note, then your murderer . . .'

'Is a woman!' D.D. filled in.

'Yep and, most likely, a tightly wound one at that.'

# 7

'They allow dogs in the comm center?'

I looked up from the coffee-stained counter in the tiny kitchenette area to find Officer Mackereth, lounging in the doorway, studying me and Tulip, who sat patiently by my side.

Seven forty-two a.m. My replacement, Sarah Duffy, had done me the courtesy of showing up on time for day shift. She'd logged in, performed roll call, then we'd spent thirty minutes reviewing the dispatch log from the graveyard shift, so she'd have a sense of history to guide the day. It helped particularly with domestic complaints, where maybe two calls from the same residence had already come in during one shift, then a third hit during the next shift. At that point the second dispatcher knew the situation was ongoing, possibly escalating, and probably it was time to get more aggressive with the police response, whether the caller agreed or not.

I'd just clocked out, feeling I'd earned every penny of my $14.50 hourly wage. I was simultaneously exhausted and cranked up on adrenaline, a dangerous combination for anyone, but particularly for me.

One more day down, three more to go until the twenty-first. Randi and Jackie had each been murdered in the evening. For the sake of argument, I'd set my mental deadline at 8 p.m. January 21. Meaning eighty-four hours and counting. Or, assuming I slept six hours each morning, only sixty waking hours left.

Tom pushed away from the doorjamb and walked into the small space. He approached Tulip, held out his hand.

'He got a name?'

'Her name is Tulip.'

'Bring her often?'

'Too cold to leave her outside,' I said, as if that explained everything.

He nodded, so maybe it did.

I finished wiping down the counter with a Clorox wipe, then went to work on the battered stainless steel sink with a scrubber sponge. Nine months ago, I'd started buying all new cleaning supplies for the break room. Trust me, someone had to do it.

Officer Mackereth was scratching Tulip's ears, but eyeing me. I didn't return his gaze. I scoured the sink. Coffee and hard water stains everywhere. Drove me nuts.

'Quite the call tonight,' he said presently.

I stilled, noticed a rust stain that would never come out, scrubbed harder.

'Sorry I was slow on the intel,' I said abruptly. 'Caller was hiding from her husband and couldn't really talk.'

'Then how'd you get the information?'

'Phone beeps.'

'Pardon?'

I finished the sink, glanced at him, then turned on the water to rinse the sponge. Officer Mackereth was probably mid-thirties, blue eyes, short-cropped brown hair. Bit burly, but carried it well. Gave him the kind of presence that made subjects give up on the idea of running and surrender instead.

I didn't like him standing so close. I didn't like him studying me with cop eyes, trained to ferret out secrets and spot dissembling.

He'd never caught up with me after a shift. Most of them hadn't. On the one hand, as Detective D.D. Warren had said, I had their backs and they felt like they had mine. On the other hand, dispatchers had a notoriously high burnout rate. Meaning most of my officers were waiting for my one-year anniversary, to see if I was still around, before investing in a personal relationship.

I was like the walk-on part in all those old war movies. The new guy whose name nobody bothered to learn.

Except Officer Mackereth was talking to me now, paying attention to me now. Following war movie logic, he'd just doomed me to blow up in scene two.

The thought made me smile, then made me want to laugh, then made me want to cry.

Exhaustion and adrenaline. A dangerous combination in any person, but particularly in one with only eighty-four hours left.

'What do you mean phone beeps?' Officer Mackereth asked again.

I put away the Clorox wipes. Got out my messenger bag. 'I asked questions. The caller responded by using one beep for yes, two beeps for no,' I supplied. 'Got the job done.'

I slipped the wide flat strap crossways over my body, black leather bag, with my loaded Taurus, draped at my hip. I picked up Tulip's leash.

And Officer Mackereth placed his hand on my arm.

I stilled. Maybe sucked in a breath. Tried to think what to feel, how to respond. For a year I'd been training to attack, retaliate, defend. I should drop into boxer's stance, hands in front of my face. *Take a picture*, my coach always yelled. I should prepare to deliver jab one to be followed quickly by punch two, left hook three, uppercut four.

No one had touched me in a year. Casually, politely, kindly.

And the sheer vacuum of my isolation suddenly threatened to consume me. Isolation, exhaustion, adrenaline.

I wanted to laugh. I wanted to cry.

I wanted to throw myself into Mackereth's arms and remember what it felt like to be held again.

'Did you learn that in training?' he asked me evenly.

'No.'

'What about the gun? How'd you know he had a gun?'

His hand was still on my arm, his blue eyes fastened intently on my face. I kept my chin up, my expression neutral. 'Just knew.'

His arm finally dropped. Beside me, Tulip whined slightly, as if sensing my discomfort.

'Good work,' he said abruptly. 'I think . . . Thank you, Charlie. I mean it, thanks.'

'I'm glad you're okay,' I said simply. 'And I'm sorry it took me so long to figure out the situation. I'll do better next time.'

Two more shifts. That's all she had. Two more shifts.

Officer Mackereth switched his attention to Tulip, who was now pressed against my leg. I noticed his hands by his side. No wedding ring, but that didn't mean anything. Few officers wore them, not wanting to broadcast personal information in their line of work.

'I'll take you home,' he said.

'It's okay—' I started.

He cut me off. 'Can't take her on the T,' he said, gesturing to Tulip. 'We might be open-minded –' his tone was wry, calling my bluff – 'but Boston mass transit isn't.'

He had me there. Taxi had cost me thirty bucks, nearly a third of my shift. Take another taxi home, and after taxes, why had I bothered to work at all?

I still hesitated, old instincts dying hard. Detective D.D. Warren had advised me to confide in my officers. They didn't have ties to Randi or Jackie. They couldn't be part of the problem, so I should make them part of the solution.

Except . . . In war movie logic, Officer Mackereth's use of my name meant I'd die next. But in the story of my life, if I used Officer Mackereth's name, he'd be the next to go. There was a reason I kept to myself; not just because I was trying to limit the pool of people who could hurt me, but because I was trying to limit the pool of people I might hurt back.

'Come on, Charlie,' Officer Mackereth said gruffly. 'Cut a guy a break. You probably saved my life tonight. Least I can do is save you cab fare.'

He turned toward the door. And Tulip and I followed, Tulip with a fresh prance in her step at the unexpected attention.

I wondered what Jackie had been doing this time last year. I wondered what she'd been thinking, who she might have recently met. And I wondered, if she had known, if our trio's erstwhile planner had foreseen her own death, what would've she done differently.

Said no or said yes?

That's a central life question, don't you think? Do you regret the things you did, or the things never done?

Eighty-four hours and counting, I followed Officer Mackereth to his vehicle.

*

I told Officer Mackereth I lived in Cambridge, by Harvard Square. Close enough, I figured. Tulip and I could walk the rest of the way from there.

Officer Mackereth, I learned, lived in Grovesnor. Meaning, given morning rush-hour traffic northbound on I-93, he was now driving at least an hour out of his way. I protested again. He led me to his patrol car, which all officers drove home.

I climbed in the front, taking up position in a genuine black leather passenger seat that was quite comfortable. Tulip got the hard vinyl-covered bench in the back. Perfect for hosing down. Not so good for smooth-haired dogs. Tulip slid off twice, then gave up and lay on the floor.

'Where you from?' Officer Mackereth asked me as we hit the on-ramp for 93.

'New Hampshire.'

'Concord?'

'North, the mountains.'

'You ski?'

'A little. Cross-country.'

'Used to downhill in college,' he offered. 'Tore my ACL. Cross-country might be better for me. Family?'

I squirmed in my seat, looked out the window. 'Not married. You?'

'Never tried it. Seeing anyone?'

'Tulip's pretty special,' I offered.

He chuckled. 'You two been together long?'

'About to celebrate our six-month anniversary. I'm hoping she'll bring me flowers. You have any pets?'

'No girlfriend, no kids, no pets. Two parents, one pain-in-the-ass older sister, and three adorable nieces and nephews. That's enough for me.' His turn again: 'Hobbies and interests?'

'I like to clean.'

He paused, glanced at me with his left hand on the wheel. 'Seriously?'

I shrugged. 'I work all night, then sleep all day. Cuts into a girl's social life, you know.'

'Fair enough.' He glanced down at my hands fisted on my lap, stating shrewdly, 'Bet you didn't get those knuckles cleaning.'

I stared down self-consciously, wishing I'd put on my mittens, or at least tucked my hands beneath my legs. My knuckles were a mess, the valley between the joints of my pinky and ring finger swollen and purple on both hands. The remaining knuckles were abraded in several places, a collection of old and new injuries. Prizefighter hands. Not pretty, not feminine, and yet I valued this new and improved look very much.

'Boxing,' I admitted at last.

Officer Mackereth arched a brow. 'Then you do have a hobby. Must be a serious one if you can do that kind of damage wearing gloves.'

I didn't correct his assumption. Of course I fought bare-knuckled. What good were gloves gonna do me on the twenty-first?

'You seem to work mostly graveyard,' I stated, switching the focus back to him.

He nodded. 'Mostly.'

'Why? You must have enough seniority to request a better rotation by now.'

Officer Mackereth shrugged. 'I started out with graveyard because that's what rookies get. And I don't know. Guess I've always been a night person. I don't mind the hours, while there are plenty of officers with families and kids and dogs, and God knows what, where graveyard would be a real pain in the ass. Seems to make more sense for me to keep the shift.'

'Team player,' I said.

'Most cops are,' he observed. 'What about dispatch officers?'

'Loners,' I assured him, which wasn't exactly true, but I was feeling impulsive. 'Being shut up in a darkened room with multiple monitors and a dozen cups of java is our idea of a good time. You know what you get when you cross an air traffic controller with a tightrope walker? A nine-one-one operator.'

He laughed, a rich, easy sound that thrilled me more than it should have.

'What got you into dispatch, anyway?' he asked.

'Tried it out in Colorado. Needed a job, didn't have a college degree. Call centers will take just about anyone, which fit my qualifications.'

As a student, I'd suffered from chronic memory issues, not to mention a limited ability to focus. It had made for a rough academic ride. Oh, the times Jackie had shaken her head at me as I'd failed yet another test. Turned out, however, that crises brought out the best in me. You don't want me on your team for a quiz bowl, but if someone's breaking into your house, I'm the gal to call. I planned on the adrenaline rush being my friend on the twenty-first.

'Not many dispatch officers make it through training,' Officer Mackereth observed now.

My turn to shrug. 'Turned out I liked it. Every shift is different, you get to think on your feet. I'm probably painfully ADD, meaning it's perfect. You?'

'Father's a cop. Cliché, but there you have it. And I like it. Every shift *is* different. You get to think on your feet.'

Officer Mackereth exited 93 for Storrow Drive. Almost there now. Through the top of the rear divider, I could just make out Tulip's head as she sat up in the back.

'You can drop us off in Harvard Square,' I said.

'You don't live in Harvard Square.'

I looked at him. 'How do you know where I live?'

'I'm a cop,' he answered levelly. 'I looked it up.'

My hands stilled on my lap. I thought of my loaded Taurus, snug in my bag because they'd never let me wear it holstered at work. 'Officer Mackereth,' I began.

'Tom.'

'Officer Mackereth.'

'Tom,' he repeated stubbornly.

'You can drop us off at Harvard Square,' I informed him crisply. 'Tulip could use the walk.'

'Only if you answer one question.'

I eyed him mutely.

'Is it just me you don't trust,' he continued evenly, 'or is it all men? Because to the best of my knowledge, I've never done anything to disrespect you, but if I have, then I'd like to know so I can do better next time.'

He was nearly at Harvard Square. And he wasn't going to slow down. I could tell that. He knew my address and he had it in his head that he owed Tulip and me a ride home. Maybe that was nefarious, maybe he wanted to prove what he knew, how close he could get.

Or maybe, he was a guy and I was a girl and tonight we'd shared something pretty intense. And I was exhausted and fired up and he was exhausted and fired up, and he had that deep laugh and that broad chest and it would be easy to touch him.

I remembered that. The warm, hard feel of a man's skin beneath my hand. The coarse rasp of beard, the hungry taste of a man who wanted me as much as I wanted him. It made me feel a little reckless, a little wild.

Maybe what most of us feared wasn't dying, but dying alone. Without ever really touching. Without ever really connecting. Having inhabited this earth, but without leaving any impression on it.

The thought hollowed me out. Took all my fatigue and restlessness and spiraled it dark and low, until I did want to sleep with a virtual stranger. I just wanted, for one moment, to feel like I mattered.

Officer Mackereth hit Harvard Square. He slowed, allowing for the morning congestion of lights, cars, and college students. He followed the road as it looped around brick buildings, slid under the overpass, took a left at one of the many green spaces, and formed a direct line to my house.

In the back, Tulip whined, sensing we were close. Four blocks. Three, two, one. Officer Mackereth tapped the brakes, turned right, traveled half a block down, then halted right in front of my landlady's gray triple-decker.

I already had my fingers on the door handle – good news, front seat passengers were allowed to come and go as they pleased from police cruisers. 'Thanks for the ride,' I said.

'Dinner?' he asked evenly. 'Tonight. Before our shifts. I could pick you up. Cook you dinner at my place if you'd like to bring Tulip. Or take you out if you prefer.'

'Thank you for the ride,' I said again.

He sighed. 'You're a tough nut to crack, Charlie.'

I didn't disagree, just climbed out and released Tulip from the back. She bounded out gratefully, racing a little circle on the snow-covered sidewalk.

Officer Mackereth didn't say anything more. Just studied me through the window as I closed the passenger door in his face. A heartbeat later, he put his cruiser in drive and pulled away.

Tulip and I stood side by side, watching him depart.

I waited until the patrol car was out of sight. Then I finally exhaled a breath I hadn't realized I was holding and turned toward my landlady's house. At the last second, a movement caught the corner of my eyes. I glanced up sharply, just in time to catch the silhouette of a person standing in the second-story window of the house next to mine.

The second I spotted the figure, he or she stepped back. Blinds came down. The window blanked out, leaving Tulip and me once again alone on the street, with the hairs prickling the back of my neck.

# 8

'I want in.'

'What?' D.D. looked up bleary-eyed from the stack of interview statements she'd been skimming. She already felt bewildered, but that didn't surprise her. Jack, so cute and peaceful over dinner, had been up all night crying again. She'd taken the first shift, rocking him. Alex had taken the second. Come morning, they were both wrecked.

A fellow detective leaned over her desk. Ellen O. She had a real last name, but it was too long and involved too many consonants. When the newly minted detective had first joined the force two years ago, someone had shortened her name to O, and, half the time, no one bothered with even the Ellen part, but simply referred to her as Detective O.

O was fifteen years younger than D.D. and fifteen pounds heavier, but in all the right places. She had dark exotic eyes and glossy brown hair nearly the same shade as cinnamon. In the beginning, male detectives had been very interested in mentoring the young sex crimes detective. When she was less than receptive to their attentions, rumors had started that she was a lesbian.

D.D. doubted that. From what she could tell, Detective O lived and breathed her job. She was actually more intense than even D.D., which was not, in anyone's mind, a good thing. While D.D. would admit this to no one – no one! – the rookie detective scared her a little.

'Your dead perv,' O prodded now. 'Possibly one of two. I want in.'

D.D. started with the obvious: 'You're a sex crimes detective. This is a homicide investigation.'

Lisa Gardner

'Where the victims are suspected pedophiles, which just so happens to be my area of expertise. Trust me, you need me.'

D.D. gave O a look. They'd both been around long enough to know that as arguments went, "trust me" was never the right approach.

O slapped a sheath of papers on D.D.'s desk. 'Forensic analysis of the first perv's computer. I'll give you three minutes to review it, then you tell me the relevant findings, because I already know.'

'Three minutes?' D.D. scowled. She hadn't gotten to reviewing details of the 'first' shooting yet. She was still working on the homicide that had happened on her watch, not the one that hadn't.

'Three minutes was all it took me,' O declared boldly. She crossed her arms over her chest. The sex crimes detective was wearing a white button-down shirt over a blue tank. Nothing wrong with the ensemble, perfectly professional. It was all D.D. could do not to reach over and fasten the top button.

Apparently sleep-deprivation made her petty. And bitchy. And way too tired for this.

D.D. sighed and gave up. She pushed the report back to O. 'Fine, you're the expert, and yeah, especially if these two shootings are related, we could use some help. What you got for me?'

O appeared genuinely startled. Maybe D.D. was, too. She'd never caved easily, or gracefully, before. *Hah*, she wanted to say. *You're younger and prettier, but I'm older and wiser.* That would probably ruin the moment, however, so she didn't.

'All right,' O said. She uncrossed her arms, took up position on the edge of D.D.'s desk, and got serious. 'Douglas Antiholde, level three sex offender, shot four weeks ago in the doorway of his apartment. Double tap to the left forehead.'

'Yeah, know that much.' D.D. made a motion with her hand for Detective O to speed it along.

''Kay. So most pedophiles specialize, particularly when it comes to MO. Some use coercion, some use force, some use opportunity. Either way, all of them start by "grooming" their targets. And they have preferred methodology for that as well, the latest and greatest being the Internet.'

'Douglas Antiholde was an Internet predator,' D.D. filled in dryly. Another hand gesture to move it along. Not her first rodeo.

'You know the target age group for online predators?' O asked.

'Fourteen-year-old girls,' D.D. guessed.

'Nope. Five- to nine-year-old boys.'

'Really?' D.D. sat up a little straighter. Okay, she had not known that.

'Antiholde's Internet log is textbook,' O was saying. 'He was a registered user of every major kiddie website out there, plus Facebook, plus Spokeo, plus Chatroulette. You gotta understand, these guys are like day traders – this is what they do, twenty-four seven. They surf the Internet, identifying targets, initiating relationships, and then grooming, grooming, grooming. Just like stockbrokers, they understand that not every target is going to pay off. So they build a "portfolio" of ten, fifteen, twenty victims they're actively following and researching. They don't expect all to bear fruit. They just need one to work out, and it's worth it to them.'

D.D. had a feeling her mouth was hanging open. She'd never pictured sex predators as working professionals before. That level of discipline. That level of focus. 'Ummm, aren't there safety protocols or security software that help block sex predators' access to kids?'

'Yes and no. See, most five year olds join websites that feature their favorite toys, where they can become a member. Now, these sites certainly advertise to parents their security protocols. Stuff like they have trained professionals hanging out on the websites patrolling for bullying, that sort of thing. And they impose limits on communication, mostly on instant messaging where it appears Virtual Animal A is talking to Virtual Animal B using dialogue bubbles. Virtual Animal A can "chat" with Virtual Animal B, but only by selecting from stock phrases. This gives parents a sense of security. Cute fuzzy Animal A can't type in a dialogue box, *Hey want to meet after school*, because that's not a stock phrase.

'Unfortunately, parents are missing the obvious. Just joining these sites, becoming a part of a virtual community where you are encouraged to make virtual friends and rewarded for hanging out, is starting the grooming process. A five year old now thinks it's *good* to be online. A five year old now thinks it's something *special* to be a member of an Internet community. And a five year old now thinks it's *fun and desirable* to invite perfect strangers to be friends. From an online predator's point of view, a kiddie website does all the up-front work for him. Then he just has to show up and close the deal.'

'But how?' D.D. asked. 'According to you, they can only communicate using pre-scripted phrases.'

'Sure, on those sites. Which is why they serve as the first step in the grooming process. Look, a guy like Antiholde picks a popular kids site, say AthleteAnimalz.com. He logs on to the site, enters his animal's code, becomes a member. Then, for the first few weeks, he does what any user does – he plays like mad. He masters games, he builds up points, he wins whatever there is to win. Boys, in particular, are acutely status-conscious. From an early age, they want to win and they want to be friends with winners. So Antiholde becomes that winner. He builds a virtual image as the most popular, most successful member of the site. The high school quarterback everyone wants to high-five in the school halls. Then he goes to work.

'He starts monitoring other users. He's looking for the members that play regularly. Remember, he's a day trader. He's got a lot of stocks to watch, so he doesn't want the random visitor to the site. He wants someone with fairly predictable hours, the kid that goes on after school or after dinner most days of the week. The kid that day in, day out, he's gonna find there.

'Now he starts friending. Invites other users to be his buddies. Asks them to play games with him. And again, the website is going to do his work for him, by providing the perfect team-building exercises. Think of any of the virtual combat games – Antiholde's character will be the one that magically has your back. He'll save your character again and again. Which will make you feel good about him, again and again. In a matter of weeks, you're happy to see him logged on to the site, excited to be on his team, and even more thrilled when he invites you to log on and play with him at certain times during the day. You're not just friends now, you're *friends*.'

'Yeah,' D.D. interjected, 'but it's all still online. A virtual rela-tionship. Creepy, but make believe. Plus what are the odds the kid is from the predator's same town? I mean, I've heard the stories of the sixteen-year-old girl being lured into taking a plane to meet her new soul mate, but a five year old?'

'Sports teams,' O said.

'Sports teams?'

'Primary geographic indicator used to target boys. You're a pedophile in Boston, first thing you do is look for kids who describe themselves as Red Sox, Celtics, Bruins, or Pats fans. Nine times out of ten, you've just identified a victim within driving range. And boys love to talk sports. Another innocuous way of bonding, where the kid is giving up a major piece of personal information, without ever being the wiser.'

D.D. shifted uneasily in her chair. 'That's twisted.'

Detective O shrugged. 'Just because they're predators doesn't mean they're stupid. Computers are tools. We use them to help us analyze evidence and process reports. Internet predators use them to reach beyond the walls of their seedy apartments, into your nice, cozy family room, and make contact with your child without you ever knowing the difference. Some of them even create their own sites. Hamsters Who Play Hockey, whatever. On Website A, where they've established the relationship, they trace the kid's user name back to the child's email addy – a fairly simple technical exercise. Then they send the kid an email, inviting the child to visit hockey-playing hamsters. Nothing scary or alarming about that, especially as the email came from Cute Animal A, who the child's been "playing" with for weeks. Kid clicks on the hockey-playing hamster link, and bada bing, bada boom, the child is now on a website controlled by a predator, where content will quickly become more and more questionable as the predator ramps up the next phase of the grooming process. Or maybe the predator goes with a direct outreach. From playing virtual games online, to sending an email saying, *Hey, buddy, want to meet after school and play catch in the park?*'

'Or *Want to see my new puppy?*' D.D. murmured.

'Second victim,' O filled in. 'Stephen Laurent. Yep, come see my puppy would do the trick. And most kids are easily manipulated. They are receiving an email from a perceived friend, so they say yes. They show up at what they think is another kid's house, to see a puppy, except there's a grown man there. But there's also the puppy, and they've been trained not to be rude to adults, so even if they're uncomfortable, even if in the back of their mind they think maybe they shouldn't . . .' She shrugged. 'They go along. Things we've trained our children to do without the help of computers.'

D.D. felt ill. She was accustomed to analytically discussing crime. But now she kept seeing Jack, except five years from now, and she and Alex were taking the time to raise him in the right neighborhood with the right locks on the door and attending the right kind of school, except the minute he went online . . . Her son would disappear down a virtual rabbit hole, with dark alleys and seedy strangers everywhere, except the dark alleys would be dressed up as brightly colored computer screens and the seedy strangers would be cute little bunnies with names like ILuvSk8boardingInHarvardSquare. Dear Lord.

'Do you have kids?' D.D. asked Ellen O.

The detective's face was serious. 'Are you kidding? I go around spouting facts like forty per cent of girls aged twelve to seventeen have been solicited by a stranger online. Doesn't really go over well on dates. Or at cocktail parties for that matter. Then, should someone pull out a smartphone while I'm in the room . . . Let's just say, at least my cats still hang with me.'

D.D. hadn't thought of that, but it rang true. O had a head filled with the kind of boogeyman stories no one wanted to hear. D.D. was a homicide detective, and even she wasn't sure how much of this she could take. It made her feel too powerless, as a mom and a cop.

'So,' D.D. ventured, 'you're saying Antiholde's computer log proves he was an online predator?'

'Profile fits.'

'And Stephen Laurent?'

'I'd like to glance at his Internet log, but figured I should get your permission first.'

'I'd like you to look at his Internet log, too,' D.D. agreed. 'At the moment, we're searching for any kind of link between the two victims—'

'Pedophiles.'

'Murder victims. If they both frequent these websites you're talking about . . .'

'Question becomes,' O said, 'how'd their cover get blown? I mean, online, they're gonna appear like any other user, an excited kid.

Except someone figured out who they were and what they were doing.'

'Victim in common?' D.D. guessed. 'Someone who knows the victim?'

She was thinking of the forensic handwriting expert she'd talked to last night, Dembowski's theory that their shooter was an anal-retentive female. D.D. didn't say anything, however. She didn't want to contaminate the investigation with an assumption, and apparently graphology itself was riddled with assumptions, not to mention the assumption that the person who left the note was the same person who shot Stephen Laurent. Which brought her to another question. She regarded Detective O.

'You read the crime scene report of the first shooting, Antiholde?'

'Yep, late last night.'

Ah, the good old days, when work didn't shut off at five.

'Any documentation of a note from the shooter?' D.D. asked.

'What do you mean?'

'When I left the Stephen Laurent scene, I found a note on my car. I'm wondering if it was from the shooter.'

Ellen O frowned. 'What'd the note say?'

'Everyone has to die sometime. Be brave.'

'Oh. Oh, oh *oh*. Hang on. Wait here.'

O dashed off. D.D. sat there, wondering what was up. Sixty seconds later, O was back with some crime scene photos. One showed the victim, Douglas Antiholde. Another showed a close-up of the contents of his pants pocket, including loose change, a paper clip, and a crumpled piece of torn yellow legal pad paper that had been smoothed out enough to read: *Everyone has to die sometime. Be brave.*

Writing was script, with a flattened bottom, every letter precisely shaped.

'I'll be damned,' D.D. murmured.

'Serial shooter, targeting pedophiles,' Detective O declared triumphantly. 'I'm in!'

'Are you ever,' said D.D. 'And good luck with that. Good luck to us all.'

# 9

I dreamed of my mother.

She stood at the counter in a tiny brown-and-gold kitchen, curtain of dark hair obscuring her pinched face as she crooned to herself. 'Sugar and spice and everything nice, that's what little girls are made of.'

In my dream, I was three years old, crammed into a high chair meant for a baby, my back plastered to the sticky vinyl seat, while a white plastic strap, splattered with dried eggs and fuzzy oatmeal, jammed into my tummy hard enough to hurt.

I wanted out. I whimpered, whined, fussed, and fidgeted. If I could just get my quick little hands on the buckles, I could escape. But I'd done that before. I had a memory of getting out, so she'd changed the straps, and now the buckles were in the back of the sticky seat and I was trapped and uncomfortable, and even though I was hungry, I didn't want to be there anymore.

My mother had a lightbulb in her hand. She'd taken it from the chipped white lamp in the family room. Unscrewed it, while singing softly to herself.

'Sugar and spice and everything nice, that's what little girls are made of.'

My mother placed the lightbulb in a blue plastic bowl, picked up a large metal spoon, and slammed down hard. A faint tinkling sound. The older me, the real me, and not the trapped three-year-old version of me, understood the sound was the lightbulb shattering.

The three-year-old trapped me simply watched with big blue eyes as my mother ground the lightbulb, all the while singing, singing, singing.

Then, she looked up at me and smiled.

Next to the bowl was a jar of peanut butter. Now my mother unscrewed the lid. Now she scooped out a big spoonful. Now she placed the peanut butter in the blue plastic bowl with the shattered lightbulb. And stirred.

'Sugar and spice and everything nice,' my mother declared. 'That's what little girls are made of.'

She crossed to the high chair. She placed the bowl on the too-tight white tray. Plopped it down on a piece of congealed egg. I could hear the squishy, popping sound of yolk smooshing against the bowl.

My mother was dressed up. She had gloss on her lips, color on her cheeks. Her brown hair was freshly washed. She'd taken the time to brush it until it fell long and shiny halfway down her back, a waterfall of shimmering brown-red silk.

I wanted to touch that hair. Hold it in my fist. Feel this softer, shinier version of my mother.

My mother looked pretty. It both fascinated and terrified me.

'Sugar and spice and everything nice,' my mother singsonged. 'Oh, but Charlie honey, nice girls finish last. You don't want to be last. The world wants brave little girls, tough little girls. Sugar and spice and broken glass, that's what little girls should be made of.'

She scooped up the first spoonful of peanut butter. 'Here comes the airplane. Come on, Charlie. Be a good girl for your mommy. Open up. Here comes the airplane, into the hangar, vroom, vroom, vroom . . .'

Later I vomited blood. We went to the emergency room. The nurses rushed me in, fussed all over me. I was poked, prodded, the doctor flashed a light in my eyes. I held my stomach and whimpered. But I didn't cry. Good girls were brave. Good girls were tough.

Pain. Wracking cramps, eye-rolling diarrhea, my face bursting with sweat, but I promise, promise, promise, no tears rolling down my cheeks.

'I just don't know what to do,' my pretty, shiny mommy was telling the doctor. 'I turned my back for only a moment, and next thing I knew, she was eating a lightbulb. I mean, really, Doctor, what kind of child eats a lightbulb?'

Good girls are brave. Good girls are tough.

'It's just so hard, sometimes, being a single mom. I mean, I'd just popped into the kitchen to make her favorite peanut butter sandwich, and well, I was doing laundry and trying to pick up all the toys in the family room and clean the bathroom. And yes, a lightbulb had burned out, so I'd gotten one down to replace it, but I never thought for a second, never imagined . . . I'm sorry, I'm sorry. I don't mean to cry. I just haven't slept in so long. You have no idea how active she is and impulsive and . . . And now this and we don't have insurance and, and . . . I'm sorry, can I just sit down for a minute?'

Good girls are brave. Good girls are tough.

The doctor patted my mother's shoulder. The doctor told my mother everything would be all right. The doctor told my mother she was doing the best she could and he understood completely.

I rolled over, held my stomach, and vomited more blood.

Wanted to talk. Wanted to find my voice, but my tongue was swollen and my cheeks hurt and my throat burned.

Another nurse standing beside me. Wiping my mouth with a cool cloth, touching my forehead with gentle fingers. I stared at her. Dark eyes, dark hair. Kind face. Speak. I wanted to. I tried to open my mouth. Could feel the urgency of it, the desperate need to. Had to speak, had to speak.

Not about the lightbulb, not about the peanut butter.

Something else I had to say. If I could just say . . .

Good girls are brave. Good girls are tough.

I opened my mouth.

The nurse turned away. Across the room, as if sensing my intent, my mother glanced over the doctor's shoulder, met my gaze, and triumphantly smiled.

I woke up in the blind-darkened room of my Cambridge rental. Pulse pounding. Hair damp. Gray tank top glued to my sweat-plastered skin.

Words were still on the tip of my tongue. The words I never got to say back then, the words it took me years to slowly but surely remember:

*Baby's crying.*

That's what I'd wanted to say. What I'd felt a desperate urge to tell the doctor, the nurse, someone. Except in theory, I didn't remember a baby. In theory, my mother only had me.

*Baby's crying.*

Down the hall, I thought now. And for a second, I could almost taste a name, feel it like a scent in the air, a ghost of a ghost of a memory. A baby girl. Down the hall. Crying.

I squeezed my eyes shut. Pressed the heels of my hands into my eye sockets as if that might help. To remember. To forget?

I never knew. All these years later, I never knew.

My mother hurt me. I knew that. She was not well. So sick, in fact, that after that last incident, she was sent away permanently. A mental institute I guess, because that's where sick people generally went, and jail would've involved a trial, and that I would've remembered.

My mother went away. That's what Aunt Nancy told me the first day in the hospital, and I never brought it up again. Mentioning my mother's name risked summoning the demon. So I never asked and Aunt Nancy never told.

Something bad had happened. Worse than usual. And I knew what it was. Deep down inside, I understood that I knew everything, that in fact I remembered *everything*. But I didn't want to remember what I remembered. So I didn't. By a conscious or subconscious act of will, I took the past, boxed it up, and put it away, never to be seen again.

Maybe not the best coping strategy. And not without consequences. Turns out, when you wall off pieces of your mind, you can't control everything that disappears. To this day, I have haphazard recall at best. Time escapes me, days, weeks. Entire conversations with best friends, the vital last lecture that happened right before the final exam.

Jackie and Randi used to tease me I'd forget my own head if it wasn't attached to my shoulders. I'd laugh with them, but often self-consciously. Jackie had really called me on the phone last night, we'd talked for two hours, and I'd forgotten all of it? Randi had told me all about her first date with local heart-throb Tom Eastman, and I couldn't recall a single detail?

Small glitches in the operating system, I'd tell myself. I mean, given the amount of resources I'd dedicated to wiping eight entire years from my general consciousness, some errors were bound to occur. Besides, no matter how much I screwed up, forgot, genuinely overlooked, those occasions were still better than the few times I started to remember.

Recall was most likely to happen when my anxiety spiked. Then the past would leak out in my dreams, snippets from an old movie reel, where once upon a time, a thin crazy mother lived in a tiny dirty house with her thin lonely daughter. And the mother fed her daughter shattered glass and slammed her fingers in kitchen drawers and pushed her down steep flights of stairs because little girls needed to be brave and tough.

Until one day, the little girl grew to be so brave, so tough, that she won the war.

That, I felt in my bones. My mother did something. But I won the war.

And I didn't ask about my mother anymore, because in my heart of all hearts, I understood that answer might tell me everything I still wasn't prepared to know.

*Baby's crying.*

Girl. Stuffed bear. White ruffles, pink polka dots. *Sugar and spice and everything nice . . .*

Don't remember. Block it out. Shove it away. Nothing good can come from the past, especially a past like mine. Not to mention, at this stage of the game, what would be the point?

A hunted woman doesn't need closure. A hunted woman needs battle skills.

I stood abruptly, glanced at the clock in my shadowed room, and calculated the time remaining until 8 p.m., January 21. Zero hour. When my own killer would finally come calling.

Seventy-eight hours to go.

I put on my workout clothes, grabbed Tulip's leash, and prepared to run.

My father lives in Boston. Only argument Aunt Nancy and I ever had was about him, so again, another topic rarely broached and even less frequently considered. But yes, I have a father. Rich guy. On his fifth, sixth wife, last I heard. I have siblings, too, half siblings I guess. I've never met any of them, and I have no illusions my father is any more of a parent to them than he is to me.

My dad has a sperm donor approach to fatherhood. Meet a young pretty girl, knock her up. If she's young enough, pretty enough, surgically enhanced enough, maybe marry her, too. Until of course, the next young pretty thing comes along, in which case, hey, he's a guy; he can't help himself.

I guess he met my mother while on vacation at the grand old Mount Washington Hotel in Bretton Woods. She was seventeen and working as a housekeeper. He was thirty and looking for entertainment. According to Aunt Nancy, my mother told him she was pregnant. He didn't marry her, but sent money. Sperm donor, check writer. See, a hell of a guy.

He never followed up on my care. At least that's how the story goes. Lost touch with my mother in the very beginning, which surprises me a little. Not that he'd let me go, but that my mother would let *him* go. Maybe she tried. But she would've been a mountain mouse and he's some big city finance guy, came from money, makes even more money, has a long and enduring value system wrapped up in his own self-importance. She probably never stood a chance.

I guess the cops in upstate New York called him first, after the incident. My mother had his name listed as the emergency contact, though no phone number. Police, however, are a bit more skilled than mentally ill twenty-five year olds, so within a matter of days, they tracked him down. He was not in the country, however. Paris, London, Amsterdam. I don't recall.

He bounced them to Aunt Nancy, who did the honors of assuming responsibility for a niece she'd never met. Even then, she ran a business, the call came out of the blue, so it took a few more days while she made it from the wilds of New Hampshire to the even deeper wilds of upstate New York.

Those days remained hazy for me. I remembered waking up in the hospital. I remembered being surprised that I was alive. Then I remembered feeling deeply, deeply disappointed.

A social worker sat bedside. She had black hair cut in a short bob that showed off a sharp, angular face. Not a kind-looking person. Not maternal. She looked hard and spoke in a clipped voice.

The doctors had removed my appendix, maybe some other things. Apparently, spending years eating small doses of glass and rat poison was not good for various internal organs. But I was healing well, she'd assured me. I'd be just fine.

And again, I was so deeply, deeply disappointed.

I never spoke to her. Or the nurses. Or the doctors. They had betrayed me. They had forced me to live. I'd hated them for that.

Eventually, my aunt had arrived. She'd taken my hand, and that quickly I went from being my mother's child to being my aunt's niece.

That was the best thing that had ever happened to me.

Aunt Nancy was my mother's older sister by six years. She had silver-gray hair cut Brillo short. Premature gray hair ran in the family, I was told. Like blue eyes and strong jawlines. But the gray color suited my aunt, brought out her steel blue eyes, her high cheekbones. My aunt could care less. If my mother was obsessed with male attention, then my aunt was equally obsessed with keeping men at arm's length.

When their parents died in an auto accident – in New Hampshire you'll notice lots of signs advising you to brake for moose; you really should – my aunt took over the parenting role. My mom was a wild one, even back then. And my aunt was the responsible one, even back then. Needless to say, their relationship was strained even before my mom got knocked up by a wealthy Boston financier.

They went their separate ways until one day, the phone rang and my aunt learned about an incident, a niece, and yet one more unexpected life change.

Like any kid, I never appreciated my aunt, until one night, my own phone rang with news of an incident, a tragedy, an unexpected loss. And I turned to my aunt for guidance, because given a choice between being my mother's daughter and being my aunt's niece, I'd take niecedom any day of the week.

My aunt is brave. My aunt is tough.

Fuck chewing shattered glass.

Run a bed and breakfast with little help and no health insurance in the mountains of New Hampshire, where in January the daily temperature will start at negative twenty and most of your Boston guests will have forgotten to pack hats, scarves, and gloves and will consider it all your fault.

I thought of my aunt now, as Tulip and I slowed at an intersection, waited for the light to change, then sprinted through the crosswalk. I thought she deserved better than yet another life-changing phone call on January 21.

I thought, heart pounding from the exertion of my six-mile run, sweat pouring down my face, dog trotting beside me, gun quickly accessible in my fanny pack, that I was glad my aunt couldn't see me now.

Because she'd have taken one look at me and understood that even if I was winning the battle, I'd lost the war: I'd become the spitting image of my mother, down to the bruised eyes, hollowed out cheeks, and hard-lined face.

The mountains had left me. My aunt had left me. Living in isolation, fighting paranoia in a big city, I had become everything I knew better than to be.

These days, I was my mother's daughter.

Except I didn't chew shattered glass anymore.

I carried a .22 semiauto. And this evening, sometime after 7 p.m., I was going to prove once again that I knew how to use it.

# 10

Hello. My name is Abigail.
   Have we met yet?
   Don't worry, we will.
   Hello. My name is Abigail.

# 11

Rhode Island State Police Detective Sergeant Roan Griffin had the voice of a bear and the build of a boulder. Big guy. Probably bench-pressed small automobiles after toppling sumo wrestlers and tackling linebackers. Good-looking guy, too. Officer Blue Eyes, the *Providence Journal* had dubbed him years ago, when he'd appeared on Dave Letterman to model the state police's award-winning new uniforms.

Truth was, the Rhode Island State Police had a reputation for the best-looking cops in New England. No one knew how they did it. Maybe a special factory that chiseled out broad-shouldered, barrel-chested, square-jawed men. Either way, whenever there was an opportunity for cross training with their Rhode Island counterparts, the female officers of Massachusetts quickly signed up. Like, all three of them.

Currently, D.D. was on the phone with Griffin. A shame, really, because Rhode Island's headquarters was only an hour south, and given the restaurants available for lunch in Providence's Federal Hill . . . Missing out on sightseeing and Italian dining, D.D. thought with a sigh. So much for the new and improved lifestyle.

Griffin was a married man. Actually, his second marriage, as the first wife had died of cancer. Wife number two was a blond advertising executive named Jillian. D.D. had never met her, only knew her because of the press coverage. Jillian had survived the notorious College Hill Rapist about eight years back. Her younger sister hadn't been so lucky. When they'd finally arrested a man for the attacks, Jillian had formed a group dubbed the Survivors Club in order to assist one another through the trial. Except there hadn't been a trial, given that the suspect had been gunned down outside the courthouse and Jillian and her fellow club members had gone from sympathetic victims to prime suspects.

D.D. would be the first to admit she'd followed the case as zealously as Nancy Grace, especially when days after the alleged rapist's murder, another woman was attacked. Seriously, there were days on this job when she thought not even a suspense novelist could make these things up.

Griffin and Jillian had two boys now. Ages four and six, D.D. was learning. The youngest, Dylan, had taken a page out of his father's book and was all football all the time. The six year old, Sean, had recently discovered cooking. As in last night he'd prepared rack of lamb for the entire family.

'With a pomegranate molasses marinade,' Griffin was finishing now, 'though I suspect his mom helped him with that.'

'He's six. How'd he even lift a roasting pan into the oven?' D.D. wanted to know.

'Oh,' Griffin said breezily. 'He gets that from me.'

'And the hot oven . . . not a problem?'

'Jillian did the honors of taking it out. And she helped him sear the outside on the stove. But he found the recipe—'

'Where? At the back of his comic books?'

'He checked out a cookbook from the library. He's a how-to kid. No fiction, but brings home books on how to plant gardens, how to engineer robots, how to build boats. Guess now it's gonna be how to cook.'

'Rack of lamb. That's amazing.'

'Hell, it was fabulous. I'm ready to start a college fund for Johnson and Wales.'

'I don't know about cooking yet for baby Jack,' D.D. said. 'But last night he threw up something that might pass for molasses.'

Griffin laughed. That was the great thing about parents and homicide cops – nothing ever grossed them out. She could tell diaper stories all day, and her fellow detectives would actually find that charming. D.D. wondered sometimes how normal people lived.

'Is he sleeping at all?' Griffin asked.

'No.'

'Try driving around?'

'No. Too afraid I'll fall asleep.'

'What about during the day? Does he nap?'

'Some. When you're holding him, or when he's in his carrier, then he passes out cold.'

'Okay,' Griffin said briskly, 'so Dylan wasn't much of a sleeper when he was an infant. I'd take him for short drives in the car seat, get him wiped out. Then return home and place his carrier directly in his crib, with him still strapped in. Worked like a charm for weeks. Then pretty soon, we could just place him straight into the crib. Maybe being in the carrier helped get him acclimated to the crib? Hell if I know, but it worked.'

D.D. pursed her lips, nodded. 'Sounds like something worth trying. Or I could just sign up for the funny farm now.'

At the last minute, she realized maybe she shouldn't have said that. Given Griffin's own past, that little incident with the Candy Man, Griffin's ensuing mental breakdown, the medical leave from the state police.

Griffin just laughed again, sounding unruffled. D.D. took that as a sign his new family was working for him. She hoped so. Griffin was a good guy and great detective. If he was happy, maybe there was hope for the rest of them.

'So,' she declared, 'as delightful as our children are, I'm actually calling you about a case. Randi Menke, murdered in Providence two years ago. Guess the state police became involved because you were already investigating the number one suspect for fraud.'

'Jon Menke,' Griffin said immediately. 'Slimy bastard.'

'You think he did it?'

'Please, at the time I would've bet my career on it, which it turned out, would've cost me, given the second murder one year later.'

'Jackie Knowles,' D.D. filled in. 'So you heard about that.'

'Only four dozen times. The friend . . . Charice, Chartreuse . . .'

'Charlene. Charlie.'

'That's it.' Griffin snapped his fingers over the phone. 'Charlie something something Grant. She visited our fine headquarters many times. Made her wishes for swift and immediate justice known.'

'What do you think?'

Another sigh. 'Crap, it's January eighteenth. Just three days to go.

Well hell . . .' Griffin stopped murmuring, seemed to collect his thoughts. 'Okay, so I can only speak to the Providence scene, and there wasn't much to it. First responders arrived to a quiet house. Front door was closed but unlocked. In the family room, they found the body of a woman. She was lying there so peacefully, one of the guys dropped to start CPR. Wasn't until he was leaning over her that he saw the bruises around her neck and realized she was dead.'

'Fully clothed?'

'Dressed in some kind of upscale, dark green track suit – pants, long-sleeved white shirt, matching top. Fluffy white socks, L.L. Bean slippers. Comfy clothes, as one of the detectives put it. Like she'd gotten all settled for the night, then someone rang the doorbell.'

D.D. considered that. Women didn't usually wear track suits and fluffy socks when expecting male guests, so she went with their theory – Randi had turned in for the night.

'TV?' she asked. 'Was it or any lights on when the officers arrived?'

'TV was off, all lights had been turned off—'

'Print the switch plates?' D.D. interrupted.

'Duh,' Griffin informed her drolly. 'Nada. Perp was definitely wearing gloves and, less quantifiable, but I'd say knew the house. Felt comfortable there. It's like he showed up, did the deed, then tidied up. Turned off lights, mopped the floor, wiped down the kitchen for all we know. But the scene was tidy. Except for the dead body, of course.'

'So maybe there had been a struggle,' D.D. challenged. 'Maybe Randi put up a helluva fight, and that's why the perp cleaned up afterward.'

'Maybe. No signs of trauma on the body, though. No defensive wounds, no bruising. All in all, it's like someone walked in, put his hands around her neck, and that was that.'

'You've said he a couple of times. So you're thinking a male attacker?'

'ME's best guess. It's not easy to manually strangle someone. Takes a bit of muscle but also finger strength. Randi was an average-sized female, five five, hundred and twenty, did Pilates four times a week. In theory, it would take someone bigger and stronger to over-power her so quickly.'

D.D. pursed her lips. 'And Jon Menke?'

'Weasel,' Griffin muttered. 'Six feet, one ninety, physically fit, spent four to five mornings a week at the gym. Apparently, he felt a doctor should look the part. We learned his female colleagues appreciated that.'

'A ladies' man?'

'Definitely not monogamous.'

'Did Randi know?'

'Apparently part of the cause for the divorce. The other part being that he liked to beat the shit out of her.'

'Document it?' D.D. asked sharply.

'Oh yeah. To give Randi some credit, she did her homework before leaving the bastard. Called a hotline, got some advice. She'd filled an entire safety deposit box with photos and walk-in clinic reports before dialing up the lawyer and making a break for it. And trust me, Menke was pissed off about that. His wife not only left, but got him branded as a wife beater while nailing him for alimony. Yeah, Menke had every reason to want her dead and was fully capable of getting the job done.'

'Except . . .' D.D. drawled out.

'Alibi,' Griffin supplied. 'A cocktail waitress, mind you, some pretty young thing who probably saw his pecs, his paycheck, and his Porsche and promptly forgot things like his history of domestic abuse, but they were in a bar and several regulars backed their claim. In the end, we couldn't break it.'

D.D. thought about it. 'You said he had a history of smacking his wife around?'

'Yep. Fat lips, black eyes, a wrecked knee where apparently he'd kicked her.'

'Sounds like a guy who had trouble managing his temper.'

'Yep.'

'But, the homicide scene . . .'

'Looks like the work of someone fully in control,' Griffin agreed. 'Which was the second problem with pursuing Menke. On the one hand, it just felt right to nail him for something. On the other hand, this something didn't feel like his kind of something. He would've trashed the place. Not to mention, according to our criminologist, wife beaters who become wife killers almost always disfigure their spouses. Shoot them in the face, stab them five dozen times. It's a personal, frenzied, dehumanizing attack. This . . . this was cold-blooded. More akin to murder-for-hire, which became our next theory.'

'Oooh,' D.D.'s eyes widened. 'Menke paid someone to take down his too-good-for-her-own-good ex-wife.'

'Yeah. My theory. Real winner at the time, and maybe still the best theory, but we could never find a money trail. Now, the feds were investigating Menke for health care fraud at the time, and the money trail there was long and convoluted. Lot of suspicion that he was dealing prescription drugs on the side, which would've given him access to both cash and a certain "clientele" we could never prove. So murder-for-hire remains the most likely scenario, in my mind.'

'Did you ever get him for fraud?'

'Feds got him. Small potatoes though. Could only prove the tip, not the iceberg. But it was enough to have his medical license revoked, plus he's serving three-to-five in a Club Fed somewhere. You can contact a Boston FBI agent, David Riggs, if you have more questions. He ran the health care fraud investigation.'

'When you pressed Menke about his wife's murder, how'd he take it?' D.D. asked. 'Get hostile on the subject, or smug?'

'Moral indignation. He was totally over her, how dare we suggest otherwise.'

'Ah, moral indignation. Always a nice choice for a wife beater. Taking the high road.'

'Well, he was a doctor, you know.'

Both D.D. and Griffin lapsed into silence. 'No physical evidence at the scene?' D.D. tried again.

'Only evidence was lack of evidence,' Griffin assured her.

'What do you mean?'

'Most homes have fingerprints. How odd that this one didn't.'

'So the killer really did *clean* up afterward.'

'Stone cold and handy with a sponge. I'm still thinking murder-for-hire, and this guy has quite the résumé.'

'And the second murder?' D.D. asked. 'In Atlanta?'

'Don't know the details. Only heard after the fact from Charlie, plus some Atlanta Feebie, Kimberly Quincy, gave me a buzz. She'd heard there might be a connection between Jackie Knowles's murder and a Providence case and was curious. She commented that the Knowles scene was equally pristine. Other than the dead body and all.'

D.D. frowned. She didn't like it. 'They gotta be connected,' she muttered now. 'I mean, how many *clean* murder scenes have you seen in your day?'

'Counting Randi's: one.'

'Exactly. So they have to be connected. But how?'

'Question,' Griffin corrected, 'is who? We knew Randi had at least one enemy – her ex. But what about Jackie Knowles? Who had reason to want her dead?'

'Murder-for-hire suggests money,' D.D. said immediately. 'But two different victims from two different families rules out inheritance.'

'Please, Randi wasn't getting that kind of alimony. She had thirty bucks in checking, that was it. Look,' Griffin took a deep breath, 'I gotta run in a minute, but for what it's worth, when I heard about the Atlanta scene, I went back to the area hotels. Tried to see if maybe a mutual acquaintance of Randi and Jackie might be in town. They grew up together, right? So maybe a neighbor, classmate, friend.'

'Charlie yada yada Grant,' D.D. guessed.

'Not that I could prove, but maybe she paid for a room with cash . . . You know how it is.'

D.D. nodded. She did know how it was. 'She found me, you know.'

'Charlie something something Grant?'

'Yep. She's living in Boston now. Running from her neighbors, classmates, friends.'

'Three days until the twenty-first,' Griffin murmured.

'Yep. She wanted to meet me in person. She hopes, if she doesn't survive the twenty-first, that'll make me try harder to solve her murder.'

'Shit,' Griffin drawled.

'My thought, exactly.'

Griffin said, 'You should call Atlanta. Try the Feebie. She seemed all right. Wish I could help you more, especially given the time line . . .'

D.D. agreed. Three days to solve two cold cases that hadn't yielded any leads in the past two years . . . 'So,' she asked briskly, 'if you were me, who would you be on the lookout for?'

'Someone physically strong, mentally patient, good with his words, better with his hands, and absolutely positively soulless. Probably above average computer skills as well – the Internet being every stalker's new best friend. Conversely, I'd tell Charlie that as long as she's running, stay off the net. Logging on these days is like sending out smoke signals: *Here I am*. And mine the connections. How many people really knew all three women? In fact, here's a thought – have you checked out Facebook? Sometimes there are pages in memoriam, you know, in honor of Randi Menke and/or Jackie Knowles. See who's posting, then track them down. Might give you a start.'

'Lotta man hours for a case that's not even a case,' D.D. muttered. Then in the next instant, she thought of Detective O, Internet predators, and online grooming and felt a satisfying click in the back of her head. Ten weeks of total sleep deprivation, and she still had it. 'Thanks, Griffin,' she said hastily. 'You just gave me an idea.'

# 12

Jesse flew off the school bus, slinging his Red Sox backpack over his left shoulder while dashing down the snowy street. Didn't have a watch. Wasn't sure about the time, but the bus had been late. Wouldn't it figure that today of all days the bus would be late? Had to hurry, hurry, hurry.

He hit the front steps of the apartment building and jumped them two at a time before slapping the palm of his hand against the buzzer for his apartment. His mom, expecting him, buzzed back. He jerked open the heavy outer door and leapt for the stairs, missing the bottom two, hitting the edge of the third and sliding down on his knees before he got his feet beneath him and finished the long rat-a-tat dash up three levels. He was already digging in his coat pocket for the apartment key. He arrived at his unit's front door, sweaty, trembling, and feeling a little sick.

Couldn't be late, didn't want to be late.

Helmet Hippo was depending on him.

Jesse jammed the metal key in the lock, got the door open, and burst into the apartment, already hemorrhaging boots, backpack, mittens, coat, hat, snow pants. No time for snack. Gotta move, move, move.

He sprinted for the table, hitting the power button above the keyboard of the computer as his mother yelled down the hall: 'Jesse, you okay?'

'Yeah, yeah, yeah. Just gonna play a game.'

'Jesse?'

'AthleteAnimalz. Geez, Mom, everything's all right!' Second the words left his mouth, Jesse bit his lower lip, realizing too late, he should've watched his tone. Sometimes, if he was 'fresh', his mother would take his computer privileges away. He paused, hand still on the computer, eyes on the screen as the old laptop slowly churned to life.

But his mother didn't appear in the hallway, didn't say anything more. Probably on a call, couldn't tear herself away. Jesse felt guilty, but grateful. He darted away from the loading computer long enough to grab Zombie Bear and a glass of milk. The stove clock told him it was 3:42 p.m.

Yep, he was late. Very late.

He flew back to the table, sloshing some of the milk over the rim of the glass, then had to run back to the kitchen for a napkin, and by the time he returned and cleaned up the mess, his heart was really going thump, thump, thump and he didn't feel well again. He was hot, like shaky and trembly and he wanted to cry, but he didn't know why.

He was late and Helmet Hippo would be mad and he'd been fresh and now probably his mom was all mad and he just wanted a friend; he just wanted everything to be okay and for someone to like him, and for his mom to not have to work so hard and for their downstairs neighbor Mrs Flowers not to bang on the floor all the time when he was trying to use quiet feet but still wasn't so quiet.

Jesse plopped down in front of the computer, entered the AthleteAnimalz website, and did his best not to weep. He knew he was late. He still didn't want to blubber like a big baby.

Homerun Bear had mail. Jesse's arm was trembling so badly, it took him three tries with the mouse to click on the mailbox icon. The letter was from Helmet Hippo. It included a smiley face and a picture of a baseball mitt.

'Hey Bud. I'm here and ready to play. Find me when you're ready. Your friend, Helmet Hippo.'

Then Jesse did cry. Giant tears of relief. Helmet Hippo wasn't mad at him. Helmet Hippo still wanted to play.

Helmet Hippo was still his friend.

Jesse sobbed gratefully.

# 13

At 4:31 p.m., I began phase one of operations. First up, dress code. I went with black jeans, black turtleneck, thick-tread running shoes, and a black wool coat, all courtesy of the local Salvation Army store.

I looked like a cat burglar, or a New Yorker, depending on your frame of reference.

I loved the shoes and tried to get over it. Phase four of operations involved pitching the entire ensemble into a public Dumpster. Not that the police couldn't find or wouldn't find the items, but there was nothing to prove these particular secondhand clothing articles were mine. A precaution built into a precaution built into a precaution.

So far, it had worked for me.

Exiting the house, I wore a bright turquoise scarf and matching hat and oversized mittens. I'd read somewhere that one of the keys to any disguise was distinguishing accessories – later, witnesses would associate me with the aqua scarf or shocking gloves, meaning I couldn't be the black-clad perpetrator. Obviously, I was wearing turquoise at the time!

I had my messenger bag slung over my shoulder, stuffed with wadded newspaper to give it the appearance of bulk. Later, the newspaper would be tossed and replaced with my overbright scarf, hat, and mittens. For now, the bulk of the leather bag disguised another telltale bulge – my Taurus .22 holstered at my waist on a belt specially designed by my firearms coach, J.T. Dillon, to hold twenty-seven extra rounds of ammo.

I would see him for the last time tomorrow. I had a feeling he knew a little bit about tonight, too. But he didn't pry and I didn't inform. Instead, our conversation two weeks ago had gone something like this:

'If I needed to, say, establish a new identity . . . for example, get my hands on a complete set of top-of-the-line papers, would you know who I might contact to make such arrangements?'

J.T., loading his .45. 'Seems like I get asked that question a lot.'

'Beats girls asking what's your sign.'

J.T., finally looking up at me. Me, doing my best not to squirm beneath that gaze. Before J.T. took on a serial killer, shot up half of Massachusetts, and eventually found a wife, he was a marine, Force Recon. Mostly, he reminded me of an old gunslinger, possessing the salt-and-pepper hair, leathery brown face, and deeply lined eyes of a man who'd spent most of his life peering into the horizon and was never surprised by what he saw there.

'Nothing's cheap,' he said.

'I got a rainy day fund. Hey, it's raining.'

'My wife likes you,' he said, as if that settled the matter for him. Maybe it did. I'd met his wife only once before. She'd studied me for half a second, then walked over and wrapped me into a tight embrace. I got the feeling Tess was as tough as her husband, and that if I ever took them up on their offer of dinner, we'd have a lot to say.

J.T. provided a name. Told me to wait twenty-four hours, so he could vouch for me. He must've, because when I made the call two days later, the crisp-voiced woman on the other end seemed to be expecting me. She asked questions. I provided answers. And three days ago, for the bargain basement price of one thousand dollars, I picked up three sets of brand-new, top-of-the-line fake papers: three birth certificates, three Social Security cards, one driver's license.

Everything a terrified woman might need to stay on the run for the rest of her life.

I wasn't sure I could imagine that, to tell you the truth. It's funny, but boxing and shooting and running had awakened something inside me. Turns out, I had a violent streak. It'd only taken me twenty-eight years to figure that out, but these days, I was doing my best to make up for lost time.

Exiting the back door of my landlord's house, I was grateful to come around and discover the front porch clear, no sign of Tulip. Tonight was a solo mission for sure.

I hunched deeper into my coat, chin tucked to collar to fight the biting cold, and set off for Harvard Square. Ten-minute walk to the T stop. Eight minutes waiting for the train, then off and moving again.

Rush hour, the subways crammed full. I stood in the middle, just another nameless commuter, hand gripping the metal support pole, legs swaying in rhythm with the railcars, inhaling the subterranean scents of sweat and urine and wet wool coats.

I hummed softly under my breath, my only concession to my growing nervousness.

Seventy-five hours left to live.

What would you do?

Sky was pitch-black when I returned to upper earth, pushing my way through the creaky turnstile, hiking up the steps to another darker, quieter section of Boston. Street lamps did their best to combat the relentless winter night, but they'd been positioned too far apart, casting the icy sidewalk into large enough pools of shadow to make a lone female think twice. I shed the turquoise scarf, hat, and mittens, shoving all deep into my pack. Then I flipped my messenger bag backwards, pouch bouncing against my rear. No need to disguise my hip holster anymore. In this neighborhood, everyone was probably packing, and blending in was my best shot at survival.

Turned out, even snow was ugly in housing projects. The mountains where I used to live, Harvard Square where I now lived, blanketed in yards of white fluffy Norman Rockwell snow. Not here. In this section of town, snow became just another form of litter. Gray, sandy, riddled with yellow pools of dog piss and bristling with discarded straws, Big Gulp lids, cigarette butts. You didn't look at this kind of snow and think of Christmas lights, cheerful hearth fires, or mugs of hot cocoa. You walked by these piles and figured even Mother Nature was an unforgiving bitch.

I set off, following a map I'd committed to memory to find an address I'd never written down. Another precaution rolled into a precaution.

Sidewalks weren't empty. In an inner city neighborhood, they never are. I walked by groups of hulking black teens, baseball caps worn backwards, down coats four sizes too large, chests gleaming with gold chains. Some were laughing, some were smoking. Some were already pushing and shoving, maybe in jest, maybe not.

They all looked up. Started. White chick, on their streets.

I smiled at them. I put my finger to my lips. I exhaled softly, Shhhh.

And just like that, they quieted, stepped away.

I think it had to do with the look in my eyes. One each of them recognized, most likely contemplated every single morning when standing in front of his mirror.

You want to know what it feels like to have nothing left to lose? Liberating.

Intoxicating.

Dangerous.

6:02 p.m., I acquired my target.

Seventy-four hours left to live.

What would you do?

Tomika met me in the foyer. She had the kids bundled up so thickly only their eyes, brilliant white, appeared against their dark faces. Michael, the older boy, had a red backpack. Mica, the four-year-old girl, clutched a blanket and a teddy bear. Tomika carried the rest, two black duffel bags slung over each shoulder. Eight years of marriage, twenty-six years of living, condensed into two midsized travel bags.

I faltered. My foot, coming over the threshold, missed. I stumbled, caught myself in the doorway.

Then I did something curious even for me. I exhaled, so I could watch my breath form a misty trail in the ice-cold night.

That satisfied me. Made me feel that the scene was exactly right.

'Has he called?' I asked softly.

'Five minutes ago.'

I glanced at my watch, set a mental deadline. 'Let's go.' I held out my arm, and it seemed the most natural thing in the world for nine-year-old Michael to loop his hand through it. I smiled down at him.

He gazed solemn-eyed back up at me, and again, the scene felt right.

Tomika had called dispatch for the first time six months ago. Usual story. Drunk, angry husband, tearing up the place. Usual results. Police showed up, talked her husband down; she refused to press charges.

But six weeks ago, Michael called the hotline. Their mother had gone out, leaving him and his little sister alone with their father. Now they were huddled in the closet, trying not to be seen or heard because other men were over and had gotten to arguing and one had pulled a gun and Michael had grabbed his little sister and jammed them both into the back of their parents' closet and he didn't know what else to do.

I did what comm officers do. I asked questions, I got answers, I dispatched several officers to the scene, and I kept Michael on the line. Forty-five minutes that call lasted. We sang silly songs. Exchanged knock-knock jokes. Michael and Mica even taught me some ghetto slang to improve my street cred.

By the time the first of my officers had arrived, the men were gone, and Stan grew pissed off at having a patrol man on his doorstep. Officer Mackereth, Tom, had been on duty that night. He'd done good. Never mentioned Michael or Mica, two frightened kids huddled with a phone in the closet. Just said he'd responded to reports of an argument in the neighborhood. Had Stan seen or heard anything?

After that, Michael started calling more often. Sometimes just to talk. Because nights were long in his house, and who cared about monsters under the bed when the real thing was passed out drunk on the family room sofa? He worried about his mom. He was terrified for his sister.

After the last recorded call, three weeks ago, Social Services had paid the family a visit. As Michael explained to me days later, Stan rounded up the family and sat them before the caseworker. They were to answer all questions openly and honestly. While Stan stood there and glared at them.

The moment the social worker left, Stan got out a hammer. He broke all of Tomika's fingers, then four of Michael's, then two of little Mica's. No one, he informed them, would be dialing the phone ever again. Or next time, he wouldn't be getting out a hammer – he'd get out an ax.

It had taken Michael twenty-four hours to work up the courage to dial 911 with his pinkies. Then he'd had to wait another two days for it to be my turn on graveyard shift. If anyone ever listened to that recorded call, it would sound like a little boy, playing with the phone, looking for his mother's number. It would sound like an exasperated dispatch officer finally rattling off a number to appease the child.

That it happened to be the dispatch officer's own prepaid cell was just because, of course. What other numbers do you know off the top of your head?

Michael and I took our conversation off line, where his mother, Tomika, joined the party. Then I liquidated my entire savings accounts, all forty-two hundred dollars, to buy a woman and her two children brand-new IDs, to cover first and last month's rent plus security deposit on a new apartment, and to pay for the bus tickets that would get them all there.

Seventy-three hours and thirty minutes remaining.

What would you do?


I escorted Tomika, Michael, and Mica to the bus stop. It would take three more exchanges to get them to Portsmouth, New Hampshire, but Tomika had an old girlfriend there, who'd set her up with a job. New names, new life, new opportunity.

Tomika was crying.

'I love him,' she said, then brushed her cheeks with hands thick with finger splints and white bandages.

'He'll kill you.'

'I know.'

'He'll kill your children.'

'I know.'

Michael had his arm around his little sister's shoulders. His expression, as he stared at his mother, was resigned.

'Mommy?' Mica finally spoke up.

Tomika glanced down at her daughter, sobbed harder. 'I swear I won't go back. I'll be strong. I'll take care of us, baby. I promise, I'll take care of us.'

Given the state of her splinted fingers, I helped her organize the new IDs in her purse. I opened her wallet, withdrew her old driver's license, slipped in the new one, made with the help of one of her Facebook photos and J.T.'s friend. In thirty seconds Tomika Miller became Tonya Davis. I wrapped my turquoise scarf around her neck, slipped dark sunglasses over her eyes, and added a bright hat to cover her uptucked hair.

For Michael and Mica, we had something simpler in mind. Michael gained a wig, becoming the seven-year-old sister, while Mica's ponytail was summarily cut off, turning her into a four-year-old younger brother.

Later, at the bus stop, should Stan Miller ask questions, no one would know of a lone woman with an older son and younger daughter boarding the bus. They'd only witnessed two women and two children who climbed on together, with an older girl and younger boy. I handled all the tickets again, so Tomika could keep her bandaged hands hidden inside her coat. Another question Stan might think to ask, but no one in the bus depot would have the answer.

At the last minute, I got back off the bus, mentioning I'd forgotten something, would catch up later.

Right before exiting, I leaned down and slipped a prepaid cell, recently purchased from Wal-Mart, into Michael's pocket. It was programmed with a single number – my own. I whispered in his ear, 'Call me. Anytime. I'll be there, Michael. I'll be there.'

Then I was off. Five minutes later the bus pulled away, Tomika Miller and her two kids getting a fresh start in life.

Until the first time it grew too tough, and Tomika gave in to the urge to call her husband. Or broke down and told her story to a friend who'd tell a friend who'd tell a friend who'd tell Stan Miller. Or Stan himself managed to track them down.

Maybe this time, Stan would bring that ax. Maybe this time, Michael would call me, begging, pleading, screaming desperately for help.

Maybe it would be after 8 p.m. on January 21.

And my phone would ring and ring and ring. Nobody left alive to answer.

I glanced at my watch. 7:42 p.m.

Seventy-two hours and fifteen minutes left to live.

What would you do?

I headed back to Tomika's old address. I headed for Stan Miller.

Things I didn't know about myself until the last year: I am, or used to be, deeply, deeply terrified of fighting back. First time my boxing coach tried to get me to spar in the ring, I couldn't do it. Shadowboxing, sure. Heavy bag work, no problem. Speed bag, fun. But to hit someone, actually pull back my arm, then snap my fist forward, rolling my shoulder, rotating at the waist, stepping into the full velocity of the punch, committing to my opponent's gut, kidney, chin, nose, right eye. Couldn't do it.

I danced around the ring. Dodged, ducked, V-stepped, side-stepped, elbow blocked, swatted, did anything but throw a punch.

All those years of going along. All those years of being a brave little girl, a good little girl. I couldn't retaliate.

My mother had trained me too well.

At the end of the sixth session, in sheer frustration, my boxing coach, Dick, a retired three-time world champion, nailed me in the eye. It hurt. My cheekbone exploded. My eye welled with tears. I recoiled, stared at him incredulously, as if I couldn't believe he'd done such a thing.

He jabbed me in the other eye. Then the gut, the shoulder, the chin. My coach started wailing on me.

And I took it. I hunched over, fists in front of my face, elbows glued to my ribcage, and let him beat me.

Brave little girl. Good little girl.

Making my mother proud.

Dick gave up first. Walked away in disgust. Muttering at me for not fighting, muttering at himself for beating up a defenseless girl.

And that did it. I finally registered my own pain. I finally heard someone calling me a *defenseless girl* and I lost it.

I attacked my fifty-five-year-old, gristle-haired, battle-scarred boxing coach and I tried to kill him. I threw jabs, right hooks, uppercuts, left hooks, solid punches, endless kidney shots. I chased him around the ring, corner to corner, and I discovered inside myself something I'd never known was there – rage. Pure, unadulterated rage. And not the good old, 'I'm twenty-eight years old and I'm finally pissed off at my mother' rage, but the better, harder, 'I'm twenty-eight years old and I'm finally pissed off at *me*' rage. Because I'd taken it. Because I was a good girl and a brave girl and I went along. So help me God I went along and I went along, and I was never going along again.

At the end of the session, my coach had one black eye and one swollen nose. I had two black eyes and bruised ribs. And we were both exultant.

'That's it!' he told me again and again, dripping blood all over the boxing ring. 'I knew you could do it. I knew it, I knew it, I knew it! Now, that's boxing, Charlie. That's committing to the punch!'

Turns out, I didn't want to be Tomika Miller, running from shadows, constantly looking over her shoulder.

I wanted it to be January 21. I wanted to open that door. I wanted to look my killer in the eye.

And I wanted to beat the shit out of him, before plugging three to the chest. One for Randi. One for Jackie. And one for me.

I'd been a good girl once.

Now I didn't plan on being a good girl ever again.

I arrived back at Tomika's apartment in the tenement housing unit at 8:26 p.m. I'd been told Stan's shift as a security officer ended at seven. Usually, he had half a dozen drinks with the boys, then came home to terrorize his waiting family around nine.

Big guy. Six two, 280 pounds. Not fit. His security job involved sitting in a booth, checking ID at a major manufacturing plant. Basically, he made twelve bucks an hour to sit around and look intimidating. Which must have pissed him off, because then he returned home and threw his weight around.

According to Tomika, he was often packing and seemed to have an endless supply of firearms. Where they came from, she didn't know and she didn't ask. But he and his buddies liked to shoot beer cans off the rear fire escape at nights, and none of them had problems producing a weapon.

So I had roughly thirty minutes to prepare for a mountain of a man who might or might not be packing multiple firearms.

My palms were sweating. My heart beat too hard in my chest.

I worked on breaking down my plan into short, manageable steps. First, quick buzz through the apartment, removing lightbulbs. Darkness was my friend, surprise my best advantage.

The instant Stan opened the door, he'd be back lit by the hall, a clear target. Best moment of opportunity would be those first two seconds, when he was caught unaware and completely haloed, while I'd be nothing but a faint shadow in the dark recesses of the living room.

My countdown to January 21 would continue. His would not.

Next step, hastily ransacking all kitchen and bedroom drawers. I found a .22 and a tiny little ankle holster gun. I kept the ankle shooter, dropped the .22 in the toilet. Then I discovered Stan's tool kit and went to work. A precaution built into a precaution built into a precaution.

In the back bedroom, I left the window access to the rickety fire escape open – always good to have an additional egress, especially if neighbors responded to the sounds of gunfire by crowding the inner halls.

Nine oh one. Jittery. Not good. My own anxiety started to piss me off. Nerves? I'd been training and practicing for a fucking year. What good were nerves to me? So sorry, Mr Killer of My Two Best Friends, but can we hold off on our confrontation for a minute, while I calm myself down? Want a drink? Want a Xanax?

Here, take two.

Fuck nerves.

I was a lean, mean killing machine.

God dammit.

Footsteps. Out in the hallway. Heavy and ringing. *Thump. Thump. Thump.*

My heart rate spiked. My black turtleneck constricted around my throat, and at the last second, I had to take my shaking left hand off my Taurus to wipe my sweaty palm on the leg of my jeans.

I'd locked the front door. Everyone did in this building. Now I heard the jangle of keys. A rasp of metal teeth engaging the first lock, then the second. Front door flung open.

Two hundred and eighty pounds of Stan Miller loomed in the entryway.

'What's for dinner, bitch?' Stan boomed across the darkened apartment.

He sounded cavalier, almost like he was in a good mood.

So I shot him.

I pulled left. Don't ask me how, don't ask me why. But I fucking pulled my shot left. Doorjamb exploded, Stan dropped like a rock and rolled toward the kitchen, screaming. I cursed a blue streak and, through my shock and rage, realized now I was in for it, not to mention that if my firearms instructor J.T. ever heard about this, he'd kill me anyway and spare me the miserable pain of the twenty-first.

'What the fuck, what the fuck, what the fuck!' Stan was yelling. 'Where's Tomika? What'd you do with Tomika?'

'Killed her!' I called back at him. 'That'll teach you not to pay your debts.'

(I was making this up. Precaution built into a precaution, right? Always gotta have plan B, and if I couldn't kill Stan, plan B was to lead him to think that his family was dead. A man like Stan had to owe somebody something somewhere. It just figured.)

'You're a girl,' Stan said. And just like that, he stood up in his kitchen. Apparently, being attacked by a girl didn't scare him nearly so much.

So I shot him again.

This time, I hit his shoulder. He howled, dropped again.

I felt better about things.

Until good ol' Stan popped back up and fired off four rounds in my general direction. This time, I dived for cover, cursing myself all over again. First two seconds. Battles are won or lost in the first two seconds. He'd been standing right there, lit up beautifully, 280 pounds of target. How the hell had I missed 280 pounds of target?

Dammit!

'Gonna hurt you,' Stan bellowed now. 'Gonna find you, gonna hurt you. With a knife. Bad.'

I crawled behind the overstuffed recliner, leading with my gun, and peered out, trying to penetrate the gloom of the kitchen. Couldn't see a thing.

Shit.

I took a second to get my bearings. Stan seemed to be doing the same, the apartment falling eerily silent. I strained my ears for sounds from the rest of the building. Neighbors yelling about gunshots, or banging the ceiling to say *quiet the noise*. Police sirens already screeching down the street.

Nothing.

Maybe 9 p.m. was too early for most residents of this building to be home yet. Or maybe, in a building where men routinely spent their evenings shooting beer cans off the fire escape, nobody noticed gunfire anymore.

I did. My ears were ringing, my heart pounding, my hands a shaking mess of adrenaline and fear. Even my stomach felt funny. Hollowed out, queasy, and butterfly-y. Shock, probably. Terror. Rage.

I tried homing in on the rage. Fear would get me killed. Anger was the only hope I had left.

'Who are you?' Stan boomed again. 'I don't owe nobody nothin', so who the fuck are you?'

I didn't answer, but traced the sound of his voice toward the hall to the left of the kitchen. I could just make him out, his gray sweatshirt a faint glow on the dimly lit floor. He'd shimmied out into open space. Probably to sneak around on me, but also to keep himself from getting cornered. The tiny kitchenette was no good to either of us; too small and cramped. Family room was better. Rear bedroom, with its open window leading to the fifth-story fire escape, best yet.

But for me to get to the bedroom, Stan had to get out of the hallway. Fine.

I shot him again.

For a big guy, Stan moved pretty fast. Sprang out of his crouch and leapt through the doorway into the kids' room. Couldn't tell if I'd got him or not, and didn't wait to see. I bolted down the short hallway into the back bedroom, as he opened fire behind me. Carpet exploded at my feet. Sheetrock rained down from overhead.

He was an even worse shot than I was. Course, spending the past few hours in a bar probably didn't help his aim, thank goodness for me.

I took four zigzagging steps and staggered into the rear bedroom.

Another ringing shot, and I was hurling myself over the windowsill, wincing as I flopped awkwardly onto the metal fire escape. I could feel the rickety deck sway upon impact. Couldn't stop. I'd be trapped on the tiny fenced-in balcony, and he'd come for me, like shooting fish in a barrel.

I didn't think anymore, I moved. Crabbing around, trying desperately to find the top rung of the descending metal ladder in the dark. I banged my head against another set of metal rungs, the ones heading up, staggered back, and a meaty fist clamped onto my shoulder.

Stan thrust his massive head and shoulders through the window and held tight.

'Gotcha! Gonna make you hurt, girl. Gonna get my ax, gonna get my hammer, gonna get my knife. Gonna make you pay.'

Which was a funny thing for him to say, given that I was the one holding a gun. One small twist, and I had the barrel of my .22 pressed against his temple.

Stan stilled. His eyes rounded. His mouth formed the proverbial O and he sucked in a breath, as I dug the barrel of my gun harder against his fat head. Big ol' Stan had made a mistake. He'd grabbed me with his left hand, and given the width of his massive shoulders wedged through the narrow window frame, his right hand, the one holding his own gun, was trapped uselessly in the bedroom. He'd need to release me and bring his left shoulder back inside the apartment, in order to get his right arm through again.

Battles are won in the first two seconds, or in the final two minutes.

The fire escape swayed unsteadily, making me feel as if I were surfing on air. I smiled at Stan. I exhaled and watched my frosty breath mist in the cold night.

The scene felt exactly right.

Shoot. Pull the trigger. For Tomika and Michael and Mica.

For Stan's hammer and his family's fingers and their long, terrified nights.

I wanted to. I needed to.

For that little boy in Colorado, whom I still couldn't forget. For all the crying kids, all the terrified women who called 911, except they had problems too big for any dispatch operator or patrol officer to help.

Pull the trigger.

Baby. Crying down the hall. I could hear her again, so close, so clear. Baby, in my mother's house, crying down the hall.

Sugar and spice and everything nice, that's what little girls are made of.

Sugar and spice and broken glass, I should've told the nurse. If only I'd told the nurse. Why hadn't I told that nice nurse?

PULL THE TRIGGER!

*Pull the fucking trigger!*

But I couldn't do it. I stared at Stan Miller, peered into the whites of his eyes, pressed my nickel-plated semiauto deeper and deeper into his temple . . . and I couldn't do it. My hand shook too badly.

I pulled back my arm and pistol-whipped him instead.

Stan howled. Let go. Stumbled back through the window.

I bolted. Down the ancient fire escape, rusty metal rungs shaking, whole structure swaying from my rat-a-tat impact, as I half slid, half jumped from metal decking down to metal decking, desperate to hit the street five stories below.

Stan was gonna get his right arm out now. Stan was gonna hunt me down. And Stan would shoot a woman in cold blood.

I felt the fire escape groan again. Heard, more than saw, Stan squirm and heave and twist his considerable homicidal bulk onto the narrow fifth-story decking.

Faster, faster. Not much time now. Gotta move, move, move.

As the fire escape heaved, sighed, gave an ominous creak.

'Gonna get you, girl,' Stan bellowed from above. 'Big Stan gonna run you down. What'd ya do to my family? Where's my Tomika? Tell me now, girl. Talk, or I'll shoot out your damn bitch brains.'

The first metal bolt attaching the fifth-story decking to the crumbling brick building went ping. Then the second, third, fourth.

Go, go, go, I urged myself. No time to lose. Jack, racing the giant down the beanstalk. *Run!*

The whole fire escape swayed above me. Making the sharp corner two flights below, I knew the moment Stan figured out what was happening, because he dropped his gun. It went sailing by me, just missing my head. Stan didn't need his pistol anymore. He'd grabbed for the railing instead.

Except that wouldn't help him any. I knew, because I was the one who'd ratcheted loose all the bolts attaching the rickety fifth-story fire escape to the ancient bricks of the dilapidated building.

A precaution built into a precaution built into a precaution.

I'm only a hundred and five pounds. Too small to fight a giant like Stan. But lighter and faster to beat him down a collapsing fire escape.

The wobbly metal ladder was shaking beneath my feet now. Above me, I heard a terrible screech as the fifth story decking swung out into midair, then felt it, like a giant chain, start ripping the corresponding layers of decks and ladders from the side of the cheaply constructed housing unit. *Ping. Ping. Ping.*

Stan screamed.

Metal groaned. People inside the building began to yell at the unexpected commotion, while the ladder beneath my own feet suddenly lurched down and away. One story above street level. Wasn't gonna make it.

I jumped, dropped, and rolled. To the side, away from the collapsing metal structure thundering down and across the street.

More screaming. More yelling. More groaning.

Stan Miller plunged five stories to the frozen pavement below.

Then the screaming stopped. Gritty sand and dirty snow ballooned up, settled back down.

I staggered to my feet, cleared my eyes, registered a pain in my ankle. Now was not the time. People pouring out. Residents of the unit who'd been immune to gunfire and screaming, but not this. No one, no how, had seen anything like this. They gathered on the street, yapping, dialing cell phones, shaking their heads, and then, when they spotted Stan's hulking body, skewered on multiple shorn metal rungs, the first woman screeched in horror, before several more joined her.

I stared at the carnage, the twisted heap of wreckage, the blood pooling on the front of Stan's shirt.

Then, I ran.

I didn't look back. Not for the screaming women. Not for the growing cries, not for the startled exclamation from the lone kid who spotted my escape.

I ran and I ran and I ran, my body shaking uncontrollably.

Round the block, I paused long enough to grab my messenger bag from beneath a snowy bush. Then I was off and running again.

9:56 p.m.

Seventy hours left to live.

What would you have done?

# 14

Baby Jack was crying again. He was not a happy camper and he wanted everyone to feel his pain.

'He gets that from me,' D.D. said. It was 9 p.m. Jack had been crying off and on ever since she picked him up from day care, where apparently he'd spent a very fussy day. No temperature. No spitting up. But he scrunched his face and fisted his hands and churned his legs as if he were jogging a marathon.

So far, they'd given him droplets specially designed to relieve baby gas. Not particularly effective droplets, D.D. thought.

'We could call the pediatrician,' Alex said. He was sitting on the couch, while she attempted to soothe Jack in the rocking chair.

'And admit we don't know what we're doing?' D.D. said.

Alex regarded her strangely. 'We don't know what we're doing. And we're not the first new parents who harassed their doctors with middle-of-the-night questions. For heaven's sake, that's what they're there for!'

Alex's unexpected display of emotion finally caught D.D.'s attention. She took in his salt-and-pepper hair, currently standing on end. The dark shadows beneath his eyes. The gaunt lines of his face.

He looked like hell, a man who hadn't slept in years. Did she look that bad? Come to think of it, Phil had clapped her on the shoulder four times today with clear sympathy. Suddenly, she got it.

'The baby's winning!' D.D. burst out.

'That would seem a fair assessment of the situation,' Alex agreed tiredly.

'He's only ten weeks old. How can he be beating us already?'

Alex eyed their squalling son. 'Same way youth always conquers age – better stamina, faster recovery.'

'We're two strong, intelligent, resourceful people. We can't be defeated by an infant. I was sure we'd make it until he was at least seventeen and demanding his own car. Which reminds me, when he's three and wants his own cell phone, the answer is no. And when he's five and wants his own Facebook page, the answer's also no.'

Alex stared at her, eyes sunken, cheeks unshaved. 'Got it.'

'Did you know the target age for Internet predators is five- to nine-year-old boys?'

Alex's eyes widened. 'No!'

'Yep. Big bad world out there. And more of it than you think is sitting in that sleek little laptop on the table.'

Alex ran a shaky hand through his hair. 'Well, wasn't like I was going to sleep tonight anyway. This from your new case?'

'Yeah, got a sex crimes detective, Ellen O, assisting now. She's an expert on Internet predators, so she and Phil spent the day poring over reports from the computers of the two vics and talking nerd.'

'Find a connection between the two pervs?' Alex asked.

'Many and varied,' D.D. assured him. 'Ironically enough, vics' computers share so many favorite sites, it's almost impossible to get traction. It's not a matter of did they run across each other online, but on how many different websites, user groups, and chat rooms. It's gonna take a bit.'

'Is Neil still going through the photos?'

'Sadly for him, yes. He made it through the first of six boxes and already looks like the walking dead. Gonna need some stress time for sure. I tried talking to him once today, but he's not ready yet. Just gotta get through it, he told me.' D.D. sighed, thought of her young squadmate with genuine concern, and sighed again. 'I almost admire his naïveté.'

She shifted baby Jack to her other shoulder, resumed rocking. Judging by the whimpering in her ear, Jack didn't like her left shoulder any more than the right.

Alex stood up. 'Want me to take a turn?' He gestured to Jack, who churned his feet fussily.

D.D. rubbed her son's back, hating not being able to soothe him.

It felt both wrong and inevitable. Proof that she wasn't maternal enough, just as distant as her own parents. Except she didn't feel cold and dismissive. She hated that her baby was upset. Wanted desperately to do the right thing, say the right thing that would comfort him. So far they'd tried burping, swaddling, rocking, singing, pacing, and driving. Nada.

The baby was winning. And they were old.

'Okay,' she said reluctantly.

Alex crossed to her. 'What about the ballistics report?' he asked as he transferred Jack from her shoulder to his chest. 'Got anything to conclusively tie the shooting of victim one to the shooting of victim two?'

'Got a note,' D.D. said triumphantly. 'Left in first victim's pocket. Exact same phrase: *Everyone has to die sometime. Be brave.* Written in the exact same tightly wound script.'

Alex was impressed. Jack was not.

'Maybe we should try going for a drive again,' D.D. suggested.

'Not sure either of us is safe behind the wheel.'

D.D. nodded tiredly. Alex was right about that. They were stupid tired. Which was why they were talking shop. It was the only topic of conversation that came to them naturally.

'Ballistics report should arrive tomorrow,' she murmured.

'Before or after your parents' plane lands?'

'*Crap!*'

Alex stopped pacing with the baby. 'Was I not supposed to remind you of that?'

'We should just run away,' D.D. said. She couldn't deal with this. She was too tired and her baby hated her. There was no way she could handle her mother, too.

'I could meet them,' Alex offered bravely. 'Pick up Jack from day care, do the honors. Then, if you get stuck at work, it's not so terrible. You could always meet us later for dinner, something like that.'

'They'll never forgive me.'

'Yes, they will. You're the mother of their grandson. And when he's not squalling like a howler monkey, he is the cutest, most adorable, most brilliant baby boy ever. Aren't you?' Alex hefted baby Jack into the air, gave him a little toss, then caught him again.

Jack stopped crying. He gazed down at his father. He hiccupped, twice.

Heartened, Alex gave him another little toss.

Jack landed in his father's arms, hiccupped again, then, with a giant belch, finally relieved the gas cramping his tiny tummy, by spewing his entire liquid dinner down his father's chest.

Alex stopped moving, held perfectly still.

'Well, at least he's not crying,' Alex said at last.

D.D. scrambled for towels, wet wipes.

'You are the best father in the entire world,' she assured her sleep-deprived partner. 'Come Father's Day, Jack is gonna get you not one, but two ties. I swear it!'

D.D. had just finished getting Jack cleaned up and settled into his carrier, when her cell phone rang. She checked the screen. Blocked number, which could mean any number of things this late at night. Out of sheer morbid curiosity, D.D. took the call.

'Detective D.D. Warren? FBI Special Agent Kimberly Quincy from Atlanta. Sorry to call so late.'

'Oh,' D.D. said. 'Oh, oh, oh. Not a problem.'

'Been out all day,' Special Agent Quincy continued in a clipped voice. 'Just got your message and was going to call you back tomorrow, then I realized the date.'

'Only two and a half days till the twenty-first,' D.D. filled in.

'Exactly. Figured if you were calling me, you had some kind of development, and you'd appreciate a call back sooner versus later.'

'I have the third friend,' D.D. said. 'Charlene Rosalind Carter Grant. I believe you know her.'

'You could say that.'

'Well, now I know her, too. Like you said, it's nearly the twenty-first. Charlie's preparing for war. As a backup plan, she'd like me to handle her murder investigation.'

'Huh.'

'With all due respect, Special Agent, I haven't slept in ten weeks. I was hoping for more than "Huh" from the FBI.'

'Big case?' the special agent asked.

'New baby.'

'Boy or girl?' Kimberly's voice warmed up.

'Boy. Loud, fussy, cranky, beautiful boy.'

'Two girls,' Kimberly provided. 'The seven year old wants a cell phone. The four year old wants a puppy. Sure you don't want help on the case? I could fly right up.'

D.D. smiled. 'You're supposed to tell me it gets easier. "This is just a phase. Parenting gets better and better every day." Lie to me. I could use a good story right now.'

'Absolutely. Best days are ahead. And FYI, never leave a five-year-old alone with a jump rope and her two-year-old sister, and if your husband works as many nights as mine does, buy the king-sized bed now, because all life-forms will be in your room.'

'Hard to fit a king-sized bed in Boston real estate. Jump rope?'

'Technically, the two year old was only tied up for ten minutes, then figured out how to wiggle out of the knots. I blame my husband. He's an outdoorsman, so he keeps teaching the girls "skills" that inevitably result in babysitters never returning.'

'What's your husband do?'

'Mac's a state cop.'

'Ah,' D.D. said, connecting the dots. 'So your daughters are double-Special Agent kids – FBI on the one side and Georgia Bureau of Investigation on the other.'

'That might be the other explanation,' Kimberly agreed.

'My partner is also a former detective, who now teaches courses in crime scene analysis at the police academy. I figure when Jack skins his knee for the first time, he'll fetch placards to mark the scene of the crime first, then grab a Band-Aid.'

'Mac's been taking our eldest, Eliza, to the shooting range with him. He swears her first time out, she clustered three to the chest. Apparently, aiming for center mass is genetic.'

'Your seven year old can shoot?'

'It's the South, honey. We like our guns.'

'I like your daughter,' D.D. assured her.

'Me, too. So what can I tell you about the Jackie Knowles murder? I'm assuming you've read my father's report.'

'Your father's . . .' D.D.'s voice trailed off, then she got it. 'The consultant, retired FBI agent Pierce Quincy, he's your father?'

'Yep. He's the reason I got involved. Generally speaking, a local homicide doesn't garner FBI attention, but my dad had done the initial analysis of the Rhode Island crime scene. He identified several overlapping variables between the Providence murder and Atlanta homicide, and a predator operating in multiple jurisdictions would be our cup of tea.'

'So you definitely think the murders are related.'

'Hard to believe otherwise,' Kimberly said bluntly. 'Victims knew each other. Were murdered exactly one year apart by someone using the same MO. There's a connection, all right. I'll be damned if I know what it is, but there's a connection.'

'What do you think of the third friend, Charlene yada yada Grant?'

'Only met her a couple of times, and she wasn't feeling good about the investigators handling her friends' murders on either occasion. She's interacted with my father many more times, and much more positively. He likes her, but remains reserved. While she seems to earnestly and passionately care about her friends and has remained a staunch advocate on their behalf . . .'

'She remains a prime suspect,' D.D. filled in.

'Yep.'

'She got an alibi for the Knowles murder?'

'Her aunt claims she was in New Hampshire the evening of the twenty-first. By midday on the twenty-second, when Charlene got the news of Jackie's death from the local police, she flew straight down from Portland, Maine. We have her name on the ticket and can corroborate the Delta flight. All in all, a decent alibi.'

'There's a but in your voice,' D.D. said.

Kimberly sighed. 'Only lead we've ever had in the case – Jackie's neighbor claims to have seen Jackie return home after nine p.m. on the twenty-first, and she wasn't alone. She'd brought home a friend: a female with long brown hair and a petite frame.'

'Like Charlene Grant,' D.D. mused thoughtfully.

'Who was a thousand miles away with her aunt. Unfortunately, the neighbor only saw the woman from behind, so not the best ID, but all we got.'

'Crime scene?' D.D. prodded.

'Clean. Conspicuously clean. Switch-plates-wiped-off, floor-boards-mopped, every-sofa-pillow-in-place kind of clean. Kitchen, entranceway, family room – all spotless. The killer took his or her time, felt comfortable in the home. Detail-oriented, thorough, smart.'

'Strong,' D.D. added. 'Manual strangulation?'

'COD, manual asphyxiation, yes. So, strong hands. But I'm less convinced on this subject than the Rhode Island investigators. They took the manual strangulation as proof the perpetrator must be male. Maybe it's living in the South, but I've watched enough little old ladies wring the heads off chickens to be more open-minded. Plenty of women have decent upper body strength. Especially if they grabbed another female from behind, I think it could be done.'

'So maybe the "friend" Jackie brought home that night. You check with the local bars?'

'Sure, credit card activity told us where Jackie had spent the evening. Unfortunately, it was a new bar opening downtown. When we flashed Jackie's picture, couple of servers remembered seeing her that night, but no one was paying much attention. Apparently, the debut was very successful and the place was cranking.'

'Her email messages, cell phone log?' D.D. asked.

'No recent contact from a new friend, or calendar notation to meet so-and-so at such-and-such. I'm guessing Jackie hadn't planned on meeting a friend that night. I think the other woman found her.'

'Found her, or stalked her?'

'Good question.'

'And the woman talked Jackie into taking her home.'

'Conjecture, but a good one.'

'Because Jackie might be suspicious of a man, given what happened to her friend, Randi. But she wouldn't think much of a strange female.'

'According to friends and family, Jackie thought Randi's ex-husband killed her. So it's not clear Jackie was on guard one way or the other. Then again, it was the one-year anniversary of her best friend's murder. Jackie's at a downtown bar, probably feeling a little lonely, a little blue . . .'

'The right approach, *Hey, I like your sweater, mind if I have a seat* . . .'

'A little conversation, a couple drinks,' Kimberly filled in.

'Jackie was an easy target. Assuming our killer is a female and really good at social engineering.'

'To judge by both scenes, we're looking for someone with advanced people skills. Which, let's face it, you can't say about all killers.'

D.D. nodded, mulled it over. This case that was not even a case was growing on her, sinking in. A puzzle within a puzzle.

'So now it's basically two days until the twenty-first,' D.D. provided. 'Location has moved to Boston, where we have the final member of the trio, Charlene Rosalind Carter Grant. She's definitely on guard. Carrying a .22, running, training, boning up on forensics and true crime, not to mention outreaching to her local homicide detective. I don't see her bringing home any "new" friends, male or female, on the twenty-first.'

'Probably not,' Kimberly agreed.

'So our killer would have to come up with another ruse,' D.D. murmured, still thinking.

'What does Charlene want most?' Kimberly asked.

'What d'you mean?'

'If you're a killer, if you want to get someone's attention who has every reason to be on guard, you have to offer something so good, so personal, so compelling, that even paranoid Charlene would be willing to throw caution to the wind, just to learn more.'

'She wants to know who killed her friends,' D.D. said.

'Then maybe the killer has it even easier this time around. She doesn't have to "pretend" to be anything at all. She can just be herself. Because *she* is who Charlene wants more than anything in the world. She holds all the answers to Randi and Jackie's last minutes. And if you're someone who has lost people you love to crime . . . it's very hard to say no to that. Even if you know better, the desire, the *need* to know what happened to your loved ones . . . That's a very powerful tool. I wouldn't blame Charlie for not walking away.'

'Who'd you lose?' D.D. asked softly.

'My mother and sister.'

'And if the murderer called you up tomorrow?'

'He'd have to be dialing from one-eight-hundred Rent-a-Psychic,' Kimberly said flatly.

'And now your seven year old can plug three to center mass.'

'Yep.'

'Sounds good to me.'

'Charlene's preparations are physical,' Kimberly stated curtly. 'Her killer's MO, however, is psychological. Intimate. Up close. Personal. What good is running a six-minute mile going to do her, when she's the one willingly opening the door? Charlene doesn't need to be tough. She needs to think tough. That'll get her through the twenty-first.'

'I want to stir the pot,' D.D. announced.

'How so?'

'Facebook, social media. I'm working with another detective who's something of an expert. We're thinking of putting together a fake Facebook page, with posts commemorating the deaths of both Randi and Jackie. See who responds.'

Kimberly seemed to consider the matter. 'What about leaking info?'

'You mean crime scene details?'

'I mean fake crime scene details, maybe a criminology report. Something unflattering. No, I take that back. Something . . . messy. Our killer likes to be in control, yes? Neat, tidy, thorough. What if you reveal something about the Knowles scene the killer missed. Something that's now a possible lead in the investigation. Get the killer feeling defensive, second-guessing him- or herself.'

'Get inside his or her head,' D.D. murmured.

'Turnabout is fair play.'

'Got an idea for a detail?'

Kimberly hesitated. 'I'd ask my father. He knows both scenes, he was a profiler. Messing with criminal minds. Hell, he'll love this. Give him a call.'

'Thank you.'

'Not a problem. Keep me posted. Especially on the twenty-first.'

'Will do. Good luck with your growing girls.'

'Good luck with your baby boy.'

Both women sighed, hung up their phones.

# 15

I was late for my graveyard shift. First time ever. Couldn't help myself.

I'd had to race all the way to the T stop. Then wait for the train to return me to Cambridge. Then run another seven minutes, snotty-nosed and watery-eyed, all the way back to my one-bedroom rental. Mrs Beals wasn't home, but Tulip was sitting on the front porch.

I didn't even stop to think about it. I scooped up the warm, solidly packed body of the dog that was not my dog and buried my face into the sleek folds of her neck. Tulip leaned her head against my shoulder. I could feel her sigh, as if releasing a great strain herself. So we stood like that, my arms cradling her body, her head on my shoulder.

Maybe I cried a little more. Maybe she licked the tears from my cheeks. Maybe I told her I loved her. And maybe she thumped her tail to let me know that she loved me, too.

I carried Tulip to my bedroom. Didn't care anymore if Frances discovered and kicked me out. So little time left. What did it matter anymore? So little time left.

Stan Miller. Metal rods, protruding through his massive frame. The blood, dripping down the corners of his mouth. Sightless eyes, forever staring at me.

I tucked Tulip in my room with a bowl of food, then retreated down the hall for a long hot shower. I scrubbed and scrubbed. Shampooed, rinsed, conditioned. Did it all over again.

Was it just my imagination, or could I still smell the gunpowder on my fingertips? I searched my naked body for other signs of the evening's activities. Blood, bruising, something. I felt altered on the inside, ergo it made sense the outside should change as well.

But . . . nothing. My leather shooting gloves had done their job and protected my boxing-battered hands as I'd careened down the fire escape. My heavy winter wardrobe had done its job and guarded my already battle-scarred skin as I'd dropped and rolled. Even my ankle felt almost fine, a minor twist that had quickly recovered.

When I got out of the shower, I cleared the steam from the mirror to confirm what I already knew.

I had just killed a man, and I looked absolutely, positively the same as I had before.

Charlene Rosalind Carter Grant meet Charlene Rosalind Carter Grant.

Loving niece, loyal friend, respected dispatch officer, and stone cold murderer.

I started shaking again, so I returned to the shower, cranking up the water as hot as it would go, but still not beating the chill.

Eleven fourteen p.m. Tulip and I caught a taxi to work.

Second-to-last shift.

Sixty-eight hours, forty-five minutes.

I kept my arms around the dog that wasn't my dog and didn't let go.

'Baby's crying.'

'Wh-wh-what?'

'Baby's crying. Down the hall. Crying and crying and crying. Nothing helps. Dunno . . .' A shaky sigh. 'Dunno, dunno, dunno. Please, ma'am, tell me how to make it stop.'

Sitting alone in the glow of multiple monitors and a muted TV screen, I rubbed my face and forced myself to focus. Crying baby. Overwhelmed new parent. One of dispatch's top ten calls. Protocol was to establish basic physical health of newborn and basic mental health of new parent. If both seemed okay, then remind caller that 911 was for emergencies, not for parenting tips, before disconnecting.

I didn't disconnect my caller. It had been a relatively quiet shift, the police scanner filled with chatter about one major crime, already being handled, with no other emergencies coming down the pike. And I understood, like a lot of dispatch operators who sat alone in darkened comm centers at 2 a.m., that sometimes people just needed to talk.

So I let my caller talk. I learned the name of her nine-month-old baby girl, Moesha. I learned that the baby's father worked graveyard for a janitorial service company. I learned that my caller, nineteen-year-old Simone, was still hoping to get her GED and wanted to be a vet tech someday. She'd been excited to get pregnant, still held out dreams of getting married. But her baby daughter cried most nights and it was getting tough, and now the baby's dad was being a jerk and Simone just wanted to go shopping with her friends, but she didn't have any money and her boyfriend said she was too fat to buy new clothes and why didn't she wait till she lost all the baby weight, and yo, when might that be?

Simone talked. Simone cried. Simone talked some more.

I sat and listened and stroked Tulip's head.

Simone talked herself down. Call ended. Screen went blank.

I sat in the dark, smoothing Tulip's floppy ears.

'Baby's crying,' I whispered to Tulip.

She gazed up at me.

'Down the hall.'

Tulip placed her head in my lap.

'I screwed up, Tulip. All those years ago, in my mother's house . . . I failed that baby. And that's why I don't think about my mother anymore. I don't want to remember. Not that it matters anymore, does it? Too little, too late.'

Tulip nosed my hand.

I smiled down at her, stroked her head. 'Funny, I've spent a whole year planning, preparing, and strategizing for my last stand. And in the end, I'm probably gonna die just like everyone else – filled with a list of unfinished business.'

Tulip whined softly. I leaned down, put my arms around her neck.

'I'm going to send you up north,' I promised her. 'You'll get to live with my Aunt Nancy, become a B-and-B dog. And the mountains are beautiful and filled with paths to run and squirrels to chase and rivers to swim. You'll like it up there. I certainly did.'

I held her closer. 'Remember me,' I whispered.

Tulip sighed heavily.

I knew exactly how she felt.

Door opened shortly thereafter. A dark figure appeared, backlit by the hall light, and it jolted me from my chair. I sprang up, into an automatic pugilist stance, while my desk chair flew across the tiny space.

Officer Mackereth flipped on the light.

'You always work in the dark?' he asked gruffly. He was dressed in his uniform, duty belt clasped around his waist. I'd checked the roster when I started my shift, so I knew he was working tonight. I also knew he'd been called in earlier, along with a dozen other officers, to help handle a homicide in the Red Groves housing project. Dead black male, skewered on a collapsed fire escape of a tenement housing building. Messy scene, according to the radio chatter. The crime scene techs had finally used blowtorches to sever the metal rods in Stan Miller's body from the fire escape. Then the ME had hauled away the corpse, still shish-kebabbed, in an extra large ambulance the city had recently purchased for transporting extra large patients.

I dropped my hands to my side, flexed my fingers. I wanted to move farther away, but the desk kept me in place. The single-person comm center was strictly utilitarian. Seven feet wide, seven feet deep. The PD's handicap-accessible unisex bathroom was larger.

Beside me, Tulip perked up. She trotted over to Officer Mackereth, sat before him, and presented her head.

He bent over, scratched her neck. Then, in a move that probably surprised him as much as me, he squatted down and gave Tulip a hug. She licked his cheek.

'At least one of you likes me,' he said.

Under the wash of fluorescent lights, I could see the heavy lines in his face. The price one paid for working death scenes. Would he dream of Stan Miller's body later this morning? How much would it surprise him to know I'd be having that nightmare, too?

'Tough night,' I commented now, staying next to my console.

'At least no other calls,' Officer Mackereth said.

'Pretty quiet.'

Lisa Gardner

'Figures. We got every uniform buzzing around the Red Groves scene, so of course nothing else comes in.'

'How's Red Groves?' I stared at my monitor, as if I should be checking it.

Tom shrugged. 'Scene's secured. Body's bagged and tagged. Neighbors are furious and fearful. The usual.'

'Any witnesses?' I asked. Casually.

'Only three or four dozen—'

'*Really?*'

Officer Mackereth blew out a huff of breath, stood up. 'Hell, we had so many gawkers saying so many different things, who the hell knows? Half of them claimed the vic was yelling at his wife, then must've gone to storm down the fire escape, but it collapsed. Others swear there was a shoot-out at the OK Corral, probably drug dealers, maybe Russian Mafia—'

'Russian Mafia?'

'Not likely. Someone sure as hell shot up the apartment, though. Bullet holes everywhere. We're still looking for the family. Wife, two kids. One of the neighbors saw them leaving earlier in the evening. I'm hoping for their sakes, that's true.'

'Oh,' I said.

'Messy way to go,' Tom said, rocking back on his heels. 'Christ, never seen anything like it. Plunging five stories to land in a bed of metal stakes.'

At the last moment, he must have seen the look on my face. He caught himself, said hastily, 'Sorry. Didn't mean to . . . Occupational hazard. Cops forget sometimes that other people don't spend their time staring at corpses.'

'It's okay,' I said numbly. 'I hear enough stuff.'

'Not the same. Hearing is easier than seeing.'

'Is it? Or does it just leave more to the imagination? Especially when I never get to learn the end of the story. Yelling, screaming, crisis, crisis, and now on to the next caller. Oh well.'

Officer Mackereth nodded slowly, as if considering the life of a dispatch operator for the first time. 'Clean anything?' he asked abruptly.

I had to think about it. 'Not yet.'

'Hit anyone?'

'Not yet.'

'Slow day for Charlene Grant?'

'Charlene Rosalind Carter Grant,' I corrected automatically.

'Not what your driver's license says.'

My chin came up, I regarded him levelly. 'The form didn't allow for two middle names, so I opted not to include either one.'

'Why the two middle names, anyway?'

'Don't know.'

'Family names?'

'Maybe.'

'You never asked your parents?'

'Don't know where they are to ask the question,' I said stiffly.

That seemed to draw him up short. He nodded again, but continued to study me. We were dancing. Around and around. Except I couldn't figure out: Were we partners on a dance floor, or opponents in a boxing ring?

'Tried Googling you,' he said now.

'What'd you find?'

'There are a lot of Charlene Grants in the world.'

'Maybe that's why I have two middle names. To distinguish.'

'You don't have two middle names.'

'Yes, I do.'

'Not according to your birth certificate.'

'You looked up my birth certificate?'

'Well, when Googling doesn't work, what else is a guy gonna do?'

I didn't know what to say anymore. I blinked at him. Tulip whined softly, sitting between us.

'What do you want?' I asked now. The backs of my legs were still pressed against the desk. Abruptly, that bothered me. I forced myself to take a step forward. Stop retreating. Own the room. Seize control of the situation.

'Email addy,' Officer Mackereth said.

'Don't have one.'

'Facebook page? Twitter account? MySpace?'

'Don't own a computer.'

'Smartphone?'

'Don't own a computer, a smartphone, an iPad, an iPod, an e-reader, or even a DVD player.'

'Off the grid,' Officer Mackereth observed.

'Frugal. If I want to go online, I visit the library. I can always check out a good book while I'm there.'

'What are you doing on the twenty-first?' he asked.

'*What?*'

'The twenty-first, Saturday morning. What are you doing?'

'Why?' My voice came out too high-pitched. At my sides, my hands were clenched. I don't know if he noticed, but Tulip slunk over to me, pressing against my legs.

'You refused coffee. Turned down dinner. That leaves brunch.'

'Brunch?'

'Saturday, the twenty-first. One p.m. Café Fleuri at the Langham Hotel. All-you-can-eat chocolate buffet. Best offer I got. What do you say?'

I . . . I didn't know what to say. Then I didn't have to. Because next to me, the monitor lit up, my headset started to chime, and I was literally saved by the bell.

I grabbed my headset, turned toward the ANI ALI screen.

'Can't run from me forever,' Tom murmured behind me.

I whipped around, but he was already gone, flipping off the light switch and returning me to the gloom.

# 16

Five thirty a.m. Jesse snuck out of bed. He used his best quiet feet, padding down the heavily shadowed hallway toward the kitchen table. The door to his mother's bedroom was still closed. He paused, just in case, listening intently. No sounds from the other side. His mother slept. Good.

Jesse continued on to his target: the ancient laptop. It beckoned from the kitchen table. Battered case folded shut and topped by a waiting Home Run/Zombie Bear.

Jesse's mother liked rules. One of them was no TV or computer time on school mornings. Monday through Friday they both got up at 6:30 a.m. They ate breakfast together, then Jesse's mom packed his lunch while he got dressed, brushed his teeth, and combed his hair. By 7:20, he was thundering down the apartment stairs to the curb below, where he caught the 7:30 bus.

That was the drill. Jesse went to school, his mom went to work.

Monday through Friday, Jesse followed the schedule, played by the rules. It made his mom happy, and Jesse liked it when his mom was happy. She smiled more, ruffled his hair, bought him treats she didn't really approve of, such as Twinkies. It was just the two of them, Jenny and Jesse against the world, she would tell him. They would snuggle together on the sofa each night, where she would read him Goosebumps novels and he would rest his head against her chest like he was still a little kid and it was all right, because it was just the two of them, Jesse and Jennifer against the world.

Jesse loved his mother.

Jesse couldn't sleep last night. He couldn't stop thinking about Helmet Hippo and their afternoon together on AthleteAnimalz.com.

Jesse had always enjoyed the website. It was something to do. But yesterday . . . Yesterday had been way cool. He'd not only had something fun to do, he'd had someone fun to do it with. A real friend who believed in Jesse, thought Jesse could do anything. An older kid who liked him.

Jesse wanted to go back online.

Even though it was a school morning.

He had a plan. First up, he'd set his watch alarm for one hour before his mother woke up. Sun wasn't even up yet, so his room had been cold and dark as he'd crawled quietly out of bed. He'd paused long enough for his fleecy bathrobe. Then, the soft glow of the hallway night-light had beckoned him out of his dark room, into the apartment, where he followed its glow toward the family room. The sound of his footsteps were dampened by his footy PJs until at last, he arrived, on a school morning, in front of the computer. He chewed his lower lip. Eyed Zombie/Home Run Bear.

Gave in to the impulse.

Quickly, he shoved aside Zombie Bear, popped open the top, hit the power button, and heard the computer whine wearily to life.

The old computer took a while to load. So, while it woke up, Jesse moved on to the next phase of his plan. He was going to feed himself breakfast. Then, he was going to fix his own lunch. Then, he was going to pack his own backpack.

That way, when his mother got up, and inevitably discovered him on the computer, she couldn't get too mad. He'd eaten breakfast, right? He was all ready for school, right? He'd even *helped* her by fixing his own lunch, right?

Sometimes, rules could be bent a little. It was just a matter of proper mom management.

Jesse tiptoed into the tiny kitchenette. He cracked open the refrigerator, using its glow to guide him as he carefully climbed onto the kitchen counter, eased down a bowl, found the Cheerios, poured the milk. Breakfast took about five minutes. He resisted the urge to check on the computer, as the kitchen table was next to his mother's bedroom and activity in there was more likely to wake her. Better to stay tucked away in the kitchen, getting through morning chores.

Next up, lunch. He was a bologna man. Liked it with a little mayo and one slice of Kraft American cheese. He preferred white bread, but his mother only bought wheat. White is like eating a piece of sugar, she told him, which only made him like white bread more.

Jesse got out two pieces of wheat bread. Struggled with the squeeze bottle of mayonnaise. He had to use two hands. First nothing came out, then half the bottle exploded out in a giant white blob. He did his best to smooth it with a knife, but when he finally added the cheese and bologna and put the two slices together, mayo oozed everywhere.

A wet, messy sandwich. The price to be paid for morning Athlete-Animalz. Jesse felt philosophical as he stuffed the gooey mess into a sandwich Baggie and plopped it into his lunch box. He added an apple and a snack-sized bag of pretzels. School would provide a carton of milk.

He zippered up his Transformers lunch box, loaded it into his backpack, and rocked back on his heels, feeling pretty good. He'd done it. Breakfast and lunch, all by 6 a.m. Not that hard, either.

Except then he glanced at his hands, still covered in greasy mayo. And the kitchen counter, which was dotted with even more mayo, pieces of cereal, and bits of bread. Better clean up or his mother would freak.

Back on the counter. Running the water thinly, doing the best he could with the sponge, smearing around the mayo, chasing the bread crumbs. Another quick rinse, and he hopped down, careful to land on soft feet before taking a deep breath, closing up the refrigerator, and finally creeping out of the tiny kitchen. His hands were maybe a little greasy. But not too bad, he thought. Close enough.

Laptop. Open. No longer wheezing. Waiting for him.

Jesse sidled up to it. He could already feel his heart race with anticipation. One last second, straining his ears for any sound from his mother's room . . . Silence.

Jesse typed in *www.AthleteAnimalz.com* and hit return.

He had mail. And not from Helmet Hippo, which surprised him. He was still figuring out the rules for mailing another player. From what he could tell, 'talking' to another animal during a game was subject to a lot of restrictions; each animal could only pick from the Go Team Go list of expressions to appear in the conversation bubble over its head. But emailing . . . that seemed to be fair game. Helmet Hippo could write anything, a real letter to Jesse. And Jesse could write a real letter back, which he thought was pretty cool. Like a big kid talking to a big kid. This latest email, however, wasn't from Helmet Hippo. This morning someone else had found him: Pink Poodle.

Curious, Jesse opened the letter:

*Nice playing! You're getting really good, especially at baseball. That's my favorite game. Is it your favorite, too?*

*I play every day. I use the computers in the Boston Public Library after school. I see you are a Red Sox fan. Does that mean you live in Boston, too?*

*You should come some time. We can play together. I'll show you some tricks for hitting the curveball. No big.*

*If you feel like hanging out, come to the library. I'm easy to find: look for the Pink Poodle. Whatever.*

*C U on-line.*

*Pinky Poo*

Jesse frowned. He read the letter again, then again. Some words he struggled with, but he thought he got it. Pink Poodle liked him. Pink Poodle lived in Boston. Pink Poodle could show him some tips if he came to the Boston Public Library.

Jesse sat down in front of the computer. His heart was beating hard again, though he wasn't sure why. He rubbed his palms unconsciously on the worn legs of his pajamas. He studied the bright, cheerful email again.

Stranger danger. His mother talked about that. Both in real life and on computers. If someone sent him an instant message, he was never to reply, but fetch his mother immediately. If someone sent him an attached file, he was never to open it. It might have a virus, which would destroy their already sickly computer. Worse, it might be something bad, not suitable for kids.

Scary? he'd asked his mom, because while he'd never admit this to his fellow second graders, Jesse didn't like scary movies. They gave him nightmares.

Something like that, his mother had said.

So he wasn't to 'talk' to strangers online, or open attached files. But Helmet Hippo and Pink Poodle weren't strangers. They were other kids on AthleteAnimalz. And they weren't sending him scary videos. They were teaching him skills so he could win more points.

Jesse liked winning points. He could use more skills.

And he was allowed to go to the Boston Public Library, he reminded himself. He and his mother went often, a couple times a month. Libraries were good. His mother approved of them. If he asked to go after school, she'd let him. You were never to get into a stranger's car, or follow a stranger into his house. That he understood. But meeting another kid at the public library . . . that didn't sound so bad.

Jesse read the note again.

Pinky Poo. A girl. But a girl who was really good at baseball. Best hitter Jesse had seen. Even better than Helmet Hippo. And wouldn't Helmet Hippo like that, when Jesse logged on later and could rack up even more points for his team . . .

Jesse made up his mind. Using his index finger, he began to laboriously type out his response, using Pink Poodle's letter to help him with spelling.

*Baseball is my favorite game, too. I will come. After school. No big*, he added, because he liked the way it sounded. Older, confident. Like maybe a sixth grader.

He sat back. Reviewed his reply one last time.

Public place, he assured himself. The library.

Besides, stranger danger applied to creepy men. Pink Poodle was a *girl*. Jesse wasn't afraid of a girl.

Jesse nodded to himself. He touched his carefully crafted email on the computer screen. Admired his own typing, proper use of punctuation. Just like a sixth grader, he decided.

Jesse hit send.

While on the other side of the thin apartment wall, his mother's morning alarm chimed to life.

# 17

Hello. My name is Abigail.
  Have we met yet?
  Don't worry. We will.
  Hello. My name is Abigail.

# 18

D.D. went to the dark side. And fell in love all over again.

Coffee. Hot. Rich. Black. She cradled her cup tenderly, feeling the warmth spread from the beverage to the palm of her hands to the pulse points at her wrists. That first slow inhale. Savoring. Taking her time. Welcoming a long lost friend.

'Oh for fuck's sake, just drink it!' Phil ordered from across the conference table.

She eyed him mildly. Detective O sat next to him, Neil on the other side. This morning, O was wearing a formfitting deep red sweater, which made her appear less city detective and more Victoria's Secret model. Neil, on the other hand, looked like he'd spent the night in the morgue, as a corpse.

'You almost never swear,' D.D. said to Phil, still clutching her mug, feeling the aromatic steam waft across her senses.

'You almost never look like a Folgers commercial. O and I have been here all night. Neil's been here half the night. We want to debrief, then get some rest.'

That made her feel bad. D.D. eyed her exhausted case team, their over-fluoresced faces, deeply bruised eyes. She didn't look any better than they did, having pulled an all-nighter herself. Only her taskmaster was smaller and more persistent.

'All right,' she agreed with Phil. 'Let's get this party started. You go first.'

At which point, she took the first sip. Immediately, her heart quickened. She both tasted and heard the caffeine hit her bloodstream, a powerful jolt that made her want to sigh and inhale and start the whole process all over again. So she did.

'For the love of God!' Phil exclaimed.

'Want a cup?'

'Yes!'

Phil stormed out of the room in search of fresh java. O shook her head. Neil folded both arms on the table and collapsed his head into them.

Just another day in paradise, D.D. thought, and sipped her wonderful, lovely, how-had-she-ever-lived-without-it cup of joe.

Phil returned with his own cup, and the party finally got started.

'We found a chat room,' O announced.

'We found a *transcript* of a chat room,' Phil interjected, eyeing his computer partner. 'As for the chat room itself, it's probably encrypted or encoded eight ways to Sunday.'

'Have to be invited to join,' O added.

'Worldwide membership from what we can tell – makes it very difficult to trace the servers involved,' Phil said.

'But it's definitely a training site,' O emphasized.

'Training for what?' D.D. asked with a frown, cradling her coffee more defensively now. Geek in stereo was no easier to follow than geek in mono.

'For pedophiles,' O clarified. 'You know, a place to hang out, compare notes, and feel accepted for your perversions.'

D.D. set down her coffee. 'What?'

'We've been noticing this trend for the past few years,' O announced dismissively, her findings obviously old news to her, if not to them. 'More and more crimes against children are being committed by younger and younger perpetrators. We figured it had something to do with the use of chat rooms within the sex offender community and this transcript proves it.'

Neil raised his head from his arms. He stared at the dark-haired sex crimes detective. 'Start over,' he said. 'Speak slowly.'

O rolled her eyes, but complied. 'Okay. Society has norms. Those norms include not regarding children as sex objects. Of course, a pedophile views children in exactly that manner – a deviant sexual fantasy. Generally speaking, a child molester will spend at least a few years fighting that fantasy. Recognizing it as inappropriate and trying to resist the urge. Maybe some do, but obviously others don't, eventually acting out on that impulse and beginning a life of crime.

'Given this cycle, most sex predators are mid-twenties to mid-thirties when they offend. As criminals go, that's a relatively mature perpetrator pool. There are some exceptions – teenage babysitters targeting their young charges, but that's more an example of impulse meeting opportunity. The attacks are rarely planned or sophisticated in nature. So again, the "classic" profile of a pedophile is an older male. Except lately, we're seeing a spike in crimes that are nearly children against children – relatively young pedophiles engaging in the kind of sophisticated targeting and grooming behavior that until now, we've always associated with older predators.'

'Good God,' Neil groaned. D.D. seconded that vote.

'Our best guess,' O continued, 'validated by this transcript, is that these teenagers aren't fighting their deviant sexual fantasies. Instead, they're logging on to the Internet, where they're finding validation for their impulses and even tips for how to engage in these inappropriate acts. Basically, hard-core pedophiles are using Internet chat rooms to train the next generation of child molesters, which is accelerating the predator cycle.'

'I'm never using my computer again,' D.D. said.

'Please,' Phil said tiredly. 'We spent all night reading the logs from these kinds of chat rooms. Now I have to go home and bleach my eyeballs.'

'You keep saying transcripts,' D.D. said. 'What does that mean?'

'Victim number two,' Phil supplied, 'Stephen Laurent, downloaded some of the chat room logs onto his hard drive. Including one that details how to use a puppy to approach young children. A second chat describes how to create a following on various kids' websites in order to attract potential victims. It's very detailed, including tips for how to determine which "e-victims" live in close enough geographic proximity to become "physical victims".'

'He was building a manual,' Neil said flatly. 'A fucking perverts manual on his hard drive. Complete with photos.'

O reached over and lightly touched the back of Neil's hand. The redheaded detective flinched, sat up straighter.

'You want help?' O asked kindly. 'I've gone through those kinds of photos before. I can assist if you'd like.'

'I can't see 'em anymore. It's just . . . I've stopped viewing them as kids. And that's wrong. Too wrong. I can't do it anymore.' Neil turned his stare to D.D. 'I'm done.'

She nodded immediately. 'You're done. Absolutely. And you're right, Neil. They're kids. They deserve to be seen as kids. The fact you recognize you've hit your limit is a good thing. It does right by them. Thank you.'

'I don't think they're his victims,' Neil said.

Phil looked at him. 'What d'you mean?'

'Made it through four out of six boxes. The photos themselves are too eclectic. There are Polaroids from the eighties, faded shots from the seventies. Subjects are boys, girls, young kids, teenagers, black, white, Hispanic, urban, house, hotel. I think Laurent collected the shots – I don't know, bought them online, traded for them from other collectors . . .' He looked at Detective O.

She nodded. 'Sure, pedophiles have always traded graphic images, videos, etc. For some predators, visual aids even do the trick for them. You'd be amazed how many "family men" we've busted for owning child porn, who claim the porn was "good for them". Kept them from committing the actual act.'

'I hate this case,' Neil muttered.

D.D. didn't disagree with him, but she was getting confused. 'So are you saying Stephen Laurent might not have been an active child molester, but a porn collector?'

'I'm saying that model exists,' Detective O stated, 'but I doubt Laurent was a passive pedophile. He was not only downloading transcripts on how to engage in illegal behaviors, but remember, he'd also gotten a puppy.'

'Do pedophiles escalate?' D.D. asked. 'So maybe Laurent started with child porn, but was now graduating to child molestation?'

'Sure. And to a large extent, that's what these chat rooms are all about. Giving a weak, low-self-esteem, usually male perpetrator the acceptance, tools, and coaching to finally act out his sexually deviant fantasies. There are chat rooms for rapists, too, by the way. Probably serial killers as well.'

'I hate this case,' Neil said again.

But D.D. had an idea. 'So judging from that cycle, what is Stephen Laurent? The mentor or the intern?'

'Intern,' O said without missing a beat. She turned to look at Phil. 'That's basically what we saw on his computer, right? The understudy gathering information on his next, starring role.'

Phil nodded his agreement.

'And the first shooting victim,' D.D. asked quickly. 'Antiholde. He went to these chat rooms, too?'

'Same chat room,' Phil provided.

'Trainer or trainee?'

'Trainer,' Phil said flatly. 'Given his criminal history. The second victim, Laurent, hadn't been caught yet. Our first victim, Antiholde, had already been caught and paroled. I bet he visited the chat room for two reasons – to brag about past exploits, while trying to improve his technique for future offenses. Definitely a more experienced predator than Laurent.'

'But still seeking more information, guidance,' D.D. said.

'Pedophiles are always seeking more information,' O said bluntly. 'It's a high-risk lifestyle, where they feel victimized by their own impulses and live in constant fear of being caught. It keeps them logging on.'

'And how many users in this chat room?' D.D. asked.

'Can't get on to find out. Transcript from Laurent's computer shows a few dozen active posters.'

'We need to track them down.'

'Obviously working on that,' O said dryly. 'Unfortunately, pedophiles are a suspicious bunch, and very sophisticated with their computer skills.'

'But our victims have a common link – this chat room. Identify the users, identify the killer . . . or the next victims.'

'But again,' Phil reminded D.D., 'we only have copies of a chat, not access to the chat room itself. While the transcripts show a couple dozen posters, that's probably only the tip of the iceberg. Most members "lurk" in these kinds of forums. Meaning there's probably hundreds if not thousands of other users who don't actively post, meaning they remain invisible to us. We'll work on tracing the user names we can identify from the transcripts, but bear in mind, it's probably a needle-in-the-haystack kind of exercise.'

'You said we can't access the real chat room,' D.D. spoke up. 'That it's encrypted eighty ways to Sunday, invitation only. So how can we get an invite?'

'Don't know,' O said. 'Probably friend of a friend kind of thing. Meet in other forums, perhaps swapping porn, and once enough trust is gained, eventually a member of the chat room will extend an invitation.'

'But they must get new members, these teenagers, like you said.'

'Sure, and one possibility is that we could go "undercover" as a teenage boy. Build a virtual identity that surfs the right places on the net, engages in the kind of Internet searches that might catch a fellow pedophile's eyes. There are "undercover" operators on the Internet, you know. But that kind of thing can take months to fully execute. Given our shooter's time line, we have more like weeks.'

'We need a hacker,' D.D. said bluntly.

'Agreed.'

'Or . . .' D.D. thought a moment. 'Do they know two of their users are dead? What if we claimed their user names and passwords? Could we log on as Stephen Laurent and/or Douglas Antiholde?'

'We'd have to identify their user names and passwords,' Phil said.

'Which our fine computer forensic experts should be able to do, right? Mine it out of the hard drive of the victims' computers?'

Slowly, Phil nodded. O, as well.

'Yeah,' Phil considered. 'Might take them a couple of days, but the computer pros should be able to do that.'

'All right, so forget building an undercover identity. We'll simply steal Stephen Laurent's user name, log on, and recon. We'll listen, we'll learn, and with any luck, we'll find our man . . . or woman as the case might be.'

'Woman?' O asked.

D.D. hadn't mentioned her conversation with the forensic handwriting expert before. She figured it was probably time. 'The notes left at both scenes: *Everyone has to die sometime. Be brave.* Based on penmanship, our note writer is most likely female. Tightly wound, probably private-school educated, and prone to wearing plaid. Which is another question, I suppose: How much "personality" can you tell from chat room logs? Any of the users come across as a type A female? Or can you even distinguish male users from female users?'

Phil shook his head. O, too. Both detectives were thinking, however. D.D. had that feeling between her shoulder blades, the one that as a detective she liked to get. They were on to something. Finally gaining ground.

Case would crack. Soon. Suddenly.

They would get their man . . . or woman.

'Anything else I need to know?' she asked.

Her case team shook their tired heads. 'O,' D.D. said, 'how about you meet with Neil, take over photos?'

O nodded. Neil looked embarrassed to surrender his assignment but didn't argue.

'Neil,' D.D. continued, 'in my office at ten. Phil, you're off duty at noon. Go home, get some rest. O, you can finish today, but I don't want to see you tomorrow before noon. Remember, it's a marathon, not a sprint.'

Phil looked at her strangely. 'You never send us home.'

'Are you complaining?'

He shut up.

D.D. adjourned the meeting, returning to her office, where she picked up a second crime scene report and prepared for her second major case of the day: the soon-to-be murder of Charlene Rosalind Carter Grant.

D.D. lifted the phone and dialed.

# 19

Training equals preparedness. You drill a pattern of movements over and over again, so that when the moment of attack occurs, rather than freezing in shock, you fall back into a series of instinctive responses that quickly renders your opponent useless.

That's the theory at least.

Tulip and I left the Grovesnor PD a little after 8 a.m. No Officer Mackereth to drive us home. The morning sun was weak, barely penetrating the thickening clouds. I could already taste the snow building on the horizon, feel the frosty bite through my coat, hat, and gloves.

Within a matter of minutes, Tulip, with her short tan-and-white fur, was shivering.

It distracted me. That was my excuse as I hustled us both to the corner, where I began the competitive game of hailing a taxi at the height of the morning commute.

After five minutes, I'd had no luck, and Tulip was shivering harder.

Bus pulled up. Number was right for my purposes, so I boarded, hefting Tulip up with me.

The bus driver, a heavyset black woman with crimped gray hair and a face that had seen it all, shook her head. 'Service dogs only.'

'She is a service dog. Lost her collar. Some jerk took it off her right outside the police station. How d'you like that? Now look at her. She's out of uniform and freezing to death.'

Tulip helped me out by giving the driver a particularly pathetic glance.

Four other people shoved up behind me, trying to board, impatient with the holdup, particularly given the freezing temperature.

But the driver ignored them, stared at me.

'What's your disability?' she demanded.

'Peanut allergy.'

'There's no dogs for peanut allergies.'

'Are too.'

'Are not.'

'Are too,' muttered the man behind me. 'Come on. Let her on or kick her off. It's fucking cold out here.'

I glared at him, then took in the row of passengers already filling the seats. 'Anyone eat peanut butter this morning?' I called out. 'Or have peanuts in your purse?'

Couple of tentative hands went up. I turned triumphantly to the bus driver. 'See, I need my dog. Otherwise, I might die on your bus, and think about the paperwork. Nobody wants to do that kind of paperwork.'

I swiped my commuter card and dropped Tulip into the aisle, as if that decided the matter. As I headed toward the back of the bus with Tulip in tow, I could tell the bus driver still didn't believe me. But it was fucking freezing out, and nobody liked paperwork.

I lied. I got away with it. It made me a little triumphant, a little cocky. Second mistake for the morning.

Really, it was only a matter of time.

I had to stand. Right hand up, holding the overhead bar for balance. I had the end of Tulip's leash encircled around my left wrist, with my left hand pressed flat against the closed flap of my messenger bag. Protecting the contents, particularly my weapon.

Now, here's a rule of mass transit: The colder it is outside, the hotter it will be inside.

Heat blasted through the vents, and pretty quickly, the wool coats and fleece-lined hats that made so much sense outside, became suffocating inside. Tulip started to pant. I started to sweat. More people jammed in, hot bodies pressing together, adding to the sauna.

Twenty minutes into my fifty-five-minute ride, I started to feel nauseous. The swaying suspension system, rolling beneath my feet. The beads of sweat, rolling down my hairline to pool on my over-heated neck. The stench of too many bodies crowded too close together, only some of whom had bothered to shower recently.

Another five minutes, and I raised my hand from my messenger bag long enough to loosen my scarf, remove my hat. I breathed marginally easier, then the bus was off and bouncing again, passengers bobbing, windows fogging.

I managed to stuff my hat in my coat pocket, then I had to move my left hand again. Unbutton the top button of my jacket, second, third, fourth.

I wore an oversized navy blue fleece pullover beneath my coat. The kind of soft, bulky sweatshirt perfect for cozying up with a good book on Sunday afternoon. It was strangling me now, the collar damp with sweat, the compressed sleeves squeezing my arms.

Thirty minutes down, twenty-five more to go.

Bus stopped. Passengers got off. More passengers got on. Tulip whined and panted. I loosened my grip on the sweat-slicked metal bar, wiped my forearm over my brow.

Bus lurched forward and so did my stomach.

Was I still holding on to the messenger bag? Maybe. Maybe not. I was hot, uncomfortable, fighting motion sickness. So first distracted, then cocky, and now partially incapacitated.

Cities operate by jungle rules, you know: The weak and infirm are immediately targeted to be culled from the herd.

Stop after stop. Block after block. With me panting almost as hard as Tulip. Not paying attention to my fellow passengers. Not noticing my surroundings. Just counting down the blocks. Wishing desperately to get off that damn bus.

Finally, as my face went from overheated red, to unsightly pale, to alarming green, the stop. Doors opened in the front. I started the forward charge, leading with Tulip, who weaved effortlessly through a sea of heavy boots and flapping overcoats.

'Excuse me, excuse me, coming through.' Pushing, shoving, and shimmying. Following the siren's song of fresh air, beckoning through the open door. At last, we made it. The bus driver and I exchanged final scowls, then Tulip and I clambered down the steep bus stairs onto hard-frozen terra firma. We jogged a couple of steps away from the metal sauna.

I was vaguely aware of the bus doors closing, the bus pulling away. I had both hands away from my messenger bag. Opening up my coat, gulping for icy, snow-laced air, trying to draw as much of it as I could into my overheated lungs, through my sweat-soaked fleece.

My leather bag dangled at my hip, my open coat flapped around my thighs.

I was all about the refreshingly frigid air, the feel of it against my face. I was finally off the bus. End of the road. From here, Tulip and I could jog the roughly mile and a half to our destination. Away from the densely packed urban sprawl, into the back roads and rolling countryside that still dotted random parts of Greater Boston.

It felt good to be out of the city. I felt safe. Relieved. Optimistic even.

Right until the instant I was attacked from behind.

He caught my coat lapels first. Jerked the front flaps of my black wool coat back and down. In one second or less, he'd incapacitated my left arm, basically bound it to my side with my own coat. The strap of my messenger bag, however, slung diagonal across my body, trapped the right lapel at the side of my neck, tangling his hand.

I used that second to stand perfectly still, my mouth caught soundlessly open, while my brain screamed (stupidly), *But it's not the twenty-first!*

While I made like a statue, my attacker grabbed the strap of my messenger bag, whipped it over my head, and tossed it aside. The weight of the bag tangled with Tulip's leash. My fingers opened reflexively, releasing her leash, and that quickly, I'd lost my gun and my dog. To be sure about it, my attacker, still standing behind me, kicked my bag away.

Then, his hands closed around my throat.

Belatedly, my survival instinct kicked in. I stopped cataloguing what was happening and started responding. First, I fought against my own coat.

While my attacker squeezed, slowly but surely obstructing my airways, I jerked my coat-bounded elbow backwards into his side. When he shimmied left, I used the air-starved moment to jerk off my coat, finally freeing my hands and arms.

His grip tightened. My mouth gasped, I struggled for air. Could feel pressure growing in my chest, the weight of my own rising panic.

*But it's not the twenty-first!*

Fight, I needed to fight. But I was expecting to punch forward. To squat, block, jab. Now I was left with self-defense 101, trying to stomp on my attacker's instep, kick back into a kneecap. Hurt him, incapacitate him. Do something so that he'd have to let go.

Barking. Tulip, running around our feet, leash trailing.

Hands still squeezing, white spots appearing in front of my eyes.

Forgetting to stomp, to fight. Succumbing to panic and clawing futilely at the fingers at my throat, as if that would make a difference.

So this is how Randi had felt. This is how Jackie had felt.

Such a crushing weight against my chest. The desire, the urge to breathe was so primal, so hardwired that the lack of oxygen led to the most peculiar kind of pain. As if I could feel the cells in my body dying one by one, screaming out their last desperate seconds.

Baby, crying down the hall.

*I know, I know. I should've told. I should've.*

I was crying. He was killing me, and instead of fighting back, I was weighed down with old regrets. The baby I'd failed. The mother I'd let hurt me. The friends I'd loved with all my heart and buried one by one.

Tulip barking, then suddenly, a yelp of pain. He'd kicked her. My attacker had hurt my dog.

That pissed me off.

I sagged. In a dimly remembered move from so many rounds of training, I stopped surging up with my legs and turned myself into dead weight instead. The sudden shift of my knees giving out threw my attacker off balance. He lurched forward, and I immediately countered by planting my feet and using my attacker's own weight to flip him over my head.

Then, I was on him. I kicked at his ribs, punched his unprotected head. This wasn't boxing. This was street fighting. I inhaled ragged, desperate gasps of air into my searing lungs as I kicked and jabbed and chased my killer across the snowy ground.

My attacker rolled, forearms over his face as he quickly put distance between us in order to regain his footing.

No way. Not gonna happen. If he got up, no doubt he was gonna be bigger and stronger than me, with maybe a knife or gun or other tricks up his sleeve. So I had to keep him down, where *I* could loom over *him*, where *I* was the biggest badass in town.

I continued to chase. He rolled, at one point made it up onto all fours, but I rewarded his efforts with such a devastating kick to the ribs, he collapsed and scuttled sideways.

He kept his head down, protecting his face, but also making it hard to read his intent. Thus, he managed to surprise me when I lashed out again and his left hand came up lightning fast, grabbed my foot, and jerked hard.

I toppled back, landing with a crack on my right hip. But even gasping in pain, I had the presence of mind to kick with my other foot, dislodging my first leg from his hand. Now we were both on all fours on the frozen ground, scrambling around each other.

Tulip circled as well, no longer barking but whining and uncertain. I couldn't risk looking at her or our surroundings. I should probably scream, call for help. We were just off the street. It was after 9 a.m.; even on the outskirts of the city no place is ever completely deserted.

But I couldn't make a sound. My blood rushed in my ears, I could hear the hoarse sound of my own breath. But I couldn't even whisper. My vocal cords were locked, frozen.

In the horror movies, the plucky victim always screams her terror. In real life, we are more likely to die in silence.

I got my feet under me at the same time he got his. I bounced up, fisted hands up, proper fighting stance finally established, just as my attacker squared off against me.

And I found myself staring into the weather-beaten face of my shooting instructor, J.T. Dillon.

'I give you a C,' he said. He straightened, hands dropping to his side.

Still not entirely sure about things, I punched with my right, going for the side of his head. Just as quickly, J.T. blocked my shot with his left arm, then his hands were down again, passive at his side.

'Maybe a D,' he said roughly, his breathing no easier than mine. 'You're still alive, but only barely.'

Slowly, I straightened. 'You attacked me as a training exercise?'

'Think of it as graduation.' He fingered his side, where I'd kicked him pretty hard, and winced. 'Though, given my age, next time I'm going with a paper diploma.'

My hands were still up. I couldn't drop them. Not yet. My breathing was too shallow. My throat hurt. I would be bruised in a matter of hours.

'Fuck you!' I said suddenly.

He studied me, eyes cool, inscrutable.

I hit him again. He blocked it again. So I really went for it. Punching, jabbing, and attacking until pretty soon we were chasing each other around in a circle again, him on the defensive this time, me powered with a rage I barely recognized. He had hurt me. I needed to hurt him back.

He'd almost killed me.

And I'd nearly let him.

It burned. My throat, my chest, my pride. All that training, all that practicing, and I'd still nearly died, taken out by a sixty-year-old ex-marine.

Tulip chased us. Not barking or whining. She had seen me spar before, and maybe she understood the situation better than I did. I don't know. I chased my shooting coach and he let me. Dodging, blocking, recoiling, sometimes slapping back. Moving with a speed I didn't know a silver-haired former marine sniper could still have.

Problem with hitting, really truly throwing a punch, is that it demands such an explosive release of energy. Even world heavy-weight champions can only sustain the action for three minutes at a time.

Sooner versus later, my hands grew heavy. My lungs heaved for air, my shoulders and chest burned. My heart rate had spiked to the edge of nausea, and I no longer chased my opponent as much as I staggered after him, my rage still willing, the rest of me giving out.

J.T. ended the situation, by plopping down beneath a skeletal tree. I collapsed on the snow next to him. My face was beet red, covered in sweat from my exertions. The snow felt good, the gray sky a balm against my flushed cheeks.

Tulip came over, sat beside me, and whined uncertainly. I stroked her head. She licked my cheek. Then she wandered over to J.T. to repeat the ritual. Satisfied all was now well, she plopped between us, burrowing against my side for warmth. After another moment, J.T. got up, trotted over to my messenger bag, and returned it to me.

He sat back down and we passed another moment in silence.

'Why is my firearms instructor beating me up?' I asked finally.

He regarded me steadily. 'Nothing wrong with training with a handgun,' he said curtly. 'But odds are, you'll never get off a shot. Or if you do, you'll be panicked and overwhelmed with adrenaline. You'll shoot wild till you run out of ammo. Then, you're back where you started – up close and personal.'

I thought of my encounter with Stan Miller. J.T. had just summarized it quite nicely. Stan and I had both fired wildly. And the situation had ended up close and personal.

'Have you ever killed anyone?' I asked.

'I've done my share of damage.'

'How did it feel?'

'Never as good as I wanted it to.'

We sat in silence again. I stroked Tulip's head.

'Am I going to die on the twenty-first?' I asked at last. A stupid question, but maybe that's what life came down to. Stupid questions in waning hours where we stood on the tracks, watching the locomotive bear down on us and wondering how bad it was gonna hurt.

'Maybe,' J.T. said. He looked at me again. 'Who beat you? Mother, father, boyfriend?'

I didn't answer right away. I stroked Tulip's silky brown ears. 'Mother,' I said finally. 'Munchausen's by proxy.'

First time I'd said the words out loud. Aunt Nancy and I had never discussed it. And I'd never told Randi or Jackie. Never even mentioned my mother to them, or where I'd lived before the mountains or any of the days, weeks, months that had existed before I became my aunt's niece instead of my mother's daughter.

But I told J.T. Dillon, because physically hitting someone is like that. It forms a bond. Sex, violence, death. All intimate in their own way. Another thing I hadn't known until the past year.

'You didn't defend yourself,' J.T. said curtly. 'You didn't fight for you.'

'Eventually I did.'

'No. I kicked your dog. You fought for your dog.'

'She's a good dog.'

He stared at me. 'You gotta get her out of your head,' he said abruptly.

I stiffened, still stroking Tulip's ears, but feeling myself pull away.

'Mean it,' J.T. said. 'You gotta hit for you. You gotta take that rage and shame and silence, and turn it into a weapon. You gotta know, Charlie, you gotta well and truly *know* it's not okay to be hurt. You don't deserve to be punished. Someone attacks you, stop accepting, start fighting back.'

'I'm trying.'

'Bullshit! You hesitate. You go to some place in your head where you're conditioned to hang out until the punishment stops. Look, I can train you to shoot. Dick can train you to hit. But neither one of us can *untrain* you to stop playing victim in your own life. You gotta do that. You gotta care.'

I flushed, felt like a little girl chastised for not doing my homework. I didn't want to be passive. I *wanted* to be a badass. And yet, when his hands had closed around my throat . . . When he'd attacked me from behind . . .

I'd felt like I deserved it. I'd been bad and I deserved my punishment. Conditioned response of abused children everywhere. We all grew up, but none of us ever got away.

'Dying for someone is easy,' J.T. murmured now, as if reading my mind. 'Living for yourself, that's hard. But you gotta do it, Charlie. Honor yourself. Defend yourself. Fight for yourself.'

I nodded finally, tucking Tulip closer to my body to help keep her warm.

'Are we going shooting now?' I asked.

'In a minute.'

He was opening my bag, withdrawing my Taurus. The .22 looked tiny in his large callused palm, his long fingers better suited for his explosive .45 than my peashooter. He sniffed at it, looked at me.

'Never put away a gun dirty,' he said.

'Figured I'd clean it after our session.'

'Never put away a gun dirty.'

'Okay.'

'Want to talk about it?'

'No.'

'Good, 'cause I don't want to know.'

He handed me the Taurus. We both rose to standing.

'She gonna be okay walking?' He gestured to Tulip.

'If we keep her moving. She needs a coat. Maybe later today.'

'Do that. Dog that's worth fighting for deserves a sweater.'

J.T. started walking; Tulip and I fell in step beside him. It was a mile and a half to his house, tucked away on three acres of land. Perfect for a man with a shooting range in his backyard. Perfect for a man – and his wife – who didn't much care for company.

'She still alive?' he asked as he walked.

I didn't need clarification to know who he was asking about. 'No,' I heard myself say, another rare admission, a memory barely known and definitely never explored. But if I really thought about it . . . of course my mother was dead. It stood to reason that if she were still alive, she would've contacted me by now. Written a letter from prison or whatever mental institute she was living in. Dropped by the first moment she was released. That's the whole point of Munchausen's by proxy – the perpetrator considers herself the victim. It's all about her – she doesn't just need sympathy, support, understanding. She deserves it. But I'd never heard from my mother since waking up in the upstate New York hospital. Not a phone call, not a letter, not a peep.

There had been some kind of final confrontation. I'd lived, and my mother . . .

'Drinker?' J.T. asked.

'No.'

'Drug abuser?'

'Crazy. Just plain crazy.'

'Glad she's dead then,' J.T. said. 'Now get over her.'

'Sure,' I promised him. 'Might as well.' I glanced at my watch. 'Fifty-eight hours to go,' I muttered. Both of us started to jog.

# 20

'Quincy.'

'This is Sergeant Detective D.D. Warren, Boston PD. I'm calling regarding the criminal profile you developed for Charlene Grant. The January twenty-first homicides. As in two murders down, maybe a third to go, which I'd personally like to avoid. Boston's homicide rate is high enough, thank you.'

'Detective,' retired FBI profiler Pierce Quincy greeted her crisply. 'Spoke to my daughter last night. She apprised me of your investigation. Sounds like you have a plan, something involving social media?'

'Seems worth trying. I understand you studied both the first and second crime scene.'

'Prepared the first report for Jackie Knowles. Wrote the second for Charlene, after Jackie's murder.'

D.D. hadn't thought of that. 'Sorry,' she murmured, not sure what else to say to the retired profiler.

'Crime scene analysis is easier,' Quincy replied simply, 'when you don't know the victim. Therefore, I must add caveats to my second report. It is probably not as objective as the first.'

'Let's start with the first murder, the Providence scene,' D.D. decided. 'My impression from your report, and the lead investigator, Roan Griffin, is that the perpetrator is someone with a high-degree of self-control, advanced communication skills, above average intelligence, and a good deal of manual strength.'

'Agreed.'

'Male or female?'

'Statistics would argue male. Lack of sexual assault, however, complicates the analysis.'

'Gut feel?'

'Can't get one from the Providence murder. However, factoring in the Atlanta homicide, where the victim was last seen with a woman, I lean toward a female perpetrator. It would explain the willingness of both women to open their doors, even the thorough cleanup afterward. Granted, many serial killers can be meticulous in their ability to sanitize a crime scene, but few think to tend the sofa cushions.'

'Tend the sofa cushions?' D.D. asked.

'They appeared recently fluffed. A distinctly feminine touch.'

'Fluffed? How can you tell that?'

'Can't, not definitively. But according to Jackie's neighbor, Ms. Knowles had a tendency to toss the decorative pillows to one side of the love seat and sit on the other. When the police arrived at the scene, however, the accent pillows were perfectly positioned. In fact, the lower cushions and back cushions of the love seat were smoothed out and neatly squared. As one detective observed, it appeared as if no one had ever sat on the furniture. It was fluffed.'

'But Jackie might have done it,' D.D. countered. 'You know, tidying up in case she brought up a "guest" that night.'

'True. I'm offering a theory based on supposition, not fact.'

'Well, at least you're honest,' D.D. informed him.

She thought the profiler might have laughed, but the moment was brief.

'We need to stir the pot,' D.D. said abruptly. 'We have two days before January twenty-first. I've got Charlene Grant running around Boston, hiding from everyone she knows and currently armed with a twenty-two semiauto—'

'She has a handgun?'

'Legally registered.'

'Won't help her.'

'Based on supposition or fact?'

'Both. First two victims never fought back. If they didn't rip off their own fingernails trying to claw away a pair of hands choking them to death, what makes Charlene think she'll get off a single shot?'

D.D. swallowed hard, not liking that image. 'Maybe they did fight back. The perpetrator cleaned up their hands afterward, after fluffing the pillows, of course.'

'Randi had perfectly manicured nails of above average length. Not a single one was broken. What are the odds of that?'

'Tox screen?' D.D. asked.

'Negative for drugs.'

'Could they have been attacked in their sleep?'

'Possible, but lack of oxygen should have bolted them awake, triggering fight or flight. By all accounts, both were capable of fighting.'

'Then how do you explain the lack of self-defense wounds?'

'I can't.'

D.D. sighed again. 'At least you're honest,' she repeated.

'Sadly, that's not helping either one of us. Or, on the twenty-first, Charlene Grant. Has there been any contact?' Quincy asked abruptly. 'A note to Charlene, anything?'

'No.'

'Unusual,' he commented. 'Very, actually, for a repeat offender to duplicate a pattern so precisely. Most killers describe murder as a physical sensation, releasing a chemical in the brain similar to a runner's high. The first kill is generally impulsive and anxiety-inducing. But after the dust settles, the killer forgets the fear, remembers the buzz, and begins to yearn again. Next kill cycle may take a bit, but over time, the need for the physiological release that accompanies each murder becomes the overriding drive, shortening the kill cycle, leading to more frenzy, less organization, less control. The killer may try to combat the cycle by turning to alcohol and/or drugs as a substitute for the homicidal high, but it rarely works. On the other hand, it does assist law enforcement efforts as the killer begins to disintegrate, making more and more mistakes.'

'Judging by that logic, this killer is still at the infancy of the kill cycle, if he or she can make it a full year between each victim?' D.D. guessed.

'Technically speaking, this killer isn't yet a serial killer. Takes three. At this point, we have a repeat offender whose pattern is almost technical in nature. More ritualized assassin than serial predator.'

'Maybe because the murderer is a female. She's not driven by bloodlust, but something else.'

'It's the something else we need to understand. If we could identify the why, then perhaps that would reveal the who.'

'All right.' D.D. was game. 'Why Randi Menke? Why Jackie Knowles? What do they have in common?'

'Both single women living in urban environments. Same age. Both grew up in the White Mountains of New Hampshire, with friends and family in common. More specifically, both were best friends of Charlene Grant.'

'Which Charlene takes to mean that she's the next victim. Are you as sure of that? Maybe this has something to do with Randi and Jackie. Not Charlie at all.'

'Possible,' Quincy replied. 'With only two murders, we lack enough data points to draw meaningful conclusions. The fact that Randi and Jackie happened to know each other could still be completely random; they knew they knew each other, but the killer did not.'

'I don't like random,' D.D. said. 'I know it happens, but it still hasn't made a believer out of me.'

'That would make two of us,' Quincy agreed. 'So, we'll make our first assumption: Randi and Jackie share a common link that led to their deaths. Now, in adulthood, they didn't really. They lived in two different states, separated by nearly a thousand miles. Randi lived in a posh area of Providence, divorced from an abusive husband, worked as a receptionist at a wellness center. Jackie lived in the suburbs of Atlanta, single, lesbian, corporate workaholic. Not so much in common.'

'Wait a minute,' D.D. interjected. 'What about the abusive husband? Did Jackie know, perhaps intervene on behalf of her friend, Randi, which might have put Jackie in the doc's sights?'

'Negative. According to Jackie herself, she never knew Randi was having domestic issues until after Randi's murder. Apparently, Randi had never confided in her friends.'

'She isolated herself,' D.D. added, recognizing the pattern of so many beaten wives.

'In adulthood, the three friends had drifted apart,' Quincy stated.

'Meaning, in order to find the common link between Randi and Jackie, you must go back approximately ten years, to when they grew up together in the same small town, attending the same tiny school. And during that time, they were not defined as Randi and Jackie, but as Randi, Jackie, and Charlie. Apparently, the locals often referred to them by a single moniker, Randi Jackie Charlie.'

'The Three Musketeers,' D.D. said.

'Precisely, and given that, I can't blame Charlene for making the assumption that she's next. Best case scenario, she wakes up pleasantly surprised January twenty-second. Worst case scenario . . .'

'Hope for the best, plan for the worst,' D.D. murmured.

'Exactly.'

'All right,' D.D. said briskly. 'For the sake of argument, let's assume the entire trio has been targeted. So why now? Wouldn't it make more sense to try to kill them when they lived in the same town? All together? For that matter, why pick them off, one by one? And why on January twenty-first?'

'Excellent questions, Detective. When you find the answers, please let me know.'

'It's ritualized,' D.D. continued, thinking out loud. 'The perpetrator's whole approach is deeply personal to him or her. The date, the methodology, even the individual targeting. Perhaps the target cluster is a trio of friends, but the killer's style ensures each one dies alone.'

'An interesting observation, Detective.'

'All right, so let's say the killer is morally opposed to BFFs. First murder was two years ago, nearly eight years after the women had gone their separate ways. Why wait until so many years have passed, then start by attacking Randi on the twenty-first?'

'There are several points to consider there,' Quincy replied. 'One, age. The women parted ways at eighteen. Assuming the killer is someone who knew them from childhood, it's possible the killer is of their peer group. Eighteen is a transitional age, the boundary between being a teenager and being an adult. You could argue the killer needed to gain more experience before having the wherewithal to act out his or her impulse . . .'

'Grooming,' D.D. muttered. 'Had to go to various murder-r-us chat rooms, learn how to get it done.'

'Pardon?'

'Nothing.'

'Eighteen is also a pivotal age in mental health. There are many conditions, including bipolar or schizophrenia, that manifest around this stage of development.'

'Meaning, the attacker transitioned from "normal" to "abnormal", including an abnormal need to kill BFFs?'

'Possible, worth considering, I think. The issue with this theory is that the nature of the crime scenes argues for a perpetrator in full possession of his or her faculties. An organized, not disorganized killer.'

'But something happened,' D.D. murmured. 'If you assume that the three friends are the target, something happened to make the perpetrator embark on this ritual.'

'Maybe it happened on the twenty-first,' Quincy said.

'Did the women see something, witness something?' D.D. mused. 'Maybe they were home for the holidays, as adults, and came across an incriminating auto accident, happened to witness a Mafia killing, something, anything.'

'Question has been asked many times. Charlene has always responded negatively.'

'Okay.' D.D. kept thinking. 'Three best friends. Who hates three girls?' And then it came to her, so obvious she couldn't believe she hadn't thought of it before. 'The fourth,' she breathed out. 'The fourth girl, who never made the cut.'

'Hell hath no fury like a woman scorned,' Quincy said. 'It's a good theory. In fact, I'm sorry I never thought to ask that question.'

'So I return to Charlene, I ask about other childhood friends.'

'No,' Quincy corrected immediately. 'Don't ask about friends, ask about the girls who were never friends. The loner in the class-room. The girl who always sat by herself at lunch, the outsider, looking in.'

'But you said the killer has above average communication skills. When has that loner had above average communication skills?'

'Maybe I was wrong about that. Maybe Randi and Jackie opened their doors out of lingering pity for a former classmate, not warm welcome of a charismatic stranger.'

'Okay, okay. I can do that,' D.D. agreed. 'But even if Charlene remembers a name, I'm down to forty-eight hours to track a person for a case that isn't even yet my case. Given the time line, maybe this girl is already in Boston, on the hunt for Charlene . . .'

'You want a strategy that is more proactive?'

'I want to draw the killer to us. I was thinking of setting up a Facebook page, something commemorating the anniversary of the murders, honoring the victims. I want to stir the pot. Crawl inside the killer's head. How do I do that?'

The phone line fell quiet. She could feel Quincy considering the matter.

'I wish I could come to Boston,' Quincy muttered. 'I would feel better, I think, if I were in Boston.'

'Hey, nothing personal, Mr. Former Fed, but Boston PD is not a bunch of local yokels. We try to keep at least one person alive a year. I'm thinking this year that'll be Charlene Grant.'

'I'm worried about her,' Quincy said quietly.

'You should be,' D.D. said bluntly. 'I spent an hour with the girl. She needs to gain about twenty pounds, sleep twenty days, and lay off the twenty-two. Other than that, though . . .'

'My wife and I. We've recently adopted.'

'You have a baby?' D.D. was shocked. She hadn't seen a photo of the former profiler to determine age, but given that his daughter was a full-grown fed with kids of her own . . .

'Not a baby. We are much too old for that,' Quincy replied dryly, as if reading her mind. 'A ten-year-old girl we fostered first. We love her dearly. And if we are very lucky, one day we hope she will be able to feel that love. But she isn't there yet.'

'Project,' D.D. said.

'Potential,' Quincy corrected gently. 'My wife is a former law enforcement officer as well. We've seen both sides of the equation. We know what we're up against. When I heard of Jackie Knowles's murder . . . It was good to have a child in the house again. It was good to remember the promise of the future and not just dwell on past regrets.'

D.D. didn't say anything. Quincy's words made her think of everything she loved about coming home to Jack. She'd worried in the beginning that having a baby would limit her ability to do her job. And maybe Jack did limit her hours, but he also balanced the equation. Children, the hope for a better tomorrow, was everything a homicide cop worked for. You took the hit, so your child wouldn't have to. You put in the long hours, as her case team had done last night, so that other kids could feel safe.

'Fourth friend,' Quincy said.

'What?'

'That's what you need. Based on your own analysis. You need to create a fictional fourth friend. A fresh target to distract your killer.'

D.D. frowned, turned it over. 'But how? If we assume the killer is someone from childhood who knew the trio, the murderer will know it's false.'

'You need to be the fourth friend.'

'What?'

'The person who initiates the Facebook page. Position yourself as a person of honor and ownership of Jackie and Randi. You met them in college maybe. First Jackie, then Randi, then Charlie. You all hung out together in Boston. You love them, you grieve for them, and now you've appointed yourself memory keeper. If your theory is correct, and the killer is a social outsider, that alone will aggravate her. She murdered Jackie and Randi so that they would belong to her. And now in death, you're taking them back. You're claiming their memory. Colloquially speaking, that should piss her off.'

'I like it,' D.D. said. 'Killing is about power. So you must interrupt the power equation, deliberately provoking and threatening the authority of the killer. She's not in control. You are. In fact, you are the best friend Jackie and Randi ever had, because you will keep them alive forever. Your love, your power, is greater than hers.'

'And I have better shoes,' D.D. added. 'Women can't stand that.'

Quincy's low chuckle. 'Sounds like you're on the right track.'

'Thank you,' D.D. said honestly. 'This has been very helpful.' She paused. 'Can I ask you one last question?'

'By all means.'

'Could it be Charlene? She's setting herself up as the third victim, but what if that's just a ruse? What if she's the perpetrator and this is how she's covering her tracks?'

The receiver was quiet again. 'I don't know,' Quincy said at last. 'That's a complicated way to get away with murder. But one thing's for certain – you'll know on the twenty-second.'

# 21

J.T. and I shot rounds for an hour. I practiced at twenty feet, then fifty feet, then thirty yards. No long-range targets for me. For me, the challenge would be up close and personal.

When I emptied my last box of ammo, I sat on a hay bale near the fence line and worked on cleaning my gun. Snow had started, dusting my dark hair with light flakes as I hunched over my Taurus, meticulously taking it apart.

Tulip had left me for the warmth of J.T.'s house and the comfort of his wife's company. J.T. was still shooting. He had a 150-yard target he liked to play with. Sometimes, he'd shoot happy faces, or a five-point star, maybe a heart for his wife on Valentine's Day. I guess we all have our talents.

When my phone rang, I ignored it at first, then remembered Michael, the prepaid cell I'd slipped into the boy's pocket on the bus, and quickly checked the display.

Not Michael, but I recognized the number. I hit answer and brought Detective D.D. Warren to my ear.

'Work last night?' she asked me.

'Yes.'

'Sleep this morning?'

'No.'

'Same as the rest of us then. Come on down. We got a plan.'

'Excuse me?'

'I'm your new best friend. Literally. Meet me at police head-quarters, thirty minutes. We got something to show you.'

The detective hung up. I looked up to find J.T. watching me.

'Gotta go?' he asked.

'Guess so.'

''Kay,' he said.

''Kay.'

I went to fetch my dog. When I returned outside with Tulip, J.T. was gone and only the scent of gunpowder lingered in the air.

'He's not good at goodbye,' his wife, Tess, murmured behind me. She'd come out onto the covered front porch, arms crossed over her black-and-gray plaid shirt for warmth. She was younger than J.T., closer to fifty than sixty, with silver strands liberally sprinkling her pale blond hair. In faded jeans and fleece-lined slippers, with her hair pulled loosely back to reveal a delicately boned face, she wasn't a beautiful woman, but striking. She had a way of looking at me that reminded me of J.T. They didn't just look, they *saw*, and they trusted in their ability to handle what they'd seen. The two of them fit each other perfectly.

I peered out at the empty shooting range. 'I know how he feels,' I said.

Tess came to stand beside me. 'I told him he should stay with you, on Saturday the twenty-first. Just in case.'

'No.'

'And he said that's what you would say.'

'Have you ever been hit?' I asked her abruptly.

'Yes.'

'Did you take it, or did you fight back?'

'Both. People change. Kids grow up.'

'J.T. says I have to get my mother out of my head.'

'He's smart like that.'

'But I don't know how.'

'Do you hate her?' Tess sounded genuinely curious.

I had to think about it. 'I don't know. I avoid her. Don't think, don't remember. Then, I don't have to feel.'

'That's your problem then.'

'Denial? But it's a personal strength of mine.'

'If you believe you're honestly going to die on Saturday, Charlie, if you believe you're honestly going to have to fight for your life, you should feel something about that.'

'I'm pissed off,' I offered.

'It's a start. There's no right answer. I forgave my father. J.T., on the other hand, will probably never stop hating his.'

That surprised me, but I didn't say anything.

'I don't like to hate,' Tess said simply. 'Not my father, not my ex-husband. I held on to the rage as long as I needed it to do what I needed to do. Then, I let it go. I look at my children. I feel how much I love them. I feel how much they love me. And that makes me feel better instead.'

'I love my dog,' I said, automatically bending to pat Tulip's head. 'And she's not even my dog.'

'Sounds like a country-western song. You're welcome to stay here, Charlie, for as long as you need.'

I nodded, then straightened, adjusting my messenger bag, fiddling with my grip on Tulip's leash. 'Goodbye, Tess,' I said.

She wasn't surprised. 'Goodbye, Charlie.'

Tulip and I stepped off the front porch, and even though Tulip whined a little, neither of us looked back.

It took Tulip and me twenty minutes to walk through the light snowfall to an area busy enough to hail a cab. Then another twenty minutes for the cab to deliver us to the BPD headquarters in Roxbury. The driver wasn't happy to transport a dog, so I had to tip him five bucks extra, and that quickly, I was broke.

Let me tell you, a girl doesn't work police dispatch for the money.

I thought of Officer Mackereth, felt myself flush, and reminded myself sternly I didn't work at police dispatch for that either.

To enter HQ, I had to go through security. The first officer, a mountain of a black man, got a little excited about my .22. I showed my license to carry, but he remained skeptical. Leave it to Massachusetts to create a gun policy so paranoid that even when you took the proper legal steps no one believed you.

Of course, I'm not sure what legal steps were taken to secure my gun permit. J.T. had done it for me, given the stringent standards. Probably called in a few favors. I never asked, unanswered questions being the whole key to my relationships.

'What do you do for a living?' the BPD officer asked me now.

'Comm officer, Grovesnor PD.'

'Oh.' His massive shoulders came down. He gave me a grudging measure of respect. Officers liked dispatch operators. We took care of them, and they knew it.

He kept my gun, handing me a tag. 'You can claim it on your way out. Same with the dog.'

'You can't take my dog.'

Officer Beefy got puffy again. 'Honey, my house, my rules.' He jerked his thumb toward the glass door. 'Dog goes outside; say pretty please, and I'll keep an eye on it.'

Having now gone twenty-four hours without sleep, I didn't take this news well.

'Look, your detective invited me here,' I informed him, beyond caring if he was three times my height and four times my weight. 'This is my dog, and I'm not tying her outside in this weather or in this neighborhood. If Sergeant Detective D.D. Warren wants to see me, then she gets both of us. That's the deal.'

'Sergeant Detective D.D. Warren?' The officer's dark face broke into a broad grin. 'Ha, good luck with that.' He motioned to the desk sergeant, sitting on the other side of the security scanner. 'Got a visitor, with dog, for Detective Warren.'

'With dog?' the desk sergeant called back.

'She sniffs out doughnuts,' I informed the sergeant. 'Took years of training.'

'Sounds like a Detective Warren dog,' the sergeant drawled. Tulip and I were finally allowed into the lobby, where we roamed the enormous glass-and-steel space while waiting for our date to arrive.

Urban police stations should be dingy, with yellow-stained drop ceilings and tiny barred windows, I thought crabbily. Not modern art monstrosities, boasting cavernous lobbies filled with glass and gray winter sky, let alone the wafting odor of coffee and fresh baked goods. Rather helplessly, Tulip and I followed the tempting scents to the open doors of the building's cafeteria. I hadn't eaten in twelve hours, and neither had Tulip, but being out of cash limited our options. As it was, Tulip and I would have to muscle our way onto the T if we wanted to get home.

D.D. Warren finally appeared at the other end of the lobby. I recognized her by the bounce in her curly blond hair and the laser-like quality of her crystalline blue eyes. She spotted me, then Tulip, and zeroed in.

'What happened to you?' she demanded. Guess I was starting to bruise.

'Boxing.'

'Aren't you supposed to wear gloves?' She pointed to my hands, where the knuckles on both pinky fingers had turned bright purple.

'I will remind my attacker of that on the twenty-first,' I assured her.

'And the bruises around your neck?'

'Hey, you should see the other guy.'

'Legally speaking, I'm not sure you want that.'

'True.'

She stared at me a minute longer, as if trying to figure out just what kind of crazy she was dealing with today.

Then she surprised me. 'Nice dog.' She held out her hand for Tulip. 'I like dogs for women. One of the best lines of self-defense. Better than guns. Guns can be taken and used against you. Not a good dog.'

I shook my head. Should've known the detective would have a point.

'I don't plan on having Tulip around on the twenty-first,' I informed D.D. 'I'm sending her to live with my aunt.'

'Then you're an idiot.'

'I prefer the term responsible adult.'

'Martyr.'

'Considerate friend.'

'Self-sacrificing fool.'

'Self-sufficient fighter.'

'Idiot,' Detective Warren said again.

'Are we done yet?'

'I don't know. I find that now that I have a newborn, I appreciate adult conversation more. Want coffee?'

'Who's buying?'

She eyed me, eyed my dog. I categorized D.D. Warren along with J.T. Dillon and his wife, Tess; like them, D.D. didn't just look, she saw.

'Come on, my treat.'

Tulip and I followed D.D. into the cafeteria. I selected a roasted chicken sandwich for me, bread and cheese for Tulip. Then I added two cookies, a bag of chips, a cup of coffee, and a bottle of water. The detective didn't say a word, just paid the bill.

She led us back to the desk sergeant, who gave me another look, then handed the detective my tagged .22.

'She had this in her bag. Licensed to carry,' he informed her.

'Tattletale,' I mouthed at him.

D.D. glanced at me.

'Nothing,' I said.

She sniffed my gun. 'Recently cleaned.'

'Nothing,' I said.

'Why am I helping you again?'

'I pay taxes.'

'In that case . . .' D.D. handed the desk sergeant my beautiful nickel-plated Taurus with its rich rosewood grip. 'It's legal, so when she's on her way out, she can have it back.'

The desk sergeant took my gun, handed me a visitor's pass. I snubbed my nose at him.

It's possible I'd gone a little too long without sleep.

We went upstairs to the homicide unit, where D.D. turned on her computer and I stopped breathing for the second time that day.

Randi's picture came up first. Her beautiful wheat blond hair blown out straight, one side tucked behind her right ear, long bangs swinging gracefully down the other side, drawing attention to huge, doe brown eyes. She was sitting next to a planter of pink petunias, maybe on her front porch in Providence, because I didn't recognize the backdrop. But I felt the weight of her large, soft smile. The familiar gesture of her fingertips, brushing across the strand of pearls above the neckline of a dove gray cashmere sweater.

Her grandmother's pearls, gifted to her on her sixteenth birthday by her parents. Jackie and I had oohed and ahhed over them. We weren't pearl people, but we understood how much Randi loved them. We knew that she'd wear them every day, whether entertaining or gardening or grocery shopping, and look perfect doing so.

And if Jackie was jealous her best friend had received such an extravagant necklace, she didn't show it. And if I was jealous my best friend had inherited a family piece from a grandmother who'd known and loved her, I didn't show it. We were happy she was happy.

Randi had glowed that day. She'd opened that box, and her normally quiet face lit up until she appeared even more lustrous than the pearls.

I couldn't help it. I reached out. Touched the image on the flat monitor, as if I could still feel the warmth of my friend's skin, feel the indent of her dimple, hear her call my name.

*Charlie, Charlie, Charlie! Look at this! Can you believe it? My grandmother's pearls. Oh, Charlie. Aren't they beautiful?*

The words came out before I could stop them. 'I failed her.'

D.D. Warren was watching me. Looking and seeing. 'Why do you say that?'

'I was the glue. That was my job. Jackie organized us, Randi energized us, and I . . . I held us together. Through petty fights and minor squabbles and all the ways three girls can become two against one. We were better together. I appreciated that. So it was my job to keep us on track, reminding us even when it was difficult that three was better than two which was better than one. Except then we turned eighteen and drifted apart.'

'Why?' D.D. asked the question flatly. As if she already understood the answer mattered, was the real reason I now couldn't let my friends go.

I took my eyes off my friend's picture. I studied the detective and I started to understand the real meaning of being tough. The trait shared by Detective Warren and my firearms instructor J.T. and his wife, Tess.

They looked at life without blinders. They had the confidence to not dodge the blow, but stand there and take the hit.

'I was embarrassed,' I told the detective quietly. 'I let us fall apart, because I didn't just love Jackie and Randi, I knew that I loved them more than they loved me. So I never told them about my mother. If I had, then maybe Randi would've told us about her abusive husband. And Jackie and I would've helped her and we would've stood together, instead of scattering and dying apart. But I couldn't tell them about my mom. I loved them so much, I couldn't risk them thinking less of me.'

Detective Warren leaned forward, peered at me intently. 'What should you have told them about your mother, Charlene?'

I held up my left hand. The fresh boxing bruises stood out starkly, bright purple kisses on the webbing between some of my fingers. But there were other markings as well, a patchwork of thin white scars zigzagging across my skin. They became more obvious in the summer, when I had a tan, than during the winter when, like most New Englanders, my skin was bone white. But I knew D.D. would spot the pale, spidery lines.

I murmured, 'I think other people's mothers don't break bottles over the back of their little girls' hands, so they can take their children to the emergency room and have the cute male intern tweeze out the broken glass. I think other people's mothers don't hold a hot iron to their daughters' fingertips, so they can return to the same ER three days later, when the cute male intern said he'd be working again.'

'How old were you?'

'Young enough to go along, old enough to know better.'

'And this was in New Hampshire?'

'Upstate New York. That's where I lived before my mother died. At which time, Social Services tracked down my aunt and asked her to take me. That's how I met Jackie and Randi, first day of school. We sat side by side. And just like that, we were best friends. We did everything together – played, studied, worked, rebelled. Except then we turned eighteen, and they had dreams and I didn't. So I let them go. And I didn't call or check up or be the kind of friend I should've been, because I didn't want them to know just how much I missed them. I was embarrassed, that all these years later I still loved them more than they loved me. And now . . . And now . . .'

I couldn't get the words out. I just sat there and touched the digital image of my best friend who I'd never see again.

I should've told Randi everything. I should've told Jackie. I'd hoarded my secrets as a child, then Jackie and Randi had hoarded their secrets as adults. Randi had never told us about her abusive husband. And Jackie never confided in us that she was gay. I only learned that during the police investigation, when Pierce Quincy, the profiler Jackie had hired, let it drop, and I'd sat there stone-faced, willing no expression to show, because of course I would know such a thing about my best friend. Of course one best friend would feel comfortable enough to share such a personal revelation with another best friend.

The thin white scars on the back of my hand were the least of my concerns. It was the internal wounds that hurt me. My world had always been too small, first just me and my mother, then me and my aunt, then Randi Jackie Charlie. I'd always had too little. I'd always loved too hard. And I'd always lost too much.

*Baby, crying down the hall.*

I guess I'd had her, too, a baby I'd known I needed to protect. But I hadn't, and now, I couldn't even remember her name. So much for life without blinders. Twenty-eight years old and still taking daily dips in denial.

I didn't want to be at police headquarters anymore. I wanted to go home to the mountains. I wanted to walk into my aunt's house, throw my arms around her, and cry like a child.

*I'm sorry, I'm sorry. I loved them and I failed and I just can't do it anymore. It is too hard to walk through this life alone.*

There was a knock on the door. Detective Warren and I both looked up. A woman stood in the doorway, wearing a cinnamon red sweater that showed off wavy locks of stunning reddish brown hair and an even more stunningly curved figure. A TV show cop, I thought instantly. The kind that solved the case, won the male lead, and celebrated both events with a new pair of Jimmy Choos.

I looked down at my nearly flat chest, then fingered my plain brown hair yanked back into a plain brown ponytail, and immediately felt self-conscious.

'Show her?' asked the woman.

'Just started. Come in. Detective O, this is Charlene Grant. Charlene, Detective O. She set up the page, being our resident Facebook expert.'

Detective O and I shook hands. She appeared to be about my age, which surprised me. Then I peered into her brown eyes and met a gaze as flat and frank as D.D. Warren's. Cop eyes. Must be one of the requirements to graduate from the academy.

'Nice dog,' she said. She peered under the desk, where Tulip was curled up asleep.

'Not my dog,' I said automatically.

The detective stared at me, then at D.D.

'Not my dog either,' D.D. said.

'Well, that explains it.' O propped one hip against the desk. The office wasn't big; we were now all crowded in, me sandwiched between two hard-edged Boston cops with better wardrobes and bigger guns. Somehow, I didn't think that was accidental.

'What do you think?' the new detective gestured to the computer screen, voice brusque.

'I'm sorry?'

Detective O glanced at D.D. again.

'Haven't gotten there yet,' D.D. said by way of explanation. 'It's your baby, so why don't you do the honors.'

'All right,' Detective O began. 'So . . . Saturday, the twenty-first, will be the second anniversary of Randi Menke's murder in Providence.'

I flinched, said nothing.

'And the first anniversary of Jackie Knowles's murder in Atlanta. Given the pivotal date, we thought we'd set up a Facebook page in honor of both victims and see if we can provoke a response.'

'How?'

'Jackie and Randi must have had other friends and acquaintances before you moved into town,' D.D. spoke up. 'Did your arrival upset any of these relationships? Maybe displace another girl, create competition, social rivalry?'

I regarded her blankly. 'I don't know. We were eight. I'm not sure I was aware of social rivalries when I was eight.'

'What about as you grew up? You girls became the Three Musketeers. How did other girls take it?'

I still didn't understand. 'We weren't mean. At least, I didn't think of us that way. We weren't bullies or anything. We just . . . played together.'

'What if other girls wanted to play?' Detective O asked curtly.

'Would you let them?' There was a tone to her voice, almost an accusation. I found myself leaning away. Maybe it was a tactic she often used with subjects, but clearly she'd already found me guilty.

'You mean like in grade school?' I ventured. 'Because I have vague memories of jumping rope and playing freeze tag, but lots of kids were doing it, not just us three.'

Detective Warren spoke up. 'Let's try high school. By the time "Randi Jackie Charlie" hit high school, what was the social landscape like? Were you always together, or did you have other friends, other hobbies, sports, after school activities?'

'We weren't always together. We had different class schedules, of course. And different extracurricular activities. Jackie was active with the debate team, soccer team, and the alpine ski team. Randi was into figure skating and home arts. I did cross-country skiing in the winter, but spent most of my time helping my aunt with her B and B.'

'So you had other friends?' D.D. prodded.

'I guess. There were over a hundred and fifty kids in our class, so we definitely knew more than just each other.'

'Let's start with Randi.' Detective O took over the conversation again, brown gaze probing. 'When she wasn't with you and Jackie, who were her friends?'

I had to think about it, delve back ten years, and the minute I tried, I could practically hear Jackie's voice in my head, laughing at my terrible memory. Me, of all people, the cops needed *me* to remember. 'There was this girl . . . Sandra, Cynthia, Sandy . . . Becca, her name was Becca. She ice skated, too, I think. And maybe a Felicity? Artsy, like Randi. I think.'

'Did you like them?'

I shrugged. 'I think so.'

'They like you?'

I shrugged again, feeling even more self-conscious. 'We would say hi to each other in the halls.' Probably. 'Why? What are you looking for?'

'The fourth girl,' Detective Warren said. 'The girl who wanted to be friends, too, but none of you let her in. We have reason to believe she's still out there, and she's really pissed off.'

*

It took a bit. We had to pore through my high school memories, which was a challenge at best. I know some people can tell you the name of the cat they had when they were four, but I wasn't one of them. I simply don't remember things well. Not good things, not bad things. Not twenty years ago, not twenty days ago. If memory was a muscle, then mine had been purposefully atrophied through consistent lack of use.

Plus, Detective O rattled me. The way she asked questions, then scrutinized my answers as if she already knew I had something to hide. I felt simultaneously guilty and remorseful. She was disappointed in me. I was failing her; I should remember faster, answer better, confess all.

Good cop, bad cop, it occurred to me. Both detectives were playing me expertly, but all they had to show for it was a very tired, increasingly confused witness, who honestly didn't recollect her childhood.

Finally, we Googled my high school, and found an archive with digital copies of old yearbooks.

With a bit of effort, I was able to identify a dozen girls that floated around our trio, some friends of Randi, some friends of Jackie. None were friends of mine. Even reviewing pictures of my Nordic ski team, I didn't recognize half of the girls' pictures, couldn't provide their names.

My world really had been Randi and Jackie. Away from them, I passed the time. With them, the world started spinning again.

I wondered if they would've said the same. Had they really enjoyed spending all their weekends helping out at my aunt's B&B? Were they really excited to take my call at ten o'clock at night because I'd thought of one last thing to say?

Maybe I wasn't the glue that held us together. Maybe I'd been the anchor around their necks. And that's why we'd drifted apart when we turned eighteen. They'd been happy to finally get away from me.

The detectives took down names and background info. They wanted personal information on Randi, things only a good friend would know about Jackie. Nicknames, favorite expressions, songs, movies, TV shows, childhood pets.

I could answer all of their questions. I tried to tell myself that meant something. I hadn't just loved my friends. I'd *known* them. I'd listened, I'd understood, I'd cared.

Jackie and Randi, I'd remembered.

But it became increasingly difficult to bolster my flagging spirits as the detectives turned my childhood relationships upside down and inside out, leaving me feeling emptier and emptier. As if Randi Jackie Charlie hadn't been the best part of my life, but maybe just a very unhealthy friendship fostered by an overly needy girl in order to compensate for her mother's destructive love.

The detectives muttered among themselves, took notes, asked questions, opened more Internet pages and launched more Google and Facebook searches.

I stopped sitting and paced the tiny confines of the office instead.

Detective D.D. Warren had framed certificates on the wall. Apparently she had a degree in criminal justice and lots of advanced training in various firearms and forensic courses. The frames were slightly askew, so I straightened them up. They were dusty as well, so I took a napkin and polished them up.

What I needed was Windex to polish the glass. Without thinking, I turned to ask, and found two sets of eyes staring at me. The detectives' gazes went from the straightened frames to me to the straightened frames again.

'Neat freak much?' Detective Warren drawled.

'Only when I'm nervous.'

'How often are you nervous?'

'Every day of the past year.'

The detectives exchanged glances.

'You went to a public school?' Detective Warren prodded.

'Yes.'

'Who has neater handwriting? You, Jackie, or Randi?'

'I don't know. Randi had a thing for drawing little hearts over her i's. Does that count?'

'What about print?'

'Me probably.' I shrugged. 'But only because Randi preferred cursive, and Jackie had terrible handwriting, all cramped and rushed.

It didn't do any good to pass notes with her in class – we could never read what she wrote.'

'Wrote like a doctor,' D.D. said amiably.

'Exactly.'

'Do you listen to the police scanner when you're off duty?' she asked abruptly.

The change in topic confused me. 'What? Sometimes. Why?'

'Just thinking, in your line of work, you must like to keep your finger on the pulse of the city. And the things you must hear, the things you must know, being police dispatch and all.'

'You're dispatch?' Detective O spoke up, finally sounding impressed. She looked me up and down, as if reassessing. 'Tough job. I got a friend who does it. Kids are the toughest calls, she says. So much shit going on out there, and so little you can do to help them.'

'True.'

'Does it make you mad?' she continued conversationally. 'Because I'm a sex crimes detective and it makes me *furious*. I mean, the number of perverts out there, and the things they can get away with, and there's nothing we can do about it. Most kids are too terrified to come forward, and even if they do, system puts them through the wringer. You must hate that. Taking those calls while already knowing that even if the officer shows up and an arrest is made, it's still gonna end badly for the kid. Just the way it is.'

'It's best not to get personally involved,' I said. I had stepped away from both of them. I wondered if they had noticed; figured they had. I found it interesting that while their bad cop routine had rattled me, the good cop routine had me genuinely fearful and ready to exit stage left.

'Look,' D.D. said briskly, waving her hand toward the computer monitor and their pile of notes. 'This is a lot of information we're plowing through in a short time. Why don't you write down any other names we should consider, no matter how inconsequential, then you can head out. We'll be in touch if we have any more questions.'

She handed me a sheet of paper, a pen. Then she picked up a stack of files, clearing a space on top of a gunmetal gray filing cabinet for me to use. 'There you go. And while you're at it, write down the full names of your parents and your aunt.'

'Why my parents?'

'Basic background.'

'My mother's dead. My father's not part of my life. Don't think it's relevant.'

The good detective wasn't going to let me off that easy. 'Didn't you come to me for help?'

I looked at her.

'You were standing outside my crime scene,' she continued, and this time there was an edge of challenge in her voice. 'You said you were there because you Googled me. Though, now that I think about it, you never approached me. You were walking away. *I* ran *you* down.'

'I wasn't going to approach you.'

'But you said—'

'I just wanted to see you. I wasn't, I didn't,' I waved my hand around her office defensively. 'I never expected any of this. You're my precaution built into a precaution. I figured I'd write you a letter, provide details on my own case. That way, if I didn't get it done on the twenty-first, you'd have a better shot at finally catching the guy on the twenty-second. You'd provide justice for my aunt, closure for Randi and Jackie's families. I wasn't researching you for me. I was studying you for them.'

D.D. narrowed her eyes. 'Two of your friends have been murdered,' she stated bluntly. 'You believe you will be the third.'

'Yes.'

'So you've left behind your home, the people who know you. You're hiding out in the big city, no registered phone or utilities. You have no computer, no email, no Internet footprint to trace. But you've kept your name.'

I had my chin up. 'Can't change everything.'

'You're training, boxing, running, shooting. Preparing to make your last stand. But you're going to send the dog away.'

'Yes.'

'And maybe you looked me up, but it was never with the mind-set of asking for help *before* the twenty-first. Not to mention, you're a woman with a target on your back who hasn't asked her own officers for assistance.'

I didn't say anything, just returned her steely blue stare.

'Can't figure you out, Charlene,' she drawled at last. 'You trying to live January twenty-one? Or are you trying to die?'

'I don't want to die.'

'But do you want to *live*?'

I remained silent. D.D.'s gaze dropped to my scarred hand, and in those fine white lines, I figured she read the answer.

Earlier today, Tess had said that adults could change, that children grew up. But some things in life were very hard to transform. For example, taking the little girl who'd once stood there passively while her mother ironed her fingertips and trained her how to throw a punch. Or taking the same little girl, who'd willfully chewed and swallowed a shattered lightbulb, and teaching her how to pull the trigger.

I was trying to move forward. Some days were certainly better than others. But in the end, I'd only had 363 days as a fighter. I'd experienced far more as the victim, the child who did whatever her mother wanted her to do, because that was the price of love, and that little girl had lived too little and loved too hard and lost too much.

'Names please,' Detective Warren said, and gestured to the blank piece of paper.

I took my time, mostly because my hands were shaking. I formed each letter carefully, wanting the result to be neat and legible. I wrote two names, following an instinct I couldn't explain, but that felt right.

I took one last moment, to study my carefully printed letters.

Then, I handed over the piece of paper.

I collected my dog.

I collected my gun.

Three p.m. Thursday afternoon. Fifty-three hours and counting.

Tulip and I headed out into the city's stark, snow-frosted landscape.

# 22

Detective O waited until Charlene had exited the homicide unit, then she returned to D.D.'s office, closed the door, and collapsed in the desk chair across from her.

'Could we really be that lucky?' she asked, her voice incredulous. 'I mean, is it just me, or is Charlene Grant a perfect fit for our shooter?'

'Don't know if it's luck,' D.D. mused, frowning. 'Remember, I first encountered her outside the second homicide. When I ran her down, she claimed she was checking me out to handle her own case. But maybe that was just fast thinking on her part. She offered up her own troubled history to distract me from the fact she was loitering outside an active crime scene.'

'What's with her hands and throat? Looks like she's been mugged—'

'Training.'

'So she really thinks someone will try to kill her on the twenty-first?'

'Randi Menke and Jackie Knowles really are dead.'

Detective O paused. Then her eyes widened. 'Motivation. Think about it. Charlene's police dispatch. She takes the calls, she hears these kids. Maybe she wants to help them, but she's not sure how. In the meantime, she's boxing, shooting—'

'Gaining skills.'

'And, even more importantly, counting down to her own death. Meaning, at a certain point, *what does she have to lose?*'

D.D. stilled, regarded the other detective. 'Charlene decides to do something with the limited time she feels she has left. Maybe right some past wrongs, given a history of child abuse.'

'She's saving other kids,' O continued. 'Doing what she no doubt wishes someone had done for her when she was that age, and Mommy Dearest was pulling out the insulin.'

'Insulin?'

'Oh, other case I worked. Evil stepfather, actually. A diabetic. Came up with the idea to inject his beautiful twin stepdaughters with insulin. Their blood sugar would crash, rendering them semi-comatose, he'd do what he was going to do, then squirt spray cans of frosting into their mouths to bring their blood sugar back up. Later, after he'd perfected his technique, he'd leave cans of frosting out on the counter just to mess with their heads.'

D.D. stared at her. 'Your job sucks.'

'No,' the young detective said seriously. 'The cases suck. My job, putting that evil stepfather away for twenty years and ensuring those little girls will never be hurt again, pretty much fucking rocks. Which you, of all people, I'd think would understand.'

'Touché. So, back to the matters at hand. Motivation. Means. Opportunity. Yeah, Charlie looks pretty good as a vigilante killer right now.' D.D. glanced down at the piece of paper in her hand, unfolding it and holding it out to Detective O. 'Handwriting, however, is not a perfect match.'

'No flat edge,' O agreed, taking the paper. 'Then again, she had to execute her penmanship with both of us watching. Girl's not stupid. If she did write the other notes, you'd think she'd take some steps to make her handwriting look different.'

'She wrote in print here, not cursive like the notes, but check it out, the letters are neat in appearance, carefully formed.' D.D. turned toward one stack of paperwork on her desk. She couldn't help glancing at her watch, simultaneously aware of the amount of work she still had to do and of her parents' flight landing in a matter of hours. She rifled through the pile of papers until she found what she was looking for, scanned copies of both notes left at the shootings.

*Everyone has to die sometime. Be brave.*

She pulled the copies, placing them on the blue-gray carpeted floor between her and O. O positioned Charlene's recent writing exhibit between the other two sheets, and both peered down.

'Rosalind Grant,' O read. 'Carter Grant. Who are they?'

'Charlene Rosalind Carter Grant.' D.D. recited Charlene's full name. 'Maybe her middle names are in honor of her mother and father?'

'I thought she wasn't going to give us her parents' names.'

'Must be my charm.'

'Look at the n,' Detective O said after another minute. 'First in the note writer's cursive "everyone" then in Charlie's printed "Grant". Looks similar to me.'

D.D. shrugged. 'Looks like an n.'

'Top arch is nice and round. The lines going up the left side of the letter and down the right side are almost exactly parallel. You write an n. See how rounded your top is and how perfectly parallel your sides are.'

For the sake of argument, D.D. gave it a try, first in cursive, then in print. Either way, her n looked dreadful. Like an upside down v. No neatly arched top, no nicely parallel sides, just a tiny, shuttered-up scrawl.

'You write like a doctor,' O declared.

'In my family, that's a compliment.' D.D. automatically snuck a glance at her watch again. 'Okay, Charlene's n is certainly closer to the note writer's n than mine. Now, if only those were grounds for arrest.'

'You could have the handwriting expert write up an analysis—'

'Which he's already said won't be admissible in court, given that graphology is considered a pseudo-science.'

'This isn't graphology. Theorizing that the letter writer is anal-retentive is graphology. This is straightforward forensic analysis of penmanship, author of letter A most likely also wrote exhibit B.'

'But he needs multiple exhibits. Still,' D.D. amended herself, 'I'll make a copy of Charlene's names, get him started. Might take a couple of days, however, for him to do his thing. In the meantime, we need something more tangible.'

'A smoking gun.'

'Which ironically, we just handed back to her.'

'What?'

'Her twenty-two. We had it in custody downstairs.'

'Really?'

'Really. But you still can't run a ballistics test without probable cause. I tell you, those constitutional rights are making our job more difficult every day.' D.D. continued to stare down at the notes, frowning.

Rosalind Grant. Carter Grant. Charlene Rosalind Carter Grant.

Why those names? What was Charlene trying to say?

'I like her,' she murmured. 'Who knew, but I actually like the girl, and would prefer not to arrest her for murder.'

Detective O sat back, steepling her hands in front of her. 'Want to hand over the case? I could take the lead.'

D.D. nearly laughed. 'What, don't they keep you busy enough in sex crimes? First you want on the case, now you want to lead it.'

'I take my responsibilities seriously.'

'And I'm a slacker?'

'Well . . . you have other obligations now.'

'Is that the politically correct way of saying I'm a working mom?'

'Fact of life: Baby's gotta get picked up when the baby's gotta get picked up.'

'Another fact of life: The trick to this job isn't working hard, it's working smart.'

'Is that a politically correct way of saying I'm not as experienced as you?'

'Yes.'

Detective O opened her mouth. Detective O closed her mouth.

'Touché,' she said at last.

'Let's review.' D.D. forced her gaze off the wall clock and back on her upstart new partner. 'Charlene Rosalind Carter Grant. Obviously knows where the second victim, Stephen Laurent, lives, as I found her in the neighborhood. Has a permit for a twenty-two, same caliber as the murder weapon, and has stated she can hit a bull's-eye at fifty feet.'

'Physically fit,' O supplied. 'Also tiny, nonthreatening. If a pedophile opened his door to her, he wouldn't automatically assume the worst.'

'Relatively young,' D.D. continued. 'And with an almost childlike build. Even more reason for perverts not to slam the door right away.'

'She would have the ability to research pedophiles through her police dispatch job. Maybe hear about them on the scanner or via incoming calls, but also, she can log on to police databases, registered sex offender lists.'

'Access to information would not be a problem,' D.D. agreed.

'And in terms of the profile developed by the graphologist—'

'Our daily dose of quack.'

'She fits the requirements of being anal-retentive.'

'Though I appreciate the help with my pictures.'

'Definitely a bit of a control freak. What's the deal with the hair anyway? She's not just wearing a ponytail, she's basically seized the strands in a choke hold. And none shall ever escape.'

'Very controlled hairdo, but very sloppy clothing. Oversized, baggy. Maybe her way of trying to look larger and tougher than she really is?'

'Pretty blue eyes,' O commented. 'Hair down, better clothes, she could talk her way into most men's apartments, pedophiles or not.'

'But would she leave the puppy?' D.D. asked.

'Pardon?'

'In Stephen Laurent's apartment. The killer left a young puppy to fend for itself. It's one thing to kill a suspected pervert. It's another to abandon a puppy without food or water. Charlene must have some sympathy for dogs, as it appears she's adopted a street mutt. So would she leave the puppy behind?'

'Calculated gamble. Odds are the victim's body will be found soon versus later, and the puppy rescued.'

'Possible,' D.D. said, but the detail bothered her. Felt not as right to her as the other variables.

'She suffered abuse as a kid,' O continued, 'making it easy for her to identify with the victims.'

'She also feels powerless,' D.D. filled in. 'Both of her friends have been murdered, the police have no answers, she's convinced she'll be the next one to die. She's trying to prepare, but mostly, she's waiting. Someone is about to kill her, and there's not a thing she can do about that.'

'Whereas attacking pedophiles . . .'

'Would make her feel powerful. Now she's the one in control, taking charge, righting wrongs. Pulling the trigger probably beats Xanax for anxiety reduction, that's for sure.'

'Unless she's the one who murdered her friends,' O pointed out.

'Possible.'

O studied her. 'But you don't think so.'

D.D. shrugged, tried to put her thought, which was really more of an instinct, into words. 'As a former profiler explained to me just this morning, two murders don't provide enough data points for thorough analysis. Who knows if Charlene is really a target, or if there will even be another murder on the twenty-first. But I believe Charlene believes it. Because of the marks on her knuckles and the fingerprints bruising her neck. She's training that hard. She's willing to be attacked and pummeled and choked, because she believes that's what she needs to do in order to survive January twenty-one.'

'And assuming she believes she really will die in a matter of days . . .'

'Then she has some incentive to color outside the legal lines.'

'Exact vengeance for young, powerless victims everywhere.'

D.D. nodded. She looked up at O. 'One thing's for certain.'

'What?'

'If it really is Charlene Grant, she only has two days left. Given she's probably cleared her calendar for the twenty-first, that means sometime in the next twenty-four hours . . .'

'Another pervert will bite the dust.'

'With the twenty-two semiauto we just returned to her.'

# 23

Four thirty p.m. Sky was already dark, snow drifted lazily outside the apartment window, and Jesse was nearly frantic.

He'd been asking to go to the Boston Public Library for, like, the *whole* afternoon. He'd wanted to take a bus after school, but his mother had said no. She didn't want him on the bus in *this* weather, meaning there were, like, six snowflakes on the sidewalk and now the whole world had to grind to a halt.

When he'd begged and pleaded and nearly cried with frustration, she'd finally said she'd take him at four, when she got off the phone, because she had some school research she needed to do. Plus, Jesse had said they were studying libraries at school and he was supposed to write three sentences on his favorite library, which is why he needed to go. So they would ride the subway together, to the central branch of the Boston Public Library, then maybe have dinner at the food court in the Pru Center. A big night out, said his mom.

She'd looked happy about that. A little excited, planning their evening adventure, and that had made Jesse feel bad 'cause he was lying. But he wasn't lying *too* much. He really would write three sentences and they could go to dinner in the mall, but first he really, really, really needed to meet Pink Poodle and learn how to hit a curveball.

At 3:55, he put on his big fat winter coat, then a fresh pair of dry socks, then his boots, his hat and gloves. By 3:59 he was standing next to the door, poofed out three times his natural size, clutching Zombie Bear, and ready to go.

Except his mother hadn't gotten off the phone.

She was talking and talking and talking ('Just a minute, Jesse!'

'Jesse, shhh!' 'Interrupt me one more time, young man, and no library!')

Jesse was now too hot. Sweat trickled down the back of his neck and he hopped from foot to foot because he had to pee, but he didn't want to get unbundled, because his mother might hang up the phone any second, then it would be time to leave, and they needed to *go*.

He walked little circles in front of the door, spent time jumping over the piles of shoes. Jump, jump, jump, the world's smallest obstacle course.

*C'mon, c'mon, c'mon*, c'mon!

Then, when he thought he couldn't take it a second more, his mother appeared in the hallway.

'Jesse? Ready to go?'

'Ahhhhh!' he nearly screamed, then bolted for the bathroom before his bladder burst.

When he returned, still overheated, but slightly less crazed, his mother was just finishing buttoning up her coat. Without another word, he followed her down the three flights of stairs into the cold.

Jesse liked the city at night. He liked the lights everywhere, different colors and shapes that bounced off the low-hanging clouds and made the city look like a fun house. He especially liked a night like this one, when the snow was drifting down in big fat flakes, that you could catch on your tongue and feel melt into droplets of rust-flavored water.

Jesse's mother walked briskly toward the subway stop three blocks away. Jesse darted around her, pretending he was a frost monster, powered by snow, running at the icy flakes, snapping at them with his mouth until his mother told him sharply, to *stop it before he hurt himself*.

Then he trotted along beside her, subdued but still happy, because they were finally going to the library and the city was all lit up and there were people everywhere, and surely that meant Pink Poodle would still be hunched over a computer in the Boston Public Library, because it was that kind of night. Cold and busy and bustling.

Zombie Bear's bandaged head poked out of his pocket, the undead homerun hitter along for the ride.

It took *forever* to finally reach the main branch of the Boston

Public Library, on Boylston Street. Technically it was two buildings; the historic McKim Building and the newer Johnson Building. Jesse loved the 160-year-old McKim Building, with its massive stone arches and ornate carvings and the kind of long, shadowed halls that hinted of ghosts and gargoyles. The McKim had mostly the research stuff, however – government documents, historic papers. Jesse and his mom headed for the Johnson Building instead. It was built in the seventies and, according to his mom, looked it. Jesse didn't much care for the outside, but the inside was pretty cool. It had a special kids' area, even a teen room.

Maybe he would need to visit the teen room. Maybe, that's where Pinky Poo hung out. Jesse hadn't thought of that.

He fingered Zombie Bear. Told himself he wasn't nervous. Grabbed his mom's hand and trotted up the steps.

In the lobby, his mother laid out the plan. She had some nursing homework to do. She walked him to the section she needed, showed him exactly where she would be. He was allowed to go to the kids' section. He could pick some books, then he was to return *right here*, where he could look at his books while she finished her project. He could write up his homework, too. Then, they'd go to dinner.

Jesse nodded solemnly. They had been coming to the library since he was a baby. He knew the drill.

He kissed his mom. Maybe hugged her harder than he usually did. Then he headed down the stairs to the first-floor children's room.

Jesse knew the library well. Sometimes, on rainy days, his mother would bring him here to 'explore', her library-speak for going someplace free where a young boy could run around without old Mrs Flowers yelling about stampeding elephants.

When Jesse had turned six, he and his mother had first started separating. Partly because she'd gone to school and she had her own work to do, but also because Jesse had noticed other kids in the library without hovering moms, and decided he no longer wanted to be embarrassed by his. At first, his mother had waited outside the section. Then, bit by bit, they'd gone their separate ways.

The children's room made a big deal about not allowing 'unattended adults'. Meaning adults couldn't just roam the section without a kid in tow. This was meant to discourage loiterers, Jesse's mom said, as well as reduce stranger danger. It seemed to make her feel better about Jesse being in the room on his own.

There was always a librarian in charge of the kids' section. If Jesse had any problems, or felt nervous about stranger danger, he was to approach the librarian for assistance. But Jesse had never had any problems. He loved the library. The big vast space with towering shelves and piles of books, and people who sat and read and left you alone, so you could pretend you were an explorer in the lost wilds of the Congo and at any moment a giant ape might swing out from between the narrow aisles, or an alligator snap from beneath a reading bench, or a snake unfurl from a hanging lamp.

But Jesse didn't play explorer now. He headed for the computers in the children's room. They sat at various little desk cubbies and all were in use. He spotted one girl, but she looked even younger than him and was playing some Dora the Explorer game, while her father stared at a cell phone beside her.

Not too many computers in the children's room. Jesse hadn't really thought about that. But upon more consideration, he figured Pink Poodle was older and, therefore, might be in the teen room up on the mezzanine level. He'd never been in the teen room, but the library was very proud of it. He'd seen pictures on posters, advertising a room for teens to hang out. It had crazy red gaming chairs and a big red-and-purple patterned carpet that apparently teens liked, but which made Jesse's eyes hurt.

He found the stairs, headed up. He could do it. Just open the door and walk right in like any other kid. Of course he was in the teen room. Of course he belonged there.

Jesse made it to the door and hit the first obstacle: a sign declaring that only kids younger than eighteen and older than twelve could enter. Anyone older or younger might be asked to leave.

Maybe being asked to leave wasn't the same as leaving, Jesse decided. He took a deep breath. Walked in.

The room was crowded. Teens and laptops and huge windows showing city lights and red chairs and crazy carpets, and Jesse got so revved up he forgot to breathe and then the whole room swam before his eyes.

He glanced around wildly, once, twice, saw girls, saw boys, saw no poodles, and hightailed it back out.

That was it. He couldn't go into that room. He couldn't handle it.

But what to do? How to find Pinky Poo?

It occurred to him that there were computer stations scattered all over the library. Patrons could even check out laptops, which his mom did when their ancient computer required medical care. Pink Poodle hadn't said which computer or any particular section. Maybe she just roamed the way Jesse liked to roam, until she found an open station.

Jesse decided to give it a try. He started at the bottom of the library and worked his way up.

He had Zombie Bear out of his pocket, clutching him with both hands. It was hot or cold in the library, depending on the area. The mezzanine level definitely felt too hot, so Jesse unzipped his jacket, shoved his hat in his pocket, walking slower and slower, trying to look for a homerun-hitting girl sitting tucked away in the shadows, without looking like he was looking.

Then he saw it.

A pink poodle sitting on the corner of a computer station.

Jesse stopped. He spotted the computer user, just as the teenage boy looked up and spotted him.

The boy spoke first: 'Homerun Bear?'

'Pinky Poo?' Jesse sounded stupid. He shut his mouth, wished he hadn't spoken.

But the boy laughed. 'Yeah. I know.' He grinned, looked a little embarrassed. The boy had tousled brown hair, kind of shaggy, which he now brushed away from his forehead. 'Swear the poodle isn't mine,' the boy said. 'Belongs to my little sister. She got it for her birthday a year ago and wanted help with some of the games. So I started messing around on the site, and . . .' Boy shrugged. 'My sister hasn't looked at the poodle since, but here I am. Baseball, three days a week.'

Jesse nodded, relaxing slightly, taking a step forward. 'You should get a Homerun Bear,' he said seriously.

The boy laughed again. 'Thought about it, but Pink Poodle has all the stats, and I don't wanna give 'em up.' Boy stuck out his hand. 'Barry. You?'

'Um . . . Jesse. Jesse Germaine.'

'Nice bear. What happened to him?'

Jesse held up his bandaged bear self-consciously. 'Oh, um . . . he's a zombie now. A homerun hitter, back from the dead.' The words felt lame the moment he said them, but the boy, Barry, laughed again.

'That's pretty cool. Maybe I could zombie-ize Pink Poodle, too. That'd be at least a little cooler than being a sixteen-year-old boy with a pink pooch.'

'Are you playing a game now?' Jesse asked, venturing closer.

'Yep. Helmet Hippo was just online. He's my nemesis, you know. Has one thousand and five hundred points more than me. But I'm improving my game all the time, so I'm thinking in the next month, I'll close that gap. Pass the fucker.'

Jesse gaped for a second, caught off guard by the swear word. Then he closed his mouth, forced himself to appear relaxed again. Barry was sixteen. Sixteen-year-old boys could use those kinds of words. Jesse could use those kinds of words. He glanced around. As long as his mother never heard him.

'Are you playing baseball?' Jesse asked, standing behind Barry's shoulder, peering at the monitor.

'Yep, seventh inning, at bat, two outs. Got Slimey Slug on my team.'

'Sorry,' Jesse said.

'Exactly. Not going well. Will take a miracle to get up to bat again.'

'Oh.' Jesse was disappointed. He wanted to learn how to hit the curveball.

Barry seemed to understand. 'Want to play? Come on, grab a chair. We'll log on your bear and I'll show you some things to do.'

Jesse scrambled to find an empty chair. He pulled it up close to Barry, shoulder to shoulder so they could both see the monitor. Then he carefully placed Zombie Bear next to Pink Poodle on the tabletop. He thought they looked good together.

Jesse glanced at his watch, realized it had been well over fifteen minutes. 'I'll be right back,' he said. Before Barry could respond, he bolted to his mother's section, where he found her hunched over a giant book, brow furrowed as she flipped pages. Jesse exclaimed in a rush, 'Sorry I'm late working with the librarian to find a new series to read can I have fifteen more minutes please?'

'What?' his mother stared up at him.

'Librarian. Helping me. Gonna find a new series to read.'

'Okay. But not too much longer. Get the first book of the series, bring it here, please.'

''Kay.'

Jesse breathed deep, glanced at his watch again, and bolted back downstairs, where Barry had already logged off Pink Poodle and was clearly waiting for him.

'Just needed to check in,' Jesse said without thinking.

'Check in?'

Jesse's cheeks turned pink. 'My mom,' he mumbled. 'She's doing research.'

'Okay,' Barry said, like it was no big deal. He asked Jesse his password, logged in Zombie Bear, then they were off and running. Barry used the keyboard first, showing Jesse what to do. Then Jesse would use the arrow keys and try to replicate. Sometimes, the moves were too fast. Then Barry would place his hand over Jesse's and show him which arrow – right, left, up, or down – to hit faster. Like left, left, left, down, right.

When Jesse made a hit, Barry cheered, his voice low so others wouldn't shush them. When he missed, Barry would mutter stuff like 'Fucker', 'Shit', 'Shit on a stick', in an even lower voice, and Jesse would giggle because he'd never heard 'Shit on a stick' before and the more he thought about it, the funnier it sounded.

Then Barry's pocket started to chime. 'Jesus H. Christ,' the boy said, and Jesse's eyes rounded into saucers.

Barry fumbled with his pocket, pulled out a phone. 'Gotta go,' the older boy said.

'Oh,' Jesse said. Then, before he could help himself. 'The curveball, we didn't get to the curveball.'

'Yeah, right.' Barry was already logging off, grabbing Pink Poodle, stuffing the dog in the pocket of his oversized ski jacket. 'Well, you know, come back tomorrow. We'll do it then.'

Jesse bit his lower lip. He wanted to come back tomorrow, but it had been hard enough to come today. And given how long it had been since he'd checked in with his mom, she was probably mad at him, and then he definitely wouldn't be allowed back in the library tomorrow. 'I got . . . something . . .' Jesse mumbled. 'After school.'

Barry was already standing, pushing the chair. 'Next day then.'

'But . . . but . . .'

'Look, kid, I gotta go.'

Jesse couldn't think of what to say. Just stared up at the older boy.

'Okay, okay, okay,' Barry said at last. 'Follow me, 'kay? I gotta grab a smoke. Right outside, I can light up, then I'll show you how to log in on my phone and we'll hit a curveball. But then I gotta go, 'kay?'

The older boy was already moving. Jesse scrambled to catch up.

Outside the air had turned frosty. Jesse could see ice particles dancing in the glow of the streetlights and feel tiny pinpricks of cold sting against his cheeks. Barry loped down the front steps, moving quickly. The teenager was tall, lanky. Walked, talked like a cool kid. Jesse bet at school, all the other students liked Barry, wanted to be like him. And here he was, with Jesse.

The boy stopped at the bottom of the library stairs, pulled out a pack of cigarettes, lit one up.

He caught Jesse staring up at him. 'Never smoke,' the older kid instructed. 'These fuckers will kill you.'

Jesse nodded.

Barry held out his phone. 'I'll show you what to do.'

Barry got Jesse logged on. They found a baseball game in progress, and Jesse waited his turn to come up to bat. Barry kept moving, so Jesse jogged along beside him. He was focused on the phone, the world of AthleteAnimalz, not paying attention.

'Gotta piss,' Barry said abruptly.

Jesse looked up. They were no longer outside the library. They were no longer on Boylston Street. 'What?' He let the phone fall down to his side. For the first time, he didn't feel so good about things. Jesse wasn't allowed to wander alone in the big city. Jesse didn't *want* to wander alone in the big city.

'Gonna piss. You know, waggle the willie, wet the snake, walk the dog.' The older boy took back his phone, started unsnapping his jeans.

Jesse looked away, nervousness growing. They seemed to be behind one of the restaurants, next to some Dumpsters. The smell hit him at the same time as his fear, and he recoiled, took a step.

'What? It's nothing but us boys here. That a problem for you?'

Jesse shook his head, but he still didn't look up. He was sweating. Could feel it suddenly streaking down his face, neck, the small of his back. His stomach roiled. He didn't feel good. Couldn't say why, but he did not feel good.

Barry had his pants down; he was holding his privates.

'Come on, Jesse. Sheesh. Just a penis; you got one, too, right?'

'I want to go home,' Jesse whispered.

Then Barry said, in a voice Jesse hadn't heard before, 'Well you should've thought of that about thirty minutes ago. Before you left the library with someone you'd never met before.'

Jesse looked up then. He looked straight into the eyes of Stranger Danger, and he suddenly understood everything his mother had ever told him, every mistake he'd ever made, every bad thing that was about to happen to him.

Just as another voice said, 'What'cha doing, boys?'

Jesse turned around to find the woman right behind him. She had brown hair scraped back into a ponytail and the scariest blue eyes he'd ever seen. Jesse registered two things at once. She was smiling at him in a way that had him just as uncomfortable as the boy Barry did, and she was holding a gun.

She looked right at Jesse, put a finger to her lips. 'Shhh.'

Then she turned to the older boy.

'What the fuck,' Barry said.

'Pink Poodle, I presume?'

'Who the hell are you?'

'Helmet Hippo. I've been watching you. You are a very naughty boy.'

The gun came up. The older boy stepped back.

At the last second, Jesse closed his eyes. At the last second, Jesse covered his ears.

He still heard:

'Wait, wait. What the hell. I'm just a kid—'

'Everyone dies sometime.'

'I didn't. I never. I didn't mean—'

'Be brave.'

'Wait! I'll stop, I'll change, I swear! I'm just a kid! *Wait*—'

A sound, somewhere between a pop and boom. Once. Twice.

Then nothing.

Jesse counted to five. Then slowly, he opened his eyes. He saw the older boy's feet poking out from behind the Dumpster. He saw the woman bending over those feet.

Then the woman straightened, slipped her gun into a leather bag on her hip, and turned toward Jesse.

He whimpered, stepped back.

But she merely smiled at him, extending a hand as if in greeting.

'Hello,' she said. 'Have we met yet? Don't worry. My name is Abigail.'

# 24

I don't remember making it home from BPD headquarters. I suppose Tulip and I managed the subway. In the constant stream of humanity boarding the late afternoon train, it's easy enough to slip through, for a woman and a dog to go unnoticed.

We would've taken the orange line from Roxbury to Downtown Crossing, then changed to the red line for Harvard Square. The transfer station at Downtown Crossing would've been a hot, crowded mess, filled with people already glazed over from the day's events, moving on autopilot, just wanting to go home.

We would've walked twelve minutes from Harvard Square, up Garden Street past the snow-covered Cambridge Commons, left onto Concord Avenue, right at the parking lot for the Harvard College Observatory, onto Madison. Or maybe we ran. Not the best side-walks; footing would've been treacherous given first the soft snowflakes, then a sharper, icier drizzle that would've pelted the top of our down-turned heads and turned the brick pavers at Harvard Square into a particularly slippery mess.

I don't remember, my memory having one of its fickle moments. The price of forgetting. The ongoing cost of coping with a childhood that should've broken me but didn't. I must have gone home, though. Right? Where else would I have gone from police headquarters? What else would I have done?

I slept. I know that much. At a certain point, I was in my own room in my own bed, Tulip nestled beside me, back to back. I woke up once, noted the clock reading 8 p.m., and was grateful, after the past forty-eight hours, that I didn't have work. Then my eyes closed and I had the craziest dream.

My mother was in the backyard. She had a shovel. She was digging a hole. It was dark and stormy out. Rain lashing, wind whipping. A flashlight stood upright on the ground next to her, illuminating pelting raindrops, wind-tossed debris. From time to time, the blade of the shovel would catch the faint yellow beam, wink in the light. Up, down. Up, down.

I stood at a window. It was tall for me. I was on my tippy toes so I could peer out, and I'd been watching for a while, because my toes ached and my calves burned, but I couldn't stop looking. The wink of the spade. Up, down. Up, down.

My mother wore her favorite nightgown. It was pale yellow with tiny blue flowers and green leaves. The rain had plastered it to her skinny frame, molding wiry legs and whip-thin arms as she bent and heaved spadefuls of dirt. Her long brown hair was loose, wet hanks stuck to her hollowed-out cheeks.

Up, down. Up, down.

The hole grew bigger. Not too big. Big enough.

Then, the baby, crying down the hall.

My mother heard it at the same time I did. Her head came up. The shovel stilled in her hands. She turned toward the window. She looked right at me. She smiled, her mouth a gaping black maw, and her hair suddenly turned to hissing snakes around her head.

I let go of the windowsill. I fell back. Bumped my head against a coffee table, but I didn't cry out. I scrambled to my little feet and I began to run.

Down the hall. Baby crying.

Had to get there first.

The creak of the back door opening. My mother, stepping through the back door into the filthy little kitchen, bare, bony feet caked with mud.

Down the hall. Baby crying.

Had to get there first.

My fisted hands chugged. My little knees went up and down as fast as my mother's spade had. Running, running, running. Hearing my panting breath, feeling my pounding chest. Running, running, running.

'Charlie,' my mother sang out behind me. 'Come out, come out, wherever you are.'

Down the hall. Baby crying.

Had to get there first.

'Come to your mommy, Charlie. Remember, Charlie . . . Don't make me angry.'

Then I was there, yanking open the closet door. No crib. No bassinet. A dresser drawer, padded with blankets and placed on the floor.

Footsteps, closer. Steady. Sure.

'Come out, come out, wherever you are.'

The wink of the shovel blade, up, down, up down, up down.

I scooped up the baby, grabbed the pile of blankets, and ran for the front door. I bolted out into the wild night. Whipping wind. Lashing rain. Thundering sky. Couldn't notice. Couldn't care.

'Charlie. I see you. Charlie! Don't make me angry . . .'

I headed straight into the woods. Knew where I was going. Practiced this. Had known. Had to try. Had to do something. With my small little hands and my small little legs, but my big heart, nearly bursting in my chest.

'Charlie . . . Don't make me angry.'

The broad-leafed tree was a dozen trunks back. Last-second pause, taking the longest blanket and using it to tie the baby in a sling against my chest. I'd practiced this before, too. Sometimes, I carried the baby around the house this way, because then she didn't cry, and when she didn't cry, life was better for all of us.

Blanket was wet. Baby was wet. I was wet.

My mother's voice, not so far behind me now. 'Charlie Grant, come here this minute. Charlene Grant, don't make me angry!'

I reached for the nearest branch, low, slippery, not too big, and with determined little fists, I grabbed it with both hands and scrambled up to the first tree branch.

Moving fast and desperate. All up, no down. Tree wasn't that big, but neither was I. If I could just keep moving, monkey-climb my way to the top . . .

My mother was afraid of heights. She would follow me out, she would follow us down, but she would never follow me up.

Below me, her sudden screech.

'Charlene Grant! You come down here. Right now! Do you hear me, young lady? Charlene Grant, you do as your mother says!'

Swinging up and up. Not looking down. Not wanting to think about the drop, the fall, the squirmy weight of the baby. Not wanting to see my mother standing below, her hands on her hips, glaring at me with her snake-like hair and black maw mouth and the shovel that would go up down, up down, up down. Forming the hole. Not too big. Big enough.

At last I ran out of branches. Had to stop, nestled in the junction, shivering uncontrollably, rain streaming down my face, one hand clinging to a branch beside my head, the other wrapped around the baby.

My mother still screamed, but the wind was now whipping her words away. From this height, she was smaller, harder to see. From this height, I didn't have to be scared of her anymore.

Eventually she would wear herself out. Eventually she would return inside and, caked in mud and filth and leaves, curl up on the couch and fall asleep. Then I would carefully make my way back down.

I would change the baby's diaper, wrap her in fresh blankets I'd left warming on the radiator. I'd feed her a cold bottle, sitting cross-legged on the floor with her propped on my lap.

The baby would fall asleep. Then I would return her to the nest in the hall closet, before heading back outside and refilling the tiny hole, working, just as my mother had done, by the glow of a flashlight.

If I did everything right, in the morning, there would be no sign of tonight. It would be erased, a bad dream that never happened. And my mother would wake up happy, maybe singing lightly under her breath, and she would dance around the house with me, giddy and gay, and she would kiss and hug the baby, and everything would be all right again. She would love us.

For a little bit, anyway.

I nestled deeper into the tree limbs. Felt the warmth of the baby against my chest. Hoped she felt my warmth, too, as I wrapped my other arm around her and held on tight.

'It's okay,' I whispered to her now. 'Almost done now. Almost safe.'

She was no longer crying. Instead, she stared up at me with big brown eyes.

Then her little face lit up in a giant toothless grin.

She beamed up at me, my beautiful baby sister, Abigail.

# 25

D.D. made it to the restaurant on time. Alex had selected the Legal Seafood on the water, next to the Boston aquarium. It was close to the airport, offered good food and great views. D.D. knew the restaurant well, had used to walk there from her North End condo. Walking, however, was much easier than navigating the crush of rush-hour traffic.

She plodded up 93, then looped through an elaborate off-ramp pattern that mostly involved sitting at red lights for three to four turns at a time.

By the time she arrived at the waterfront location, she was tense, frazzled, and pretty sure she had sweat through the blue silk blouse she'd bought the week before, in anticipation of meeting her mother.

Across from the restaurant was a public parking garage. D.D. wound her way up the levels until she was lucky enough to discover an empty space, way in the back, as far away from the stairwell as one could get. The space was marked *Compact Only*. She wedged her Crown Vic carefully into the narrow confines, then eased open her door.

As she stepped out of her car, the icy cold sliced through her like a knife. She went from overheated to shivering in a matter of seconds.

She should start walking, warm herself up.

She stood there instead, feeling like a little girl again, dragging her feet as she got home from school, because she had another note from her teacher in her backpack and her mother would be angry again. Worse, her mother would never say a word. She'd just thin her lips and look at her in a way D.D. knew too well.

*I am a grown adult*, D.D. reminded herself. *A top detective, respected by cops, feared by felons.*

It wasn't working for her yet. She wanted it to, but it wasn't working.

She thought of Alex and baby Jack instead. The way Alex was no doubt sitting patiently with her parents, easing them into their visit, encouraging them to fuss over their grandchild. The way Alex would look up when she finally walked into the restaurant. The way he would smile, instantly, genuinely, as she appeared table-side.

D.D. started walking, one black-booted step in front of another as she made her way across the garage, down the stairwell, then across the snowy street until she arrived in front of the bustling restaurant.

Final deep breath. Reminding herself that a woman who worked death investigations could surely handle one dinner with her own parents.

Her hands trembled.

She went in.

Alex and her parents were seated in the very back, in a corner booth. It was slightly quieter back there, but still busy enough given a Thursday night at a major Boston restaurant. A waiter had performed the high chair trick – turning it over so that Jack's car seat fit snugly between the wooden legs. Alex sat on the right side of the booth, her parents side by side on the left.

Her mom, Patsy, sported a Florida tan, beautiful silver-blond hair, and an elegantly carved face that had obviously served as the model for D.D.'s own. She was wearing linen slacks and a sea foam green sleeveless sweater over a thin white shirt – a snow bird trying to adjust for the northern climate, but forgetting just how cold and bitter January in Boston could be. D.D.'s father, Roy, equally fit and trim, also appeared as if he'd been plucked from the golf course, wearing a navy blue sports jacket over a white-and-blue striped polo shirt.

Alex, as she'd predicted, spotted her first. He wore one of her favorite dark red cashmere sweaters over a black turtleneck. When he saw her, his blue eyes lit up, and the corners crinkled with the full force of his smile.

She faltered. She went to take a step and actually stumbled a little. Because it hit her, halfway across the extremely loud and crowded restaurant, that the most handsome man in the place belonged to her. Smiled for her. Sat patiently, with their baby and her parents, for her.

And it terrified her, because for every ounce of love she felt for him, she felt simultaneously, like a bank of black clouds across the sun, that she wasn't worthy. That a man this handsome, accomplished, and smart belonged more to the likes of her parents than to the likes of her.

Which pissed her off all over again. All these years later, she did not want to feel that small. Maybe she hadn't been the child her parents had wanted her to be. But she was the adult she needed to be, and that ought to be enough.

D.D. thrust up her chin and strode across the restaurant.

She arrived in front of the table. Opened her mouth to declare loudly, 'Welcome, Mom, howdy, Dad, have a good flight?'

Just as her pager chimed to life.

Alex spoke first. 'Everything okay?'

D.D. unclipped the pager, read the brief message. Closed her eyes. 'I gotta go.'

'What?' Her mother, addressing her for the first time, already sounded strident.

'I'm sorry.' D.D. did her best to gather her wits. She leaned over, kissed her mother on the cheek, then her father. When she spoke, however, she looked at Alex, as his expression was easier to take. 'Another shooting,' she informed him.

'Same case?'

'Exactly. Near Copley, so at least I'm close.'

'I don't understand.' D.D.'s mother again.

'I'm in the middle of a major case, a string of murders. Another just happened. I have to go.'

'But . . . but . . . you just got here.'

'Apparently, the killer didn't get that memo.'

'D.D. Warren—'

'Mom,' D.D. held up a hand, strove for a neutral tone of voice. 'I appreciate you coming up from Florida. I know it's cold and you don't like it here. But . . . This is my job. I'm not just a detective, I'm the lead investigator. Buck stops here.'

Her father took her mother's hand, as if to calm her. 'Will you be back?'

His voice had a quiver she didn't remember hearing before. And now, as she looked closer, she saw fresh lines around his eyes, skin sagging beneath his chin, age spots on the backs of his hands. Seventy-eight, it occurred to her. Her parents were seventy-eight years old. Not ancient, but definitely getting up there, and how many more of these trips would they be able to make? How many more years would they have with her and their baby grandson?

'Probably not for dinner,' she whispered.

'So we'll see you in the morning.'

'I could do an early breakfast, if you'd like, or maybe catch up for lunch if that's better for you.'

'I don't understand,' her mother interjected, still sounding disapproving. 'It's seven o'clock at night. You just got off work, now you're going back to work, and still the best you can do is an early breakfast?'

'Welcome to Boston Homicide.'

'What about Jack? You have a baby now. What about him?'

D.D. hadn't even greeted her son yet. She'd kissed her parents, spoken to Alex, but her baby . . .

She bent over his car seat. Jack was asleep, oblivious to the growing drama around him. His lips were pursed into a little rosebud, his hands fisted on his blue-clothed tummy. A new bib around his neck proclaimed, 'Someone in Florida loves me.'

D.D. glanced up at her parents. 'That's adorable, thank you.'

Her pager chimed again. She closed her eyes, feeling the relentless pull.

'Go,' Alex said softly. 'It's okay. I'll handle it.'

'I owe you,' she mouthed at him, over their son's sleeping form.

He nodded, a shade grim, so apparently her parents' charms weren't lost on him.

D.D. placed her lips against Jack's forehead. She inhaled the scent of baby powder, felt the silky wisps of his hair. And for a second, she could actually agree with her mother. What was she doing, walking away from this?

'I'll call you in the morning,' D.D. said to the table.

She walked back through the restaurant, bracing herself for the cold as well as the relentless weight of her mother's disappointment.

As the crow flies, Copley Square was only a hop, skip, and a jump from the waterfront. Given Boston traffic, further snarled by a wintry mix of light snow and icy sleet, it took D.D. nearly forty-five minutes to navigate the handful of miles. She didn't bother with the legalities of parking, but pulled up on the curb right behind a string of police cruisers.

She stepped out of her car to find Detective O already waiting for her.

Whatever plans D.D. had had for the evening, O's had obviously been better. The young detective had her dark hair piled on top of her head in a loose knot of curls. Mascara touched up her exotic eyes and deep red lipstick enhanced her lips, while beneath her long, black wool coat, she wore a knee-length dress paired with black leather stiletto boots. She looked softer, rounder, more feminine. A look D.D. herself had never been able to pull off, but that some guy somewhere had probably really appreciated.

O caught her stare. 'Police pager: best birth control invented by man,' she drawled.

'Funny, I used to say the same thing.'

O arched a brow, given D.D.'s new mom status.

'Condoms aren't a hundred per cent effective either,' D.D. said defensively.

'I'll remember that.'

D.D. shut her door. Donned her fleece-lined black leather gloves, pulled down her black wool hat. 'So, what do we have?'

'Dead kid, back alley. Scared kid, back of patrol car.'

'I thought this was related to our sex offender shootings.'

'Dead kid was the offender. Scared kid the victim.'

D.D. digested this, eyes widening. 'Scared kid didn't pull the trigger, did he?'

'Nope. But he saw who did. Lone female.' O broke into a grim smile. 'Small build, small gun. World's craziest blue eyes, he said, and brown hair, scraped back into a ponytail.'

'Charlene Grant,' D.D. breathed.

'Aka Abigail.'

D.D. tended the crime scene first. Given the high traffic around Copley, the ME's office had already removed the body. No sign of Neil, so maybe he'd accompanied the body to the morgue. She'd given Phil the night off, which left her and O to do the honors. As O had obviously been at the scene for a bit, D.D. did her best to come up to speed.

Squatting down inside the crime scene tape, D.D. could just make out the faint impression of the already-removed corpse, which formed a literal snow angel on the white-dusted alley. Victim had been tall. Long splayed legs, one dangling arm.

She didn't see the outline of the right arm. Maybe the victim had it over his chest. Maybe he'd been raising it in front of his face at the time of the shooting. Pedophile or not, that image disturbed her, to be shot down in cold blood.

'How old?' she asked Detective O, who stood behind her, shivering in her short dress and boots.

'Victim gave his name as Barry. Said he was sixteen.'

'And he targeted another kid?'

'Seven-year-old boy. Apparently "met" him on a gaming website. Arranged to meet him at the Boston Public Library. Then lured him outside.'

D.D. shook her head. Even after O's lecture on sex predators becoming younger and younger, sixteen was hard to take. 'Has the body been identified?'

'Uniformed officers are canvassing the area now. He was on foot, so maybe someone local will recognize him.'

'There's a doorstop conversation,' D.D. muttered. 'First off, we regret to inform you that your son is dead. Secondly, he was most likely killed while sexually assaulting another child. Shit.'

Detective O didn't say anything; maybe she shared the sentiment.

'So the older boy got the younger boy outside, then led him here.' D.D. looked around. They were tucked in a back Dumpster area, servicing local establishments. It was secluded, rank-smelling. But not totally private. One end was open to the side street, not to mention they stood before a heavy metal service door used by personnel as they hauled out trash.

'Wonder if he scoped the area out before,' D.D. thought out loud. 'Learned the traffic patterns of this alleyway, felt comfortable. Or maybe, as you explained before, it was a case of impulse meeting opportunity. The seven year old had followed, so the sixteen year old decided to see what he could do.'

Detective O shrugged; given that the perpetrator was now dead, there wasn't any way of answering such questions.

'The sixteen year old had just exposed himself,' O said, 'when the woman appeared. The victim didn't recognize her and has no memory of her following them. But she seemed to know the sixteen year old, implied that she'd been watching him. She identified herself as a gamer from the same website.'

D.D. stood up, frowning. 'Really? So while one user is targeting kids, another user is targeting the predator. And both were able to find their victims in real life? But how? Isn't that supposed to be the hard part?'

'Sixteen year old probably targeted the younger based on his stated interest in the Red Sox. Once sixteen year old established that the boy lived in Boston, he sent an email inviting him to the library, which, as a public place, seemed harmless enough.'

'Lured him in.'

'Exactly. As for our Femme Nikita,' O went on, 'there are several tools available to her. Personally, I'd start by running my target's user name through Spokeo, to find other sites he visited. Given "Barry" was sixteen, one of the first sites that would probably come up is his Facebook page. So I'd visit there, study his photo, identify friends, hobbies, interests. Better yet, Facebook has a feature called Facebook Places or Check In. Meaning that when "Barry" posts while at the Boston library, that site automatically shows up as part of the post. Now, La Femme Nikita can follow all of Barry's comings and goings, including that he was at the Boston Public Library tonight. Assuming she has a smartphone, she doesn't even need to lug around a laptop. She simply carries her smartphone in one hand, her gun in the other, and lets Barry tell her exactly where he's going and what he's doing. Takes all the fun out of stalking if you ask me.'

D.D. shook her head, gazing down at the snowy shadow of a dead kid. 'But you said the sixteen year old targeted his victim at a gaming website, not the chat room you and Phil discussed earlier?'

'Not the chat room. AthleteAnimalz.com, however, is a major corporate kiddie site. Chances are, our first two pedophiles roamed there as well.'

'Meaning that's the connection, not the chat room.'

'Or all of the above. The pedophile community isn't that large. It's not unreasonable that their paths crossed in several different sites on the Web.'

D.D. could buy that. She straightened, working on getting the choreography established in her head. 'Sixteen-year-old boy targets seven-year-old boy. Lures him to dark alley. Then . . . this woman appears. What happened next?'

'According to our seven-year-old witness, she was already holding the twenty-two. Pretty much ignored the younger boy, homed straight in on Barry. Of course, at this point, Barry had his pants unzipped and was holding his penis, making himself the obvious target.'

'What'd she say?'

'Not much. Confirmed the older boy's Internet identity as Pink Poodle—'

'A sixteen-year-old boy is Pink Poodle?'

'Welcome to the Internet. And for the record, that strategy helped him. The seven year old agreed to meet tonight in part because he assumed he'd be meeting a girl, and who's afraid of a girl?'

'Shit,' D.D. said.

'The shooter then identified herself as Helmet Hippo, another user from the website. Teenager tried to defend himself. Argued his age, said he'd change.'

D.D. looked down at the snow angel. 'Obviously, that didn't work.' But it bothered her again. Sixteen years old. Shot down in cold blood. What if he could've changed? The courts probably wouldn't have tried him as an adult, but another citizen had. Tried him and executed him in a matter of minutes.

'The woman stated he'd been a very naughty boy, ordered him to be brave, then shot him.'

'Just like that?'

'Just like that. Granted, our witness is young and traumatized, but his best guess is that the entire altercation took about three minutes.'

'Be brave, you said. Was there a note?' D.D. asked. 'Everyone has to die sometime, yada yada yada.'

'Tucked inside the victim's coat. Most likely written in advance, as, according to the witness, she didn't have time to write anything at the scene. He saw her bend over the body, however, probably placing the paper in the victim's jacket.'

'So definitely the same shooter. Refining her game now. Not just picking off pedophiles, but rescuing their victims.'

'In her mind, I'm sure she had a good night.'

'What happened after she shot the sixteen year old?'

'The shooter introduced herself to the witness, told him not to worry, then walked away.'

D.D. arched a brow. 'Which way did she exit?'

'To the left. The boy didn't follow, though. He stood there a minute longer, then bolted back to the library, where his mother had alerted the staff she couldn't find him. They were going to lock down, police had just been called, when he came tearing up the steps. He was hysterical, she became hysterical. It took five or ten minutes to sort things out. Then uniformed officers immediately dispatched to this location, while broadcasting the woman's description, but no hits.'

D.D. wasn't surprised. Anyone could disappear in Boston. Which was why Charlene Grant originally moved here.

D.D. thought about it. 'That the Internet user was sixteen should've startled her. Made her pause, ask more questions, something. But it didn't. Meaning your theory stands to reason – she'd been stalking her target for a bit, visiting his Facebook page, maybe even following him in person on other occasions. She wasn't surprised by his age or his actions. She expected both.'

'Premeditation,' O supplied. 'Planning. Strategy.'

'Smart. Adept with computers. Patient.'

'Controlled,' O added to their profile of the shooter. 'She shot the sixteen year old, then walked away. No collateral damage, no fussing with the witness. Just in, out, done.'

'Where's the witness now?'

'Back of a squad car with his mother. We're arranging for a forensic interviewer who specializes in children to meet them at HQ.'

'Can he talk?'

O shrugged. 'Last time I saw him, he clung to his mother and didn't say a word.'

'I'd like to try.'

O hesitated. D.D. looked at her. 'What?'

'You have any experience with kids?'

'Worked a case where a four year old was the prime witness.'

'Look, you may be older and wiser,' O drawled, 'but I'm sex crimes, and unfortunately, most of my cases involve questioning kids. So take it from me, you can't screw this up. You lead the witness here, and that contamination will carry. Then the entire interview will be tossed, and we'll have no grounds for arresting our prime suspect, Charlene blah blah Grant. You gotta be smart.'

'Then I'll leave the stupid questions at home.'

O still didn't seem happy, but she turned away from the alley, returning in the direction of the flashing cruiser lights. The little boy and his mother were huddled in the back of the first patrol car. The door was open, probably to make them feel less like prisoners. But it also let in the chill, and both the boy and his mother were shivering. The mom held a cardboard cup of steaming beverage, probably coffee, but she wasn't drinking it. Just holding it, as if willing the warmth to make a difference.

The little boy didn't look up when they approached. He was leaning against his mother's side, his tiny form nearly lost in an oversized black winter coat, hat, scarf, and mittens. D.D. had an impression of dark eyes and a pale pinched face, then he turned away from her.

The mother had her left arm around her son. She had the same pale features and haunted expression as the boy. But her jaw was set, her lips thinned into a resolute line.

'Sergeant Detective D.D. Warren,' D.D. said to introduce herself. It sounded as if they'd already met O.

'Jennifer Germaine.' The woman nodded, as she didn't have a free hand to offer. She nudged her son, but he didn't look up. 'My son, Jesse,' she said after another moment.

'How are you doing, Jesse?' D.D. asked.

The boy didn't answer.

'Fair enough,' she agreed. 'I'm not having the best night either.'

He turned slightly, stared at her with a wary expression.

'I'm supposed to be having dinner with my mother. She came all the way from Florida to see me. But I had to leave. She's not very happy with me. It doesn't feel good, to have my mom not very happy with me.'

Jesse's lower lip trembled.

'But I also know she understands,' D.D. continued. 'It's the cool thing about moms. They always love us, huh?'

Jennifer's arm tightened around her son. He pressed himself harder against her side.

'I'm sorry,' he whispered, his voice coming out hoarse and raspy. Maybe from crying now, or screaming earlier.

'Why are you sorry?' D.D. asked, keeping her voice conversational.

'I was a bad boy.'

'Why do you say that?' Open-ended questions. That was the deal with kids – can't imply, can't lead, can only ask open-ended questions.

'Stranger danger. Don't talk to strangers online. Don't meet strangers. Don't go away with strangers. My mommy told me. I'm sorry, Mommy. I'm sorry, I'm sorry, I'm sorry.'

The little boy started to cry. His mother stroked his hair, then leaned over his head, murmuring low words of comfort.

'Thank you for returning to the library tonight,' D.D. said.

The boy looked up slightly.

'That was quick thinking. You had to find your way back through the city streets, which I personally find very confusing at night. But you did. You found your mother, you notified the police. Very brave of you. Have you ever walked the city alone, Jesse?'

The boy shook his head.

'Then kudos. You kept a cool head. Bet your mom's pretty proud of you for that.'

Jennifer nodded against the top of her son's head.

'I need you to be brave for me now, Jesse. Just a little bit longer, okay? Just relax, snuggled up next to your mom, and think about a couple of things for me.'

The little boy nodded, just slightly.

'Can you tell us what happened tonight, Jesse? In your own words. Take your time.'

Jesse didn't start talking right away. His mother bent over again. 'Jenny and Jesse against the world,' D.D. heard her whisper to him. 'Remember, Jenny and Jesse against the world. Hold my hand. We can do this.'

The little boy took his mother's hand. Then, he began to speak.

It was a pretty straightforward tale. A sixteen-year-old boy named Barry spent his afternoons gaming online as a pink poodle. He racked up points, he gained attention. He sent out emails to other gamers, offering friendship and help.

Jesse had taken the bait.

He'd assumed he had nothing to fear from a poodle, a meeting in a public library, and a rendezvous with a presumed girl. And so it went, right up to the second Jesse found himself standing in a back alley, too scared to run, too shocked to scream.

He couldn't tell them much about the woman. Her arrival had startled him. Her gun had terrified him. Mostly, he remembered her eyes. Bright, bright blue eyes.

'Crazy eyes,' Jesse breathed softly. 'Creepy, like blue cat eyes.' He looked up at them. 'I think she's an alien or maybe a robot or a monster. She . . . she hurt him. And . . . and I was happy.'

His gaze dropped again, and he buried himself suddenly, tightly, into his mother's embrace.

'I'm sorry,' the little boy moaned, voice muffled against his mother's coat. 'I was bad. And there was this noise, and he's dead. And I was bad and I'm sorry, I'm sorry, I'm sorry. Mommy, I won't ever do it again. I promise, I promise, I promise.'

D.D. looked away. She didn't know what hurt worse, the boy's obvious pain, or his mother's, as she put her other arm around him and rocked him against her, trying to soothe, clearly knowing it wasn't enough.

'I would like to take him home,' the woman said. 'It's late.' She added as an afterthought, 'He has school tomorrow.'

Then her face suddenly crumpled, as if understanding for the first time that school in the morning probably wasn't going to happen. That tonight had been bigger than that. That this was one of those things that would take more than a good night's sleep to recover from.

Detective O stepped forward to explain about the interview with the forensic specialist, which needed to happen sooner versus later, as children's memories were highly pliable.

Jesse's mom shook her head, clearly becoming as overwhelmed and shell-shocked as her son.

D.D. reached out and squeezed the woman's hand. 'Just another hour,' she said encouragingly to the woman. 'Then you can both go home. And tomorrow will be better than today, and the next day will be better than that. It will get better.'

The woman looked at her. 'I love him so much.'

'I know.'

'I would do anything for him. I would give my life for him. I was just looking up a school assignment. Fifteen minutes we'd be apart. We'd done it before and he's at that age. He doesn't always want his mother around anymore. And I want him to feel strong. I want him to feel safe.'

'I know.'

'I would do anything for him,' she repeated.

'The interview will help,' D.D. assured her. 'I know it sounds scary, but telling his story will allow Jesse to own it. It will become less and less something that happened to him, and more and more something he can narrate, take control over. We've seen it with other kids. Talking helps them. Holding it inside, not so good.'

Jenny sighed, rested her cheek on top of her son's head. 'Jenny and Jesse against the world,' she murmured.

'You're a good mom.'

'I should've done more.'

'Story of a mother's life.'

'Do you have a child?'

'Ten weeks old, already the love of my life.'

'What would you do?'

'I hope I never have to find out.'

'Please . . .'

D.D. hesitated, then answered as honestly as she could: 'I would try to help him find his strength. The bad part already happened. Now it's about helping Jesse find his way to the other side. Where he's no longer the victim, but the one in control. Where he can feel strong. Where he can feel safe.'

The woman stared at her, seemed to be studying her face. 'We'll go to headquarters,' she said at last. 'We'll meet with the inter-view . . . expert.'

'We'll have a victim's advocate meet you there as well,' D.D. told her. 'There are resources for you and your son. Please don't be afraid to use them.'

D.D. handed over her card, then straightened, jamming her freezing cold gloved hands back into her coat pockets.

'Thank you for your help, Jesse,' D.D. said. 'I appreciate you answering my questions.'

The boy didn't look up, didn't respond.

She said to his mother: 'Take care of your son.'

'Oh, I will, Detective. I will.'

D.D. stepped away, heading over to O. She'd just paused beside the sex crimes detective when a startled cry went up. Both investigators turned to see a uniformed officer waving for them furiously from the first patrol car.

'Detectives,' he called. 'Quick! You gotta see this!'

D.D. and O exchanged glances, then made their way precariously down the icy sidewalk. The uniformed patrol officer had the passenger-side door open and was gesturing inside excitedly.

'On the dashboard,' he said urgently. 'Don't move it. I'd just set it there, you know, to deliver to the evidence room later. Course, I got the heat running, then when I looked in . . .'

It appeared to be the shooter's note, now encased in clear plastic. A full sheet, the letters scripted in the familiar precisely formed, elegantly rounded letters. Except, as D.D. looked closer, she suddenly spotted other letters so small and jumbled together, they first appeared as a blemish or blur.

She looked up abruptly, glancing at the uniformed officer. 'Did you touch this, mess with it in any way?'

She stood back, allowed O to take a look.

'No, no, no,' Officer Piotrow assured her hastily. 'It's the heat. When I saw that something seemed to have happened, I picked up the note, and I'll be damned if the letters didn't immediately disappear. But then I set the paper back down on the hot dash . . .'

D.D. felt her heart quicken.

'I think it's lemon juice,' the officer was saying. 'My kid did this experiment once in grade school. You can write secret notes with lemon juice – the words will disappear when the lemon juice dries, but reappear when you hold the note over a hot lightbulb. I think my dash is the lightbulb.'

'A note within a note,' Detective O murmured, still leaning over the paper. 'Different penmanship.'

'Different sentiment,' D.D. replied tersely, chewing her lower lip.

The first note, *Everyone dies sometime. Be brave*, was scrawled in the usual large rounded script.

In contrast, the hidden message was much smaller, jumbled letters hastily scrawled and crammed into a space no bigger than a dime.

An order. A taunt. Or maybe even a plea:

Two simple words: *Catch Me.*

# 26

Hello. My name is Abigail.
    Don't worry, we've met.
    Trust me, and I will take care of you.
    Don't you trust me?
    Hello. My name is Abigail.

# 27

It felt good to hit.

I liked the satisfying thwack of my gloved fist making hard contact with the heavy bag. I liked the feel of my front leg pivoting, my hips rotating, and my shoulder rolling as I snapped my entire body behind the blow. Jab, jab, jab, uppercut, roundhouse, feint left, left hook downstairs, left hook upstairs, second roundhouse, V-step right, jab left, punch right, dodge low, uppercut, repeat. Hit, move, hit harder, move faster. Hit.

Four thirty a.m. Pitch-black outside. Brutally cold. Definitely night, not day. All over the city, sane, well-adjusted people were snug in their beds, sound asleep.

I stood alone in the middle of a twenty-four-hour gym in Cambridge and pounded the crap out of the heavy bag. I'd been at it a bit. Long enough that my long brown hair was plastered to my head, I'd soaked through my quick-dry gym clothes, and my arms and legs were glazed in sweat. When I landed a particularly forceful blow, perspiration sprayed from my arms onto the blue mat.

I'm not a pretty girl – my figure is too gaunt, my face too harsh these days. But I'm strong, and in the wall of mirrors across from me, I took pride in the muscles rippling across my shoulders, the curve of my biceps, the fierce look on my face. If there were men in the gym right now, working their way through their own regimens, they'd feel a need to comment. Make light of my sweaty form, raise a brow at my go-for-broke style, ask me what his name was and what he did to make me so angry.

Even better reason for me to arrive at four in the morning, running from uneasy dreams and a screwed-up internal clock that wasn't used to sleeping at night anyway.

Alone, I could hit as hard as I wanted to for as long as I wanted.

Alone, I didn't have to apologize for being me.

Girls get a raw deal, I think. When boys brawl, tumble, tackle, it's all 'Boys will be boys'. A little girl lashes out, and immediately it's 'Hands are for holding, hands are for hugging'.

Boys are encouraged to grow strong, to inspect their scrawny arms and thin chests for the first sign of muscular bulk. Girls, by the time they're eight, are already overanalyzing their waistlines, worrying about the dreaded muffin top. We have no concept of gaining muscle, just an enduring aversion to gaining fat.

Girls are complimented on beauty, flexibility, and grace. But what about the upper body strength it takes to scramble up a tree, or the core muscles involved in swinging across the monkey bars? Young girls perform natural feats of strength on parks and playgrounds all across the country. Parents rarely comment, however, and eventually girls spend more and more time trying to look pretty, which does earn them praise.

Until recently, I wasn't any different.

I had to learn my aggression the hard way. Through practice and repetition and painful reinforcement. By experiencing the cracking neck pain that follows an uppercut to the chin, or the immediate eye-welling sensation of taking a fist to the nose. Pain, I discovered, was fleeting. While the satisfaction of standing my ground, then retaliating fiercely, lasted all afternoon.

I had to learn to go deep inside myself, to a tiny place that had managed to survive all those years with my mother, a place where I could finally stop apologizing and start fighting back.

Around the fourth month of boxing, I happened to catch my reflection in the mirror. I noticed lines in my shoulders, curves on my back. Muscles. From fifty push-ups every morning and every night. From jump roping and heavy bag intervals and speed bag drills. From tripling my daily intake of protein, because for all of my philosophizing, boys are different than girls. They start with more muscle mass, add to it more efficiently, and retain it more effortlessly. Meaning if I wanted to bulk up, I had to eat, eat, eat. Egg whites and chicken sausage, six ounces of boneless chicken breast, six ounces of fish, protein shakes supplemented with peanut butter, plain Greek yogurt supplemented with protein powder.

Eventually my boxing coach moved me on to 'tire work'. Big heavy tractor tires. I sledgehammered them, flipped them, jumped on top of them. By the six-month mark, I'd both leaned down and filled out. People stared at my arms when I went out in public. Teenage boys took notice of the way I moved, granted me more space on a crowded subway. Men looked me in the eye with a bit more respect.

And I liked it. Physical pain is nothing, I've realized. It's letting go of your fear, finding your rage, and feeling strong that make the difference.

Unless it's 2 a.m., and you're dreaming of a baby who couldn't have existed, or your homicidal mother who certainly did, or Stan Miller and the iron spikes protruding from his bloody chest.

Did killing someone make me a badass? Or did it take more courage to continue pounding the heavy bag while my own hollowed-out face mocked me in the far mirror?

I worked the bag for another thirty minutes. Next, I hit the weight machines. Then the StairMaster, followed by jump roping. This was it, my final workout before my once-in-a-lifetime main event. The next thirty-eight hours would be spent on rest and recovery. Like a professional athlete, I would take the final two days before the marathon off. Gotta be fresh for 8 p.m. Saturday. Gotta be ready.

Six a.m., people started arriving, beginning their own daily rituals. I left them behind, staggering into the locker room, where I headed straight into a hot, steamy shower.

I stood there a long time, soaking exhausted muscles.

And I wondered, if I was so strong, if I'd made so much progress in the past year, why was I still so terrified of a baby girl named Abigail?

I walked home from the gym. Watched my breath puff into the single-digit air. Watched the sun crawl its way over the gloomy gray horizon. I strode past yawning college students and hunch-shouldered morning commuters, all of them heading into the brick sprawl of Harvard Square as I worked my way out.

I kept my hands jammed deep in the pockets of my coat for warmth, while my ears were wrapped in a plain brown scarf. The cold didn't bother me. It felt refreshing after my time in the gym. I moseyed along, my body finally wrung out and ready to collapse on my bed.

Times like this, I could almost admire the world around me. I could almost feel the tang of a snowflake on the tip of my nose. Appreciate the way the dawn painted the horizon with streaks of pink and orange and made the densely packed buildings glow.

I didn't want to die.

It came to me, walking fifteen minutes toward my lonely room.

I had regrets. I wasn't a great person. I'd engineered another man's death. I'd done something terrible to my own mother. And I'd lost both of my best friends.

Put it in those terms, and why I even cared about what was going to happen at roughly 8 p.m. tomorrow was a mystery. But I wasn't ready to give up. Maybe my life was one giant fuckup. But I felt . . . I didn't know. As if I was on the edge of discovery. Finally realizing the power of my own arms and legs. Finally, twenty-eight years later, learning how to be me.

I wanted more mornings like this one. More rounds with a heavy bag, more crisp winter days. I wanted to walk the dog that was not my dog, smooth my hands over her sweet face. I wanted to run and laugh and, someday, what the hell, fall in love. Have a couple of kids. Raise them in the mountains where everyone would know their business, but also look them in the eye and smile.

I thought of Officer Mackereth. His invitation to brunch. The fact that I'd worked my final shift tonight and probably wouldn't see him again.

Thirty-seven hours to live.

What was I waiting for? I was who I was. I'd done what I had done. And in a day and a half, what would happen would happen.

No more training. No more planning. No more preparing.

Living. That's the only thing I had left to do. All thirty-seven hours of it.

I started to think about it. Really, truly consider it.

Then I turned the corner toward my house, and discovered my Aunt Nancy standing there.

*

I have known my aunt for nearly twenty years. She is a practical woman – gets up early, goes to bed late, works hard in between. Life has problems, but none that can't be quickly identified and properly tackled. Elbow grease resolves most things. If not, perhaps a plate of freshly baked brownies will do the trick.

In our years together, we've cried a little, hugged on occasion, but laughed most of all. My aunt believes in laughter; you need it to run a business, especially in the hospitality trade.

I valued that about my aunt. What you see is what you get, which made her one of those people you immediately liked when you walked into a room.

So it was doubly strange to stand awkwardly in front of her now, positioned on the covered front porch of a Cambridge triple-decker I'd never expected her to visit. We stood four feet apart, my hands still jammed in my coat pockets, my face more shuttered than I would've liked.

'Charlene,' she said at last, breaking the silence first.

'How did . . . ? When did . . . ?'

'It's time, Charlene. Come home.'

I stared at her a moment longer, trying to process. My post-workout glow vanished. In its place, I felt uneasy.

'Why don't you come inside,' I said at last, reaching into my pocket and fumbling with the house key.

She nodded briskly. I realized for the first time that she wore her long winter coat but no hat or gloves. Her normally pale cheeks had turned pink with the cold, and her slight frame trembled beneath her coat.

I felt bad, hugging her belatedly and feeling her gratefully return the gesture. It should've broken the ice, returned us to normalcy, but instead I felt more confused. Of course my aunt knew where I lived. She was the only person with whom I'd kept in contact. I'd even planned on calling her today to make arrangements for Tulip.

But to see her here. Now. So suddenly. The day before the twenty-first. It spooked me, and I found that as I ushered her into my landlady's house, I kept her slightly in front of me, in my line of sight.

My landlady was an early riser. She looked up from the kitchen table as we entered. She still wore her pink-and-purple striped day robe, but being a woman of a certain age, she could carry it off. She registered my aunt's presence, my first ever guest, and performed a little double take.

I did the honors: 'Ummm, Fran, this is my Aunt Nancy. Aunt Nancy, this is my landlady, Frances Beals.'

My aunt crossed to shake hands politely, and up close, even Fran could see her shiver.

'Have you been outside in this weather? Goodness, you look chilled to the bone! Let me get you a cup of coffee. How do you take it?'

'Black, thank you. Lovely home.'

'Hundred and fifty-three years old,' Fran volunteered, 'but I like to think the old gal doesn't look a day over a hundred.'

'I know how she feels,' my aunt responded.

Frances laughed as she bustled about the kitchen, fetching coffee. I took my aunt's coat, pulled out a chair for her, offered breakfast.

Aunt Nancy shook her head, but in such a way that I didn't believe her. I hung up both of our coats, then returned to the kitchen, inspecting the shelf in the pantry that was marked with my name, before finally settling on some wholegrain bread for toast.

Behind me, Frances resumed talking with my aunt, about the house, Boston, New Hampshire, landlady versus innkeeper. I welcomed their distraction, so that my aunt couldn't see how badly my hands were shaking, and Fran wouldn't notice that all of a sudden I couldn't remember how to work the toaster.

My aunt and I had last spoken by phone two weeks ago. She hadn't mentioned coming. I hadn't mentioned returning. We had a drill. It involved never speaking of the twenty-first. That was the foundation of our relationship, after all – love each other, support each other, and never mention unpleasant truths.

My early childhood had been 'unfortunate'. My mother had been 'misguided'. What happened to Randi, then Jackie, 'tragic'.

You gotta love New Englanders. We can take anything we don't want to face, whitewash it resiliently into a faint echo of itself, then simply lock it away.

I finally managed to get out two slices of bread and slide them into the toaster. While they browned, I found the carton of egg whites and set to scrambling. Working on the stove kept my back to my aunt and my landlady. They seemed content to chat, but from time to time, I could feel my aunt's gaze upon me, assessing.

When the toast popped up, I split the pieces between two plates, topped them both with scrambled egg whites, and carried my concoction to the table.

My aunt looked up from talking with Frances, and her voice immediately trailed off. She stared at my exposed throat, and so did Frances. Belatedly I fingered the bruises from yesterday's session with J.T.

'Good Lord,' my aunt whispered.

'Sparring,' I said defensively.

'Your neck . . . your *hands*.'

Several of my knuckles were bright purple, my left hand abraded, my wrist slightly swollen. I set my aunt's plate down, tucked my hand behind my back. 'Hey, you should see the other guy.'

My aunt and landlady continued to regard me with equal levels of horror.

'It's okay,' I said at last, voice firmer. 'I've taken up boxing, that's all. And I like it. Now, eat.'

I pulled out a chair, sat down next to my aunt, picked up my toast. After another moment, my aunt nodded, maybe to me, maybe to herself, then regarded her own breakfast. She eyed the egg white-topped bread curiously, then gamely took a bite.

'Very nice,' she declared after swallowing. 'Never been a huge fan of egg whites, but with the toast, it works.'

'She's a healthy eater, that one,' Fran said.

I looked at my landlady in surprise. I hadn't realized she'd noticed what I ate, one way or another.

'Hard worker,' Fran continued, apparently taking it upon herself to vouch for my character to my own aunt. 'Tends her night job, comes home to sleep, then is always ready to report to work the next evening. No nonsense, this one.'

'Charlene's got a good head on her shoulders,' my aunt agreed. 'She was always a huge help to me in the B and B. This past year, I've missed her.'

I ate another bite of toast, starting to feel like an outsider in my own life.

'Lease is almost up,' Fran commented. She faced me, instead of my aunt. 'You coming or going?'

'Sunday,' I said.

'You'll give me the answer?'

'Sure.'

My aunt, who understood the relevance of Saturday, frowned at me.

'Gonna include the dog that's not your dog?' my landlady continued. 'You know, the one that's supposed to be outside but is in your room instead?'

I flushed. My aunt arched a brow.

'Yeah . . . um . . . Gonna talk to my aunt about that. See about finding a home for Tulip.'

'Hmmm,' my landlady said. 'By Sunday?'

'Yeah, by Sunday.'

'Dog pees, dog chews, it's out of your pocket.'

'Agreed.'

'I like her,' my aunt said, referring to Frances.

I finally smiled. 'Figured you would.'

By the time I led my aunt down the hall to my little room, I felt nervous again. Like a teenager, anxious to impress her parent with her first dorm room. Look at me, look at the life I created all on my own. Clean sheets, made bed, hung-up clothes, the whole works.

Tulip met us at the door. Judging by the look on her face, she hadn't appreciated being shut up for the morning adventures. Maybe you can take the dog off the street but not the street out of the dog. I thought I knew how she felt.

She refused to greet me, but worked her charm on my aunt instead. My aunt had the typical questions. What was Tulip's name, breed, what a sweet face, what a nice disposition.

While she fawned over the dog that I hoped would become her dog, I went through the requisite hostess motions – found my aunt a chair, refreshed her coffee, then closed the door behind us for privacy. We sat, me on the edge of the bed, her in the lone wooden chair, and Tulip on the floor in between. The conversation almost immediately sputtered out.

'Sorry you had to drive down,' I said at last, not really looking at her, but at the floor beside her chair.

I was thinking of Detective Warren's assessment of Randi and Jackie's attacker. It would be up close and personal. Someone I wouldn't immediately fear. Someone I would welcome with open arms.

I couldn't really be afraid of my aunt.

Could I?

'Have the police learned anything more?' my aunt asked.

'About Randi and Jackie's murders?' I shook my head. 'No. But I'm working with a couple of Boston detectives now. They have some fresh ideas.'

'You still think you'll be next,' my aunt said, a statement not a question.

I nodded.

'You've lost weight, Charlene. You look different. Harder.'

'Probably.'

'It's not good for you, Charlene. The way you're living right now. It's not good for you.'

I surprised myself. I looked up, stared my aunt in the eye, and asked, 'What happened to my mother?'

My aunt's pale blue eyes widened. I don't think I could've shocked her more if I'd blurted out that I was a man trapped in a woman's body. But she caught herself. Fussed with her hair for a second, fingering the fringe around her neck, tucking a short Brillo curl behind her ear.

Her hands were trembling. If I looked harder than she remembered, then she looked older than I remembered. Like the winter had been long and taken some of the fight out of her.

Or maybe she'd spent the past year performing her own count-down to the twenty-first. Which was more stressful, fearing for yourself or for someone you loved?

'What do you think happened to your mother?' she said at last.

'She's dead,' I said flatly. 'And it's my fault. I think . . . I did something . . . resisted, or maybe finally got angry, lost control. I hurt her, though. Badly, and that's why I don't remember. I don't want to face what I did.'

'She's not dead, Charlene. Least, not last I knew.'

'What?'

'Charlene Rosalind Carter Grant,' my aunt stated, and her tone was different now, testing.

'I don't understand.'

'Do you want to understand?'

'Why do you keep asking me questions like that?'

'Because from the first moment I arrived at the hospital, that's what the doctors advised me to do. I was not to tell you what happened, but to give you love and support until one day, when you felt safe enough, you would remember on your own.

'I've waited twenty years, Charlene, never knowing if this might be the week you'd suddenly bring it up or, worse, if this might be the day *she* would magically show up. It's been a lonely vigil. Stressful, too. But I did it, because that's what the doctor said. And I don't have kids, Charlie. I don't know what's right or what's wrong for an eight-year-old girl. The only attempt I had at child rearing was the years I spent trying to rein in my baby sister, and we both know how well that went.' My aunt's voice broke off, the first tinge of bitterness I'd ever heard from her. Then I noticed a sheen in her eyes that had nothing to do with the lighting.

I'd hurt her. I'd made my aunt cry.

Immediately, I wanted to take it all back. I was sorry I'd brought up my mother. I was sorry I'd left New Hampshire. I'd do anything, say anything, return home. I just wanted my aunt to be happy. She was all I had, and I loved her.

And in the next second, I realized how warped that was. How quickly I'd fallen back into the trap – appeasement at all costs. Loving too little and holding on too tight.

Worst part was, my aunt didn't even expect me to appease her. She simply sat there, shoulders squared, jaw set, awaiting my next question.

'If my mother's alive,' I ventured, 'why hasn't she ever contacted me?'

'I don't know.' She hesitated. 'I always figured she would. If not in person, then by mail. Then later, when all this Internet and email and Facebook nonsense started, I worried about that, too. But nothing that I've ever seen, or you've ever said.'

'Nothing, not a single word from her,' I agreed, and took a moment to digest that.

'Charlene Rosalind Carter Grant,' my aunt said again.

'Did I hurt her?' I asked, and my fingers were unconsciously moving across my left side, the top of my thigh, the back of my hand. I couldn't help myself.

'We don't know. When the EMTs arrived, they found you on the floor, seriously injured. In fact, they assumed you were dead.' My aunt spoke the words flatly, having obviously spent the past twenty years turning them over in her head. 'There was no sign of your mother in the house.'

'She ran away?'

'The police put out an APB for her. Especially . . . after the other discoveries they made.' She paused, stared at me again. When I didn't respond . . . 'To date, they've never found her, and I would know if they did. There are charges pending against your mother, Charlene. Serious criminal charges. Which may be why she's never appeared in person. I'm sure she knows I'd toss her sorry ass in jail the second she did.'

I blinked, caught off guard by the vehemence in my aunt's voice.

It occurred to me that I'd spent most of my life fearing that one day I might turn into my crazy mother. Hence the need to forget, avoid, fail to confront. If I didn't remember, I couldn't feel. If I couldn't feel, I couldn't lose my mind. Now I wondered if perhaps I didn't carry a trace of my resilient aunt. A woman who looked, who saw, who endured. A survivor.

Given the date, I would like to be a survivor.

'Do you remember getting your driver's license?' my aunt asked suddenly.

I was startled by the change in topic, nodding faintly.

'You wanted your license to read Charlene Rosalind Carter Grant. And when you were told it couldn't be done, you became upset.'

'I thought it was stupid you could list only one middle name. That if it was supposed to be legal ID, it should carry my full legal name.'

'No,' my aunt said.

I frowned, stared at the floor. And I remembered suddenly, being at the DMV in Tamworth, where you had to go in person to get your first license. It should've been fun and exciting for a teenager, except I was red-faced, sweating, nearly panting from a pressure I couldn't explain. My aunt was talking to me, murmuring something low and calm except I couldn't hear her. My head was on fire, my skull threatening to explode into a thousand bits. I was going to cry, I was going to scream. I mustn't cry, I mustn't scream, so I fisted my hands into my eye sockets to hold in the pain. Then, when that didn't work, I walked over to a wall and beat my head against it, as if that external force would drive out the internal agony. I pounded my forehead hard enough that two uniformed state troopers came running out with their hands on their holstered weapons.

Charlene Rosalind Carter Grant. My driver's license needed to read Charlene Rosalind Carter Grant. It hurt too much to have it any other way. To be anyone else.

'I got sick,' I whispered. 'I had to leave.'

'I finally got you to the car,' my aunt filled in. 'I drove you home, I put you to bed. Then I stayed awake all night, waiting for you to come back down, waiting for you to talk to me, to tell me what you remembered. But you didn't. At seven a.m., you appeared in the kitchen and informed me that if you couldn't have both names on your license, then you would accept Charlene Grant. You never spoke of it again.'

'My headache went away,' I said simply. 'I woke up . . . It was just a driver's license, I decided. Not my name. So it didn't matter. I could . . . It would be okay.'

My aunt smiled at me, but the expression was sad. She reached out, touching the back of my hand, where the thin white scars threaded through fresh purple bruises.

'You're a strong girl, Charlene. If you need to forget the past in order to find your future, I haven't felt it was my place to mess with that. In fact, the doctor told me that forcing you to face things before you were ready would most likely do more harm than good. So I've held my counsel. I've kept my vigil. And I'd do it all over again,

Charlene. Because I was not there when you needed me, and I'll never forgive myself for that. But that's my burden to bear, not yours.'

'My legal name isn't Charlene Rosalind Carter Grant,' I heard myself say.

'That isn't the name on your birth certificate.'

'That's why, at the DMV . . . It had nothing to do with middle names. It was the birth certificate. You showed it to me, and I became angry. Because there was no Rosalind, no Carter. And my head began to hurt. And my stomach . . .'

My aunt didn't say anything.

'But I am Charlene Rosalind Carter Grant,' I tried again, weakly this time, lacking genuine conviction. 'I . . . I *feel* it.'

'It's the name you chose for yourself. There's nothing wrong with that.'

Then it came to me, the list I'd made for Detective Warren. The two names I'd felt compelled to record: Rosalind Grant, Carter Grant. Because it had felt right to write them down. To see them listed on a sheet of paper in a detective's office.

To finally get out what I had failed to tell the nurse.

I looked at my aunt. And I felt the trapdoor suddenly yawn open in the deepest corner of my mind. There was darkness behind it. Ghosts and monsters and things that would make anyone scream in the middle of the night.

Yet I took a step closer. Charlene Rosalind Carter Grant. Rosalind Grant. Carter Grant.

'Baby crying,' I whispered.

'I'm sorry, Charlene.'

'I wanted to tell the nurse. I didn't tell the nurse.'

Another step. The floorboards of my mind, creaking in warning.

'I was too young. I swear it. I was too young.'

'Shhh.' My aunt was standing, her arms reaching toward my shoulders. At her feet, Tulip whined, rose to sitting. 'It's okay, Charlene. It wasn't your fault. It was never your fault.'

'I was just a kid myself!'

'I know, honey, I know.'

'*Baby crying!*' Except she wasn't anymore. She was pale and still as marble. Blue-lipped as I stroked her cold cheek, tried to get her eyes to open, tried to make her flash that wide, beaming grin.

Charlene Rosalind Carter Grant. Rosalind Grant. Carter Grant.

My aunt's arms were around my shoulders. Maybe her hands were even upon my throat. It didn't matter anymore. I sagged into my aunt's embrace. Dying wasn't my greatest fear anymore. Remembering was.

Baby crying, down the hall.

First a little girl. Rosalind Grant.

Then, later, a little boy. Carter Grant.

Then . . .

Charlene Rosalind Carter Grant.

'Shhh,' my aunt murmured. 'If I'd known, I would've come. Please believe me, Charlene. If I'd known, I would've come and taken *all* of you away.'

# 28

'We should arrest her. Immediately. Girl's already squirrelly. If she figures out how close we are to identifying her as the shooter, she'll bolt in a second.'

D.D. sighed. She rubbed a throbbing spot on the back of her neck that had less to do with Detective O's investigative zeal and more to do with the hours of sleep she didn't get, followed by a breakfast with her parents she never should've scheduled. But other than that . . .

She picked up her fourth cup of black coffee, eyed the way her hand performed the over-caffeinated mambo, and took a sip. 'On what grounds?' she quizzed her eager young colleague.

Phil nodded with equal skepticism. He sat beside Neil, the whole team assembled to debrief from last night's shooting and this morning's ongoing discoveries. Murder investigations had a tendency to ebb and flow. This one was currently flowing. Hell, it was nearing flood stage.

'Charlene Grant matches the description of the shooter,' O stated.

Phil was already shaking his head. 'At best, gives us grounds to bring her in for a lineup. But we can't go around arresting all the females in Boston who have brown hair and blue eyes.'

'She owns a twenty-two, same caliber as the murder weapon.'

'As do thousands of people, probably in just this city block.'

'Handwriting analysis,' O snapped, glancing at D.D. 'Especially given the note within the note.'

D.D. shrugged. 'I dropped off Charlie's handwritten list of two names plus the three crime scene notes with Ray Dembowski. He's going to test the notes from the first two shootings this afternoon to see if they have the same hidden message, *Catch Me*. Then, he'll analyze the lemon juice scrawl versus the ink script to determine if the same person wrote both messages on the sheets of paper. Finally, he'll analyze the handwriting of both messages against Charlie's list. But it'll be at least Monday before he has a formal report for us, and he's already complaining about feeling rushed.'

'Motive, means, opportunity!' Detective O threw her hands up in the air. 'Come on, I can't be the only one who thinks Charlie's guilty!'

O had exchanged last night's little black dress for a more sedate light blue Brooks Brothers button-up shirt. It was expertly tailored, perfect for the up-and-coming young detective. Would also look good on TV, D.D. thought, should camera crews catch her making a major arrest.

'It's not a matter of what we think,' D.D. said, less patient, more curt. 'It's a matter of what we can prove.'

Neil spoke up. 'I think we should arrest her.' He had a sullen look on his face, his carrot top mane uncustomarily smoothed down, his lanky shoulders rounded. He'd barely spoken since the meeting started, opting to stare at a fixed spot on the table instead.

O pounced, having finally found an ally. 'She's a flight risk. If we spend too much time getting our ducks in a row, she's bound to fly the coop.'

'Which is why we generally don't share our investigative strategies with our prime suspects,' Phil muttered.

'How is she not going to figure it out?' O exclaimed. She pointed a finger at D.D. 'She wants to call her in for a lineup. Think that won't give our game away?'

'I didn't say call her in for a lineup,' D.D. corrected. 'I said that's all a matching physical description can do for us. Now, put that finger away before you hurt someone.'

O glared at her, hand falling to her side. 'What's the alternative? Request a warrant to search her room or seize her twenty-two? Sure, we'll gain some evidence. And boo hoo, she'll be in Canada before we can snap on the handcuffs.'

D.D. sighed. She looked at O, she looked at Neil. Finally, she turned to Phil. 'Kids these days,' she murmured.

The father of four nodded in agreement. He'd gotten to sleep last night, which thus far had made him the only sane person in the room. D.D. took a fortifying sip of coffee, and got to it.

'Neil,' she announced, 'when were you going to tell us you broke up with Ben?' Ben being the medical examiner, whom Neil would've encountered last night when accompanying the latest shooting victim to the morgue.

'No one's business,' her red-haired colleague mumbled.

'Oh, but it is. Maybe your relationship wasn't dipping the pen in the company's well, but it was dipping in the company's brother's well. We work with the ME's office. The end of your relationship has on-the-job consequences and you know it. So dish. What happened?'

'We're on a break.'

Phil rolled his eyes. 'Oh, good Lord—'

'He says I'm too young,' Neil burst out. 'He says I'm too green. I gotta go . . . sow wild oats or some such bullshit.'

'Become a man?' D.D. suggested.

'Fuck you!'

'Won't solve your problem. You *are* young, you *are* green. You're also a very promising detective who spends way too much time hiding behind his partners. You want to grow up?'

'Maybe.'

D.D. gave him a look. He straightened his spine. 'Yes!'

'Then let's get you to the National Academy. It'll get you more training and experience. Plus, being a smart guy with some promising detective skills, you might even like it.'

'When?'

'You're gonna have to make some calls to figure that out. Preferably, before Phil and I are driven to beat you.'

'Horgan will agree?'

Cal Horgan was the deputy superintendent of Homicide, who'd have to nominate Neil for the academy, as well as authorize the funds should Neil then be invited.

'I'd use your nice voice,' D.D. advised.

Neil pursed his lips, tapped on the tabletop a few times with his hand. 'Okay.'

D.D.'s turn to roll her eyes. 'You're welcome. Now, as long as you're learning new skills, why don't you accompany Phil to inter-view the family of the shooting victim.'

They'd finally gotten an ID on their sixteen-year-old shooting victim/child molester. Barry Epsom. Formerly of Back Bay. Rich kid, one of four, they were told. Father a bigwig with Hancock Insurance, mother known to be a patron of the arts. Private school, where he hadn't necessarily shined academically but also wasn't known for causing trouble. Ironically enough, he had a reputation as a computer whiz kid.

Family had already lawyered up. They were grieving, admitting nothing, and the mid-morning interview was doomed to be the kind of long, dragged-out, dramatic affair that yielded no useful informa-tion but killed the rest of the day. Better to let the rookies cut their teeth on it.

'Goal,' she informed Neil, and to a lesser extent Phil, because he knew his business, 'is to be sympathetic, accuse their son of nothing, and get your hands on his electronics.' She eyed Phil, their own computer whiz, on the last part. 'Smartphone was seized at the scene last night, but that still leaves computers, iPad, iPod, gaming systems – you'd be amazed where perverts hide their electronic data these days. Search warrant is broad and I want you to use it. We'll let the forensic wizards manage this one – see if they can't dig out exactly what Barry was doing online and, even better, how our vigilante shooter might have tracked him.'

'Sixteen. Couldn't be a registered sex offender,' Neil spoke up, frowning.

'No record,' D.D. confirmed. 'Not even a sealed juvie file.'

'Then how'd the shooter know—'

'Charlene Grant,' O repeated promptly, 'knew about his behavior because she'd already taken calls from his victims. Further proof our shooter has insider knowledge, say from her job as a comm officer with a local police department.'

'Or our shooter baited him online,' Phil said neutrally. 'Reached out to various registered users on the animal website. First one that sent her porn became the next target.'

'Which is why your goal,' D.D. said to Neil and Phil, 'is to seize all electronics. Our sixteen-year-old victim has several key differences from our first two victims. Young, not yet in the criminal justice system, etc., etc. Connect him to the first two victims, and we'll finally answer some questions.'

'Analyze his cell phone,' O said dryly. 'Search the call log for the last time he called nine-one-one.'

D.D. rolled her eyes at the sex crime detective's one-track mind. 'Which brings us to the next matter at hand – how to wrap up our current homicide investigation, by trapping Charlene Grant.'

'Finally!'

'Here's the deal.' D.D. regarded Neil and O. 'You're both right: We're dealing with a suspect who's half-feral and probably will bolt at the first hint of suspicion. Which is why we have to proceed with caution. For example, we could request a warrant to seize her twenty-two on the grounds that she matches the general description of our shooter. Which, as O pointed out, would probably gain us the murder weapon but lose us the murderer as Charlene heads for the hills. Or, we can wait for her to show up for her eleven p.m. shift tonight at the Grovesnor PD, at which point they'll seize it for us.'

Detective O frowned, clearly trying to follow this logic. 'She had her gun on her yesterday,' the detective murmured slowly, 'when you called her in from work. Meaning, she must carry it with her at all times. Which would be—'

'Against department policy,' D.D. finished for her. 'Grovesnor PD has the right to seize her weapon, not to mention then authorize any tests they'd like, such as a ballistics test, to see if the rifling on Charlene's Taurus matches the rifling on the six slugs recovered from three separate shootings.'

'She'll fight that,' O warned. 'She believes she needs the gun for the twenty-first . . . which would be tomorrow.'

D.D. shrugged. 'Then she needs to spend more time reading her employer's rules and regs. Her mistake, our opportunity.'

O nodded. 'Smart,' she said finally, which D.D. would've taken as more of a compliment if the beautiful young detective hadn't sounded so surprised.

'Gee thanks.' D.D. pulled together her notes, rapped them into one eight-and-a-half-by-eleven stack, then rose to standing. 'Now you just have to keep it our little secret while speaking to her this afternoon.'

'We're speaking to her this afternoon? Why?' O looked puzzled. 'We don't have any developments from the Facebook page yet. People are just starting to friend it. Frankly, I'm not sure eight p.m. tomorrow night is enough time, even by the viral standards of the Web.'

'It's not about the Facebook page. I have news for her, however. Worth her paying us a visit.'

Neil had also risen to standing. 'You know who killed her friends?' he asked.

'Nope. I found her mother.'

Did all daughters fear their mothers? It was food for thought, after D.D.'s own breakfast with her parents. Even now, three hours later, she couldn't decide which moment was the most humiliating. Maybe when she'd first showed up in the lobby of the Weston Hotel in Waltham, and her mother had pointedly asked, 'Isn't that the same outfit you were wearing last night, dear?'

D.D. hadn't even thought about it, given that she pulled a lot of all-nighters on the job and wardrobe change was generally the least of her concerns. She'd brought that up. Her father might have even appeared sympathetic. Then they'd sat at the table. Her mother had wanted to know where Alex and Jack were. D.D. had answered that Alex had to teach today at the academy, so Jack was at day care.

Her mother had gotten that look again. Like she was sucking on lemons. Which had pissed D.D. off, because if memory served, her mother hadn't exactly played house when D.D. was a baby. Her mother had gone back to teaching, too close to tenure to give up now. D.D. had gone to day care. Hell, D.D. remembered loving day care. There were other kids who rolled and tumbled and got dirty and laughed hard. Day care was nirvana. Home was all 'Sit still, don't make that face, for God's sake can't you stop fidgeting for just one minute?'

No was the general answer. D.D. couldn't be patient, couldn't sit still, couldn't stay in one place. Even now, she was forty-one, and within the first two minutes of breakfast she was compulsively folding and unfolding her napkin on her lap. It was either that or scream.

Her mother had ordered a bowl of fruit. Her father had asked for toast. D.D. had gone for eggs Benedict with extra béarnaise sauce.

Her mother had arched a brow. Fat, cholesterol – should D.D. really be eating such things at her age?

Interestingly enough, her mother's lips had never moved, her throat had never vocalized the syllables. Turned out, she didn't have to actually speak. She could communicate an entire range of disapproval all with the single lift of her brow.

If D.D. hadn't been so thoroughly infuriated, she would've been impressed.

They didn't speak while waiting for their food. They just sat there, a father, a mother, a daughter, who all these years later couldn't bridge the divide. And eventually D.D. had stopped feeling so angry and simply felt depressed. Because they were her parents and she loved them in her own way and understood they loved her in their own way, and what a shame it didn't make bearing each other's company any easier.

Food came. They ate gratefully.

D.D. had thought she just might survive the meal, when her mother chewed her last piece of cantaloupe, set down her fork, looked D.D. in the eye, and stated, 'This is what I don't understand: If Alex is good enough to father your child, why isn't he good enough to marry? I mean really, D.D., what are you waiting for?'

D.D. had frozen, forkful of eggs Benedict midair, and stared at her mom. Then, belatedly, she'd turned her gaze to her father, who was resiliently studying the white linen tablecloth. Coward.

'I'm glad you like Alex,' D.D. had mumbled at last, then set down her fork and bolted for the bathroom. By the time she'd returned, her mother sat pinch-faced, staring straight ahead. Her father had his hand lightly on hers, but whether that was offering comfort or asking forgiveness, D.D. couldn't tell.

They were an attractive elderly couple, she realized, approaching the table. They fit together in a way you could see from across the room. And maybe that was the problem. They were the unit. And she was forever the outsider, looking in.

She kissed her mom on the cheek, feeling the rigidness of her mother's spine. She kissed her father as well, feeling the dry brush of his lips on her cheek. Then she paid the bill and got out of there.

At a certain point, you had to agree to disagree, even with your own parents. Logically she could accept that. But it hurt. It would always hurt.

At least she knew, somewhere deep down inside, that her mother loved her.

She wondered what Charlene thought about her mother, a woman who'd physically abused her most of her young life. But at least she'd let Charlene live, which based on the police reports D.D. had read just this morning, was more than Christine Grant had done for her other two children.

Parents and children. Mothers and daughters.

Love and forgiveness.

And homicide.

D.D. picked up the phone and made the call.

# 29

I was twitchy when I first took Detective Warren's call. Twitchier, by the time I departed for BPD headquarters. I left my aunt behind, nestled with Tulip in my room. Given her exhaustion from the early morning drive to Boston, it hadn't taken much to convince her to rest. I'd told her I needed to tend to a few things before work. No need to mention my conversation with a local homicide investigator. That Detective Warren had located my mother. That she had more information on the baby sister and baby brother I myself had just remembered a few hours ago. No need to mention my growing conviction that the past was closing in on me for a reason. That I was remembering my failings just in time for Judgment Day.

Three p.m. Friday afternoon. Twenty-nine hours before 8 p.m. Saturday night. Sky had finally cleared and turned that crystalline blue that marks bitterly cold winter days in Boston.

The brightness hurt my eyes, encouraged me to keep my head down and my shoulders hunched, when I should've been walking shoulders back, eyes straight ahead, taking constant inventory of the world around me. Trees cast skeletal shadows on the white snowy ground. Corners were mushy with slush and filled with blind spots caused by heaping snowbanks.

What if the killer had gotten bored with January 21 as the annual day to murder a young, defenseless woman? Maybe he'd realize there was more opportunity on the 20th, when his third victim, namely me, wouldn't be expecting it yet. Eight p.m. was also an arbitrary time, a rough average between two approximate times of death in two separate homicides. Maybe morning was better for the murderer this year. Or later Saturday night or even Sunday morning. A lot could happen in a year. The killer could've moved, gotten a new job, maybe fallen in love, had a child.

He or she could be following me. Right now. Maybe he/she had started a week ago. Or a year ago: Officer Tom Mackereth, carefully scoping me out on the job. Or my aunt, suddenly showing up on my front door, after nearly a year apart. Or a long-lost friend, that kid from high school I couldn't remember but would vaguely recognize, having spent yesterday flipping through the yearbook. Someone I wouldn't immediately assume was a threat. Someone smart enough, practiced enough, to walk right up to me without tripping any of my internal alarms.

Twelve months later, I still had more questions than answers. Mostly, I felt the stress of too many sleepless nights, the ticktock of a clock, so close now, so unbelievably close to a very personal, very gruesome deadline.

I walked down the sidewalk toward the T stop in Harvard Square, jumping at every unexpected noise, while thinking that it was a good thing I'd left my Taurus at home, because at this stage of the game, I was a danger to myself and others.

I wished it was already January 21. Frankly, I needed the fight.

A crunching sound behind me. Footsteps, fast and heavy breaking through the crusty snow. I jumped to the side, turning quickly. Two college students strode past me, the bottom half of their faces hidden behind thick plaid scarves. The boy glanced up at my acrobatics, gave me a funny look, then put his arm around the waist of the girl, pulling her closer to him as they walked past.

My heart rate had just resumed its normal pace, my feet turning back toward the Cambridge T stop, when the cell phone in my pocket chimed to life.

I pulled it out, half-curious, half-fatalistic. I flipped it open. 'Hello.'

And heard nine-year-old Michael's voice. 'She called him. Last night. She'd been drinking and then she started crying and then she called him.'

I didn't say anything. Couldn't find the words through the rush of guilt and shame that flooded through my veins. Michael, and his sister Mica and his mother Tomika, the family I'd tried to save. Little

Michael, whose father I'd taken from him, iron spikes protruding from his bloody chest.

'But he didn't answer the phone,' Michael continued now, voice flat and quick, getting his story out. 'Tillie, our next-door neighbor, answered, and he-she said Stan fell off the fire escape. He-she said Stan's dead.'

'He-she?' I asked, the only words I could muster.

'Our neighbor, Gary Tilton. 'Cept now he's a she, so we call Tillie him-her or he-she, but never *it* 'cause that gets him-her mad.'

'Okay.'

'Charlie . . . is Stan really dead?'

'Yes.'

'Good!'

The vehemence in his young voice startled me, made me wince.

'She was gonna take him back. She was gonna take *us* back. Not even two days and already life was too hard and she needed her man even if he did break our fingers. I yelled at her, Charlie. I told her no. I told her she promised not to do that to us, but she just cried harder and picked up the phone. Why is she like that, Charlie? Why doesn't she love us more?'

Michael's voice broke. He wasn't talking in a flat rush anymore, he was crying, a little boy consumed by giant, wrenching sobs, and I continued to stand there, back against a snowbank, searching for words that would both comfort a child and assuage my guilt.

I'd saved this boy by murdering his father. I'd played angel and avenger. I'd hurt in the name of hope.

Which I guess made sense, as nine-year-old Michael both mourned his father and was grateful he was dead.

'I'm sorry,' I said at last.

'Is she gonna be all right?' he asked at last, quieting his sobs. I understood he didn't mean his little sister, but his mother.

'Give her time, Michael. Your mom's never been on her own before. It'll take some practice.'

'She's just gonna find some other asshole,' he predicted, probably accurately.

'Are you guys staying put, or is she talking about moving back?' I hadn't considered that news of Stan's death might encourage

Tomika to return to their old housing project, maybe even tell people of what she did, how I'd helped her.

'Can't. They're closing down the building. Gotta fix it.'

'Do you like the new place?'

'I like the yard. There are trees and stuff. And the apartment's sunny. Mica likes the windows. She spent all yesterday standing in front of them. She even smiled.'

'Good, Michael, I'm happy to hear that.'

'Mom says we don't gotta pay yet.'

'No, you're okay for a bit.' I'd prepaid the first two months of the rental, the top floor of a converted house, within walking distance of a park, as well as a decent elementary school. I'd worked hard to find the apartment, hoping that a nice unit, conveniently paid up, would help Tomika realize that she could live alone and be happy. But maybe that was naïve of me. I wanted to judge Tomika, call her up and tell her to grow a backbone. But mostly, I remembered being a little kid in a big emergency room, injured once again by my own mother and never saying a word.

'Mom wants to go to the funeral. She says now that he's dead, maybe we could get some money.'

I didn't say anything. I didn't know.

'I don't think we should go. We're supposed to be gone. We should keep it that way. Safer, if you ask me.'

'Maybe the three of you could have a funeral for your father.'

'No,' Michael said, and his voice was hard again, a boy sounding as angry as a man.

'It's okay to miss him, Michael. He wasn't always a bad guy. I bet sometimes he was nice to you. I bet you liked those moments. I bet you miss that dad.'

He didn't answer.

'My mother used to stroke my hair,' I whispered. 'In the middle of the night, when I had a bad dream. She would stroke my hair and sing to me. I loved that mom. I miss her.'

'You gonna see your mom?'

'No.'

'Are you . . . are you still afraid of her?'

I wanted to tell him no. That I was all grown up now, ready to shoot, hit, and chase all the shadows in the dark. But I couldn't lie to Michael. I said, 'Yes. Always.'

'How'd my daddy die, Charlie?'

'All is well, Michael. You're a strong boy and your mother and sister are lucky to have you.'

The ground beneath my feet started to tremble, announcing the arrival of a subway in the tunnels below. 'I gotta go now, Michael. Thanks for calling. I might be away for a bit. If you call and I don't answer . . . Know that I'm thinking of you, Michael. I have faith. You're a strong boy and you're gonna be okay.'

'Charlie . . . Thank you.'

He hung up quickly. I slipped the phone back into my bag and ran for the train.

I made sure I looked both ways before boarding the subway car. I took a seat with my back to the far wall, where I could watch all doors, monitor all people coming and going. My black leather messenger bag sat on my lap, my hands fisted around it.

I studied faces, met stares.

Until one by one, each of my fellow passengers stood up and moved away from me.

I sat alone, and even then, I didn't feel safe.

'Charlene Rosalind Carter Grant.'

Detective D.D. Warren uttered my moniker slowly, allowing each name its own weight and space. She'd met me in the lobby. Asked about my dog, asked about my gun, appeared genuinely surprised, perhaps even skeptical, that I'd dared to journey to Roxbury without either of them.

Instead of her tiny office, she'd led me to a modest-sized conference room, furnished with a table large enough for eight. Only other person in the room, however, was Detective O. She stood against a huge whiteboard, wearing a button-up men's dress shirt in light blue.

When Detective Warren moved to her side, I realized they matched, as D.D. wore nearly the same shade of blue, but in silk. She'd paired hers with black slacks, while O had charcoal gray trousers with pencil thin stripes of blue and gray. D.D. had her short blond hair down, in loose curls that almost softened the hard lines of her face, while O's rich brown hair was pulled back in a fat knot at the nape of her neck.

Two coordinating and contrasting images of female cop. One older, one younger. One athletic, one more feminine. One with direct blue eyes, one with deep brown eyes.

Both of them all business.

I wished I'd brought Tulip, just to have a friend in the room.

'Charlene Rosalind Carter Grant,' D.D. repeated, testing each word. 'Why didn't you tell us?'

'Turns out, my past is a work in progress.'

She eyed me suspiciously. 'You gave us the two names to run, Rosalind Grant, Carter Grant.'

I nodded.

She tossed a file on the table. It landed with a faint thwack and I flinched. 'There you go. Full report. Sister. Brother. Mother. Ever read it?'

I shook my head, eyed the manila file folder, made no move to touch it.

My aunt said the doctors had advised her that I should remember on my own. That forcing the issue, before I was ready, might do greater emotional harm.

Greater harm than what? Waking up each morning, knowing that when I had nightmares of my mother digging midnight graves with coiling, hissing snakes in lieu of hair, I wasn't totally wrong?

A perfectly pale and still baby girl. The nearly marble-like form of an even smaller baby boy. That is what I'd spent the past twenty years trying to forget. Rosalind Grant. Carter Grant. The baby sister and baby brother I'd once loved, then lost to my mother's madness. The babies, crying down the hall, that I'd known, even as a toddler, that I needed to help. Tell a nurse. Bolt with them out into the rain.

I'd tried in my own way. But I'd been small and vulnerable, my mother all-knowing, all-powerful. In the end, what I couldn't change I'd opted to forget.

One crazy mother. Two murdered siblings.

Was it any wonder my head was so fucked up?

I stared now at the manila file. I thought it was unfair that my sister and brother's entire lives could be distilled into a single thin folder. They had deserved better. We all had.

'Why you?' Detective O spoke up crisply. 'You lived. They died. You must think about that, have some theories on the subject. Were you more cooperative, the good little girl? Maybe they were sniveling little brats—'

'Stop.' I wanted my voice to come out firm. It sounded more like a whisper. I cleared my throat, tried again. 'You want to beat me up, fine. But not them. You don't get to pick on them. They were just babies. You leave them alone, or I'm outta here.'

Detective Warren was scowling at her partner, clearly agreeing with me. Or maybe not. Maybe this was just the latest episode of good cop, bad cop. But then I realized a couple of things: They didn't need me to come down to HQ to talk about two twenty-year-old homicides from an entirely different state. Nor were they mentioning the Facebook page, or how to bait a killer in preparation for tomorrow evening's murderous deadline. Instead, they had a single manila folder holding police reports from my childhood.

They wanted something from me. The question was what, and how much it would cost me.

'What do you remember?' Detective Warren asked me now. 'About your childhood?'

I shrugged, gaze still on the closed file. 'Not much. I can't . . . I don't . . .' I had to clear my throat, try again. 'I don't even remember a baby brother. Not a smile, not a whimper . . . Just, his body. His perfect little form, so still, like a statue.' I paused, cleared my throat again. Still wasn't working. I looked away from both detectives, stared at the carpet. 'I'm sorry.'

'Might be that you never saw him alive,' D.D. suggested. 'ME's office consulted a forensic anthropologist on the remains. Based on the size of the skeleton, the baby boy was approximately full term, but could've been born a few weeks premature, maybe even died in utero. Either way, let's just say he didn't make it long in this world.'

'Boys are icky,' I heard myself say. 'Boys just grow up to be men who want only one thing from girls.'

Not my words, but the memory of an audio fragment, playing

back. I caught myself, shook my head slightly, as if to clear the words from my brain. 'When was he born?'

'Don't know. No birth certificate.'

'His name was Carter. I know that, even if I don't know how I know that.'

'It was written on the outside of the Tupperware container.'

I winced. 'She killed him. Gave birth, killed him, that's what you think.'

The older detective shrugged. 'Technically, your mother was charged with abuse of a corpse and concealing the death of a child. Given the skeletal remains, there's no way to prove if the baby was stillborn, or was killed after birth. Logic would dictate, however . . .'

'What do you think?' Detective O spoke up, her voice more demanding. 'You lived with the woman. You tell us what might have happened.'

'I don't remember a baby boy. Just his name. Maybe she told it to me. Maybe I found the container. I don't know. I saw the body. I remember the name Carter. I took it, made it part of mine. My own way of honoring him.'

'But you just said you didn't remember him.'

I looked up at Detective O. 'It's possible to lie to yourself, you know. It's possible to both know and not know things. People do it all the time. It's called coping.'

'Tell us about Rosalind,' the younger detective demanded.

'I loved her. She would cry, and I would try . . . I loved her.'

'Was she born first?' D.D. asked.

'I don't know. But she lived longer. Right?'

'Probably a year,' the detective said quietly.

I resumed staring at the floor. Carpet wouldn't come into focus. My eyes were swimming, turning the blue-gray Berber into a moving sea of regret.

'I was in the ER,' I heard myself whisper. 'My mother had fed me a crushed lightbulb. I was in the ER, vomiting blood and there was this nurse, this kind-looking nurse. And I remember thinking I needed to tell her. If I could just tell her about the baby. But I couldn't. I didn't. My mother trained me well.'

The detectives didn't say anything.

'I don't understand,' I said after another moment. 'My aunt is nice, my aunt is normal. I'm really fond of puppies and kitties and I've never played with matches. And yet my mom, my own mother . . . She did such horrible things to me just to get attention. And that still made me the lucky kid.'

'Is that how you view yourself?' Detective O pounced. 'As lucky?'

I looked up at her. 'What are you, fucking nuts?'

The young detective's eyes widened in shock, then D.D. stepped between us, placing a hand on her colleague's shoulder.

'What we're both trying to understand here,' D.D. stated, with a pointed look at her partner, 'is how you survived such a tragic childhood and how it might impact your current situation.'

I stared at her blankly, not following. 'I don't know how I survived. I woke up in a hospital, my aunt took me away, and I've done my best never to look back since. The few things I recall mostly come to me as dreams, meaning maybe they're not even true? I don't know. I haven't wanted to know. The first eight years of my life I've purposefully blanked from my mind. And if that means the past twenty years are spotty as well, that's just the way it goes. You rattle off your first day of school, the dog you had in third grade, the dress you wore to prom. I'll do it my way.'

Both detectives regarded me skeptically.

'You really expect us to believe that?' Bad cop Detective O spoke up first. 'You've blanked your entire childhood from your own mind?'

'Please, I've blanked most of my life from my mind. I don't remember things. I don't know how else to tell you that. The first week of my life, the last week of my life. I don't know. I don't dwell on things. Maybe that's freakish, but it's also worked. I get up each morning. And from what I do remember of the brief time before my aunt came to take me away, I didn't want to get up anymore. I was alive, and I was deeply disappointed by that.'

'Eight years old,' I whispered. 'Eight years old, and I already wished I were dead.'

'Tell us about your dreams,' D.D. said.

'Sometimes, I dream about a baby crying. That one feels real enough. Last night, however, I dreamed of my mother digging a grave in the middle of a thunderstorm. And her hair was filled with snakes, hissing at me, and I grabbed a baby girl out of the hall closet and ran away. Except, obviously my mom's hair wasn't made out of snakes, and oh yeah, there's no way a toddler can climb a tree holding a baby, not to mention that in the dream, the baby's name was Abigail, when of course, it was Rosalind.'

'Abigail?' Detective O asked sharply. She and Detective D.D. exchanged a glance. 'Tell us about Abigail.'

I shook my head, rubbing my temples where a headache had already taken root. 'You tell me. Do you have a record of an Abigail? Because I mentioned it to my aunt, and she said no. There were two babies. Rosalind and Carter. No Abigail.'

'No birth certificates, remember? No way to be sure.' D.D. was staring at me as hard as Detective O. 'In your dream, what did Abigail look like?'

'Like a baby. She smiled at me. Big brown eyes.'

'Brown eyes,' Detective O interrupted. 'What about blue?'

'I don't know. In my dream, they were brown. But . . . maybe. Don't all babies start with blue eyes?'

'But you remember brown,' D.D. said. 'Blue eyes could darken into brown, but a baby wouldn't start with brown eyes, that then turned blue.'

I was confused by both of them and their intensity. 'My aunt said two babies, that's all the police found.'

'It's possible there were other babies,' D.D. said softly. 'According to the police report, your mother moved around a lot, rarely spent more than a year in the same area. Probably helped her disguise the pregnancies, while keeping people from asking too many questions. The officers searched former rental units, of course, but she might have buried other remains, disposed of them in the woods, that sort of thing.'

'What kind of woman does such a thing?'

'A psychopath.' D.D. shrugged. 'Munchausen's by proxy is all about narcissism, a woman objectifying, then harming her own child in order to receive sympathy. Infanticide isn't that much different. She would've viewed the pregnancies as inconvenient, maybe even considered an infant as a rival for attention. She acted accordingly.'

'What do you think, *Abigail*?' Detective O spoke up.

'What?'

Detective Warren frowned at O, then turned back to me. 'You ever try to find your mom?'

'No.' I hesitated, fingered my side. 'I, um, I assumed something bad had happened. I know I ended up in the hospital, seriously injured. Then my aunt arrived. I never saw my mother again and my aunt never brought it up. I assumed . . . I assumed maybe I'd done something to her.'

'Police received a nine-one-one summons to the residence. They found you, covered in blood. Further search turned up two plastic bins with human remains in the hall closet. A warrant was issued for your mom, but she was never arrested.'

'But you said you found her.'

'You said you've been talking to your aunt,' O interjected, demanding my attention. 'She here, visiting? Or did you talk to her by phone?'

'She's here—'

'Where?'

'My room—'

'When did she arrive?'

'This morning.'

'What about last night?'

'What about last night?'

'Where'd you go after speaking to us yesterday? You talk to your aunt, hang out with friends, take the dog for a walk?'

'I went home. I'd worked the night before and I hadn't slept. I was exhausted.'

'Was your landlord home?' D.D. spoke up, swinging my attention back to her. 'Did she see you coming or going, can she vouch for you?'

'I don't know. Wait. No. I had Tulip, and Tulip's not allowed inside, but it was too cold for her outside so I snuck her in the back door.'

'Meaning no one saw you come home.' Detective O's turn.

'That would be sneaking.'

'What about this morning?' Detective Warren again.

'I left at four—'

'A.m.?'

'Couldn't sleep. Used to working nights, remember? I went to the gym.'

'So at four a.m., people saw you.' Detective O. 'But not before that.'

'I don't know!' I threw up my hands.

'Yes, you do. You were trying not to be seen and you were successful.' Detective Warren. 'Ergo, no one saw you.'

'*You said you knew where my mother was!*'

'I do.'

'Where?'

'She ever call you Abigail?' Detective O.

'What? No. I'm Charlene. Charlie. Just because I added two names doesn't mean I don't know my own.'

Detective O arched a brow. 'Oh, seems to me there's plenty you don't know.'

'I want to know where my mother is!'

'Colorado,' D.D. said.

'You have an address?'

D.D., watching me. 'In a manner of speaking.'

'I want it.'

'Don't worry, she's not going anywhere.'

I paused, regarded both detectives more warily. 'Is it a prison? Did they finally catch her?' Then a heartbeat later. 'No, because if she'd been arrested, there would've been a trial and someone would've contacted me. I would've been a witness.' Another hesitation, the wheels of my brain churning. 'Mental hospital? She cracked, finally revealed her inner lunatic, and they locked her up.'

'You think she's crazy?' Detective O asked.

'She hurt me. She killed two babies. Of course she's crazy!'

'You didn't even remember. What does that make you?'

I drew up short, staring at the young detective. And in that moment, I finally got it. Detective O wasn't spending this conversation horrified by my mother's actions. She was horrified by me.

The girl who lived it and barely remembered it. The girl who at least got to roam through a house, while her baby sister and baby brother lived and died in a coat closet. The girl who then stole her dead siblings' names.

I'd spent my whole life fearing I'd hurt my mom. Now I wished I could go back and do exactly that. Maybe if I'd done such a thing, I would've had at least one moment in my life worth remembering, one recollection that brought comfort.

'She's dead,' Detective Warren stated now. 'Listed as a Jane Doe in Boulder. It occurred to me that she probably adopted an alias after the night she stabbed you—'

'What?'

Both detectives paused, looked at me. I placed my hand on my side, eyes widening in comprehension.

Detective O spoke up first. 'Seriously? You were stabbed, and you forgot that, too?'

'I was in the hospital. They'd removed my appendix, some other . . . things. I remember the doctors talking.' I shrugged, feeling my inadequacy again, the depths of my self-imposed stupidity. 'I understood that I'd been cut open, then stitched back up.' I shrugged again. 'When you're eight years old, does it really matter why?'

Detective O shook her head.

D.D. cleared her throat. 'According to the police report, there was some kind of altercation in the house. You ended up stabbed. Your mother must have fled, because apparently you're the one who dialed nine-one-one.'

That intrigued me, given my line of work. Again, a person can know and not know all at the same time.

'Doctors were able to patch you up, but your mother was never found. Now, given your mother's history of moving, I figured she left the area immediately. Only way she could stay beneath the radar that long was if she adopted an alias. So I started with neighboring states and worked my way out, looking for a woman of the same approximate age and description as your mother, including a pineapple-shaped birthmark on her right buttock. Thanks to a federal initiative, descriptions of unidentified remains have been recently compiled into a national database. I found a match in Colorado. Of course, you should submit a DNA sample to be sure, but in addition to the birthmark, the body has two distinct tattoos: the name

Rosalind and the name Carter, both scripted above the left breast.'

'I hate her.' The words left my mouth before I could catch them. Once said, however, I didn't take them back. 'How dare she? First she kills her babies, then she tattoos their names above her heart? As if she *loved* them? As if she deserves to keep them close to her?'

I was out of the chair, pacing the conference room. My hands were fisted, I wanted a heavy bag. I wanted to punch my fist through the drywall. With any luck, I'd find a wooden stud and shatter my wrist. At this stage, I'd welcome the physical pain.

'How did she die?'

'Unknown. Body had been dead for a bit before being found, making an official ruling on cause of death difficult. According to the note from the coroner's office, however, most likely cause of death was complications from advanced alcoholism, for example, liver failure.'

'Did it hurt? Did she suffer? Were her last moments terrible and filled with agonizing pain?'

Detective O's eyes had widened. She stared at me as if transfixed, then leaned forward. 'You're angry.'

'Damn right!'

'Feeling helpless?'

''Cause I didn't get to kill her first!'

'Wishing you could change the past? Maybe go back. Would you save your sister and brother this time?'

'Yes!'

'Maybe you could save other kids. Make sure they never have to suffer the way you and your siblings did.'

'It wasn't right. She hurt me, she suffocated them, and no one helped us. No one did a damn thing!'

'How did you know they were suffocated?' Detective Warren asked.

'I mean, I'm assuming. That's how women normally do these things, right?'

Detective O picked up the beat. 'The police failed you.'

'Yes.'

''Course, you work with the cops now. You know that in most situations, their hands are tied.'

'Yes.'

'I mean the calls you must get, night after night. Little boys getting beaten by their fathers, little girls molested by their caretakers. What can you do, what can anyone do? Take down their name and number. Hey, little kid, your life is a living hell, let me take a message for you. Bet by the time you go home at night, you're all fired up, itching for action. Bet you're thinking you're not a cop, your hands aren't tied. You can shoot, you can hit, you can run. You can make a difference.'

Too late, I saw the trap looming. Too late, I stopped talking. Backpedaled furiously in my mind, trying to remember exactly what they'd asked and I'd answered. But, of course, I had a terrible memory and it was too little too late.

Detective O kept charging, full steam ahead. 'When did you first make the decision that at least one scumbag deserved to die? How'd you pick the target? A call you took personally, a case that caught your attention? Maybe shop talk, a couple of officers, debriefing from a situation they'd encountered on duty. How little they could do, and how much it sucked, and you listened and you *remembered*. You knew what you didn't want to know . . . your mother's house, the containers in the closet, the way no one helped you.'

'I don't know what you're talking about.'

'How did it feel afterward, knowing you *finally* saved a child. Must have been quite the rush. You can tell us about it, you know. I mean, we're detectives, but we're people, too. We get what you're doing, why it must be done.'

I pulled myself together, chin up, shoulders back. Detective O's eyes were probing. I forced myself to meet her stare.

'You don't know me.'

'Oh, but I do. The question is, how well do you know yourself?'

'I'm leaving.' I grabbed my messenger bag.

'Running away.'

'Got a warrant?'

'Avoiding. Fleeing. Doing what you do best.'

'*I was just a kid.*'

'So how did you know they were suffocated?'

I blinked, hands clutching the straps of my messenger bag, still poised for flight, except suddenly Detective O wasn't talking to me anymore. She was talking to D.D.

'I've studied Munchausen's by proxy. Never encountered a case where the mother abused one child for attention, while secretly killing others. However, in several instances, the mom made a big fuss over being pregnant. Milked it for attention. Then, when the babies were born, suffocated them in the middle of the night, and claimed crib death. Oh, the drama, the outpouring of public support, the endless supply of neighborly casseroles. You could see how it would work with someone of that psychological makeup. How they'd even feel compelled to do it again and again.

'But I've never heard of a Munchausen's mom resorting to secret infanticide. Where's the fix, the outpouring of public support, the emotional satisfaction? Makes me wonder what else Charlene fails to remember. What else she might have done.'

'I would never—'

'Look me in the eye, Charlene.' Detective O, suddenly rounding the table, walking closer. 'Look me in the eye and tell me you're not a killer.'

I opened my mouth. I closed my mouth. I opened my mouth again, and a word came out, but it wasn't what I expected.

'Abigail,' I whispered.

'What about Abigail?'

'Abigail,' I repeated mournfully. And my hand came up. I reached out, as if to touch someone who wasn't even there.

'Charlene—' Detective Warren began.

But I didn't wait to hear anymore. They didn't have a warrant. They couldn't arrest me, they couldn't hold me.

In the back of my mind, I realized this might be the last chance I ever had.

One year of intense training later, I sized up my opponents. Then I turned and fled.

# 30

'Oh yeah, she'll never guess we're onto her after that conversation. Subtle. Smooth. Confidence-building. I bet Charlene's headed home right now to make us both friendship bracelets. What do you think?' D.D. snapped.

Detective O scowled, pulled out a chair at the conference table, and dropped into it. 'She's guilty. You know she's guilty. Did you see her face? "Tell me you're not a killer, Charlene." She couldn't do it. *She couldn't do it!*'

'Crap, we're going to have to assign a patrol car to watch her. Course, we don't have any proof she's a suspect, let alone the budget for a patrol officer. Double crap.' D.D. also pulled out a chair, took a seat.The manila file was in front of her. She didn't open it. She'd studied the crime scene photos at 5 a.m., her first night away from baby Jack.

Interestingly enough, it was not the tiny skeletons that had bothered her. The finger bones the size of grains of rice. The unfused cranial plates of the little boy, collapsed into a heap like a pile of yellowed rose petals.

The girl had mummified slightly, delicate skin shrink-wrapping her tiny frame, keeping her bones more intact. At first glance, the remains appeared to be a macabre doll, complete with long dark hair. It was only upon closer inspection you realized this had once been a real baby, twelve to eighteen months old, who'd probably sat up, crawled, taken a first step.

No, it wasn't the impossibly tiny corpses that had gotten to D.D. It was the blankets. Pale pink with dark pink polka dots for her, dark blue teddy bears against a light blue background for him. First

Christine Grant had murdered her children. Then she'd wrapped them up in their own baby blankets. There was something fundamentally maternal about that gesture.

Something . . . incredibly fucked up.

One p.m. D.D. was feeling the weight of a long night. She didn't want to open that file again. She just wanted to go home to Jack and hold her baby close.

She pushed the folder away, pinched the bridge of her nose, and tried to figure out what to do next.

'I think she's Abigail,' Detective O said.

D.D. opened her eyes, peering at the sex crimes detective blearily. 'Say what?'

'Sybil. Wasn't that the case? A girl so horribly and ritualistically abused by her mother that she developed multiple personalities to protect herself.'

D.D. stared at her.

'Sounds like Charlene was horribly and ritualistically abused. Maybe same thing happened, except with a twist – she didn't just adopt the names of her dead siblings, she adopted a personality for each of them, as well. So, say, this Abigail she was telling us about—'

'The baby with brown eyes . . .'

'In real life, yes. But then Charlene's mother killed it, and Charlene . . . absorbed . . . Abigail instead. Protector personality. Charlene isn't killing sex offenders. Abigail is. Hence a brown-haired, blue-eyed shooter, running around Boston murdering sex offenders, while introducing herself as Abigail. Oh, oh, oh. And the notes within the notes. Maybe tightly wound Abigail, the protector personality, is the one writing *Everyone has to die sometime*, in the perfectly formed script, while Charlene, some little piece of her who knows killing is wrong, quickly scrawls the second message, *Catch Me*. A plea for help. One note with two different messages, representing two different personalities.'

D.D. stared at the young detective. She frowned. Then she stared some more. 'I think we just fell into a Lifetime movie.'

Detective O shrugged. 'Most fiction starts with a kernel of truth. Dissociative identity disorder is a recognized and diagnosable psychiatric illness. Besides, do you have any other explanation for the note within the note, let alone a Charlie clone running around Boston shooting pedophiles, then introducing herself as Abigail?'

Come to think of it. 'No. I'll tell you what, why don't you call Charlene and ask if she'll kindly return to HQ for a mental health eval? Given how much she currently likes you . . .'

'Playing nice wasn't working,' O insisted stiffly.

'Really? When'd you try it?'

'Oh please, this from the Queen of Bitch.'

'Queen of Bitch?'

'Hey, I'd take it as a compliment.'

'Hey, I do. But fact remains, our *strategy* walking into this meeting was to *not* spook the suspect. As co-interviewers, we're supposed to back each other up, not screw each other over.'

'It worked,' Detective O declared flatly. 'She's starting to break. You heard her – no alibi for last night's shooting. And hell yes, she feels helpless and wants to rescue other kids and the cops can't do enough, etc., etc. She wants to tell us. Now it's just a matter of bringing her to the point where it feels better to tell us exactly what she did than to keep it bottled up inside.'

'Maybe,' D.D. muttered, less convinced. She picked up a pencil, tapped its eraser on the polished surface of the maple wood table. 'If Charlie's past makes her a killer,' she mused out loud, 'then what else in her past makes her a target?'

'What do you mean?'

'I mean we have two investigations leading us to one subject: Charlene Rosalind Carter Grant. Just to keep things confusing, she appears to be the perpetrator of one series of crimes, while being the potential victim of another series of crimes. She shoots pedophiles, while counting down the days to her own murder. There's a crazy kind of logic there, but I still can't decipher it.'

'Her past may not have anything to do with her friends' murders.'

D.D. arched a brow. 'You mean she just naturally attracts psychopaths? First her mother, then a random stranger who decided to murder the ones she loves?'

O shrugged. 'Sure the mom's dead?'

'The twin Rosalind and Carter tattoos seem a slam dunk. I mean, there could be other deceased Jane Does of the same approximate age and description. Perhaps even deceased Jane Does with the same pineapple-shaped birthmark. But a deceased Jane Doe of the same approximate age, description, birthmark, and tattoo honoring two dead babies . . .'

'All right, all right. The mom's dead. Well, think about what Charlene said: How did her mother wind up so crazy when everyone else in the family appears so normal? Except, if Charlene's running around Boston shooting sex offenders to death, she's not really that normal, is she?'

'Meaning, maybe neither is the aunt?' D.D. murmured.

'Once you've established two homicidal maniacs in the family, what's a third? Though it makes you wonder what they talk about at family reunions.'

'I once read about a family with two serial killer brothers. And here was the kicker – they murdered independently of one another. Two separate homicidal rampages.'

'Several cases of cousins operating as killing teams. So definitely something to be said for pruning certain family trees.'

'You gonna look up the aunt?' D.D. asked, pushing back in her chair.

'I'll background the aunt. Given that she's in town, timing seems right for a face-to-face interview. What are you going to do?'

'Go home. Get some sleep.' D.D. paused. She wanted to be present for the aunt's interview. Then again, she could barely keep her eyes open, and she was hitting the point of nonsensical cranky that was more hurtful than helpful. She'd advised her unit that this investigation was a marathon not a sprint. Perhaps she should take her own advice. Interesting.

Not to mention that tomorrow was the twenty-first. Game day. Definitely, she wanted to be fresh for game day.

'I'll sleep a couple of hours first, then pick up Jack from day care,' D.D. determined out loud.

'Coming back to the office?' O asked.

'Maybe after dinner. We might have something from the hand-writing expert by then. Plus a report from Neil and Phil on their visit with our third victim's family. Oh, and I'll follow up with Grovesnor PD, make sure they get Charlene's handgun. One thing's for certain.'

D.D. rose to standing, glancing at her watch. 'For Charlene Grant there's not much time left.'

'No,' O agreed. 'There certainly isn't.'

# 31

Nine p.m. Friday night. Twenty-three hours to go.

Sun gone. Temperature plummeting. Sky dark.

My aunt had left, checking into a hotel for the evening. Tulip had left, going wherever the dog that was not my dog went. I paced my tiny room. I loaded and unloaded my gun.

I thought of my mom. I struggled to remember two tiny siblings, a baby sister and a baby brother, who'd never had a chance at life. Apparently, memory is a muscle, and having atrophied mine for most of my life, I couldn't magically now fire it to life. I tried to picture a house, a yard, a family pet. A woman, a smell, something, anything that felt like my old life.

In the end, I downed two aspirin, then shadow boxed in front of my mirror.

The woman looking back at me was gaunt. Purple bruised throat. Slicked back brown hair. Crazed blue eyes.

I looked like my mom, twenty years later.

Abigail, Detective O had called me. *Abigail . . .*

I punched the mirror. Suddenly. Quickly. One two three, bam, bam, bam. Shattered it with my bare hands. Then, watched the broken fragments rain down onto the wood floor, a shower of silver.

And for a moment . . .

*The kitchen. Fingers of silvery moonlight. Fire, climbing the walls.*

My landlady, Frances, knocked on the door. 'You okay?'

'Sorry. Um . . . accident. No problem. All's well.'

I studied my bleeding knuckles. A mirrored shard of glass protruded from the back of my left hand. I picked out the glass. I licked at the welling blood.

Then, even though I'd be an hour early, I left for work.

*

Officer Mackereth caught me in the parking lot. He'd just pulled up in his police cruiser. He popped open the driver side door, got out, spotted me walking down the dimly lit sidewalk behind him, and changed his direction from the warmth of the station to the cold of the street, where I was hoofing it from the T stop.

'Charlie,' he said, and there was something in his voice that was already a warning.

I drew up short, one streetlight behind me, one streetlight ahead of me. I planted my legs, left foot forward, gloved hand on the flap of my messenger bag.

Mackereth saw my change in stance and paused ten feet back, his right hand dropping to his holstered weapon, his own weight going forward, onto the balls of his feet. We stood like that for a full fifteen, twenty seconds, him haloed by one streetlight, me haloed by another. Neither of us at an advantage, neither of us at a disadvantage.

'You carrying?' he asked finally.

'Why do you ask?'

'I know. Call came in today. Shepherd is waiting for you inside to take the twenty-two. What'd you do, Charlie?'

I didn't answer his question, my mind already racing ahead. Boston PD, had to be. They'd figured out what I'd done to Stan Miller. Detective O had basically admitted as much, trying to wheedle a confession out of me. I didn't know how, but they were putting together the pieces. Maybe Tomika had told a friend of a friend. Maybe someone had spotted me entering the building not once, but twice that night.

Maybe it just made sense. I mean, a girl like me, growing up the way I grew up. Maybe murder and mayhem had always been only a matter of time.

*How'd you know they were suffocated, Charlie? How'd you know?*

Because I knew. Rosalind's pale little body, wrapped snug in a pale pink polka-dotted blanket. She'd loved that blanket. Had clutched the soft fleece in her tiny fists, had sucked on the satin trim.

I'd wrapped her up. Afterward.

Take care of the baby, Charlie. Don't let her cry. Can't let her cry. *Mommy will hurt us both if she cries.*

Oh God, what had I done?

'Charlie?'

Officer Mackereth. Not stepping any closer, right hand still hovering at his waist. Ten feet between us. Car went by, then another. My hand was trembling on my leather messenger bag, though I couldn't have told you why.

'I'm going to die tomorrow,' I heard myself say. 'Sometime around eight p.m. I will be strangled to death, and I won't fight back. No sign of forced entry, no sign of a struggle. I will welcome my own death.'

Officer Mackereth, watching me.

'I'm a good shot. Good fighter, strong runner. I don't want to die like my friends. I've already spent too much of my life taking shit. If I'm going out tomorrow, I want to take the killer with me.'

'Charlie—'

'I need my gun. I know you don't trust me. Hell, you don't even know me. But I need my gun. One more day. Twenty-three hours. No, thirty-six. Sunday morning dawns and I'm still alive, Boston PD can have it. I'll hand it over to you. Let you personally take it to them. I'll accept whatever happens next. I promise.'

'What'd you do, Charlie?'

'Randi's dead. Jackie's dead. Nobody knows why, nobody knows how, and nobody sure as hell knows who. But they were my best friends, Tom. I loved them too much, I understand that now. But they never complained. They loved me back and I owe them for that. Tomorrow night, eight p.m. A killer's coming for me and I'm gonna make him or her pay. It's all I got left, Tom. Nothing worth living for. Only something worth dying for.'

Officer Mackereth stepped closer to me.

'If I ask you to hand over your bag?' he asked quietly, hand on his holster.

'Please don't.'

'You're bleeding.'

'Probably.'

'Where's your dog?'

'She didn't leave a note.'

He sighed. His hand didn't come down, but his shoulders did. 'I don't know what to do about you.'

I said nothing, left him to the weight of his own consideration.

'Look me in the eye, Charlie. Look me in the eye and tell me you didn't do whatever it is Boston PD thinks you did, and I'll let it go. Turn around, pretend I never saw you.'

I looked him in the eye. I didn't say a word.

He sighed, heavier this time. His gaze appeared genuinely sorrowful. 'Kinda liked you, Charlie.'

'Kinda liked you, too.'

'Guess I shoulda known. I have a habit of being attracted to train wrecks. Hero complex, my sister tells me.'

I had to smile. 'I have a habit of wanting more than I can have. Guess we're both consistent.'

'Doesn't have to be like this.'

'I don't know any other way.'

He took another step forward. Eight feet between us. Then six, five, four. Strike distance. One step forward and I could punch him, overhand right to the head. Or simply pop open the messenger bag and start firing.

I thought of Randi. I thought of Jackie. I wondered if their last moments had been like this. Willing themselves to fight back, or simply waiting for it to be over.

Officer Mackereth finally paused, close enough he could touch his nose to mine, the frost of our mutual breaths mingling in the frigid night air. His hand remained on the butt of his weapon, not drawing it, but protecting it.

'Five p.m., Charlie.'

'Five p.m.?'

'That's when I'll pick you up. Tomorrow night. I know about your friends. Did my own research. Someone wants to take a swing at you, he can deal with both of us.'

I didn't say anything, just gazed up into his face. His expression was set, his blue eyes resolute.

'Sunday morning,' he continued firmly, 'you'll hand over your twenty-two, as promised.'

I nodded.

'I can't help you after that.'

I nodded again.

'You saved my life the other night, Charlie. Guess I feel I owe you one. But as of Sunday morning, consider us even.'

His hand shifted. I thought he might touch my cheek. Maybe I even anticipated his gloved fingers on my icy cheek. Or his warm lips brushing across my mouth. Or his body, strong and solid, pressed hard against my own.

*I'm cold*, I thought, but realized what I really meant was that I felt too alone.

Officer Mackereth turned. Officer Mackereth walked away.

I waited another minute, standing in the darkness, resisting the urge to call him back.

His burly form disappeared inside the police station. Behind me, another car whizzed by. I waited until the street appeared clear, the parking lot empty.

Then I opened my messenger bag. I retrieved my Taurus .22 semi-auto, wrapped it in my scarf, and buried it in a snow mound beneath a prickly bush at the edge of the parking lot.

By firing my twenty-two in Stan's apartment, I'd tied myself to his death. Meaning if Detective Warren got her hands on my Taurus, I'd be going to jail. Maybe I should just hand it over. Maybe, at this stage of the game, prison would be safer for me.

I remembered Tulip this morning. Instead of being grateful for a warm bedroom, she'd simply been aggravated at being shut up.

Some of us just weren't meant for confinement. We'd rather take our chances out in the open.

Twenty-one hours and counting.

I re-snapped my black leather messenger bag, squared my shoulders, and headed in for my last shift.

# 32

'No dice.'

'What do you mean no dice? Check her bag, confiscate her weapon. Done.' It was eleven thirty p.m. D.D. was at home, feeding Jack his bedtime bottle. He was snug against her chest, a warm little bundle approximately the same size and shape as a hot water bottle, and they were rocking together. A cozy domestic scene, so of course, her cell phone had rung.

'I confronted Charlene Grant the moment she walked in the door,' Grovesnor PD Lieutenant Dan Shepherd continued. 'Said there'd been reports of her bringing a firearm to work and that was against department policy. She said I was mistaken; she'd brought a *dog* to work. It wouldn't happen again.'

'Oh for heaven's sake!'

'She let me inspect her bag. No sign of a twenty-two, Detective. Game over.'

'And that's what happens when you fuck up an interview,' D.D. murmured, more to herself than Shepherd. 'Overplay your hand, spook the subject, walk away with nothing. I'm going to have "I Told You So" tattooed backwards across Detective O's forehead, so that in the future, when she's about to question someone, she can first study herself in the mirror.'

'Excuse me?' Shepherd said.

'Just thinking out loud. Did you pull Charlene's time cards?' Earlier in the day, when D.D. had called Shepherd about the possibility one of his civilian employees was carrying, she'd also asked him to check Charlene's work schedule against the first two shootings.

Douglas Antiholde had been shot January 9. They were still awaiting exact TOD on the second victim, Stephen Laurent, but probably somewhere around January 11 or 12.

'Charlene pulled graveyard the ninth of January,' Shepherd reported now.

'Eleven p.m. start?'

'Yep. Eleven p.m. start, seven a.m. finish.'

D.D. nodded against the phone receiver, adjusting Jack slightly in her arms for comfort. Antiholde had been shot late afternoon, early evening. Plenty of time for Charlene to have pulled the trigger and still been on time for work.

'She also worked graveyard on Jan eleven, with OT that kept her till noon.'

'She worked a thirteen-hour shift?'

'Sixteen hours is the maximum.'

'Gee, sounds like detective's hours right there.'

'Police dispatch is not for the faint at heart,' Shepherd commented. 'Now Jan twelve was Charlene's night off, which was another reason she probably worked so late.'

''Kay.' D.D. would have to follow up with the ME, Ben, to better pinpoint Laurent's time of death. Given the location of the Grovesnor PD, earliest Charlene could've made it to Laurent's neighborhood would've been one p.m., and that'd be pushing things.

Meaning, the way these things went, Charlene had no alibi for the first victim and the third victim, but remained a maybe for victim number two.

D.D. had pursued many suspects with less. She returned to the more pressing matter at hand. 'You ever hear Charlene talk about bringing a gun to work?'

'Of course not. I would've addressed the situation immediately.'

'She talk much about her past, how she grew up?'

'Detective, graveyard is a solo shift. Working alone by definition discourages idle chitchat.'

'What about the other officers on duty?'

'They're paid to patrol, not hang at the station.'

'What about breaks? Dinner break, lunch, whatever the hell you call a middle-of-the-night meal?' She started to build Charlene's shift schedule in her head, looking for opportunities for the girl to, say, sneak out and commit homicide, without anyone noticing.

'One thirty-minute meal break. Most brown bag it, eating in their patrol cars or, in Charlene's case, at her desk.'

'That's it? Per eight hours?'

'Two fifteens, which half our officers use to grab a smoke. Not Charlene, if memory serves. She's the fitness buff.'

'What if she has to pee?'

'She declares code ten-six, takes a comfort break.'

'But if she's the only one on duty, who covers the phone?'

'Working supervisor, generally a uniformed sergeant.'

'So there is someone else who works with her at night.'

'True. But the sergeant sits in the main station, whereas the comm center is its own enclosed space, basically a former closet now bristling with monitors, phones, and radios.'

'Would you know if she left the comm center? For example, had clocked in, but left the station?'

'Not possible.'

'Why? According to you, she and the sergeant can't even see each other.'

'But they hear each other. Charlene backs up all patrol officers. Meaning, they not only check in with her during their shifts, but she checks in with them if she hasn't heard them on the airwaves. Calls out their patrol number, makes sure each officer is accounted for. Nine twenty-six to dispatch, nine twenty-six to dispatch, that sort of thing. How long has it been since your patrol days, Detective?'

'A while.'

'Airwaves are never quiet. Even on graveyard, Charlene's job is to be talking and listening. And our headsets aren't so cutting edge she can wear them out into the parking lot and still get reception, let alone down the street.'

'So when Charlene's on the job, she's on the job.'

'Exactly.'

D.D. pursed her lips, considering. Made sense, and didn't destroy their case one way or another.

'Can I ask you a question?' Shepherd spoke up now.

'Sure.'

'Why are you investigating our comm officer? I mean, I don't have the opportunity to work with Charlie directly, but I can tell you, she's good. She's reliable, trustworthy, takes care of our officers. We like her.'

'From what she says, none of you even know her.'

'Graveyard isn't for social butterflies.'

'You background her?'

'Course.'

'Anything stand out?'

'She had a good recommendation from Colorado—'

'What?'

'Arvada, Colorado. Her first dispatch job.'

D.D. felt a chill. 'How close is Arvada to Boulder?'

'Hell if I know. I'm from Revere.'

D.D. pursed her lips, mind racing. Charlene's dead mother, the unidentified body found in Boulder. Charlene, hearing that news today, never even mentioning she'd lived in the same state. What were the odds of that?

Not to mention that in the past ten years, Charlene's mother and two best friends had all died. Meaning one woman had left behind a trail of three dead bodies across multiple states. Seemed to D.D. that it was pretty risky to know Charlene Grant these days. Heightened your odds of meeting an untimely demise, and even worse, given Charlene's fickle powers of recollection, she wouldn't remember you afterward.

You can both know things and not know things, Charlene had said. Coping mechanism for the childhood-challenged.

Multiple personalities, each remembering only its individual piece of the puzzle, Detective O had countered. Explaining Charlene's spotty memory, conflicting notes within notes, the girl's seeming ability to mourn some murders while committing others.

D.D. turned over both Charlene's statements and O's theory in her head, not liking either of them.

'I want that gun,' she murmured in frustration.

'Sorry, Detective. Did my best.'

'Yeah, yeah, yeah.' D.D. asked a couple more questions, talked a little shop, and then, when she had nothing else to show for her efforts, ended the call.

Jack was asleep, bottle lying to one side of his swaddled form. She rose from the rocking chair, placed the empty bottle on the coffee table, and took a moment to hold her son close.

She cleared her head of the case. She let go of Charlene Rosalind Carter Grant and pedophile shooters and BFF murderers.

She held her baby. She inhaled the sweet scents of formula and talcum powder and newborn innocence. She watched her son's little chest rise and fall. Admired the scrunched up lines of his face, his ten perfect little fingers curled into two loose fists.

She marveled at the tiny miracle that was her child.

Then she kissed him gently on his puckered forehead, tucked him into his bassinet, and grabbed herself a glass of water just in time for her cell to ring again.

She checked the display. Detective O. She answered it.

'Self-fulfilling prophecies,' D.D. stated by way of greeting. 'First you labeled your own suspect feral, then you spooked her into bolting. Congratulations. Charlene came to work and *didn't* bring her twenty-two.'

'Yes she did!' O's voice came out triumphantly.

D.D. paused, took another sip of water, tried to figure out what she'd just missed. 'How do you know?'

'I followed her.'

'You followed Charlene Grant?'

'Waited in the parking lot of the Grovesnor PD actually. That way, if they were able to confiscate her weapon, I could deliver it immediately for ballistics testing.'

'At eleven p.m. Friday night?'

'I made a call in advance, got Jon Cassir, the firearms expert, to agree to stay.'

D.D. frowned again. The heavy-handedness of O's approach irked her, made her want to cut the younger investigator down to size. Then she had to catch herself. O had been smart to plan ahead. Nothing wrong with an aggressive strategy when pursuing a serial shooter. In fact, there had been a time when D.D. would've thought to do exactly that.

Instead of leaving HQ to return to her baby. And saying she'd be back after dinner, except Alex was clearly exhausted from the past few nights, and she'd been tired from her all-nighter, let alone her breakfast with her parents, and tending Jack had seemed a better idea than driving all the way back to Roxbury. She could work from home, then call her parents to smooth things over. Right.

'So I'm at the station,' O was saying, 'and I saw Charlene walking down the street from the T stop. Then a patrol officer got out of his cruiser and approached her. I thought maybe he was a friend at first, but she dropped into a fighter's stance and he had his hand on his sidearm. Looked like he was going to take her bag by force, and she wasn't going to let him. Then, just as abruptly, he walked away. At which point, she took her semiauto out of her bag, wrapped it in a scarf, and buried it in a snowbank.'

'You're kidding.'

'No. So, naturally, the second Charlene disappeared into the station, I unburied her Taurus twenty-two and drove it straight to the lab. I'm here now. Cassir hopes to have results by morning.'

D.D. wasn't sure what to make of this sudden turn in events. 'We have six slugs recovered from three shootings. Are all six in good enough shape for matching?'

'No, but Cassir has usable slugs from the second and third shooting. The first shooting, Antholde, is trickier. Both slugs flattened out, ricocheting around the victim's skull, so it's probably inconclusive.'

'But we got the notes, tying all three shootings together. So if we can match the rifling on Charlene's twenty-two with the markings on even one of the recovered slugs . . .' D.D. thought out loud.

'Exactly.'

D.D. nodded. O had done good work. And it was wrong of D.D. to feel resentful. At this stage of her life, her job was to be supportive, the experienced cop mentoring the less experienced cop. Passing the baton, so to speak. In other words, growing old.

'You interview the aunt?' D.D. asked.

'Not yet. Been a little busy outsmarting Charlie. But aren't you glad I did?'

Busy, D.D. agreed with. The obsessive nature of O's approach, on the other hand, worried her a little.

'You returning to Grovesnor PD?' D.D. probed now.

'Why?'

'You've already taken things this far.'

O didn't reply, which D.D. took as answer enough.

'You want to see Charlie leave at the end of her shift, don't you? Dig around in the snow, searching for her own weapon.'

O didn't say anything.

'She believes she needs that gun for self-defense in a matter of hours,' D.D. stated. 'What do you think she'll do when it's gone?'

'If she's smart,' O said flatly, 'she'll turn herself in. We can protect her – we'll throw her in jail. Trust me, whoever killed her BFFs will never think to look for her there.'

'Your first arrest?'

'Hardly.'

'Is it difficult, as a sex crimes detective, to consider arresting a citizen who may be doing some of the work for you?'

'Have more faith in the sex crimes unit. We can do our own work just fine.'

Given how many pedophiles D.D. hadn't had sufficient evidence to arrest in her career, she wasn't sure she agreed. But she finished her glass of water, then returned to the business at hand.

'Facebook posts?' she asked.

'Over a thousand friends,' O reported. 'Lots of hits from Atlanta and Providence, family, friends of the victims. I can't vet each poster – we'd need at least half a dozen bodies to manage that workload. So I've been skimming for odd posts, out-of-place comments. Only person of interest thus far has been Randi's ex.'

'Isn't he serving time in Club Fed?'

'Where apparently they have Internet access, because yes, he was one of the first friends. Posted RIP and the murder date.'

'Asshole.'

'I can stir the pot if you want . . . post "At least Randi is free from her rat bastard husband", something like that.'

'Do it. Be good to see what he says. Also, can you monitor any posts from Colorado?'

O wanted to know why. D.D. explained that Charlie had once worked in Arvada.

'When did the mother die again?' O asked excitedly.

'Eight years ago. Have to put together an exact time line and geography, but I believe that covers Charlene's stint with the Arvada dispatch center.'

'How'd she die?'

'Coroner's guess was natural causes, liver failure caused by long-term alcohol abuse, but the body had been lying in situ for some time before discovery. Makes establishing cause of death more art, less science.'

'Suffocation,' O said. 'Pillow to the face, that's what I would've done.'

'Kill the mom the same way she once murdered her babies? But the coroner would be able to determine evidence of asphyxia: petechial hemorrhages.'

'Not if decomp was advanced enough. Like you said, more art, less science.'

'You think Charlene did it?' It was a genuine question. The coincidence of the mom dying in Colorado the same time Charlene worked there bothered D.D. And yet . . . 'Charlie asked all the right questions when we interviewed her. Never assumed her mother was dead, asking about prison first, then a mental institute, then finally death. She even inquired about how her mother died, meaning, if Charlie did do it – tracked her mother down in Boulder, paid her a visit, pressed a pillow against her face for a full five minutes while her mother kicked and fought and struggled – she's one hell of an actress.'

Detective O was quiet for a moment. 'You still like her.'

'Like has nothing to do with it. I'm just thinking out loud. Good detectives argue. It's the fun part of our job.'

'She grew up with a killer. Maybe watched her mother suffocate two babies. Maybe did it herself—'

'Big assumption.'

'Still, ritualistically abused. Think of the bonding that never took place. Lack of empathy. The free spirits of the world would have you believe a little bit of love eases all pain. Cops know better.'

'She claims to have loved Rosalind.'

'Didn't make a difference. Maybe it was even baby Rosalind's death that put her over the edge. She blew up. Fought violently with her mom, would've killed her if the mom hadn't stabbed her first.'

'Another big assumption.'

'Mom exited stage right, Charlie went to the mountains of New Hampshire. New house, new rules, new stability. Maybe it worked for a bit. Until her friends scattered, and poor old Charlie was once more all alone. Maybe she decided to track her mother down, finish old business.'

'Would really like a witness, any proof at all that Charlie even knew her mom lived in Boulder.'

'Seize her computer.'

'She doesn't have one.'

'Bet her aunt does. Bet it's in New Hampshire. Get it, pore through old docs. There's an email somewhere, an Internet search. Always is in this day and age. Plus, bet she still has access to a computer, maybe checks out one of the laptops at the Boston Public Library and uses it to hunt pedophiles, before returning it to the help desk. Nobody lives totally off the grid, and everyone leaves tracks, as you were explaining to Neil today. We just gotta keep digging. Maybe eight years ago Charlie searched for her mom, Charlie found her mom, Charlie killed her mom. And it felt good. Justice done.'

D.D. couldn't argue with that; the death of Charlie's mom did appear to be justice done. And she certainly hoped everyone on the Internet left tracks. She'd talked to Phil right before dinner, and he and Neil had seized eight separate electronic items from Barry's bedroom. They now hoped the techies found lots of tracks, including ones that tied Barry to two other pedophiles, as well as revealing how one blue-eyed 'demon', in the words of their witness, tracked him down.

'So, Charlene Grant killed her own mother,' D.D. filled in now, 'and liked the feeling so much, she decided to wait eight years, then systematically hunt down Boston sex offenders for more righteous kills?'

'Maybe she didn't wait eight years. Maybe there are other dead sex offenders in other jurisdictions. We just know the three on our watch. Not to mention, stress is a major trigger for killers, and you can tell just by looking that Charlene Grant's a little stressed out right now.'

'She's a good girl, until her stress level rises too high, then she loads a gun and lets off a little steam?'

'Why not? Worse reasons to kill sex predators.'

'More big assumptions.'

'Which is why,' Detective O replied curtly, 'I followed her tonight, got my hands on her twenty-two, and delivered it to the lab. Tomorrow, fuck assumptions. We'll have a ballistics report.'

'Hope so,' D.D. murmured, 'seeing as we just seized a potential murder victim's legally registered means of self-defense, on the eve of the big day.'

'Forget the other murders,' O shot back, sounding almost irritated. 'This is all about Charlene. What happened when she was a kid, to her and her siblings. I doubt she's even a target tomorrow. I bet she's the instigator. I mean lots of people are abused as kids, and they still manage to grow up remembering such a minor detail as being stabbed by their own mother. Then there's Charlene, who claims she forgot it all. I think that's her first lie.'

'I thought you said she was Sybil, which accounts for her lack of memory; Charlie wasn't stabbed by her mother but her "victim personality" ... Rosalind ... was, meaning Charlie really didn't know any such thing. And Charlene's not really running around shooting sex offenders, some "protector personality" Abigail is.'

'Bunch of hooey.'

'You started it.'

'Just to argue with you. Most fun part of the job, right?'

D.D. shook her head at the detective's quick change of heart. 'Fine. At least we agree on one thing – we need the ballistics report. Good work seizing the gun and making arrangements at the lab, Detective.'

For a moment, D.D. could almost feel O's discomfort over the line, and she couldn't help but think of another detective she knew that was always more comfortable with criticism than praise – herself.

'Detective,' D.D. said briskly.

'Yes?'

'Go home. Get some sleep. We have approximately seven hours until Charlene gets off work and Jon Cassir has results from the ballistics test. Meaning, most likely, tomorrow will be a big day. And –' D.D. hesitated – 'being the anniversary date of two murders, maybe even a longer night.'

'Not a problem,' O said immediately. 'We'll have Charlene arrested by eleven, processed by one, and tucked safely in jail by three. Meaning, if any killer wants her, he'll have to tunnel through cinder blocks to get her.'

# 33

Hello. My name is Abigail.
 Don't worry, we've met.
 Are you afraid of me? Or are you afraid for me?
 Trust me, and I will take care of you.
 Don't you trust me?
 Hello. My name is Abigail.

# 34

Saturday. 7 a.m. Thirteen hours and counting.

Maybe less? Maybe more?

What did I know? My shift was due to end, but my replacement hadn't appeared, leaving me trapped at a desk, comm lines still ringing with various Boston citizens in various states of panic.

I'd arrived to a slew of motor vehicle incidents. Car versus cat. Motorcycle versus telephone pole. Drunk teenager A versus drunk teenager B.

By 2 a.m., the bars had closed and the phone lines heated up. Tina Limmer from 375 Markham Street called to report that her boyfriend was an asshole. Guess she caught him balling her best friend. Sadly, being an asshole was not yet a prosecutable offense, so I'd been forced to end the call. Just in time for Cherry Weiss from 896 Concord Avenue to report the smell of smoke in the stairwell of her apartment building. Two officers were dispatched, not to mention the fire department. Officers arrested two drunken seventy-year-old men who were trying valiantly to prove that you could light a fart on fire. Fire department laughed, took in the show.

Which brought me to Vinnie Pearl of 95 Wentworth Way. He wanted to report that he'd lost his nose. With a bit of searching (I managed to direct him to the bathroom of his own apartment), he located said nose in the mirror. Turned out, Vinnie had spent most of Friday brewing homemade limoncello. Which explained his call back ten minutes later to report he'd lost his lips, couldn't feel them anymore, his entire mouth was gone.

I ordered Vinny to take four aspirin, drink three glasses of water, and good luck in the morning.

That call ended just in time for the first of three bar brawls, followed by two calls of domestic violence and yet another motor vehicle incident, Hummer versus three parked cars.

Parked cars lost. Hummer didn't fare so well either, and completely drunk-as-a-skunk Hummer driver was arrested, as they say, without incident.

Sometime around 3 a.m., I ate my cold chicken breast and half grapefruit while still sitting at my desk. At four thirty, the call volume lulled enough I could actually pee. Five thirty, I attempted to log onto Facebook from the PD's computer; I wanted to check the page honoring Randi and Jackie.

I got eight minutes to marvel at the long list of friends, the outpouring of shared memories and bittersweet tears, then the monitor lit up again, this time car versus pedestrian. The pedestrian was injured, but still able to make the nine-one-one report, as the offending vehicle sped away.

Randi hadn't suspected a thing on the twenty-first. That was my best guess. The police had never uncovered any sign of threatening notes, suspicious behavior. She'd lived a small, self-contained life, her closest friend probably her yoga instructor, who said Randi hadn't commented on anything out of the ordinary. Meaning the twenty-first had dawned as just another day. Get up. Go through the motions. No idea, no inkling, this would be her last day on earth.

Is it better that way? To never see death coming, or to spend the past year as I have, counting down every minute, planning out every second toward looming demise?

Jackie had cried the morning of the twenty-first. I'm sure of it. She would've woken up with the same heavy feeling I had. This was it. The one-year anniversary of Randi's death, and still the police had no leads, no major breaks in the investigation. Our childhood friend had been senselessly murdered and we remained with more questions than answers.

Jackie would've started off the day quiet, reserved. Maybe she would've donned a string of pearls in memory of Randi. Or bought fresh flowers, or listened to Randi's favorite band, Journey, during her drive to work.

Being in New Hampshire, I'd driven to Randi's grave that

morning, bearing a grocery store bouquet of yellow roses. I'd been nervous I'd meet her parents and not know what to say. But the cemetery was empty, and I'd stood alone on the hard-packed snow, shivering in the single-digit chill, while feeling the tears fall, then freeze on my cheeks.

Jackie had probably been preoccupied on the twenty-first. But still probably hadn't thought about herself, felt a lingering tension, a fissure of fear. Maybe that's why she'd gone out to a bar. She'd been sad, not afraid, and maybe figured a night out would cheer her up.

The police said she met a woman that night. A stranger made the most sense, as no friend or known acquaintance had stepped forward to say that she'd been with Jackie those final hours. So she'd gone to a bar, met someone she liked, someone who seemed nice enough, decent enough to welcome into her home.

No struggle.

That's the part I kept coming back to. To not just die, but to die without putting up a fight.

I couldn't imagine it. When J.T.'s hands had closed around my throat, I'd been shocked, momentarily paralyzed. But then came the instinct to breathe, the desire to strike back, struggle furiously for air.

Randi had been sweet, but Jackie had always been hard-edged. A woman who could battle her way to being vice president of a major corporation by the time she was twenty-six wasn't a quitter.

So what had happened that night? Who could she have met, what could have transpired, for her to submit so passively to her own death?

I churned the matter over, as I'd been churning it for the past year. Finding no answers, just a fresh case of nerves.

The phone lines rang. My hands trembled. And I worked and I worked and I worked, my teeth clenched, my body jumpy, and my hands desperate for the feel of my Taurus.

Seven a.m. to eight a.m. to nine a.m.

Nine fifteen, Sergeant Collins appeared in the doorway to announce that my replacement had come down sick. They were working on finding a sub now; in the meantime, they needed me to continue to hold down the fort.

It was a statement, not a question. Such is the nature of the job. Nine-one-one phone lines *had* to be covered, meaning you couldn't leave until the next person had arrived and planted butt in chair. No replacement meant no going home for me.

Nine a.m. to ten a.m. to eleven a.m.

My last hours, winding down as I sat in a darkened comm center, dealing with other people's crises, solving other people's problems.

So this is how the world ends, I thought, remembering the T. S. Eliot poem from high school. Not with a bang but a whimper.

I wanted to fight. Whatever happened tonight, I wanted to be the one who finally inflicted damage, caused bodily harm. Win or lose, Detective D.D. Warren and her team would get some fresh evidence from my crime scene. That was my resolution.

Eleven thirty. Shirlee Wertz appeared, black curly hair held back by a red bandana, overflowing book bag slung over her shoulder. We ran through the call log, I caught her up on drunk Vinnie and his disappearing body parts. Then I transferred my headset to her, stepped away from the desk, and took one look back.

Would I miss this?

I'd be taking a two-week vacation, that's all I'd told the higher-ups. No drama over my departure this way. No burning questions about my future, life after the twenty-first.

It's funny, but my throat felt tight. I stared at the ANI ALI monitor and I was choked up.

I'd liked this job. I cared about my officers, felt the burden and honor of watching their backs. I felt that, in a small, feeble way, in this dark room, manning these lines, I'd spent the past year making a difference.

Eleven forty-five a.m. Eight hours fifteen minutes.

I found my messenger bag. I exited the Grovesnor PD. And I forced myself not to look back.

I went straight for my gun. Far edge of the parking lot, beneath the prickly bush. I looked right, looked left. Coast clear, so I bent down to retrieve it.

Except it wasn't there. I dug around. Little more to the left, little more to the right, then abandoning all pretense and frantically unearthing the snow mound with two hands, like a terrier pawing away the earth.

Nothing.

Gun was gone. All that remained was an icy hole, topped with plow sand and city dirt.

In the distance, sirens sounded. One, two, three patrol cars.

Who could've taken it?

I'd told no one. Hidden it only at the last moment, when no one was watching. How could someone foresee something I hadn't even known I would do?

The hairs prickled to life on the back of my neck. I finally understood.

The killer was in Boston.

He/she was watching me.

And he/she was already one step ahead.

This was it. No more countdown.

My own murder had officially begun.

I couldn't help myself. I staggered away from the dirty, grimy snowbank. Then, unarmed and genuinely panicked, I began to run.

# 35

Jesse woke up Saturday morning in his mother's queen-sized bed. She was rolled away from him, facing the far wall, her arm flung out, snoring softly. Jesse didn't know what time it was. Probably later than usual, because the room was bright, the sun pushing and shoving at the corners of the drawn shades.

There was a time Jesse would've gotten up on his own. Padded into the kitchen for a bowl of cereal. Then he would've turned on Saturday morning cartoons. Maybe, if he felt like pushing things, logged onto the Internet and entered the world of AthleteAnimalz.

Now he pressed up against his mother's sleeping form. He liked the feel of her body, warm and soft, against his back. He smoothed the red-flowered comforter with one hand and peered at the far gray-washed wall.

He was too old to sleep with his mommy. Other kids in his class, they would tease him if they ever found out. On the other hand, maybe he'd stay one more night. Or the night after that. Then it would be the school week, and school would help. His mother said so. The counselor lady, too. Routine would be good for him. They both said that, though when his mother uttered the words, she'd had two small lines pinching her brow, right between her eyes. He didn't like those lines. He wanted to reach up and brush them away.

He'd hurt his mom. Worse, he'd scared her, and now, just like he couldn't stop jumping at loud noises, she couldn't let him out of her sight. So they'd spent all day yesterday huddled together on the sofa, watching stupid TV shows and eating junk food until even Jesse started worrying that he was rotting his brain. He could actually feel it, growing warts and holes and lesions, like a zombie brain, right there inside his skull.

He'd set aside his half-eaten Twinkie and requested an apple.

His mother had burst into tears. He'd immediately picked up the Twinkie, but she'd taken it from him, so apparently the Twinkie hadn't been the problem.

He'd been a bad boy. That was the issue. He'd broken the rules, followed a stranger, met a demon, and watched a boy die. And he didn't know how to undo it. It had happened. He'd been bad. And now . . . And now . . . ?

If he could, he'd go backwards in time, like a video in rewind. Look, here's Jesse walking backwards to the library, then up the outside stairs, then up the inside stairs, then sitting down with the stranger danger boy except now getting back up and moving away from the stranger danger boy, back downstairs to his mother. Look, here's Jesse with his mother. Stay, Jesse, stay. Be a good boy, and your mommy won't cry.

The police had taken his computer. Thursday night/Friday morning, he guessed. He'd fallen asleep in the back of the police cruiser, which had taken them home from the station after all the questions, questions, questions. His mother, he guessed, had carried him upstairs to their apartment, all three flights, though he was way too big for that, too. She'd put him on the sofa, where apparently he'd been so exhausted, he'd never stirred even when she'd taken off his shoes.

At 6 a.m., he'd bolted awake screaming the first time. Bad dream. He couldn't remember it, but it had something to do with a scary thin demon with jagged shards of teeth and too bright blue eyes.

Back to sleep, his mother had said. So he'd tried, only to wake up screaming an hour after that, then an hour after that.

At nine, she'd let him get up. Good news, no school for him, no work for her. They'd have a mental health day, she told him, but that frown was back, those two little lines wrinkling her brow, and he could tell she wasn't really happy and they weren't really having fun.

They went out to breakfast, at the little diner around the corner. On the way back, she broke the news. The police needed their ancient laptop to help them with their investigation. She'd handed it over to the officer who had driven them home. They might get it back when all was done, but Jesse's mother had told them not to bother. She never wanted to see it again.

She'd looked at Jesse as she said these words. He didn't argue, just nodded. She'd sighed a little, her frowny forehead momentarily clearing. One burden off her shoulder, a million more to go.

Jesse thought he understood his role now. He'd been bad. And you couldn't go back in time, you couldn't rewind, undo what had been done. He could only try to fix it, to balance being a bad boy with being a good boy, like in order to eat Twinkies, he had to drink a glass of milk. Good behavior to offset the bad behavior.

Last night, the police lady had said they needed his help. He was a witness. And they needed him to be brave, to tell them everything that had happened. No need to be embarrassed, nothing was his fault. He just needed to talk.

Jesse had done his best. Except he was very embarrassed. He was embarrassed by the stranger danger boy who'd so easily lured Jesse out of the library when Jesse knew better. He was embarrassed by the stranger danger boy exposing his privates. And he was even more embarrassed by the slinky, dark-haired demon girl, who'd appeared with her gun and her too blue eyes, and the way she'd smiled right at him, which just hadn't been right.

The boy was evil and the woman was evil and Jesse was embarrassed by all of that, but mostly by the fact that he'd been very, very scared and so he'd closed his eyes. For most of it. For all of it. For every second of it that popped into his head.

Once he'd left the library, he didn't want to know what had happened next. He wanted it gone, if not rewound, then erased. A series of video frames burned from his memory. Then he wouldn't wake up screaming anymore. Then his mother wouldn't look over at him and wince.

He'd resume going back to school, and they'd have their little routine again, Jenny and Jesse against the world.

That's what he wanted. More than anything. Him and his mother, all well again. Jenny and Jesse against the world.

'Mommy.' He rolled over, stared at her sleeping form.

She didn't move.

He placed his hand on her shoulder. 'Mommy.'

'Mmmhmm?' came a soft answer, but she still didn't move.

He touched her long brown hair, spilled on the pillow. Kind of like the demon's, he thought, but his mother was nothing like her. For one thing, his mommy was real, and that girl with the gun had clearly been a monster.

Jesse sighed softly. He hated to wake his mother. But he understood what he needed to do. He'd been a bad boy. No rewind. Now he would be a good boy. Fix the trouble, be the glass of milk.

'Mommy, wake up.'

His mother sighed, rolled over onto her back. Her eyelids flickered. She yawned, peered up at the ceiling.

He could tell the moment she woke up, really truly woke up, because her face, so soft and relaxed, immediately froze. Her eyes shuttered up, her brow furrowed. She turned to him.

'Are you okay, honey?' she asked immediately, and even her voice was tense.

'I love you, Mommy.'

'I love you, too, sweetie.' She took his hand. 'Bad dream?'

'No. I don't want to eat Twinkies today.'

'Okay.'

'We should go outside. Get fresh air.'

'Okay, Jesse.'

'I'll eat oatmeal for breakfast. No sugar. Plain, like you do.'

'Jesse—'

'I love you, Mommy.'

'I love you, too. We're going to get through this, Jesse. It's going to be okay.'

He started crying then. He didn't know why. He hadn't meant to. But she held out her arms, and he curled up against her chest, just like he'd done as a little kid, and she patted the top of his head and he cried harder because she was his mommy and he loved her and he just wanted it to be Jenny and Jesse against the world. He loved it when it was Jenny and Jesse against the world.

Eventually, they got up. She made him breakfast, he set the table. They both had oatmeal, slow-cooked stove-top because his mother for once had the time. He loaded up his first spoonful of the paste-like concoction, screwed his eyes shut, and bravely swallowed. Immediately, he heard a high tinkling sound.

His mother, laughing. His mother, nearly keeling over at the tiny wooden table, giggling uncontrollably at the horrified look on his face.

Which made him laugh, so he ate another bite, and she ate her oatmeal, and it wasn't really so bad, unsugared and gooey and all. He might even eat it again. Maybe.

After breakfast, they bundled up and walked to the park. It was very cold, barely ten degrees, his mother said. But the sun was out, bouncing off the snow and back up to a sky, so blue it hurt his eyes.

That's when it came to him, on the swings, soaring up to that blue, blue sky.

He was so excited, he let go and almost pitched forward at the tip of the arc. At the last second, he grabbed the chains again, lowering his feet to drag against the ground. Then, once he'd slowed himself enough, he vaulted off the black swing and raced toward his mother.

'I remember, I remember, I remember. I know something for the detective people. You have to call the detective people.'

'Okay, okay. What is it, Jesse, what is it?'

'Her eyes, her blue, blue demon eyes. I know why she looked like a monster!'

'Why, honey?'

'They're not real, Mommy. I've seen them before. In Halloween catalogues. They make contacts. Like vampire eyes or zombie eyes, but also cat eyes. Blue cat eyes. That's what she wore. That woman wasn't really a demon. She's just some girl all dressed up in disguise!'

# 36

D.D. woke with a jolt at 6 a.m. No baby crying, no alarm blaring, no Alex up and preparing for work. She lay there for a second, conducting a mental review, then it hit her. January 21. The anniversary of two past homicides. The day Charlene Grant had predicted for her own demise.

D.D. got out of bed.

She threw on Alex's navy blue flannel robe and padded into the kitchen to brew coffee. While there, she checked her cell phone for messages. Nothing.

She retreated to the bathroom to brush her teeth, take fresh inventory of the purple shadows beneath her eyes, the wan color of her sleep-deprived features, and a new but distinct loosening of the skin beneath her chin. She jiggled the suspicious flap, figured this is what happened when you turned forty-one, then scowled unhappily before returning to the kitchen for her first cup of coffee. She phoned in to work and checked voice mail for messages. Nothing.

She should check in with her parents, whom she'd now managed to avoid for nearly twenty-four hours. They wouldn't be happy about that. Probably had every right not to be happy about that.

Upon further consideration, breakfast first.

She cooked bacon, eggs, and had just started waffles when Alex stumbled bleary-eyed into the kitchen. He wore a gray FBI Academy sweatshirt over the white T-shirt and turquoise scrubs he favored for bed. His cheeks were shadowed with salt-and-pepper stubble. His sweatshirt bore baby spit-up on the left shoulder.

They were both old, she decided. But all in all, they still looked pretty good.

She poured him a cup of coffee.

'Don't you have today off?' he mumbled, accepting the mug gratefully.

'Not on deck. But hopefully, a big day in our shooting case. Awaiting a call from Ballistics anytime now.' She topped off her cup.

He caught her refilling, raised a brow. 'Thought you'd given up the java express.'

'Yeah, but there's something about homicide that simply demands a good cup of joe.'

Being a man who drank coffee all day long, Alex didn't argue.

He took a seat at the table. D.D. fed him breakfast, a rare turn of events as the kitchen was generally his domain. Another cozy scene, D.D. thought in the back of her mind. Last night it had been her and Jack, mother and son. Now it was her and Alex, essentially husband and wife.

It was aggravating to think that her mother might be right.

They ate in comfortable silence. Alex read the paper, then worked on the daily crossword puzzle. D.D. puttered around the kitchen, washing dishes, drying them, putting them away. Her mind was churning. She knew herself well enough to know she was working something out. She just wasn't sure what.

Seven thirty, Jack joined the party. Alex fed him, while she showered. Eight a.m., she decided it was still too early to bother her parents, checking her cell phone and her voice mail for work messages instead. Nothing.

Charlene Grant should be off duty now. Looking for her .22. Not finding it. Realizing the police were onto her. Or maybe too distracted by the date, the perceived danger to herself, perhaps fresh grief over what had happened to her friends, to home in directly on the police. Maybe she'd just panic instead.

What did you do on your final day alive? Take a nap to be better prepared for the coming showdown? Pick up some hottie for last-day-on-earth sex? Indulge in a final fat-, sugar-, and calorie-laden meal?

Call the people you love and tell them good-bye?

Except Charlene didn't really have anyone left. Just her Aunt Nancy and a stray mutt.

Rosalind Grant. Carter Grant. Two dead siblings.

Christine Grant. One dead mother.

Charlene Rosalind Carter Grant. Aka Abigail. The woman at the epicenter of the storm.

D.D.'s brain went back to churning.

Nine a.m., she, Alex, and Jack were all clean and had been fed. They were as ready as they were going to get. Last check of voice mail. Nothing. Last check of cell phone. Nothing.

D.D. finally caved, calling her parents and inviting them over. Alex agreed to pick them up at their hotel as they hadn't rented a car, not wanting to drive in Boston traffic. They were in Waltham, D.D. had wanted to say, not Boston. Boston driving was a spectator sport, like sumo wrestling, where the largest, most aggressive vehicle won. Waltham, on the other hand, toodling around the burbs . . . She sighed and promised herself for the umpteenth time she would not be this annoying to Jack when she grew old. Come to think of it, she'd probably be worse.

While D.D. waited, she loaded Jack into the BabyBjörn, cradling him against her chest as she vacuumed the entryway rug, tidied up the living room.

The room could use a fresh coat of paint. While they were at it, they should probably recover Alex's faded blue bachelor sofa, buff the hardwood floors. Maybe a braided rug to soften the space, a potted plant for a touch of green. Or better yet, window treatments.

D.D. caught herself actually contemplating wallpaper, then came to her senses, snapping off the vacuum cleaner and giving herself a firm mental shake. Forget the fucking decor. She was Sergeant Detective D.D. Warren, for heaven's sake. She didn't slipcover. She handled homicides.

Nine forty-five a.m. She gave up on checking messages and called the lab directly. Jon Cassir in Ballistics did not pick up, so she left him a voice mail. Then she and baby Jack paced some more.

Detective O believed Charlie was their vigilante killer. Charlie was targeting pedophiles to make up for the powerlessness of her own abuse-filled youth, the mother who hurt her, the baby siblings she never saved. Plus, being a dead woman walking, what did she have to lose?

But Detective O also believed Charlene wasn't a target for January 21. In fact, Charlie had probably set the whole thing up.

D.D. frowned. Those two theories were mutually exclusive. Charlene had either orchestrated the January 21 murders, meaning she wasn't a dead woman walking, or she honestly perceived herself as doomed, hence it was okay to shoot sex offenders.

D.D. paced the length of the family room.

Charlene believed she was going to die today. Right or wrong, D.D. felt that in her bones. The girl's gaunt appearance, her battered knuckles, the bruises around her throat. No one trained that hard without the threat of real and imminent danger hanging over her head.

Meaning D.D. had two serial crimes to analyze. The double murder of two childhood friends, making Charlene the logical next victim. Plus the serial shooting of three pedophiles, perhaps targeted by Charlene in a misguided attempt to administer justice during her last days on earth.

Except, at the scene of the third shooting, Charlene had introduced herself to the young, traumatized witness as Abigail. This, from a woman who was already carrying around the baggage of her dead siblings' names. Assuming she felt a need to provide a name, why not Rosalind, or Carter, or, as she was prone to do, the whole enchilada, Charlene Rosalind Carter Grant? For that matter, what kind of murderer pulled the trigger, then turned around and introduced herself to the audience?

A crazy one, she could practically hear Detective O counter in her head. One that wasn't a person at all, but a 'split personality'. A woman who clearly hadn't come to terms with her past.

Front door opened. Alex ushered in her parents.

'Where's my grandson?' D.D.'s mom gushed, walking into the house, arms wide open. 'It's time to make some memories!'

Memories, D.D. thought dryly. All in the eye of the beholder.

In that instant, she had a very interesting idea.

Eleven a.m. Jack was back asleep in his carrier. D.D.'s parents were sitting on the sofa. Her mother was discussing the cold winter, the terrible Boston weather, the bad traffic, how gray it always was (for the record, the sun was shining outside, the sky brilliant blue), and the doughnut hole in the Medicare system which no one in government talked about, but which essentially meant no senior citizen had decent health coverage anymore.

'Don't grow old,' her mother offered up in conclusion. 'It's just terrible. Why all we do is paperwork, paperwork, paperwork. And the minute you get all your doctors and medications right, they go and change it and you have to start all over again.'

Alex sat in the rocking chair, a slightly glazed look in his eyes. He was holding his fourth cup of coffee, but judging by the way he kept peering down at his mug, it wasn't getting the job done.

D.D. couldn't sit anymore. She was picking up baby Jack's toys. Both of them. Then she straightened his blanket. Then she moved his carrier. Then she brought her sleeping baby two more toys and set them beside him in the car seat. Just in case.

'So when are you coming to Florida?' her mother said.

'What?'

'We were thinking March,' her mother continued, with a look at her father. 'The weather's warm, the sun shines every day, so much better than March in New England, dear. I mean, if you're lucky the temperatures will what? Finally break into the twenties? You can bring Jack to the beach, let him dip his toes into the ocean. And we'd like to have a party, of course. Nothing too big. Just enough for our friends to meet you and Jack. Oh, and, of course, Alex.'

Alex started at the sound of his own name. He looked up, expression faintly panic stricken at what he might have missed.

'We'll handle the tickets,' D.D.'s mother continued. 'It'll be our gift to you and Alex. A baby gift.' She beamed.

D.D. stood in the middle of the family room, holding on to Jack's binky for dear life. She glanced at Alex.

'Florida?' he asked blankly.

'Yes,' D.D. filled in. 'They would like us to visit. In March.'

'The weather in Florida is nice in March,' he said.

'True.'

'Okay.'

'What?'

'We can go. In March. It will be nice to see where your parents live.' Then Alex got up and walked to the kitchen.

D.D.'s cell phone rang. Probably the only thing that saved her from triple homicide. Detective O's name lit up the screen.

'Gotta take this,' she muttered and made a beeline for the rear bedroom.

'Cassir just called,' O announced without preamble. 'Ballistics is a match for the second shooting and third shooting. First shooting, slug's too damaged, as he'd predicted. But come on, two out of three . . .'

'Yeah,' D.D. agreed, wheels churning again. 'Two out of three works for me. Request the arrest warrant for Charlene Rosalind Carter Grant.'

'On it.'

'O, have you checked Facebook this morning? The page you set up?'

'Yeah. Eleven hundred friends and climbing. No obvious threats and crazies. Ex-husband hasn't posted again. Half a dozen people who appear to have gone to high school with both victims, but hell if I can tell if they're psycho. We'd need more time.'

'Can you check birthdays?'

'If people include that information in their profiles. Some do, some don't.'

'Search for Jan twenty-one.'

'Today? You think . . . you think this is someone's idea of celebrating their birthday?'

'There's gotta be a reason it's Jan twenty-one, right? Date didn't mean anything in Randi's world, didn't mean anything in Jackie's world, and doesn't mean anything in Charlie's world. Hence, it means something to the killer.'

'Happy birthday?'

'Yes,' D.D. said, and as she said it, she felt the last pieces of the puzzle click. Her mental churning ending. The answer arrived. 'Charlene Rosalind Carter Grant,' she stated. 'That's our problem. We keep thinking this is about Charlene Rosalind Carter Grant.'

'Yeah.'

'Maybe it's not. Maybe this has nothing to do with Charlene

Rosalind Carter Grant. Maybe, it has everything to do with Abigail.'

'Charlie is Abigail. Ballistics report confirms it.'

'Maybe. But that still doesn't answer the question: Our shooter made a point of introducing herself as Abigail. Why?'

'She was comforting the boy. She hates the perverts, not the victims.'

'She could comfort the boy without providing a name. But she was specific. "My name is Abigail."'

'In honor of her sister. The baby whose body we haven't found yet.'

'So dead baby Rosalind becomes a middle name, and dead baby Carter becomes another middle name, whereas Abigail . . . ?'

'Becomes a splintered personality.'

'Why?'

'How the hell do I know? I believe that's why they call it insanity.'

'What about the twenty-first?' D.D. continued. 'Charlene's BFFs were each murdered on January twenty-first. Why that day?'

'That question's been asked. Unfortunately, no one knows the answer. On the other hand, maybe we'll finally get some new data today.'

'I think the two things go together,' D.D. said.

'What two things?'

'Abigail and January twenty-first. See, we only know Charlene Rosalind Carter Grant. We've only dug into her past, asked her questions. But what about Abigail? Why that name, why that date?'

'You're implying *Abigail* is the connection between the BFF murders and the sex offender shootings?'

'I think so.'

'But . . .' O's voice hesitated. 'Abigail is Charlie.'

'Actually, if this is a case of multiple personalities, that's not true. Abigail is a piece of Charlie. But technically speaking, the two have never met.'

'Do I get to arrest Charlie?' O asked.

'Sure. We have ballistics. Use the report to obtain the warrant. Getting Charlene behind bars isn't a bad thing, but I'm telling you now, who we really want to meet is Abigail. Whatever's going on, she holds the key.'

'I'm off to arrest Charlene Grant,' O said, her tone implying D.D. was the one who'd now gone crazy.

'Fine,' D.D. agreed. 'I'm off to learn about Abigail. We'll see which one of us finds the killer first.'

# 37

When the first Grovesnor PD cruiser came wailing into sight, I froze. It was coming for me. No logical reason to assume such a thing, but I did. Just because you're paranoid doesn't mean they're not out to get you.

I planted myself next to a telephone pole near the entrance to the underground T station, shoulders hunched, head ducked down as if I could magically disappear into the bulk of my winter coat.

Didn't work. Brakes screeched. The cruiser careened to a halt beside me. I eyeballed the distance to the subway stairs, descending beneath the earth. Forty, fifty steps. I was small, fast. Had a fighting chance at it if I took off right—

'Get in,' Officer Mackereth growled through the open passenger side window. 'For fuck's sake, Charlie. Get in. Get down. Now!'

I popped the door, tucked myself into the front passenger's seat, then shut the door and curled myself into the foot well beneath the dash. Head down again, trusting my dark brown hair to blend with the black leather seat as further camouflage, while Tom hit the gas and the cruiser shot off, sirens still wailing, looking for all intents and purposes as if the officer were in hot pursuit.

'Describe your gun,' Tom said, both hands on the wheel, gaze straight ahead, expression grim.

'What?'

'*Describe your firearm!*'

'Taurus twenty-two semiauto. Nickel-plated . . . rosewood grip . . .'

'What kind of grip?'

'Rosewood.'

He grunted, threw the car around a corner, accelerated slightly.

'Tom, what's going on?'

'Call came in from the sergeant two minutes ago. You're wanted on an outstanding warrant.' He finally spared a glance at me. 'Murder one.'

My eyes widened. I didn't say anything.

'Gonna argue with me, Charlie? Say you didn't do it? You're innocent.'

'I don't understand,' I said.

'Neither do I,' he stated flatly, and he sounded angry. At himself, me, the situation – I couldn't tell. 'This is what I don't get: Been chatter over the radio for the past thirty minutes about a break in a major case – string of shootings of child molesters. Finally got a match on the gun, something like that. Bunch of Boston cops been joking that maybe instead of arresting the shooter we should give *her* a badge.'

Tom took his eyes off the road just long enough to stare at me. 'Knew it was you, Charlie. Knew it had to be. The request last night to seize your weapon, the LT pulling your time cards, spending half the night on the phone with a Boston detective—'

'Wait.' I straightened, promptly whacked my head on the under-side of the dash. 'A string of shootings? Child molesters? What?'

'Yeah, exactly. Because I know for a fact we didn't seize your weapon last night. Shepherd checked your bag – you were clear.'

I didn't speak anymore, just listened.

'Which made me wonder', Tom continued, 'how the Boston PD managed to have matched slugs to your handgun. So I called the lab—'

'You called the lab?'

'Sure. I shoot with the head ballistics tech, Jon Cassir, a couple of times a month. So I asked him about it, you know, cop to cop, talking shop. And he said yeah, he'd spent all night shooting into the drum in order to run a ballistics test in a high profile case. Couldn't pull any prints, though, given the checked rubber grip.'

'Rubber grip?' I was more confused than ever.

Tom slowed the cruiser slightly, blinker on. He tapped the brakes, paused at an intersection. I ducked down again, prayed for invisibility. Then he turned right, accelerating steadily, but killing his light bar, slowing his pace. He seemed to have a specific destination in mind, but I didn't know where.

'I checked your bag one night,' he said now.

'You rifled through my messenger bag?'

'You took a ten-six. I happened to be looking for you. You weren't there, but your bag was. So I looked inside.'

'You invaded my—'

'Be grateful, Charlie. I saw your peashooter. Nice piece, I remember thinking, especially the rosewood grip. So if you're carrying a twenty-two with a rosewood grip that we definitely *didn't* seize last night, why does Boston PD have a twenty-two with a rubberized grip they clearly believe belongs to you and, better yet, ties you to a string of shootings?'

'Why'd you check my bag?'

'History of being attracted to train wrecks, remember?'

'But you didn't report me.'

'Hadn't made up my mind yet. Your turn. Spill.'

I was silent for a moment, chewing the inside of my lower lip. 'I don't know,' I said at last. 'I didn't shoot three sex offenders. I own one handgun, which I hid after our . . . conversation . . . last night. Except, I just looked for it ten minutes ago and it was gone. So maybe the Boston cops have it, except according to you, it's a totally different handgun they've matched to the shootings – though, given the arrest warrant, they don't know that yet.' I frowned, turned the matter over in my head, frowned again. 'I don't get it.'

Cruiser had slowed some more. Tom put on the blinker, turning left. 'Who'd you piss off?'

'I don't know anyone well enough to be a friend or an enemy. I've kept to myself for the past year. I think you can attest to the general state of my warmth and fuzziness.'

Tom grunted in agreement. 'Someone seems to think you're a killer. Or,' he caught himself, 'someone wants others to think you're a killer. Because that's what this is, right? A classic frame-up. Someone has submitted a gun, claiming it's yours, that's now been matched to three homicides.'

'But it's not my Taurus. My license,' I started, then stopped. My license to carry included only the class of gun I was permitted to own, no detailed description of a specific firearm, such as a .22 with a rosewood versus checked rubber grip. 'It's not my gun,' I repeated more firmly. 'And my firearms instructor, J.T. Dillon, can testify on my behalf. He's trained me for the past year on my Taurus; he knows what it looks like.'

Tom grunted. 'Well, at least you got the first witness for the defense.'

I understood his point. With time and effort, I could argue the Boston PD were wrong; whatever .22 had been submitted in my name wasn't mine. But in the meantime, they'd already issued a warrant for my arrest. Meaning first I'd be tossed in jail. Later, it would be sorted out.

I didn't have later. Not given that today was D-day, January 21. The day I'd spent a year training for. I was supposed to greet my killer, armed and ready for battle. Now, after twenty minutes or less, I was defenseless and on the run from the law.

But how? But who?

Slowly but surely, my brain kicked to life. 'A cop submitted the real murder weapon. Only way there could be a match, right? Joe Blow can't show up at the Boston PD lab and say here's Charlene Rosalind Carter Grant's gun. Please conduct the following test.'

'Bingo.'

'But thinking ahead, the same cop also seized my real Taurus semiauto. So I couldn't quickly produce it, head straight to HQ with my own twenty-two, saying hey, there's been a mistake.'

'Maybe.'

'I don't understand,' I said again, and I hated how weak I sounded, how confused.

'Who all knows you have a twenty-two? I do. What about other cops in our department, or Boston PD?'

'I've been working with Boston Detective D.D. Warren and this other detective, O. Both of them know about my Taurus. Detective D.D. had promised to look into the murders of my friends, see what she could find out for today. And O's been building some Facebook page, trying to bait the killer . . .'

My voice trailed off. Except last time I'd been there, they'd asked me lots of questions that had little to do with the death of my friends. They'd drilled me on my mother, my childhood, my dead siblings. O, in particular, had cycled back to my feelings of 'frustration and helplessness'. How I of all people knew how much children out there suffered and how little the police could do to help.

Unless, of course, I was running all over town assassinating pedophiles.

They thought I did it. Of course. And I hadn't denied anything, because I wasn't exactly guilt free. Different crime, same blood on my hands.

But how did I go from being suspected by two detectives to being framed by at least one of them? And which one?

Then I got it. I knew exactly what had happened. I stared at Tom. 'Detective O,' I said. 'She did this. Oh my God, she fucking framed me for her own crimes.'

Tom eyed me from the driver's seat of the parked car, his expression already skeptical. 'Why?'

'You said it yourself. Cops were joking that instead of arresting the shooter, you should give her a badge. Maybe that's because the pedophile shooter already has a badge. A frustrated sex crimes detective. You know, the young, earnest rookie learning the hard way she can't always make her case, save the victim, catch her man. But she can, in the cover of night, shoot him down.'

Tom frowned, but didn't immediately call me crazy. 'This job can be frustrating,' he allowed. 'But why involve you? Like you said, you got a couple of witnesses, myself included, who can testify that you carry a Taurus with a rosewood grip, not a checkered grip. Meaning, sooner or later, you'll talk your way out of this, and then Detective O will be left looking like a bad cop at best, or exposed as the real shooter at worst.'

It came to me. 'Because I don't have sooner or later. As she well knows, I'm doomed to die today. Hell, I'm perfect. We even look a bit alike, except, well, she's pretty. But you know, brown hair, general height. She knows I have a twenty-two, has even asked me about it. Just yesterday, she spent an entire interrogation positioning me in the eyes of her fellow officer D.D. Warren as a slightly crazy woman with a dubious memory and traumatizing past. Perfect vigilante killer. Best of all –' I glanced at my watch – 'in roughly eight hours, I'll be in no position to argue my innocence. Dead and presumed guilty. What more could a vigilante cop want in a fall guy?'

Tom frowned again, but nodded slightly. He popped open his door. 'Stay,' he ordered.

I ducked my head, doing as I was told, then immediately felt frustrated. All this prep, all this hard work, just to revert back to the role of trained dog? Fuck it. I sat up straight, peering around.

We were parked near a snowbank in front of a brick apartment building. Not tenement housing, but not gentrified. Blue collar, where the real people lived. I'd just connected the dots, when Tom swung open my door and growled at me, 'It's my ass on the line. Do you mind?'

I got out of the car, keeping my head down and face averted from possible witnesses. Officer Mackereth had brought me to his place. Aiding and abetting a fugitive, simply because in his heart of all hearts, he figured it was right.

I followed him meekly inside, up three flights of stairs, to a simple one-bedroom apartment, with a large bay window overlooking the street and blinds pulled everywhere. I blinked at the enveloping darkness, then realized that of course he blacked out his windows. He always worked graveyard, sleeping during the day, out and about at night.

He flipped on some lights, throwing his keys on the cleared counter of the modest kitchen. Place was probably six hundred square feet. One big square of a kitchen and living room, attached to a smaller square that was the master bedroom/bathroom. Carpet was brown. Kitchen featured dark wood cabinets with gold Formica countertops. In the main living area, the beige couch was overstuffed, and a flat screen TV dominated. Bachelor pad. Not pretty, but clean, functional. Officer Mackereth lived modestly, but respectably.

'I can't stay too long,' he was saying now. 'Gotta get back out there, as long as there's an outstanding warrant for your arrest. Punch out now, LT will get suspicious.'

'Thank you,' I said.

'They'll probably keep things ramped up another hour or so. All hands on deck. Then, if there's no immediate break, we'll fall back into an ongoing rotation. I'll get to sign out, rest before my shift resumes tonight.'

'Okay.'

'I think you'll be safe here. But you're gonna have to stay inside, shades down. If you watch TV, keep the volume low. One advantage of this neighborhood is that most of my neighbors work during the day. Building's pretty quiet.' He looked at me. 'Gonna be okay without your dog?'

'She's always kept her own schedule.'

'Anyone you need to call?'

'My aunt.'

'She your closest relative?'

'Yes—'

'Then don't. They'll be talking to her next.'

'I don't want her worried—'

'She know you, she like you, maybe even love you?'

'Yes—'

'Then trust her. That's what this is going to come down to. Fugitive apprehension one-oh-one: First, check known locations of the subject. That'll be your place of work, then your landlord. Next, interview known acquaintances. In your case, that's a bit more of a head-scratcher. Your aunt, for sure. If you've mentioned boxing or your firearms instructor to others, then they'll be next on the list. But you've been living for twelve months without leaving much of a trail. That'll slow things down.'

'I don't think so.'

'Why do you say that?'

'Because someone else is out there, watching, waiting, already plotting my death. I'm supposed to be strong today. Ready, fit, on top of my game. It's what? One twenty-eight in the afternoon, and look at me. Thanks to Detective O's machinations, I'm unarmed and hiding with my tail between my legs. Next, you're gonna leave and that someone else is gonna knock on the door. And I'll answer. I'll know I shouldn't. I'll know this is exactly what Randi did. Exactly what Jackie did. But I'll have to do it. Because we're all curious, we have to know what we have to know, so she'll knock and I'll answer.' My voice rose. 'The killer will be there. Maybe it's Sergeant Detective D.D. Warren. Hell, maybe it's Detective O. Or my aunt, whom I haven't seen in a year, but who magically arrived yesterday in Boston. So I'll open the door wider. Because I'll have to. I'll want to know what she has to say. I'll let her in your apartment.

'She'll say something. I don't know what. The last words Randi ever heard. The last words Jackie ever heard. They must be good. The mother of all siren's songs. Because she'll speak and I'll stand there, and I'll do exactly nothing as her hands come up, and her fingers wrap around my throat, and slowly but surely she'll start to squeeze.

'You'll finally punch out. You'll finally come home, and I'll be dead on the kitchen floor. No sign of struggle. No sign of forced entry. Just January twenty-first.'

Tom looked at me. Then, slowly, he reached up and smacked my forehead with the heel of his hand.

'What are you, fucking Snow White? Snap out of it.'

I blinked my eyes, felt the power of my prediction burst, fizzle out. 'Sorry. I haven't slept in a while.'

'No shit. Now, backtrack a second. You just rattled off three names. Detective Warren, Detective O, and your aunt.'

'Yeah.'

'That was good thinking. Let's stop arguing hypotheticals and nail down at least one piece of this puzzle.' Tom pulled out his cell phone and started dialing. 'Jon Cassir, please,' he said. Then a moment later, 'Hey, Jon, Tom. Hey, gotta question for you. Don't want to put you on the spot or anything, but you know the ballistics tests you ran last night? The match is for a gun regis-tered to Grovesnor's own comm officer. Yeah, can you imagine? We're all blindsided, let me tell you. I mean, at least she was shooting pervs, right? But still . . . So, anyway, couple of guys, we got some questions for the officer leading the investigation. You got a name on the evidence sheet? Detective Ellen Ohlenbusch. Great. Thanks, Jon. I'll keep you posted. Yep. Next week. Love to hit the range. Bye.'

Tom snapped shut his phone. 'There you have it. Detective Ohlenbusch. Turned in "your" gun.'

'Homicidal bitch,' I muttered. 'Not that I'm arguing with her need to kill sex offenders, but at least she could take the credit, something. Instead, she's sacrificing my safety for her reputation. I mean, really.'

'Think of it this way: survive tonight, and tomorrow, you can take her down.' Tom picked up his keys. 'Goes without saying, not the landline.' He pointed to his phone.

'I have a disposable cell.'

'GPS tracking?'

'As if I could afford such upgrades on what Grovesnor pays me.'

He finally cracked a smile. He turned toward the door. Then, at the last second, one step back, twisting, reaching out his hand.

I never dropped into a boxing stance. I never even got my hands up. I just stood there, as he yanked me into his body. Then his hands were on my shoulders, his fingers digging in tight, and my hands were smack on his chest as his lips descended.

There was nothing gentle. No asking, no reassuring, no promising. Just his lips, hard and maybe a little angry, but also hungry and needing and demanding. Then my hands made it to his hair, and my left leg wrapped around his left hip and he was devouring but I was even hungrier, even needier, and I wanted and I wished, and we kissed and we kissed and we kissed.

Then he shoved me away. He stepped back. His short-cropped brown hair stood up on end, while his chest heaved, and he held out a hand, as if to steady both of us.

'Not why I did this,' he declared finally, voice still ragged.

'Okay.' I had my hands balled at my side, mostly to keep myself from lunging for him.

'Gotta get back in the cruiser. Report in. You know that as well as anyone.'

'Fucking dispatch,' I said.

'Couple of hours, I promise to be back,' he said.

'Couple of hours, I promise to be still alive,' I said.

He nodded, looked at me, and then . . .

He left.

I locked the door behind him. Then I stood there and wondered which one of us would be made a liar first.

Six and a half hours. No gun. No dog. No home court advantage.

Screw it all. I started rifling kitchen drawers, until I found the standard junk drawer. Duct tape, ballpoint pen, four D batteries, fishing wire, twisty ties, hammer, spare change.

I prepared for war.

# 38

D.D. returned to HQ and took over a conference room. Then, starting on the left-hand perimeter of the eight-person table, she laid out crime scene reports. First Randi Menke. Next Jackie Knowles. In the middle of the table, in a long row, she placed four eight-by-eleven crime-scene photos from each homicide, like a string of place mats.

Then she stepped back and stared.

Neil came in, said something about a witness she needed to call back. She grunted. He left.

Phil came in, said something about everyone going for lunch. She grunted. He left.

She stared some more.

She thought of Abigail. A long-lost baby? A splintered personality? A fragment of Charlene Grant's fickle memory? It didn't matter what Abigail was, D.D. decided. It mattered who she was.

Abigail. Brown hair, blue eyes, willing to introduce herself to a witness after cold-bloodedly killing a child molester. Connected in some manner to Charlene Grant. Connected therefore to the BFF murders as well? The central link, the missing piece of a puzzle. The reason January 21 mattered, happened at all.

Abigail.

D.D. stared at the Randi Menke and Jackie Knowles crime scene photos. And the more she stared, and the more she thought, the more she knew she was on the right track. Abigail had done this. The crime scene photos positively reeked of Abigail.

Feminine, Quincy had called the homicides. The neat and tidy rooms, the fluffed pillows, the spotless floors. Both victims could be sleeping, sprawled awkwardly to be sure, but their faces were not horrified, their necks not broken by brute force, their limbs not skewed painfully.

Even in the close-ups, the bruising around each of their throats was minimal, almost delicate. The killer had applied just enough pressure to get the job done.

And the victims had not fought back, not offered up even token resistance.

What had Abigail known, what had Abigail done that enabled her to kill two grown women so precisely, so neatly, so . . . gently?

Not a crime of violence. D.D. paused, moved to the whiteboard, wrote that down. Whatever drove Abigail to kill, it wasn't bloodlust or savagery. She didn't hate her victims. She didn't torture, maim, or inflict any postmortem damage.

She got in, got the job done, and cleaned up afterward. Almost clinical in nature.

Not personal. D.D. added this line next to the whiteboard.

Abigail killed both of these women, but it wasn't personal to her. If so, she would've been compelled to perform such classic dehumanizing touches as slashing their faces, or maybe attacking their hands or cutting off their hair. Or, on the other end of the spectrum, a killer who was driven by an overwhelming compulsion to murder often felt shame or remorse afterward and covered the victim's body, particularly the victim's face, as if to hide what she had done. But no on both counts. No anger, no shame. Clinical.

Abigail had killed two women because it had needed to be done. She'd kept it relatively painless. Performed her ritual simply and expediently. Then she'd cleaned up. Perhaps also a matter of business – covering her tracks. Or maybe the first sign of remorse, D.D. thought. An apology woman to woman. Sorry I had to kill you, but here, I did the dishes, righted the sofa cushions, mopped the floor.

Motivation, that's what D.D. needed. If it wasn't personal, why had Abigail done it? Financial gain? According to Quincy's reports, nobody gained substantially from either death. Personal gain – bumping off a rival for a man's affection, competition in the workplace, the cheerleader that just took your daughter's slot? Again, no one thing tied together Randi Menke and Jackie Knowles. They certainly weren't rivals for a man's attention, they didn't share the same job, they didn't even live in the same state. They were just Charlene's friends, and even that connection was dated.

D.D. frowned. Made a note in a fresh column. Frowned some more.

Decided to attack the problem from a different angle.

Forget the why for a moment. How? How did one female – and D.D. was certain now the killer was female, had to be female, as Quincy had predicted – how did one female so effortlessly murder another?

Physically larger and stronger? Even then, someone choked you, you fought, you struggled, you clawed at hands with your finger-nails, you kicked back with your feet, you jabbed with your elbows. Even if the rooms had been cleaned up afterward, there would be massive physical evidence left behind on each murder victim. Contusions, lacerations, postmortem bruising.

There should have been hair and fiber tangled in each victim's clothing; skin cells, even blood samples recovered from beneath each victim's fingernails. And the bruises could be just as helpful. D.D. had seen them in the shape of the perpetrator's ring, imprints from belt buckles, even the shape of one woman's barrette clearly indented into the cheek of her rival after a particularly vicious catfight.

But as D.D. went over the photos again and again and again, she came up with the same results: nothing, nothing, and nothing.

It was as if Randi Menke and Jackie Knowles had stood there and simply let themselves be strangled. One, a woman who'd had the fortitude to leave an abusive marriage. Another, a woman who'd climbed up the corporate ladder before she was thirty.

D.D. didn't believe it. These women knew how to fight. So why hadn't they?

Female killer . . .

Drugs, she realized. Weapon of choice of most female murderers.

Abigail had drugged her victims, then killed them.

Only thing that made sense.

Except . . . D.D.'s head ached. She pulled first Randi's tox report, then Jackie's tox report. Jackie had died with a blood alcohol level of .05, consistent with a woman who'd had a glass of wine or two at the bar. Randi Menke nothing.

D.D. pulled out a chair, flopped down in it, and scowled at the report again.

Phil came in. He had a brown bag in his hand, which he held up. Apparently, she'd said yes to lunch. She could eat.

'She drugged them, definitely,' D.D. muttered, accepting the bag.

'She?'

'Abigail.'

'Abigail?'

'Woman who killed Randi Menke and Jackie Knowles.'

'Okay.'

'Only thing that makes sense. Neither victim resisted manual strangulation. Had to be because they were already incapacitated.'

'Okay.'

'Except the tox screens came back clear for drugs.'

'Then Abigail didn't poison them.'

'But she did! I know it.'

'All right, think of it this way: Abigail rendered them incapacitated using a substance not covered by most tox screens.'

'Rules out barbiturates, opium, narcotics.' D.D. opened the brown bag, unwrapped a roast beef sandwich, took the first bite. 'Meaning no weed, no meth, no cocaine, no ecstasy, no oxycodone, no vicodin . . . what's left?'

Phil shrugged, took a bite of his own tuna fish sandwich. 'What would make you passive, but not leave behind a pharmaceutical fingerprint?'

D.D. frowned again. 'Hypnosis?'

Phil shook his head. 'Doubt it. Whole drawback to hypnosis is that you can't force someone to act against their will. Voluntarily submitting to manual strangulation definitely violates most people's free will.'

'I'd like to think the victims would snap out of it and fight back,' D.D. agreed. She chewed another bite of sandwich. 'I don't get it. Abigail killed two women, for no apparent good reason. Wasn't angry, wasn't driven by compulsion, wasn't for any clear personal gain. Just killed them because it had to be done. What's worse, do you think? Being murdered, or having your own murderer not that personally invested in your death? Just, you know, getting the job done.'

'Murder for hire?' Phil asked.

'Would still have to be someone somewhere who gained. I can't figure out how the deaths of these two women lead back to any one person's gain. The only real connection between the two is Charlene Rosalind Carter Grant.'

'Maybe the killer gained Charlene,' Phil said. 'Access to Charlie, attention or affection from her, something of that nature.'

'Actually, we think Abigail is Charlene.'

'Really? When'd that happen?'

'Late this morning. Ballistics matched Charlene's gun to the sex offender murders. Meaning, Charlene shot the pedophiles, and given that the killer identified herself as Abigail during the third shooting, Charlene is Abigail.'

'That gives me a headache,' Phil said.

'Me, too!'

D.D.'s cell phone rang. She glanced down, half-afraid it might be her mother, half-hopeful it would be Detective O with word of Charlene's arrest. Instead, it was a number she recognized from having called the day before.

'Speak of the devil,' she murmured, answering her phone. 'Good afternoon, Charlene Rosalind Carter Grant. Or, seeing as it's January twenty-first, would you prefer to be called Abigail?'

'Not my gun,' Charlene said without preamble.

'Excuse me?'

'Your ballistics report. It wasn't run on my weapon, and I can prove it.'

'How?'

'You. You saw my gun at HQ. Remember? Taurus twenty-two, nickel-plated with a rosewood grip. Gun that was tested last night had a rubber grip. Not my gun.'

D.D. pursed her lips, glanced at Phil, then motioned for a pen and paper. She quick scrawled, *ballistics report?* Because truth was, she hadn't seen the final report yet. She'd only heard of it.

'Maybe you have two guns,' D.D. said.

'I don't. Just my legally registered Taurus with the rosewood grip.'

'Prove it.'

'Contact J.T. Dillon, my firearms instructor. He helped me purchase the weapon a year ago and has seen me practice with it for the past twelve months.'

'Only establishes that you definitely own at least one weapon with a rosewood grip. Doesn't say you don't own a second twenty-two with a rubber grip.'

There was a moment of silence. 'Isn't that burden of proof on you?' Charlene spoke up. 'Look at the report again. Are my finger-prints on the second gun? Because it's not mine, meaning they aren't, meaning you can't prove that it's my gun. I didn't shoot three pedophiles, and you can't prove that I did.'

'I'll tell you what. Come down to HQ, and we'll sort it out.'

'I'll tell you what. Today is January twenty-first. My handgun has disappeared and I think your own detective is fucking with me, and I'm not going anywhere near Boston PD.'

'My detective?'

'Detective O. She's the one who submitted the fake gun. And probably stole my Taurus.'

'What do you mean *your* Taurus is missing? You mean the one with the rosewood grip.'

'Exactly. I hid it yesterday, when I went to work. I . . .' There was a pause. D.D. could practically hear the girl do some quick thinking. 'After you and O questioned me yesterday, I realized you seemed to think I'd done something wrong. You treated me like a suspect, not a victim. I got spooked. I didn't want to be without my handgun, but I know it's not allowed at work. So I hid it under a bush in the park-ing lot, in a snowbank. Tucked it where it would be safe.'

D.D. nodded, knowing this part from Detective O.

'Except when I finally got off work, my handgun was gone. Then . . . I heard over the police scanner the bulletin for my own arrest and the chatter on the ballistics report. So I called the lab—'

'You called the crime lab?'

'Sure. I called the lab, said I was Detective O and asked for the details of the report. The second I heard the description of the gun, I knew it wasn't mine. Except, mine is also gone. Don't you get it yet?'

D.D. said, slowly, 'Why don't you tell me,' though she had a sudden sinking feeling. She glanced up at Phil, who was listening to the conversation positively wide-eyed.

'Detective O submitted the real murder weapon for ballistics testing,' Charlene stated. 'A twenty-two semiauto Taurus with a rubber grip. Except that's not my gun. That's Detective O's gun. *She* had the murder weapon. She killed the sex offenders. And now she's framing me for it. Has me unarmed, in hiding, and basically a sitting duck on the day we already know I'm supposed to die. Come eight p.m., Randi and Jackie's killer will finish me off, and no one ever has to be the wiser. I'm dead, Detective O gets away with triple murder. Four homicides, if you count me, and personally, I think you should count me.'

D.D. stared at the whiteboard. 'Detective O shot the sex offenders.'

'That's what I'm saying! Her gun, not mine. Her crime spree, not mine.'

'Detective O introduced herself to the little boy as Abigail.'

'Yes. Trying to frame me.'

'Trying to frame you?' D.D. tested. 'Then why didn't she introduce herself as Charlene Rosalind Carter Grant, or Charlie. Why Abigail?'

'Abigail's my sister.'

'Charlie, how would Detective O know that?'

Silence on the other end of the phone line.

'Everyone has to die sometime,' D.D. murmured. 'Be brave.'

'Wh-wh-what?'

'What does that mean, Charlie?' D.D. had never told Charlie about the notes linking the three shootings. The contents of a message were the kind of detail a good detective held back, tried to trick a suspect into confessing, not the sort of thing one gave away.

Now she heard Charlie whisper in a faraway voice, 'Everyone has to die sometime. Be brave, child. Be brave.'

'Charlie?'

'My mother. My mother said those words to me.'

'To you, Charlie? And maybe to your baby sister, Abigail?'

'Oh my God . . .'

Oh my God was right, D.D. thought. She stared at Phil. Phil stared back at her, then together they looked at the table, the sprawling, full-color collage of two women's murders.

'Charlie,' D.D. said urgently. 'Tell me about Abigail. You need to remember Abigail. Because somehow, some way, she's become a Boston detective known as Ellen O, who at the very least has killed three sex offenders, as well as probably murdered your two best friends. Your sister's not only alive, but she's coming for you, Charlie. In a matter of hours, you're dead.'

# 39

The problem with boxing is that it's a relatively civilized sport.

You face off squarely against your opponent. You use only your fists. You aim only above the waist.

From a self-defense point of view, this strategy is not as effective as, say, an all-out brawl. Certainly, there were other disciplines I could've studied that might have been more appropriate for fighting off a murderer, while also being more efficient for a girl.

But from the very beginning, I loved boxing.

I think I've waited my entire life to stand before my attacker and stare her in the eye.

Fortunately, my boxing coach, Dick, taught self-defense classes for women. He also hinted of a misspent youth, where knocking heads and kicking ass seemed the easiest solution to all of life's problems. For the past year, after our bouts, he'd shared some of his secrets with me. J.T., my firearms instructor, had done the same. Trust me, if you want to learn how to fight dirty, ask a guy who used to be Marine Force Recon. Apparently, when it comes to warfare, they really do believe the end justifies the means.

I didn't complain then, and I wasn't complaining now, as I went through my final preparations.

Three forty-five p.m. Daylight already fading.

Nightfall would bring me cover. I could leave Tom's apartment, home in on my final target, and start making amends for past mistakes. Assuming I wasn't already too late.

I started with the easy tricks. Ballpoint pen thrust into the elastic at the base of my ponytail, where it would be easily accessible. From Tom's bureau, I'd helped myself to one long white athletic sock. Now I stuffed the foot with the four D batteries, tied a knot in the ankle, then whipped it around a few times experimentally. The heavy weight in the toe stretched it out and would pack quite a punch, enabling me to inflict damage, while also staying out of strike range.

I used the duct tape to fashion a sturdy knife sheath, then attached it to my ankle. Into the sheath I thrust a short, serrated kitchen blade. Not optimal, but if I was at the stage where I needed a knife, I was already in trouble. I didn't have those kinds of skills. Wasn't even sure I had that kind of stomach. But desperate times called for desperate measures.

*Everyone has to die sometime. Be brave.*

I heard footsteps out in the hall and froze. A quiet quick rap.

'It's me,' came Tom's low voice, then I heard his key in the lock.

Quickly, I grabbed the remaining items and shoved them in my pants pockets. Already, I was breathing too hard, my heart rate accelerating. At the last minute, I dropped and loosened the laces on both my heavy boots.

I was just straightening up when Tom walked in.

And that quickly, it was game time.

January 21.

*Everyone has to die sometime. Be brave.*

I'd like to think that Detective D.D. Warren's shocking declaration had opened the floodgates of my mind. I magically remembered my long-lost sister Abigail. I magically understood Detective O and the relevance of the twenty-first, and why my best friends had to die. I even understood why a respected sex crime detective had started shooting perverts, leaving the same disturbing note with each body, while framing me for her crimes.

I didn't.

Abigail remained in my mind, a beaming, brown-eyed, chubby, gurgling baby. My little sister, whom I'd loved with all my heart. And lost. Died, I had believed. Except, of course, if she'd died, I should've absorbed her name, as I'd done with the others. Charlene Rosalind Carter Abigail Grant.

In Detective Warren's mind, that was further proof that Abigail still lived and, in some way we didn't yet understand, had become

Boston sex crimes Detective O. Brown hair, brown eyes, just like the baby in my dream.

Except I truly only remembered an infant, maybe nine months old at best. Not a beautiful exotic creature with that hair and those curves, and a solid career as an up-and-coming sex crimes investigator. A young, astute detective who, from the very beginning, didn't seem to like me.

*Everyone has to die sometime. Be brave.*

Those words, I recognized. Those words, I understood on a level that chilled my spine, set my shoulders, and raised my chin.

My mother's favorite expression. That, more than anything, proved Detective Warren's argument. Abigail lived.

But my baby sister didn't love me anymore.

'Raid the fridge?' Tom asked now, standing just inside the door. His features were drawn, tired. He'd been up at least eighteen hours by now. We both had. He appeared self-conscious as he took me in from across the room, then seemed to shake it off.

'Drank your OJ,' I said.

'Find any unexpired food?'

'The dill pickles were pretty good.'

'How about the gun safe?'

'Twelve months together, and I still don't know your birthday, favorite pet, or mother's maiden name. Totally screwed me with guessing the combo.'

'Figured as much. Calls?'

'One. Talked to Detective D.D. Warren. Good news. I think she believes me.'

Tom drew up short. He stood on one side of the counter dividing the kitchen from the living room. I stood on the other.

'She didn't pull the warrant,' he said.

'I said she believes me. Not that she trusts me.' I had my hands down at my side, hidden behind the counter. I didn't want him to see that they were shaking. That, in fact, I was trembling with nerves over what was about to come.

*Everybody has to die sometime. Be brave.*

'So, why does this other detective, O, have it in for you?'

'D.D. believes she's my long-lost sister. Out for revenge.'

Tom's eyes widened. 'Seriously? That's why she's going to kill you?'

'D.D. thinks so.' I took the first sideways step toward the end of the counter, putting my right hand into my pocket, fiddling around until I found what I needed to find. 'I disagree.'

'You don't think she's your sister?'

'No, I'm pretty sure D.D.'s right about that. But I don't think Abigail, O, is going to kill me. I've been wrong all along. I'm not the third target.'

'That's good news.'

'Quincy, the profiler, kept warning me we didn't have enough data points. Our victim pool, so to speak, was too small. I kept seeing best friends, two out of three, making me the next logical target. But Randi and Jackie weren't killed because they were my best friends. They were killed because I loved them.'

From the other side of the counter, Tom frowned at me. 'Isn't that a matter of semantics?'

'No, it's a broader category. I had two best friends. But there are three people I love.'

'Aunt Nancy.'

'I think so. I've tried calling her hotel twice, but there's no answer. Detective O was supposed to interview her sometime today. Of course, Detective Warren gave those orders before she knew O's true identity.' I made another sideways move. Almost at the end of the counter, where in two steps, I could lunge around, reach him where he stood in the kitchen.

My hands, shaking harder. My throat tightening, forcing me to swallow, take deep breaths.

*Everyone has to die sometime. Be brave.*

All these years later, my mother was coming for me. That's how it felt on some level. In a way I didn't understand yet, she had won, and I had lost, and twenty years later she was still making me pay.

Except I wasn't a little girl anymore. I wasn't going quietly into that good night.

I had learned my lessons. I was prepared to die. But more than that, I was prepared to fight.

'You sure this Abigail is going after your aunt?' Tom was asking now. 'Because you still have only two victims for analysis. And if this detective is your long-lost sister seeking revenge, still makes sense she'd go after you.'

'If all she wanted was to kill me, she could've done that in the beginning. Knocked on my door and told me her name. I would've let her inside, Tom. I would've stood there and willingly let my baby sister place her hands around my neck and squeeze. But she didn't. She went after my friends. She doesn't want me dead. She wants me to suffer. Probably, just like she has.'

'That why she framed you? Gonna kill your friends, your aunt, then get you tossed in jail?'

I shrugged, hoping it looked casual as I executed my final sideways shuffle. 'I think the framing thing was just to buy time. It got me isolated and on the defensive, making it even easier for her to go after my aunt.'

'All right,' Tom said decidedly. 'Where's your aunt staying? We're on our way.'

'I don't think so.'

'I can call for backup. We make up an excuse. Burglary in progress, a fire, hell, code the living daylights out of it, get the place crawling with uniforms. That'll set her back on her ass.'

'I don't think so.'

He picked up his keys, ignoring me completely, as I knew he would do.

'Got a surprise for you—' he started.

I lunged around the end of the counter. Two steps, half pivot, left hand up, eye-to-eye with my opponent. Jab, jab, jab to his nose, fingers curled tight, thumb to knuckles. Tom didn't get his hands up. He didn't defend himself against this surprising attack from a girl. He didn't defend himself against me.

Final blow. Overhand right to the head. I pivoted my back leg and rolled my shoulder into it. My fist, bearing the extra weight of a tight bundle of coins, connected with the side of Tom's head.

He went down. First collapsing at the knees, then swaying, before finally toppling back and to the side. His shoulder cracked against the hard wood of the kitchen cabinets. I winced, closing my eyes before I caught myself.

If you can attack the man who three hours before would've been your lover, the man who would still be your lone defender in the world, then you can damn well keep your eyes open and absorb the blow.

He crumpled on the floor. I shook out both of my hands, my knuckles and wrists already aching from impact. But that's the point of training – it prepares you for the pain, enables you to soldier through.

Not much time now.

Nightfall. January 21.

I laid out Tom on the floor. Checked his pulse to make sure it was steady, found a pillow for beneath his head. Then I swapped out my dark jacket for a lined L.L. Bean camouflaged hunting coat I'd found in his closet. I wrapped his brown scarf around my neck, catching the scent of his soap and cologne. I pulled another brown knit cap low over my head. Conducted one last check of my pockets.

*Everyone has to die sometime. Be brave.*

I kissed his forehead. Gently. Tenderly. Regretfully.

Then, because I was only human, and my eyes were burning and my resolve shaking, I moved away.

I know Tom would've helped me. For that matter, I could probably partner with Detective Warren as well. But I didn't want to. From the first moment D.D. had said my baby sister was still alive and coming for me, I'd known what I must do. The next few hours would be deeply personal.

A matter of family business.

I left a note, scrawled earlier with a brief apology that would never be enough. I took Tom's keys, exited his apartment.

I got a fresh shock in the dimly lit parking lot. The low sound of a dog whining, which grew louder as I approached Tom's police cruiser. There, in the front seat, staring at me through the windshield: Tulip.

He'd started to say he had a surprise for me. My dog. Tom had searched the city for Tulip and brought her to me.

Possibly, my eyes blurred as I worked the key remote for the police cruiser, opening the door, releasing the dog who was definitely my dog and feeling the solid weight of her as she hurled herself against my shaking form. I scooped her up and held her close. I was sorry for her, and sorry for Tom and sorry for my baby sister, whom I still loved, and sorrier still for my aunt, who might even now be paying for my sins.

I closed the police cruiser door. Too conspicuous.

Instead, I located Tom's dark green Ram truck, and opened both doors. Tulip rode shotgun.

We set off into the night.

Twenty years later. Once the victim, now the cavalry.

# 40

D.D. called Neil and Phil into her office for an emergency meeting. In the next thirty minutes, she needed to report to her boss, the deputy superintendent of Homicide, about the latest developments involving possible criminal actions taken by a fellow investigator, Detective O. First, D.D. wanted to get her ducks in a row.

She started without preamble. 'Where the hell is Detective O, what did she do, and why didn't we figure this out sooner?'

Phil went first. Given that O wasn't answering her cell phone, returning official pages, or replying to requests for contact from police dispatch, chances were she'd gone rogue. They hadn't issued a full BOLO yet, but word was out among Boston cops: if anyone spotted Detective O or her Crown Vic, they should contact HQ immediately.

In the meantime, Phil was blitzing his way through her official file. Given her young age and limited time on the job, it made for quick reading. O had joined Boston PD two years prior, transferring from a smaller jurisdiction in the burbs. Was known for her hard work and tireless dedication. Perhaps a bit rigid in her approach, perhaps didn't always play well with others, but the sex crimes investigator also got results with some pretty tough cases in a pretty tough field.

Certainly, nothing in her annual eval suggested that she was a nutcase waiting to crack.

'On the other hand,' Phil reported, 'she spent eight years living in Colorado, including the time frame when Charlene worked in Arvada dispatch, and Christine Grant's body was discovered.'

D.D. sat across from her squadmates, totally poleaxed. 'She did it. I'll be damned, but O – or Abigail, or whatever the hell her name is – killed her own mother. Told me all about it, too. That she'd held a pillow over her face and suffocated her, just as her mother had suffocated her own babies.'

'Why?' Neil asked.

'When we find her, we'll have to ask.' D.D. chewed her lower lip. 'We need Charlene. We need more info on twenty years ago, and the final incident, which left Charlene nearly dead, and her mother and younger sister on the run. Only thing that makes sense. Something happened, maybe her mother snapped, actually tried to kill Charlene instead of just maim her. Then panicked, grabbed the younger kid, and hit the road.'

Neil spoke up. 'I don't get it. How did Charlene forget an entire sister? How did the police, investigating that "final incident", never figure out there was another kid?'

D.D. shrugged. 'We know Christine Grant had two babies that were off the record. I'm guessing Charlene's younger sister, Abigail, makes three. As for the police investigation, the comment that struck me most in the official report was that there was nothing in the rental house that indicated a family had even lived there. No toys, no clothes, no . . . stuff. Sounds to me like Mommy Grant wasn't just psychopathic, but truly, genuinely bona fide crazy. As in not fit to take care of herself or others. I'm wondering more and more how much of that load eight-year-old Charlene shouldered. Only to then be stabbed and left for dead. I gotta say, I can't really blame her for not wanting to dwell on those happy times.'

'So Christine Grant is whacko enough to murder two babies, but then sane enough to try to raise two others?' Neil clearly remained skeptical.

D.D. thought about it. 'O asked Charlene if she was the good kid. She implied that maybe baby Rosalind and baby Carter were fussy and that's why they had to die.' She looked at her squadmates. 'Knowing what we know now, maybe that's how the story was told to her, by their mother. Be good, and I'll let you live. Act up, whine, defy me, and . . .'

'Except at some point, Abigail did turn against her own mother,' Phil said. 'In fact, you just said she probably killed her.'

'Sure. Think about it. For the first eight years, Charlene served as her mother's target of choice – to be broken and repaired at will. Want to believe that Mommy Grant gave up her Munchausen's ways just because she lost her eldest daughter? I bet she simply picked back up with daughter number two. Meaning Abigail now got to eat shattered glass and drink liquid Drano. Meaning Abigail now got to learn just how much a mother's love can burn.'

D.D. sighed, her voice turning somber. 'Munchausen's is most common with children who are very young. Babies, toddlers, who are unable to speak up in their own defense. Once Abigail reached a certain age, however, chances are she didn't submit as willingly to having her fingers smashed in doorways. Chances are, she started to come up with some tricks of her own. God knows, she learned from a master.'

D.D. turned back to Phil. 'This is what we need to prove: how did Abigail Grant become Ellen O? Because before we accuse a fellow officer of being the real perpetrator of two separate strings of murders, we're going to want to nail that down.'

'Yeah, yeah, yeah, knew you were gonna say that. In the,' Phil glanced at his watch, 'twenty minutes you gave me with this project, I haven't been able to answer that question. Assuming Ellen O is an alias, it's a well-vetted one. I found a Social Security number, driver's license, credit history, not to mention college transcripts from the University of Denver. My guess is, given the depth of the paper trail, Abigail Grant became Ellen O while still a teenager. Now, several ways that could happen: formal adoption, becoming a legally emancipated minor while also petitioning for a name change. Or hell, the witness protection program, for all I know. I'll keep digging around in family court records, etc., but so far, no luck.'

'Wouldn't she have real family or friends to rat her out?' Neil asked.

'Not according to her personnel form.' Phil held up a sheet of paper. 'No family members listed, and as for her "emergency contact number", when I called it, I reached the holding company of her apartment building. I think it's safe to say, Abigail . . . O . . . is officially alone in the world.'

'But why was she shooting pedophiles?' Neil asked with a frown. 'Given the family history, I get her targeting Charlene and, okay, even Charlene's best friends, as part of her "quest for vengeance". But why the pedophiles?'

'Think of it this way,' D.D. explained. 'One killer, but two different crime sprees, driven by two different sets of needs. What Abigail did to Randi and Jackie, what she has in store for Charlene, is more intimate, more ritualized for her. She's both seeking to punish the older sister who abandoned her and to exorcise a lifetime of taking her mother's abuse with this ultimate method of seizing power. The pedophile shootings, on the other hand, are almost everyday stress management. Another case she can't close. Another incident of a kid getting abused by a registered sex offender who just moved in down the hall . . . O accused Charlene of over-identifying with the victims, of hating to feel powerless. In hindsight, I think that was her way of telling us about herself. She also over-identifies with the victims, and two years on the job, she's tired of feeling helpless.'

'What about the notes? *Everyone has to die sometime . . .*'

'According to Charlene Grant, that was an expression of their mother's. A family mantra, so to speak. What's more interesting, I think, is the note within the note, the secret message written in lemon juice – *Catch Me*. At first, I thought that might be some sort of taunt by the shooter. Now I wonder if it wasn't a plea. Abigail wrote, *Everyone has to die sometime*. While Detective O added, *Catch Me*. Two notes representing the two sides of her nature.'

'Good cop, bad cop,' Neil finished darkly.

'Exactly,' D.D. answered. To think of all the times she and O had sat alone in this very office, poring over those carefully executed notes, the handwriting analysis, witness statements. O had never given anything away. The level of compartmentalization necessary for that degree of subterfuge was just plain scary.

It also fit the expert's profile of the note writer perfectly: someone rigid, anal-retentive, type A.

First thing D.D. had done, once she'd gotten off the phone with Charlene, was to run to Detective O's desk and gather up three samples of the investigator's handwriting. She'd laid them out on a cleared table, side by side with the three notes from the pedophile shootings. The handwriting wasn't a dead-on match, at least not to D.D.'s untrained eye. O's 'natural' script was neat and precise, but hardly contained letters with flat bottoms and perfectly proportioned size. Maybe she'd written the notes for the shootings using a ruler, maybe even a stencil, to further obfuscate matters. Given that the notes all said the same thing, it would be easy enough to perfect those two sentences, a mere seven words, by practicing them over and over again.

But some of the author's personality had still come through. Controlling, determined, psychopathic.

'The witness to the third shooting', D.D. said now, 'called this afternoon. The boy's mother said he'd realized that the shooter's eyes weren't really demonic, but special contact lenses meant to look like blue cat eyes. They found a picture in a Halloween catalogue and dropped it by an hour ago as a visual aid.'

She pulled out the torn catalogue page, placed it before Neil and Phil. 'I'm guessing O wore the contacts so she would better match Charlene's general description of brown hair, blue eyes—'

'But why cat eyes?' Phil asked, shuddering slightly as he took in the array of creepy contacts.

'Does that freak you out?'

'Yes.'

'Exactly. Remember, O not only wanted the shooter to match Charlene's physical description, but she also had to disguise her own appearance. I mean, just an hour later, she personally stood in front of this boy. She had on makeup then, her hair piled in big curls, a nice dress, wide trench coat. I remember thinking at the time she must've come from a date. But I think she was just trying to soften all the lines. The boy had seen a thin, gaunt-faced woman with tight hair and scary eyes. Then in real life, O did her best to appear the opposite.'

'But she's not thin or gaunt,' Neil countered.

'Maybe she wears padding under her clothes.' D.D. looked down at her own chest, definitely no longer what it used to be during pregnancy. 'Not that I would know anything about that.'

Redheaded Neil blushed slightly, shook his head at her. 'All right, assuming O transferred here two years ago so she could kill Charlene, how'd she know Charlie would be in Boston? Charlene didn't even move to Cambridge till last year.'

'O probably didn't know Charlie would be in Boston, and probably didn't need to. Think about it: by moving to Boston, O arrived in the heart of New England. From here, it's an easy day trip to New Hampshire, Rhode Island, half a dozen other states. She would've had to fly to Atlanta for Jackie Knowles, but even that's just a couple of hours out of Logan Airport. Meaning regardless of wherever Charlie or her other victims would be on January twenty-one, O would have easy access.'

'I checked with her supervisor,' Phil spoke up. 'Right now, looks like Detective O didn't work January twenty-one last year, or the year before. She's technically on duty today, but we can see how well that's working . . .'

D.D. nodded, made another note for her presentation to Horgan.

Neil spoke up. 'Why kill Randi Menke first? Why not just kill Charlie?'

'I think Abigail is looking for something more than a quick kill. If that were the case, you're right, she could've driven up to New Hampshire and dispatched Charlene with a double tap to the forehead, just as she did with the pedophiles. I think she wants to torture Charlie first, make her feel just as alone and vulnerable in the world. As for why Randi versus Jackie . . .' D.D. shrugged. 'Abigail had to start somewhere, and Randi probably seemed the easiest target. Lived only an hour outside of Boston, already traumatized by an abusive relationship. I imagine O drove down, maybe flashed her badge and said she was investigating Randi's evil ex-husband. And just like that, Randi would've let her in.'

'But still didn't fight back while she was being strangled,' Phil pressed.

'Details, details,' D.D. muttered, acknowledging his point. 'As for Jackie Knowles . . . O would've had to fly to Atlanta, but no big whoop. She could've performed a routine background check in advance, determined Jackie's occupation, place of residence, favorite restaurants from her Visa bill. Or just sat outside Jackie's office, then followed her to the bar and set about introducing herself. She bought Jackie a drink or two, let one thing lead to another.'

'Got invited back to Jackie's home,' Neil filled in. 'Took out BFF number two, moving closer to final target.'

D.D. thought about it. 'If you think about their mother's psychosis, what these girls grew up with ... Their mother didn't just hurt them, she *hurt* them, in a highly ritualized manner. Maybe that's what Abigail understands best. She's not looking for death for her sister. She's looking for suffering and acknowledgment. That's something they both can relate to. Maybe, for Abigail, suffering even signifies love. Why does Mommy hurt you? Because she loves you so much.'

'But in both cases, Randi and Jackie didn't suffer,' Phil said with a frown.

'Because it's not their attention she wants. It's Charlene's. And the mysteriousness of those murders – no sign of forced entry, no sign of struggle – definitely added to Charlene's mental anguish, while helping capture her attention.'

'I don't think Charlie will be that lucky,' Phil said.

'No, I don't think she will be either. At least she has some training on her side.'

'So does O,' Neil pointed out.

D.D. pursed her lips. 'True. And O stole Charlie's gun earlier. Though maybe that's for the best. That will lower her expectations of resistance, which might help Charlie in the end.'

'So now it's a race?' Phil asked. 'Do we, or does O, find Charlie first?'

'You didn't offer Charlene police protection?' Neil asked in surprise.

'Offer it to her? Please, she won't even return my phone calls. She called me once, told me her side of the story. She's not so interested in our side of things. I'm thinking she doesn't trust us much. Which may or may not have something to do with the fact that it's one of Boston's own officers who's trying to kill her.'

'That's why you didn't pull the arrest warrant for her,' Phil said. 'You still want her picked up, off the streets.'

'I think that's safest for her, yes.'

'But no news.'

'Nada. The girl's holed up good.'

'Hopefully,' Phil commented, 'O's thinking the same.'

'All right.' D.D. tapped the table. 'Next up, I gotta meet with

Horgan to secure permission to request a search warrant for Detective O's apartment. Neil, I'll need you to execute that warrant. Phil, I want you to continue to dig into O's past. Anything we can learn about her – friends, hobbies, pets, food allergies – anything that might give us some insight into what she's doing and how she might be doing it. I want time lines and facts, boom, boom, boom, including a list of all known firearms registered in her name. While you do that, I'm going to speak with her commanding officer.'

'More background?' Phil said.

'I'm working a hunch.'

'Care to share?'

She eyed him for a second. 'Actually, I'll go one better and give you the credit since you're the one who got the ball rolling. Remember when I was going through the tox screen reports on Randi and Jackie earlier today, and I couldn't find evidence of any drugs in their systems, and yet the only thing that makes sense is that they were drugged?'

He nodded.

'You said I needed to start thinking about drugs that didn't leave a pharmaceutical fingerprint. Ones not covered in the tox screen.'

Phil thought about it. 'Pretty smart of me. Did I mention which drug that might be?'

'No, but O did.' D.D. drummed her fingers. Of all the pieces of the puzzle, this one bothered her the most. That she had sat, shoulder to shoulder with a fellow investigator, and remained unsuspecting, even as O had leaked tiny insights into her homicidal game. Had she been reaching out, in her own way, another version of *Catch Me*? Or had she been simply taunting an older, more experienced detective, who should've known better?

'O told me about a case she'd worked as a sex crime detective: the evil stepdad was drugging his twin stepdaughters with insulin. Their blood sugar would crash, rendering them nearly comatose and unable to resist. Later, he'd bring their blood sugar levels back up by administering frosting.

'Insulin,' D.D. said softly. 'Available over the counter. Easy to administer, just a quick prick to the back of the victim's arm, into the subcutaneous fat. Within fifteen to twenty minutes, the victim would be rendered unconscious and O could do whatever she wanted. And there'd be nothing they could do to stop her.'

Neil stared at her. 'Insulin,' he repeated. 'Yep, that would do it.'

D.D. rose to standing. 'We need to locate Detective O,' she stated firmly. 'And we need to find Charlene Grant. It's three forty-three on January twenty-first, gentlemen. Abigail is once again on the hunt. And no amount of boxing or running is going to save Charlie, if Abigail, and her insulin, finds her first.'

# 41

I started at my aunt's Cambridge hotel. A frugal woman, she'd looked up budget motels in the Yellow Pages and called for rates before making her decision. Given that she would've used a credit card to check in, I figured it wouldn't be too hard for a Boston cop to track her down. Detective O could follow the credit card transactions right to my aunt's hotel door, flash her badge, and my aunt would let her in.

I parked a block away. Telling Tulip to stay, I approached cautiously, trying to appear inconspicuous, while simultaneously scoping out the area for a sign of my aunt and/or Boston cops. The cheap no-tell motel formed a two-story horseshoe built around a central parking area. I followed the covered stairs up to my aunt's room on the second story. Door was closed, but the curtains of the main window had been drawn back to reveal a brightly lit, perfectly kept, empty brown-and-gold space. I stood there a minute, absorbing the deliberateness of such a gesture. No woman in her right mind stayed in a hotel with the curtains drawn back to expose her entire room. And my aunt never left the lights on. Wasting money, you know, not to mention burning energy and ruining the planet.

Detective O. Had to be. Letting me know the room was empty. Letting me know, she had my aunt.

I headed back to Tom's truck, hands thrust deep in my coat pockets, head down, ears acutely tuned for the sound of fast-approaching footsteps that might or might not signal an ambush from behind. But nothing. Just a dark, bitterly cold Saturday evening, where the rest of the world was hunkered down safe in their homes, laughing with the ones they loved, while I walked the empty streets of Boston, realizing that I was too late and it was going to cost me.

Clearly, Detective O had reached my aunt first. But she hadn't strangled her in the middle of the hotel room; instead she'd taken my aunt elsewhere. Why?

Because a hotel room wasn't her home. They had to die in the safety and security of their own homes.

Why? Because we never had safety and security? Or to heighten the terror, make it worse?

My hand went unconsciously to my side, I rubbed my scar.

And for an instant, I could almost feel it. My ribs, wet and sticky, my legs trembling, starting to go. Watching flames leap up a wall. Thinking it was strange, to feel so cold while staring at fire.

*SisSis*, a voice called to me. *SisSis!*

Sorry, I said. Sorry.

My cell phone rang. Twenty feet away from Tom's truck, I answered it.

'Do you remember yet?' my sister asked.

'The house was on fire.'

'Dear old Mom. Always had a flair for the dramatic.'

'You beat out the flames.'

'Seemed like a good idea at the time.'

I hesitated. 'SisSis. You called me SisSis.'

This time, she didn't answer right away. When she finally did, her voice was bitter.

'You promised to always take care of me. You promised to keep me safe. But you didn't keep that promise, did you, Charlene? You left me. Then you forgot me completely. So much for sisterly love, *SisSis*.'

I didn't know what to say. It didn't matter, she was already filling the silence: 'Tell me, Charlene, are you still a good soldier?'

'Why?'

'Because everyone has to die sometime. Be brave, Charlie. Be brave . . .'

I felt the chills go up my spine. Not just because of the words she spoke, but because of the way she spoke them. A voice, rising out of the grave. My mother, whispering across the years.

'Please don't hurt her,' I forced myself to say evenly. 'This has nothing to do with Aunt Nancy. This is between you and me.'

'Then you still don't remember.'

'What do you want?'

'You should know that.'

'Tell me, and I'll come to you.'

'You should know where I am.'

Then I did. I understood. I opened the truck door. I climbed inside, phone still glued to my ear. I felt the weight of what had to happen next.

January 21. A day twenty years in the making.

'I love you, Abby,' I whispered to the sister who was about to kill me. 'Remember, whatever happens, I love you.'

My baby sister hung up on me.

I thought long and hard about what I had to do next.

For my entire life, I understood on some basic level that my mother was insane. Maybe I didn't dwell on what specifically happened when I was two or four or five. But the flashes of memory I did have were never warm and fuzzy. I didn't picture my mother reading me a bedtime story or associate her with fresh-baked cookies.

Cold winter nights, when the wind howled through the mountains and the walls quaked from the unsettling power of it, I thought of my mom. Dank basements, the smell of rust, the tang of blood, I thought of my mom. Falling off the monkey bars at school one day, the funny popping sound my shoulder made when I landed, and the even louder sound it made when I whacked it against a tree trunk to pop it back in, I thought of my mom.

She'd been insane in the truest sense of the word. Unpredictable, unstable, unreliable. Driven by wild ambitions and deeper, darker bouts of despair. She loved, she hated. I was her best girl, her favorite daughter. Now, be a good girl and stand still, while she dropped a bowling ball on my foot.

In my mother's world, to love someone was to hurt someone. Therefore, the more she hurt me, the more I should feel adored.

Insanity is genetic, you know.

I'd spent most of my adolescence terrified I'd wake up one morning suddenly overwhelmed by the need to hurt someone. I'd start hitting my friends, screaming at my aunt. I'd stop compulsively cleaning my aunt's mountain B&B and start ransacking the rooms instead.

I'd go to bed Charlene Rosalind Carter Grant, and wake up Christine Grant, terrorizer of small children everywhere.

Fortunately for me, that never happened.

But I don't think my younger sister had gotten so lucky.

My first thought was that my sister would take our aunt back to New Hampshire, to her cozy B&B tucked away in the White Mountains. But that involved a three-hour drive north. Plus, just because you're crazy, doesn't mean you're stupid – my aunt ran a business in her home, meaning the place would be crowded with witnesses.

Far better for this final family reunion – my own little Cambridge rental. One room in a historic house occupied by a single older woman. I hoped for my landlady's sake that she had been out today. I doubted any of us would be that lucky.

I parked across the street, at the Observatory. After 5 p.m. on a Saturday, the parking lot held only a scattering of automobiles. Dark had fallen completely, the street lamps casting a feeble glow which reflected off the white snowbanks.

I'd planned for Tulip to stay, but the moment I opened the truck door, she bounded out, using my lap as a springboard. She ran a couple of quick circles in the snowy parking lot, clearly happy to be on the move. I contemplated rounding her up, forcing her back into her four-wheeled prison, but in the end, I didn't have the heart for it.

Instead, I called her to me one last time, kissed her on the top of the head, and thanked her for being the best dog in the world. She whined a little, wagged her tail, then shook her white-and-tan body as if to ward off a chill. She trotted across the parking lot, moving away from my unit, off on some adventure that maybe someday she'd tell me about, if only I were alive to hear.

I watched until she disappeared around the side of the brick buildings. My throat was thicker than I wanted it to be. I patted my coat pockets, fidgeted with the scarf wrapped tight around my neck.

I had spent a year planning, preparing, and strategizing.

Now I simply heard my mother's words, back inside my head: *Everyone has to die sometime. Be brave.*

I headed across the street for my landlady's darkened home.

The bottom row of empty windows gaped like a toothless smile as I approached. No front porch light burned, no back patio light beckoned. Maybe the front door was unlocked. Maybe my sister was standing on the other side, waiting for me to walk right in.

I decided to do the unexpected. She wanted me here, obviously. There was unfinished business on both sides, so I didn't think she'd simply shoot me. She wanted to talk. I wanted to listen. She wanted to kill my aunt and hurt me as much as possible. I wanted her to know that I was sorry, that I loved her, and that, even though I didn't know how to fix the past, doubted it could be done at this stage of the game, I wished it could be.

I wished we both could start over.

No sign of life on the street as I walked to the rear garden fence, opened the gate, and closed it gently behind me. Now free from prying eyes, I approached the back door, the one I used to come and go.

Deep breath in. Deep breath out.

I knocked. Three times. *Rap, rap, rap.*

And ten seconds later, she answered.

The hallway loomed dark and shadowed behind her, while I imagined the Cambridge night sky cast a faint urban glow behind me.

She was dressed in black jeans and a tight-fitting black sweater. She looked leaner and meaner than Detective O, with her hair scraped back in a tight ponytail and her eyes blazing with crazy blue contact lenses.

I looked at her, and I saw my mother.

I looked at her, and I saw myself.

'Hello,' she said. 'My name is Abigail.'

She raised her right hand, revealing a hypodermic needle, which she pointed at me.

'Arm,' she said.

'What is it?' I gestured to the needle.

'You of all people know better than to question. Now, be a good girl, and do what I tell you.'

'No.'

'Charlene Rosalind Carter—'

'Our mother is dead. I won't go back and neither should you. We're sisters, and sisters don't treat each other like this.'

'*Arm.*'

'No.' I turned and walked away.

'Leave now and she dies,' she shrilled behind me. 'Eight minutes. Maybe nine. All your aunt has left. Or maybe you don't care. Maybe leaving your family to die is what you do best, *SisSis.*'

She had used my old nickname, which I considered a victory of sorts. The beginning of getting both of us to remember. I needed to recall most of my childhood if I was going to survive the next fifteen minutes. And Abigail . . . I needed her to recall at least some parts when she didn't hate me so much. When maybe, she even loved me a little.

I turned back toward her. She once again pointed the needle. After another moment's hesitation, I held out my arm. She moved quickly, before I changed my mind, jamming the needle straight through my coat into the fleshy part of my upper arm. I barely felt it, a faint pinprick that could've been a piece of grit caught in the weave of my shirt. She hit the plunger, and the whole thing was done in a millisecond.

Abigail eyed me. I returned her gaze levelly, waiting to feel something. Woozy, a burning in the back of my throat, maybe tingling down my arm. Most of our mother's tricks were meant for instant gratification, but I didn't feel a thing.

Abigail nodded, apparently satisfied, then made me strip my coat and hand it to her, immediately divesting me of most of my home-made weapons, which I'd stuck in the pockets. Next she patted me down, claiming my cell phone, but overlooking the ballpoint pen tucked into the back of my hair and the duct-tape knife covered by my ragged jeans, thick wool socks, and worn winter boots. Once I'd passed inspection, she opened the door wider, letting me into the darkened hall.

'Randi never even felt it,' she said, as if that should mean something to me. 'Your other friend, Jackie, she turned around when I pricked her. I told her there had been some kind of thorn stuck to the back of her shirtsleeve and she believed me. Aunt Nancy saw me coming with it, though. I let her. I wanted her to know.'

Abigail led me past my own bedroom to the large living room, with its multiple seating areas plus kitchen. I'd been right earlier – no one's lucky day. Both Aunt Nancy and my landlady, Frances, were present. Frances was slumped, pale and weak-looking, in a faded wingback chair, the farthest from me. My aunt was closer, reclined on the camelback sofa, eyes closed, eyelids fluttering in a way that didn't appear good.

I rushed to her immediately and felt for a pulse. I found it, but it was weak. My aunt's skin was clammy, and she was shivering uncontrollably.

'What did you do?'

'You mean she never tried it on you?'

'What?'

'Insulin. Crashes the blood sugar. Leads to coma, possibly death. Or a free trip to the emergency room.'

She delivered the words flippantly. I understood the untold story behind them, the countless episodes she must've endured at our mother's hands. I would've liked to offer her compassion. Instead, I faced off against her, legs spread for balance, and pleaded my case.

'I'm here, you have what you wanted. Now, let me give Aunt Nancy and Fran some sugar cubes, and we'll send them on their way.'

'Frosting,' Abigail stated. 'Works better. I gave it to both of your friends right at the end. Otherwise the postmortem blood tests would've revealed low blood sugar, giving away my little game. But a little frosting applied at the right moment . . . You'll find a spray can of it behind you on the kitchen counter.'

Her ready agreement to let me treat my aunt and landlady puzzled me. Instead of being relieved, I felt even more on edge as I turned around and headed toward the darkened kitchen. Halfway to the center island, my legs suddenly faltered. I missed a step, stumbled slightly, then caught myself. I shook off the episode, blinking my eyes against a sudden bout of light-headedness. The insulin, going to work. I retrieved the silvery spray can of decorator's frosting sitting in the middle of the counter and returned with it to my aunt's side.

'You may give them the frosting. Take any for yourself, and I will shoot you.' Abigail had pocketed the needle. In its place she now held a .40-caliber Sig Sauer.

'And take away all your fun?' I asked lightly.

'I didn't say I'd kill you. I just said I'd shoot you.'

It took me a bit to figure out the spray nozzle, which came complete with four decorative tips. Color was white, flavor vanilla. Decorate cookies, rouse a loved one from impending death. My hands were shaking. I had to concentrate to make my fingers do what I needed.

I tended first to my aunt, who seemed worse off. Next, I crossed to Frances, jamming the nozzle into her slightly gaping mouth and squirting in more frosting.

Then I stepped back, and both my sister and I studied them.

'How did you become Detective O?' I asked. I stood six feet from her, slightly in front of her, her Sig Sauer aimed at my left shoulder. Without any lights on, the room was dark, a series of larger and smaller lumps which indicated furniture, other objects that could be used for cover.

I thought the lack of lighting gave me the advantage, as I knew the space better than her. But she still held the gun, and looked very comfortable with it.

'Patron,' she said.

'Patron?'

Her features remained flat, hard. A cop's face, a victim's face. I had never realized until now how little separated the two.

'When I was fourteen, I left dear old Mom. We were living in Colorado by then. She'd stopped hurting me and started selling me instead. See, her looks were no longer what they used to be, and a girl's gotta pay rent. She still brought home the boyfriends, only they didn't stay in her room anymore.'

I didn't say anything.

'One night, it occurred to me that as long as I was selling my body, I ought to call the shots. So I waited for the right guy to come along – you know, one with lots of cash – and I made him a deal. I'd become his exclusive property, if he'd take me away.

'Turns out, I picked well. He was a successful attorney, had plenty of assets, and had always envisioned himself as one of those wealthy men with a little something-something tucked away on the side. I got my own apartment, and with a bit more negotiation, I got a new identity – you know, so Mommy Dearest couldn't track me down and take me away. Perfectly legal, of course, which is the advantage of prostituting yourself to a legal eagle. Eventually, I enrolled in some online courses and earned my GED. Only problem became when I turned eighteen, and I wanted to go to college, and he wanted to keep me in a gilded cage.'

She stopped talking. On the couch, my aunt moaned, her eyes fluttering open. She stared at both of us, but her eyes were still glazed over. I doubted she was seeing anything.

'When'd you kill him?' I asked conversationally.

Abigail smiled. 'That's not the relevant date. You should know the relevant date.'

'January twenty-one.'

'Absolutely. But why, SisSis? What's so important about January twenty-one? You tell me.'

I studied her. I tried to remember our time together, the past I'd worked so diligently to forget. 'Your birthday?'

She eyed me funnily. 'No.'

'My birthday?'

'Please. Your birthday is in June.'

Frances was awake. Her breathing had changed, evened out. She wasn't sitting up any straighter, but I could tell she was more alert. I wondered if Abigail could tell the same.

But my sister wasn't paying any attention to my aunt or my landlady. She was staring at me. She appeared, for the first time, uncertain.

'Did you really forget . . . everything?'

I shrugged, feeling half-foolish, half-ashamed. 'Most things, yes.'

'Even me?'

'I'm sorry, Abigail. I've tried and tried to remember, but I swear, I just . . . You're a baby and then you're not there anymore. I was so sure she'd killed you. Like Rosalind. Like Carter. These beautiful little babies, so perfect and precious and then . . .'

'I watched her kill the boy.'

'You did?'

'I remember everything. He was crying, and she took a pillow. It was bigger than his entire body. She pressed it down on him. "This is what we do when babies cry, Abigail," she told me. "Don't be a crier."'

'You would've been just a toddler yourself.'

'I think I was two. You would've been four.'

'How can you remember what happened when you were two?'

'How can you forget what happened when you were four?'

My aunt, sitting up straighter, moved her hand at her side.

'I wanted to die,' I heard myself say. 'I woke up in the hospital, and the doctors were talking about how they put me back together and it had been touch and go, but I'd be okay now. Except, instead of feeling grateful, I wanted to kill them for saving me. I was so . . . angry. I was so . . . depressed.' I took a small step away from my aunt, easing toward the rear door, willing Abigail's attention to follow me, and turn farther away from the two now waking women.

'I think I had to forget,' I told my sister honestly. 'I think it was the only way I could remember how to live again.'

'She killed you,' Abigail said. 'She stabbed you with a knife. I saw that, too.'

'There was fire.'

'You do remember!'

'I remember blood and flames and thinking it was strange to feel so cold.'

'She tried to burn the house down.'

'After stabbing me?'

'Yes. She'd gotten you first, but I didn't see that part. She'd come back upstairs for me, then we were in the kitchen and she had the matches, and I couldn't get away. She was going to burn us alive, but you appeared behind her and you hit her over the head with this heavy old lamp.'

'I did?'

She peered at me, and I was rewarded with a trace more uncertainty in her eyes. 'You really don't remember?'

'I wish I did. I would like to remember hurting her. Mostly, I feel like I've spent my entire life trying to learn how to be me. That she crawled into my head when I was too young to fight back and it's taken me twenty-eight years to find my own thoughts, to be my own person. Our mother was crazy, Abigail. And we were too little to fight her. But we're grown up now, and she's dead. She doesn't have to call the shots anymore. We can be ourselves. We can finally win.'

'I tried to kill her that night,' Abigail murmured, as if I hadn't spoken. 'You were dead, I thought. And she was waking up and I couldn't survive without you. I knew that, Charlie. Even back then, I knew I wasn't that strong. So I picked up the lamp, and I was going to hit her. Except, next thing I knew, she kicked my legs and I fell to the floor, and while I was lying there, she picked up the lamp and whacked me with it.'

I jolted. I felt a shiver . . . no, a shock wave . . . move through my entire body. For a moment, I wasn't sure if it was the insulin nose-diving my blood sugar level, or the seismic shift of a long-buried memory.

'I watched you die,' I heard myself whisper. 'I . . . she . . . she killed you. With the lamp. I remember that. And I couldn't move. I couldn't do anything. I couldn't raise my arm, yell, beg, nothing. I was stuck on the floor, feeling so cold and so hot. And screaming on the inside. I remember that. Feeling my whole body scream and scream as you fell down and she got up, but no sound came out. Nothing happened. I screamed, and there she was with the lamp, raising it up, bringing it down. Killing you.

'I'd kept you safe for so long, Abby. You have no idea. The nights I fled with you through the woods, or shoved you under the bed, or hid you in the crawlspace. I'd failed with the others. Hadn't been smart enough, strong enough. But with you . . . by the time you were three or four, I remember thinking I'd done it. I'd saved you and you were mine, and I loved you. *I loved you*, Abigail.'

My voice wavered, broke. My body started shaking uncontrollably while my thoughts scattered, flew apart, refused to come back together. Losing it. Blood sugar plummeting. Confusion, disorientation. Grief. Genuine grief. My baby sister had died. And in the crazy way my mind worked, I hadn't remembered it, but

I had known it. I believed I had watched Abby die and that had broken me in ways no doctor had been able to put back together again.

'But I didn't,' Abigail said. Her own hands were shaking, the gun unsteady. I should move, take advantage.

I couldn't get my legs to respond. Instead, I reached for the wall, feeling the world lurch again, desperate for balance.

Hadn't practiced for this, I thought. Hadn't prepared for this complication.

'I *lived*,' Abigail continued, her voice hoarse, both accusing and mournful. 'She took me away and it was terrible and awful and I prayed for you every night, Charlie. You were my big sister and you'd promised to save me and I *prayed* for you. Night after night after night. Then I was ten, and the first man, and it *hurt*. I cried and begged for you to save me. But you never came. You never saved me. Instead, I turned fourteen, and sold myself to a professional pervert just to get out. Except it wasn't quite enough, so I had to kill him. Except that wasn't enough either, so I had to track her down and kill her, too. I thought I'd feel better then. But it turned out, that still wasn't enough.'

I stared at my sister. 'You killed our mother?'

'Of course.' She smiled. 'Tell me when.'

'January twenty-one. You killed her January twenty-one.'

'Yes. Finally, you understand. I used her own pillow and did it just the way she taught me.'

I wondered if I should feel horrified. I wondered if I should feel grateful. 'But . . . it should've been over then. That should've been enough.'

'Of course not, because that still left you. The one who never came. The one who never saved me.'

'But I didn't even know you were alive!'

'Yes, you did.'

'No, I didn't. How could I have?'

'Because she would've told you.'

Abigail turned and thrust her finger at Aunt Nancy, who was now fully awake and staring at both of us.

'I'm sorry,' my aunt burst out. 'Charlie, I'm so sorry!'

Just as Frances suddenly lunged out of the wingback and, with an unexpected roar, hurled herself at Abigail.

The gun went off.

I fell to the floor.

Screaming. Frances, Aunt Nancy, Abigail.

'SisSis,' Abigail's voice. My little sister, calling for me.

'*SisSis!*'

I grabbed the can of frosting, which was rolling across the floor, and started to crawl.

# 42

D.D. was losing her mind.

5:02 p.m., Saturday, January 21.

No sign of either Charlene Rosalind Carter Grant or Detective O.

Several uniformed patrol officers had cruised by Charlie's Cambridge rental the hour before. No lights were on, no landlady answered the door. Grovesnor, of course, was scoping out all local contacts connected to her job. Charlene, however, was not due to work again, nor had she contacted any of her fellow officers.

That left the aunt with a house in northern New Hampshire and a hotel somewhere in Cambridge. D.D. had outreached to the New Hampshire State Police, who'd checked in with the B&B. Nancy Grant wasn't there, and the young lady who served as her assistant claimed she hadn't heard from her today and wasn't expecting her home until at least tomorrow.

D.D. followed up with a credit check, discovering a recent charge at a low-budget motel in Cambridge.

She was driving there now, not because she thought she'd find Charlene magically hiding beneath the bed in her aunt's hotel room, but because D.D. needed something to do.

Night had fallen. The sky was pitch-black, thermostat plummeting. It was January 21 and D.D. would be damned before she had another murder on her watch, in her city. Not gonna happen. She was forewarned and forearmed.

She found the motel easily enough. One of those late-seventies nondescript places, built in a double-decker horseshoe pattern around a central parking lot. Bit more snooping, and she'd identified Nancy Grant's vehicle, then a room up on the second story.

Three minutes later, D.D. stood in the open doorway of the room, frowning. The office clerk, who'd let her in, appeared equally unsettled.

'Maybe she left,' the little bald Asian man said.

'Maybe.'

D.D. walked around the room, not touching anything. Sure enough, no luggage, no toiletries, not even a wrinkle on the bed. If Aunt Nancy had slept at all, then she'd cleaned up her own motel room after herself.

Which, in the next instant, gave D.D. a long, snaking chill up her spine.

Abigail. Had to be. The world's most obsessive-compulsive killer. Strangled her victims, then fluffed their sofa pillows.

Except no body lay in the middle of the room. Meaning that instead of killing Nancy Grant, she'd taken her instead. Why? It wasn't like a murderer with such a highly ritualized approach to deviate from pattern this late in the game.

Abigail had needed something else.

Someone else.

Like D.D., she was trying to find Charlene Grant.

Except she'd found Nancy Grant first, to use as bait.

D.D. got on her phone and arranged for a crime scene team to process the hotel.

Then she was back in her car, pulling out of the parking lot, the gears of her mind churning as fast as the wheels of her Crown Vic.

Abigail wanted her sister. Abigail wanted revenge. Where to next?

Only one place that made sense to D.D. The Cambridge rental. Had to be. Except, of course, the patrol officers had checked it out. Driven by. Knocked on the door. Not seen any signs of life.

Maybe because there were only signs of death.

She'd just turned onto Charlene's street, when she caught sight of a flash of movement on the sidewalk.

D.D. hit the brakes hard, the car behind her just swerving around. The driver made an obscene gesture. D.D. didn't even notice. She was already out of her car, holding out her hand.

'Tulip,' she called out. 'Here, girl. Come on. It's okay. That's a good doggy. Remember me? You came to my office. I'm a friend of Charlie's.'

The white-and-tan dog wagged her tail uncertainly, then finally advanced, giving D.D.'s hand an experimental sniff.

In return, D.D. stroked the shivering dog's smooth head, patted her ears.

'Where's Charlie, Tulip? Do you know? Because I'm pretty worried about her. Want to help? Show me, Tulip. Where's Charlie?'

And much to D.D.'s surprise, Tulip turned around and headed back up the street. She looked behind her once, as if making sure D.D. was following. Then both dog and detective broke into a run.

# 43

So many defensive maneuvers I'd practiced in the past year. How to duck and weave and dodge and deliver blows. How to stand steady and level my arms and squeeze a trigger. How to run and run and even when I stumbled with exhaustion, how to run some more.

Now it was January 21.

I lay in the dark, half-collapsed against the hardwood floors. I heard screaming. I smelled gunfire.

And I did the most logical thing I could do.

I raised the spray can of frosting to my lips and took a hit.

Another gunshot, then three and four. I staggered forward on my hands and knees, heading into the melee.

Moaning now. I discovered my landlady, Frances, on the floor beside me. She was clutching her shoulder, curled into a ball. I could feel blood, though it was hard to see in the dark.

'Help me,' she moaned again. 'Charlie, Charlie, help me . . .'

'I will, I will. Shhhh, easy.'

More dark shadows, moving around me. One, towering up. Abigail, still holding the gun, but no longer looking steady.

'Where are you?' she cried out. She was leading with her weapon, taking aim at all shadows. I froze, holding very still next to Frances, as I wasn't sure anymore that my own sister wouldn't shoot me.

'Are you okay?' I spoke up as steadily as I could. 'Abby?'

'Shut up! Shut up, shut up, shut up! I know you're in it with her. Dumped me and Mom for her. Well, if that's the way you want to play it!'

Suddenly, she turned toward me, trigger finger moving.

I had a split second of shock, then rolled reflexively, away from

Frances, toward the now empty wingback chair. I was still moving as Abigail started firing, desperately seeking cover while my aunt cried out from across the room, behind the trio of chairs closest to the bay windows.

'It's not her fault!' my aunt exclaimed shakily. 'She didn't know. I never told her.'

'Told me what?' I called back, though I had the sinking feeling I knew.

Abigail stopped shooting long enough to hear my aunt's answer. I used the opportunity to peer out from behind the wingback chair and assess my options.

Frances was seriously hurt and needed immediate medical attention. Abigail was still armed and dangerous. My aunt . . . I had no idea. But I needed to do something fast.

'I found your mother in Colorado,' my aunt replied. Her voice seemed to be moving, probably as she sought better cover. 'I'd hired a private investigator who finally managed to track her down. I made the trip out to see her in person when you were ten.'

'Why?' I was dumbfounded enough to stop watching Abigail and turn toward the sound of my aunt's voice. I must have popped up slightly, because Abigail squeezed off another round and I quickly dropped as the arm of the wingback chair exploded beside me. I inhaled more frosting.

'I wanted to talk to her, sister to sister,' my aunt said. 'She'd hurt you, not to mention what she'd done to the babies . . . I don't know what I was thinking. I was angry. I wanted to talk to her, have my say, before calling the police.'

Abigail was moving. Not toward me, but toward the sound of my aunt's voice. I went back to hastily debating my options. Phone? Too far to safely reach. Weapons? She had taken my sock stuffed with batteries, which had been in my coat pocket, but I still had a small knife taped to my ankle, not to mention the ballpoint pen. I wasn't sure I could stomach drawing down a blade on my baby sister, no matter how deranged. The ballpoint pen would have to do.

'You came to our apartment,' Abigail said now, her voice sounding almost little girlish as she stalked our aunt in the dark.

'I didn't know you were there. I didn't know you existed.' Aunt

Nancy's voice softer, more distant. 'The police report . . . There was no sign of a second child.'

'Everything I owned I kept in a backpack . . .' Abigail said the words, just as they appeared in my head. I mouthed the rest of the sentence, so that we finished in silent unison, 'like a good soldier.'

'When I saw you,' my aunt continued, 'I didn't know what to do. I'd had a plan. I was going to yell at my sister, give her a piece of my mind, then call the police, who would cart her away to be locked up for the rest of her life. The least she deserved! But she knew. Chrissy actually knew what I was going to do and she was already ahead of me.'

Moaning. From behind me. Frances again, gasping with the pain. The sound goaded me. We couldn't stay here, pinned down in the dark while Abigail stalked us with a gun.

'But then I saw you,' my aunt was trying to explain to Abigail, her voice carrying through the dark. 'And I didn't know what to do. I told Chrissy she was sick. Demanded that she turn herself in. I offered to take you, Abigail, raise you just as I'd been doing with Charlene. Except Chrissy wouldn't hear it. She told me I was wrong, had gotten everything confused. There'd been a boyfriend in New York. That's who had stabbed Charlie, who'd murdered the babies. She'd been on the run from him ever since that night, which is why she'd grabbed you, Abigail, and fled from the police. So this "boyfriend" wouldn't find her.'

Across the room, I saw Abigail pause. She'd been moving steadily closer to the sound of my aunt's voice, seeking a target. Now, however, I saw her hesitate. I used the opportunity to ease off my first heavy winter boot.

'For a moment, I almost believed her,' my aunt whispered. 'Then Chrissy started to laugh. She looked me in the eye and told me that's exactly what she'd explain to the police. They, of course, would start looking for the boyfriend, and in the meantime, she'd demand full custody of Charlie again. She'd take both of you and disappear. I couldn't believe she'd do such a thing, but of course she would. Drama and intrigue. Everything she liked best. Who cared if it hurt you, Abigail, or you, Charlie, or me. All that mattered was that it served Christine.

'I asked her what she wanted and she offered me a deal. If I never told the police I'd found her, then I could keep Charlie. She'd never contact me, I'd never contact her. We'd go our separate ways, each one of us with one child. She made it sound generous, as if she was doing me a favor. And I . . .

'I couldn't let her have you again, Charlie. You were doing so well. You had friends and you were happy, and I . . . I loved you too much to send you back to her. So I made the devil's bargain. I agreed to her terms, Abigail. I sacrificed you, so I could save your sister. And I hoped, in my heart of hearts, that one day, you would forgive me for that.'

My aunt's voice changed, became resolute. Too late, I realized what she was going to do. Too late, I stood up behind the wingback chair, all the way at the other end of the long, shadowed family room.

As my aunt rose up from behind the sofa and peered straight at Abigail.

'I hoped,' my aunt whispered bravely, 'that as a sister, you'd be grateful that at least one of you got away.'

Abigail stared my aunt in the eye. For one second, I thought we just might make it. I thought Abigail—

She pulled the trigger. Her Sig Sauer exploded. My aunt made a funny hissing sound, spun slightly left, reaching out a hand as if for balance. Abigail took aim a second time and I hurtled my boot at her head.

It connected just as she squeezed the trigger. Another gasping sound from my aunt, then Abigail spun around, pointing her gun toward me. I flipped off my second heavy-soled boot and hurtled that one as well.

I caught her shoulder. Not hard enough to hurt her. But it threw her off balance. She had to take a second to adjust her stance, during which time I grabbed three sofa pillows and started winging them through the air.

She ducked reflexively. Left. Right. Left. I used the opportunity to spring across the room.

Not away from her.

But toward her. Bounding over the coffee table, pivoting around the camelback sofa. Ducking and weaving straight into the firing zone.

Her eyes opened. Her face shone, pale and shocked in the dark, and I suffered a fresh fissure of memory. Another time, another pale face. Another person I loved and just wanted to make happy.

But it wouldn't be enough. It was never enough. She would hurt me instead.

I drew to a halt twelve inches in front of my baby sister and stood stock-still as Abigail leveled her Sig Sauer at my chest, hot barrel touching my sternum, point-blank range.

'You should've saved me,' she whispered hoarsely.

'I did. I sacrificed myself for you. Time and time again. It just wasn't enough. I loved you, Abby. And if you loved me, then you should've been happy for me, just like Aunt Nancy said.'

'I fucking hate—'

'Shhh . . .'

My little sister's hand shook. Then her finger moved on the trigger. Just as I whipped the plastic ballpoint pen from the back of my ponytail, and, holding it horizontally between my two hands, brought it down like a steel bar against the top of her forearm, right below her wrist.

An old bartender's trick. Sounds like nothing. Looks like nothing. Hurts like hell, right before the hard pen cuts off blood flow to the forearm and the entire hand goes numb, rendering your opponent's fist slack and unresponsive.

Abigail's right hand opened reflexively. She couldn't help herself, her mouth forming a silent O of pain as her Sig Sauer clattered to the floor. I kicked it away. She caught me in the side of the head with her left fist.

Then she was battering at me, and I was doing my best to defend as the back door burst open and a dog came racing into the house, barking frantically,while a female voice rang out, 'Boston PD, hands where I can see them!'

I couldn't put my hands where Detective D.D. Warren could see them. Abigail had given up on her gun, and now had her fingers locked tight around my throat. She was squeezing, squeezing, squeezing, the dark room going even darker. My hands on hers, clawing, grappling for purchase, trying to find her fingers, force them off, as lights began to explode inside my skull.

She had such tremendous hand strength. She wasn't just wringing the breath from my body. She was doing her best to crush my neck.

Staggering back into the low coffee table. Losing my balance. Falling sideways to the floor.

'Stop, police!'

My little sister looming above me, still holding tight, her eyes filled with almost unholy glee. Until the lines blurred, and she wasn't my sister anymore. Instead, I peered up into my mother's face.

*Everyone has to die sometime. Be brave . . .*

I gave up on clawing her hands and started fighting in earnest. Jab, jab, jab to her kidneys. Uppercut to her chin, right punch to the side of her face, again and again. Hitting and hitting and hitting. A year's worth of training, the fight of my life.

The world growing dark as my insane sister absorbed blow after blow, her resolution never wavering, her fingers never falling from my throat.

'Abigail Grant! Detective O. Step away right now. Hands where I can see them!'

Shoot, I willed Detective Warren. Just shoot. But, of course, she couldn't. Abigail and I were tangled into each other, her hands on my throat, my fists buried into her stomach, two desperate women, one hulking form.

Then, out of nowhere, a white-and-tan rocket, as Tulip scrabbled down the hardwood hall and launched herself, snarling and yipping into Abigail's exposed side.

White fangs sinking. Abigail screaming. Finally, my sister releasing my throat, staggering back and straightening as she grabbed Tulip's small, lunging body and hurtled her against the far wall.

A yelp. Then silence.

Me, rolling onto my side. Trying to get up. Trying to get away. Crawling. Kind of. Sort of. Couldn't get my arms under me. Couldn't draw air into my lungs.

'Abigail Grant. Hands up. This is your last warning. Stop or I'll shoot!'

*Everyone has to die sometime. Be brave.*

My sister turned toward D.D. There was something in her hand, something that hadn't been there before. The knife. From my ankle sheath. It must've fallen out when we were fighting.

Her gaze fell to my exposed side and I couldn't help myself. I stilled, waited for her to strike the blow. Blood and fire. Maybe this was what we'd both been waiting for. Twenty years of unfinished business.

I didn't put my hands up in self-defense. I just stared at my baby sister. Willed her to look at me. Willed her to see the big sister who'd genuinely loved her.

'Don't.' D.D. Warren's voice. Closer. But also softer, as if she could feel the turning point. 'Put down the knife, Abigail. You're a cop, remember? *Catch Me*. You wrote that in your notes, because you know better. It doesn't have to be like this.'

'My mother was right,' Abigail whispered, to her, to me. 'The monsters are everywhere. Coming in the dark of the night to hurt small children. On the Internet, on the streets. I see them everywhere. I tried using my badge, I tried using my gun. None of it works. The monsters. Our mother. They are all inside my head.'

'O. Put the knife down. I'll help you. Your sister will help you. We can make this right.'

My sister staring at D.D. My sister staring back down at me.

One moment. Twenty years in the making.

My sister raised the knife.

'I just want to stop hurting, Charlie. I just want peace.'

I screamed hoarsely from the floor. Detective Warren leapt over the coffee table.

As Abigail plunged the blade into her gut and ripped up. A startled look on her pale face. Then she rocked forward, pitching to her knees, before collapsing down.

Detective D.D. Warren's voice, louder now, harsher, requesting immediate medical personnel, calling for backup. I didn't listen to her anymore. I didn't care about her anymore.

I lay side by side on the floor with my baby sister. I found her hand in the dark.

'SisSis?' she whispered roughly.

'I love you, Abby.'

And she made a sound that was wet and ominous and filled with pain.

'Everyone has to die sometime,' I told my sister, in this last moment we had together. She clutched my hand tighter. I held hers right back. 'Be brave, Abby. I love you. Be brave.'

# 44

I buried my sister next to our siblings, baby Rosalind and baby Carter Grant. They don't have large tombstones; just flat granite slabs, the best my aunt could afford for the two babies she buried twenty years ago, and the best I can afford for my sister now. But they are together, a sad trio, laid to rest with their grandparents in the two-hundred-year-old J-Town cemetery. Two plots remain. One for my aunt and one, when the time comes, for me.

Detective Warren found a private blog in my sister's computer. She'd titled it, 'Hello, My name is Abigail,' and within its long, creepy entries, she detailed the murders of my best friends, as well as her countless hours prowling the Internet, hunting down predators, seeking to aid kids in need.

She'd been right in the end. She saw monsters everywhere. And they overwhelmed her as a dark tide, which no amount of stalking and killing could keep at bay. It turned out, she'd shot and killed more than thirty-three suspected pedophiles, from Boston, to New York, to LA. The last three had been close together, only because the approaching January 21 anniversary date had forced her to restrict her hunting grounds to Boston. Until then, she'd been more careful to spread out the carnage. She was a cop, after all, and she used her knowledge wisely.

My friends Randi and Jackie never saw their own deaths coming. Randi opened her door to a female cop and discussed her ex-husband's dealings over mugs of tea before the insulin finally kicked in and she lost consciousness. Jackie met a beautiful woman at a bar. Different story, same approach.

In the end, they probably never thought of me, had any idea that being my friend had signed their death warrants.

Should such a thing make me feel better or worse?

One of those questions I'll never be able to answer.

Detective Warren ordered a DNA test on my mother's remains, confirming once and for all the identity of the unclaimed body in Colorado. I didn't fly out once the results were known. Christine Grant's body can remain in some city morgue or potter's field for all I care. I'm not claiming her, and I'm sure as hell not burying her next to Abigail, Rosalind, and Carter. Maybe that makes me harsh. Mental illness is a disease, probably deserving of some compassion.

Don't know, don't care. The police have closed their files. I don't feel a need to open up any of my own.

Detective Warren also found my Taurus .22 sitting on my sister's nightstand. As it was legally registered to me, she returned it to the appropriate owner. Best I can tell, she had no grounds for conducting a ballistics test, which was why no one has ever matched my .22 to slugs recovered from the apartment of another homicide victim, Stan Miller.

Should such a thing make me feel better or worse?

One of those questions I'll never be able to answer.

My landlady, Frances, spent two weeks in the hospital recovering from a gunshot wound to the shoulder. Interestingly enough, her long-lost niece appeared during that time, and after a bit of debate, decided to move in to help Frances during her convalescence. Apparently, my landlady is an alcoholic, who'd taken up drinking to cope with the death of her husband and four-year-old son in an auto accident thirty years ago. She'd burned numerous family bridges, caused significant collateral damage. Some of the things she never told me during the conversations we never had.

But mortality is a great wake-up call. Fran had been willing to forgive and forget for years, and now, at last, so was her niece.

I know all about such things, having finally had that long overdue heart-to-heart with my aunt, as I spent six weeks bedside in her hospital room. My aunt took two to the shoulder. First week was touch and go. Gave me plenty of time to hold her hand, and sort through my own tangled emotions.

My aunt saved me by sacrificing my sister. The first few days, I couldn't move beyond that thought. I wanted to be grateful, but I was also angry. How could Aunt Nancy have left her own niece, a young girl, with a woman who'd already killed two babies, let alone tortured her other niece? It seemed too cold, too cruel.

Then it bothered me. My aunt was practical, but never callous.

Day five, I made a call to old friends in the Arvada dispatch center. They put me in touch with a couple of veteran officers in Boulder. Sure enough, my aunt hadn't told the entire story. Sure, she'd tracked down her sister. Flown to Colorado, confronted Christine, been shocked to discover Abigail's existence. And maybe, faced with my mother's terms, she'd appeared to capitulate to her demands.

But my aunt hadn't just walked away. She'd gone straight from her sister's ratty apartment to the Boulder police. Apparently, it took a few hours to arrange a face-to-face with a detective, then a bit more time as the police made arrangements with the tactical unit as well as family services. But within five or six hours, the police had raided my mother's apartment, intent on arresting a wanted murderer and rescuing a young child.

Unfortunately, as my aunt later confided, sister knows sister. Christine had never believed for a moment that her older, dutiful sibling would simply walk away. So while my aunt had been summoning the cavalry, Christine had packed her bags, rounded up Abigail, and disappeared once more into thin air.

Abigail never got to see my aunt's return, or the tactical raid that had been put together for her benefit. She just followed her mother to yet another town, her last impression of her aunt being the older woman who'd left her.

My aunt had tried, my aunt had failed. And she hadn't told my sister the full story during those dark hours in Cambridge because she hadn't been trying to explain herself. She'd been trying to draw Abigail's attention so that I could get away.

All these years later, my aunt was still prepared to sacrifice her life for me.

I guess you could say she is as different from her sister as I am from mine.

Of course, there are other consequences from January 21. I haven't spoken to Tom since. Apparently, you can steal a man's truck, but beating him unconscious is much harder to overlook. I understand, of course. Deceit and general mayhem is no basis for a relationship.

I miss him, though. One of those things, I often tell myself, feeling lonely, feeling blue. Different time, different place . . .

Maybe someday soon, I'll drop him a note: *I'm still a train wreck, if you're still interested.*

You never know.

In the meantime, I've moved back to J-Town. Returned to the mountains, my aunt, the community where everyone knows my name. Tulip approves. She lives a happy life as a B&B dog now. Welcomes guests, chases squirrels, comes and goes as often as she pleases.

I'm also helping out at the B&B, working the busy weekends while my aunt continues her recovery. During the week, turns out my own little town needed a dispatch officer. I work graveyard, Tuesday through Friday. And don't let the small town fool you. Just the other night, someone stole a golf cart and ran amok on the course, dumping bleach in zigzag patterns across the greens. However, my brave caller and ninety-year-old witness helped crack the case, based on the baked pineapple pieces left behind.

I still run. Still box. And sometimes, after a long stretch of sleepless nights, I'll head out to the range and make happy with some targets.

But I'm trying for a kinder, gentler life now. I remember my sister and thirty-three murders that didn't do a thing to make her feel safer. I think of Stan Miller and my own choices along the way.

Not just insanity is genetic, you know.

Violence is, too.

I have vowed to make the best of this second shot at life. I will follow the straight and narrow, I remind myself, as I take certain calls. I will color within the lines, I think, as another child cries in my ear. I will not overstep the bounds of morality, I tell myself, as yet another hysterical woman sobs for help.

I wonder how long my resolution will last.

Another one of those questions I can't answer.

Yet.

# 45

It took D.D. several weeks, not to mention several favors, to get the report she desired. When she finally had it, read it, processed it, she nodded in satisfaction. And then, because it didn't mean much, couldn't mean much, she locked it away in a file and went home to her two favorite men.

'You look happy,' Alex said, when she walked through the door.

'Because I was right.'

'Ah. Generally does the trick.'

'Got back a ballistics report. Confirmed what I had suspected: Charlene Rosalind Carter Grant might not have shot those three pedophiles, but she did commit a murder.'

Alex spooned pale mush into Jack's mouth. They were trying out baby's first food: rice cereal. So far, it looked very attractive on Jack's ruddy cheeks.

'When will you arrest her?'

'Not anytime soon.'

Alex tried an airplane noise. Jack wasn't buying it, so D.D. took over. She still wore one of her favorite tailored black suit jackets but was feeling lucky.

Alex sat back, eyed her curiously. He'd had the day off, spending it with Jack. Hence the new food, splattered kitchen, general state of disaster.

'Not arresting people generally doesn't make you happy,' he said now.

D.D. sucked in her cheeks, making a fishy face. Jack imitated, puckering his little lips into an O, and she got the first spoonful of white mush successfully delivered. Like a pro, she thought, and went for mouthful number two. 'Legal standing of ballistics report is highly debatable. Did I really have probable cause to test a legally registered firearm owned by someone who wasn't a suspect in that particular case? Not to mention, said firearm was seized from the apartment of a cop, who turned out to be a murderer who'd already tried to frame Charlie for three other shootings. Meaning my chain of custody is crap, meaning my report is crap.'

She made a giant happy O. Jack giggled. Spoonful number two. She shoots, she scores.

'And yet you're happy?'

'Because I knew it. When O and I interviewed Charlie the first time, the girl looked guilty as hell. Okay, so maybe it wasn't because she was running around Boston shooting pedophiles. But I knew she'd been running around the city doing something.'

'What was the something?'

'Having a shoot-out with a lovely gentleman named Stan Miller. Known as the neighborhood bully. Security guard, wife beater, allegedly had a thing for hammers. He was found impaled on a collapsed fire escape about seven weeks ago. Quite dead, apartment shot to pieces, wife and two kids nowhere to be found. Still missing, as a matter of fact. I'd look harder, but based on neighborhood scuttlebutt, their disappearance is probably in their own best interest.'

'But he died of fire escape, not GSW.'

'Another tricky detail should I pursue a case. Can only prove a person with Charlie Grant's gun shot at Stan Miller, not that a person with Charlie Grant's gun killed Stan Miller.'

'And yet you're happy.'

Baby Jack was giggly. Baby Jack blew rice cereal all over the high chair and half of D.D.'s face. And yet she was still happy. She sat back, stirring rice cereal, waiting for the next chance to use it.

She eyed her partner.

'I like knowing things. I like knowing what Charlie Grant did, and it's possible I dropped her a note, because I like letting her know that I know what she did. Girl's a vigilante. She should know a Boston homicide cop is staring over her shoulder. It's good for her.'

'Ah. You're torturing her. Now I see why you're happy.'

'I'm monitoring her. Will help keep her honest, and I like to think at least some part of her will appreciate that.'

Baby Jack stopped blowing zerberts. D.D. reverted to more fishy faces and scored, in rapid succession, two more bites of rice cereal.

'So, I'm thinking September,' she said casually.

Alex eyed her. 'Vacation? Getaway.' He closed his eyes, swallowed hard. 'We really are going to see your parents.'

'Not if I can help it. But my guess is, they'd come here. Can't miss their only daughter's wedding.'

She looked up at him. He opened his eyes, startled, maybe even bemused. Her heart was pounding. She'd figured that might happen, but the depth of her own nervousness surprised her.

'Wedding?' he asked.

'The fall. With all the leaves turning on the trees. I think that would be pretty.'

'Am I involved?'

'I thought I'd be the one in white . . . okay, ivory, and you'd be the one in the monkey suit.'

He nodded slowly. 'Should I ask how you arrived at this decision, or just jam the ring on your finger before you change your mind?'

'Well, it might take us a couple a weeks to find the ring . . .'

'Shut up,' Alex said. Then, 'Stay right there.' He pushed back his chair rather awkwardly, then staggered out of the room, while D.D. sat there, still holding rice cereal, with bits of baby spittle across her cheek.

She turned to Jack, who waved his pudgy fists in the slightly re-clined high chair.

'I think your father is loco,' she informed him.

He blew more zerberts.

Alex returned, now holding an unmistakable blue box that made D.D.'s eyes widen. 'No way!'

'Fourteen months ago. I have been waiting fourteen months. Have I mentioned yet what a stubborn, infuriating, completely maddening woman you are?'

D.D.'s heart was pounding again. 'Not the words of praise I was expecting during a proposal.'

But it didn't matter. Had never mattered. Alex was on his knee, in their kitchen, with their baby covered in rice cereal and D.D. half-sprayed in rice cereal and it was exactly as it should be.

'D.D. Warren, will you marry me?'

'Alex Wilson, will you marry me?'

'Yes,' they said together, and he opened the box, and she gasped because it was a sapphire-studded band, just like something she'd actually wear. Then she cried a little and he cried a little and baby Jack blew more zerberts so they hugged and kissed him, too, until they were all covered in rice cereal, even the sparkly sapphire band.

'I don't get it,' Alex said, when the dust had settled and Jack was halfway cleaned up and they'd decided to pop champagne. 'Why now? You discover you can't arrest a murderer, and that makes you decide to finally marry me?'

'No. I discovered I could handle a little on-the-job frustration, because I now have more in my world than just the job. I have you, and Jack. Not to mention, when I got the report, I realized I didn't even care if Phil and Neil knew. I just wanted to come home and tell you.'

She eyed her fiancé, sitting beside her on the couch, and she said more softly, more seriously, 'You did what I feared most, Alex. And I had to have that happen, to realize it wasn't so bad.'

'What did I do?'

'You changed me.' She shrugged. 'My whole life, that's what I've fought. I was the oddball in my own family, the little tomboy freak. And my parents didn't get me, and definitely didn't approve of me, and while some kids might have worked harder for their parents' approval, I went the other way. I dug in my heels. And I decided no matter what, I'd always be me, even if that meant I might sometimes be, say . . . little prickly, a little forceful. It was okay, because I was being me.'

'A little prickly,' he said. 'A little forceful.'

She smiled. 'You didn't back down. And you didn't try to change me. You're good for me, Alex. You're patient and tolerant and exactly the kind of parent Jack needs. Watching you, I've realized that I can be that way, too. It's good to sometimes be patient. And a little tolerance does make the world easier to bear. I'm not saying I can't still be mean—'

'I would never doubt it,' he assured her.

'But I'm also realizing I can approach things other ways. And I can be happy. I can come home, and for the first time in my life, I can be. Just . . . be.'

Alex took her hand. He squeezed it and didn't say a word because he didn't have to. He got her, that's what it was all about.

'I love you, Alex.'

'I love you, too, D.D.'

They put Jack to bed, snuggled together on the sofa. Discussed possibly painting the family room. Watched some show on the History Channel. Fell asleep with marines storming some beach in some faraway land.

Midnight, Jack woke up for a bottle.

D.D. fed him, then put him and Alex to bed.

Two a.m., her police pager chimed to life.

She dressed in the dark. Kissed Alex. Kissed Jack. Clipped on her badge, hit the road.

Sergeant Detective D.D. Warren. On the job and loving it.

# Author's Note & Acknowledgments

By far, my favorite part of the writing process is interviewing fun and interesting people in order to learn fun and interesting ways of terrifying my readers (and sometimes myself!). *Catch Me* is no exception. I owe a huge debt of gratitude to:

Ellen Ohlenbusch, Internet safety expert, who absolutely, positively horrified me with her matter-of-fact explanation of all the ways the World Wide Web can be used to stalk and victimize young children. It's an interesting subject that most parents don't want to hear about, but what you don't know can hurt you. Just ask Jesse's mom, Jennifer, in this novel. Oh, thanks also for the use of your name. What can I say, Ohlenbusch was too good to pass up, especially for a Boston cop.

Speaking of Boston cops ... Wayne Rock, Esquire. I first met Wayne when I was researching another D.D. Warren adventure, *Hide*, seven years ago. Since then, Wayne has retired from the Boston PD, but still can't escape my phone calls. From police procedure to pertinent legal details, Wayne is always in the know, much to my deepest relief and appreciation.

For police dispatch, I'm indebted to a number of folks, including Shannon L. Barnes from the Gardner Police. I think communications officers are one of the most invaluable and overlooked members of the law enforcement community. Thank you for allowing me to share your story, wish I had even more time and space to do it justice.

On the boxing front, I owe my deepest gratitude to three-time world champion Dick Kimber. He has shared his love of boxing with my entire family. Yes, a family that fights together, stays together. He also shared many tidbits on self-defense, including the pen trick, which I can personally assure you really, really hurts. My forearm was bruised for weeks. Thanks, Dick!

As always, all mistakes in this novel are mine and mine alone. Hey, I gotta take credit for something.

Now, for those of you who thought some of these characters had more stories to share, you're right! Charlie's shooting instructor, J.T. Dillon and his wife, Tess, first appeared in my novel *The Perfect Husband*. Rhode Island Sergeant Roan Griffin met his wife Jillian in *The Survivors Club*. Former FBI profiler Pierce Quincy, and his daughter, FBI Special Agent Kimberly Quincy, share an entire series, including *The Perfect Husband*, *The Third Victim*, *The Next Accident*, *The Killing Hour*, *Gone*, and *Say Goodbye*. Also, brief shout out for FBI healthcare fraud investigator David Riggs, who appeared in *The Other Daughter*. I'm sure he had no problem gathering evidence against Randi Menke's evil ex, and only wishes he could've put the bad doc away for life. For more information on all the characters as well as other Lisa Gardner novels, please check out LisaGardner.com.

As for how so many of my characters came to inhabit one novel, you may thank/blame my mother. I told her I'd come up with a great way to bring back J.T. Dillon, as I knew readers missed him. She nodded politely, then mentioned that she really wanted to see Griffin from *The Survivors Club*. And the more she thought about it, it'd been a long time since she'd gotten to read about Quincy or Kimberly. What about them?

Once I got over gnashing my teeth, it occurred to me that my accountant mother had a very good idea. So this book is for you, Mom. Because you always cared and you always inspired, even if having a novelist daughter continues to bemuse you. I love you.

Speaking of love, this book is also dedicated to the real Tulip. Adopted by her devoted family from an animal shelter sixteen years ago, Tulip has lived a grand life as one of the smartest, gentlest dogs around. Her family won the honor of including Tulip in this novel at a charity auction for the Animal Rescue League of NH-North. They said that they understood their time with Tulip was reaching an end, and they wanted to capture her unbelievable spirit, as well as immortalize one of the best dogs they'd ever known. So here's to Tulip, who continues to inspire.

As for other real-life fictional characters . . . Congratulations to Tom Mackereth and Randi Menke for winning the annual Kill a Friend, Maim a Buddy/Mate Sweepstakes at LisaGardner.com. As winners they got to nominate the person of their choice to die and/ or be maimed in my next novel. They both nominated themselves. Hope you enjoy the fictional ride. As for the rest of you, the sweepstakes is up and running once more. Swing by LisaGardner.com, and who knows, maybe next year, this can be you!

Also, congratulations to Stan Miller, who won the honor at another charity auction and to Frances Beals, whose daughter Kim graciously purchased the honor for her at a benefit for the Rozzie May Animal Alliance.

As always, my love and gratitude to my family: the husband who's grown accustomed to a wife who stares off into space for long periods of time, and the daughter who every single day asks about the book, demanding a full accounting of what where when why and who, and then, if I'm really lucky, nods her approval. Phew!

Finally, my deepest appreciation to not one, but two new editors extraordinaire: Ben Sevier of Dutton in the United States and Vicki Mellor of Headline in the UK. Here is to the beginning of a beautiful relationship.